WHISPERS OF RUIN

THE FAMINE CYCLE
BOOK I

J.D.L. ROSELL

Illustration © 2021 by René Aigner
Book design by J.D.L. Rosell
Maps by Kaitlyn Clark

Published by Rune & Requiem Press
runeandrequiempress.com

READ THE PREQUEL FOR FREE

Don't miss *Secret Seller,* the prequel novella to The Famine Cycle. Get it for free from Amazon or jdlrosell.com.

A nobleman's murder. A secret buried in her past. An ancient power ascending...

Airene, a hunter of whispers and merchant of rumors, is no stranger to scandal and isn't afraid to get into a scrap.

But when a nobleman is killed, Airene is pushed to her limits in pursuit of the murderer—and the secret that will change her world forever...

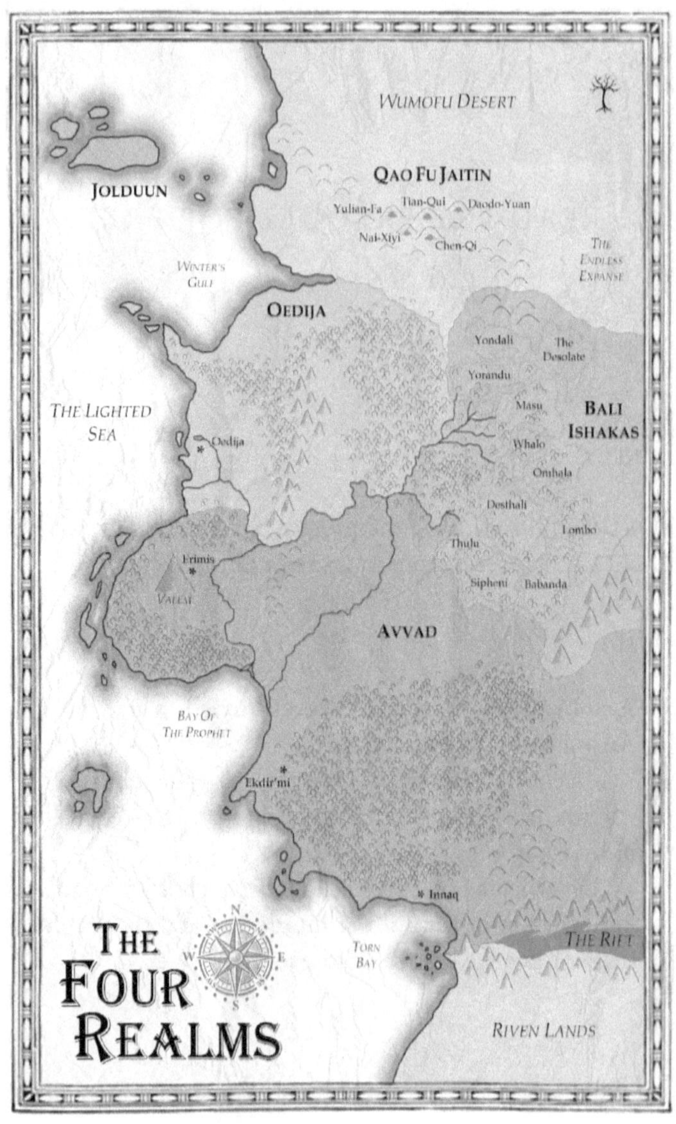

WUMOFU DESERT
JOLDUUN
QAO FU JAITIN
Yulian-Fa
Tian-Qui
Daodo-Yuan
Nai-Xiyi
Chen-Qi
THE ENDLESS EXPANSE
WINTER'S GULF
OEDIJA
Yondali
The Desolate
Yorandu
THE LIGHTED SEA
Masu
BALI ISHAKAS
Whalo
Oedija
Omhala
Desthali
Lombo
Erimis
Thulu
VALLAI
Sipheni
Babanda
AVVAD
BAY OF THE PROPHET
Ekdir'mi
Innaq
N
THE RIFT
TORN BAY
W
E
THE FOUR REALMS
S
RIVEN LANDS

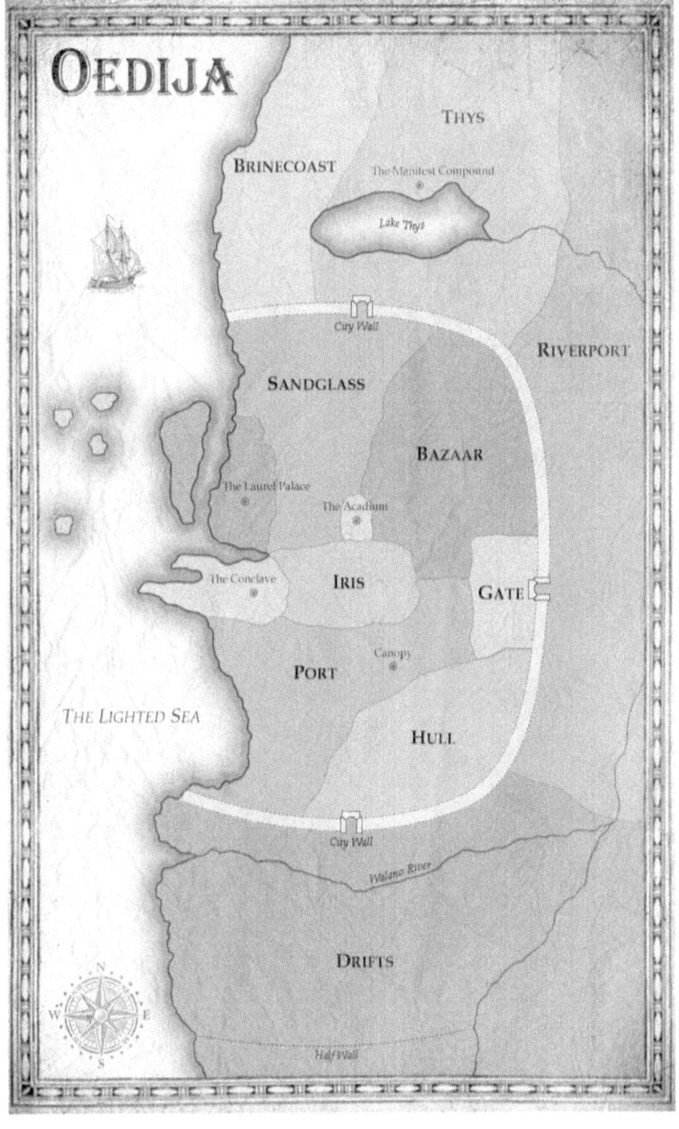

OEDIJA
THYS
BRINECOAST
The Manifest Compound
Lake Thys
City Wall
RIVERPORT
SANDGLASS
BAZAAR
The Laurel Palace
The Acadium
The Conclave
IRIS
GATE
Canopy
PORT
HULL
THE LIGHTED SEA
City Wall
Walano River
DRIFTS
N
W E
S
Half Wall

PROLOGUE

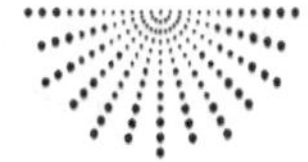

I was not born a warden.

For much of my childhood, I showed little sign of the arcane. I didn't even show promise of rising above my station. The daughter of an indebted carpet merchant and an ailing shipwright, I was fortunate merely to attend the public scholarium and learn my letters. That I received high marks was of little import.

In Oedija, the Pearl of the Four Realms, social hierarchy was rigid. No man or woman became something that their parents were not.

Yet my nature rebelled, as did my brothers'. I made nothing of our similarities for much of my life. Our mother had passed on her stubbornness to us; it was inevitable that we should try to throw off her hypocritical yoke.

Now, I know this to be no coincidence. It was our fate. But I did not understand that then. The fire that filled me seemed all my own.

The passion that has consumed me flourished one day while passing through the markets. My ears caught a fragment of conversation, a hint of gossip, but of a kind that held dark depths. At five, I didn't understand what it meant for one patrician to sleep with another out of wedlock, as the washerwoman I eavesdropped upon had confided to another. Yet when I told my father of this, his eyes widened, and he bade me to not repeat it where I could be overheard. Punishment could be doled out for slander, he said. And because I loved him, I complied.

But in his reaction, I understood something I had not known before. Secrets held power, a power others feared. Young and powerless, I yearned to claim it.

So began what would become my life's calling. By the time I was eight, I'd sought more dangerous tales than salacious scandals, opting instead for street-side scams and moneylender muggings. I would return home after long, dusty days and illustrate my hard-earned stories in colorful detail to my brothers for their amusement.

By the time I was twelve, I'd sold my first secret.

At fifteen, when adolescents settle on their occupation, I named myself a Finch after the Order of Verifiers, a long-disbanded branch of the government, to carry on their mission of exposing truth wherever deception obscured it. When I set to the work a year later, I found myself more often chasing profit than justice. But always, I told myself it was in the eventual pursuit of that noble goal.

But my calling had its limits. When I sought to uncover the secret most important to me and failed, my belief in my purpose faltered. I had honed my skills and developed my network, and for what?

What did any of this matter if I could not even find my eldest brother's murderer?

I was eleven when they found his body in a canal. His face was nothing like I remembered, bloated with death and prolonged exposure to saltwater. Yet it was the scars, thin and violet, that spiderwebbed from his eyes that haunted my memories most. They tantalized with the secrets they held.

Even as young as I was, I sensed if I could understand their origin, I would know how my brother died.

A decade later, I received a hint more of the mystery. Yet in the end, answers eluded my grasp. The trail ran dry, the clues turned up cold. Not for all my prowess as a Finch could I track down the killer.

Despair, however, is a tempering flame. It was from this failure that my calling truly began to find its purpose. That I became discontented with blackmailing scoundrels and exposing ignominy, and I searched for a higher purpose.

I was not born a warden. I had no touch of magic. But when the three horns of the Laurel Palace sounded their mournful voices over Oedija, I set down the path to become one.

A warden who would reshape the face of the Four Realms.

A warden who, Eidola willing, would cage a god.

1

FEAST & FAMINE

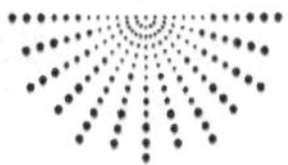

The Festival of Radiance, a celebration as old as Oedija itself, is a reminder of the Hunger War that drove our ancestors across the Lighted Sea, in the days when the daemon god Famine slew the Foremost of our gods and nearly swallowed the world...

- The Traditions of the Eleven: Eidolan worship in the demotism of Oedija; by Oracle Iason of deme Iris; 1164 SLP (Succeeding the Lighted Passage)

Perched on the edge of the rooftop, I searched for the smuggler.

It was the wrong time for a hunt. Forum Demos was packed as tightly as fish in barrels after a day's ample catch, a full third of Oedija's population gathered for the Despot's address. Expecting to spy one man among thirty-thousand was a fool's wish.

But though my back ached and my legs had gone numb from hanging off the eaves, I didn't let up.

I had no other choice.

"We should give in, Airene. We're never going to find him." Xaron stretched and yawned, then reached back for his cup of festival wine, nearly spilling it in the process. Though he dressed like a fop and possessed the athleticism of a gymnast, Xaron had the manners of a boar. His yellow coat and scarlet trousers sported many stains from the day's activities.

"We need the coin," I reminded him drily.

"But we won't find it today." Nomusa, our third accomplice, spoke up from my other side. "Zotikos will need to surrender the goods before we can pick up the coin from Maesos."

"Thanks for having my back." I gave her a long-suffering grimace.

She smiled back, a teasing curve to it. Her dark, olive skin and revealing robe accentuated her natural beauty. When we'd been younger, standing next to her had made me self-conscious of my own middling looks. But nine years of working and living together had cured that small jealousy. Her bared arms revealed the intricate, blue tatu that wound up to her elbows. They told the truths of her past, for those who could read them.

Xaron leaned into me, his breath sour with wine. "How much longer until we can convince you to leave it off? Radiance ends today, and with it goes the free wine."

I was hanging onto my resolve by a thread myself. But I forced myself to say, "Until we find him."

Xaron lapsed into morose silence and took another drink. Nomusa held her tongue. Not to be made a liar, I renewed the search, if half-heartedly. The dying light strained my eyes, promising an aching head that night.

The great amphitheater spread out below us. A quarter-mile of marbled tiers cascading down to a colonnaded dais, every tier was filled to overflowing, their occupants from all echelons of society. Patricians, citizens, honors, plebeians — this gathering was the closest that rich and poor came to being equals.

Amid that mass of humanity, Xaron, Nomusa, and I needed to spy one particular man from a rooftop at the back of the forum. But though the man would be wearing the colored robes of the mercantile class, I'd searched the tiny figures below for far too long. My eyes felt too large for their sockets. My head buzzed with festival wine. My vision swam.

It was as fruitless as a pyr hunt, and I knew it.

I kicked the blood back into my legs and stared up at the sky. Finches, each with tiny scrolls tied to their thin legs, flitted above, flecks of fast-moving colors in the sunset light. Even now, just before the largest gathering of the year, the messenger birds of Oedija received no rest. A gentle breeze, the last of the warm summer winds, blew against my face. Shouts, laughs, and shrieks from the orphans underneath our feet filled the air. No doubt many of the urchins had taken their fair share of the festival wine. Freely dispensed by the People's Conclave during the five days of the Festival of Radiance in a flagrant facade of generosity, this was the children's last chance to indulge and escape the misery of their daily lives.

A new voice broke through the other noises to rise over the tumult of the crowd, slowly quieting them. Squinting at the dais, I saw an oracle of the Eidolan faith, the religion of Oedija's ancestors, stood between the grand marble columns. The old man's voice was worn as pilled wool, yet loud enough to be heard all across the public square, thanks to the mystical aid of our present Hilarion.

"Our story begins long before our demotism and the Conclave," the oracle spoke, voice echoing through the now-quiet amphitheater. "Before the Tyrant Wardens took Oedija for their own, and set those attuned to the Pyrthae to rule over those who were not. Long even before the first Wreath occupied the Laurel Palace. We go back to just before the Lighted Passage, when our ancestors sailed from their blighted homeland in the west to a faraway land in the east — this land, settling the stones on which we now stand."

The oracle paused, then continued as if reluctant to do so. "The story begins with Famine. Some have called Famine a serpent, a great serpent. But he was no more a snake than a phoenix is a finch. Some have called him a dragon, yet this can still not do him justice. For when Famine opened his mouth wide, he could swallow the whole of Telae."

Famine. Despite the joviality of the festival below, the specter of the daemon god loomed large over the city these days. A drought promised forthcoming food shortages. Prices were already rising, and would only climb higher as stores ran low. With hunger would come strife. Robbery. Rioting. Perhaps even revolt, if things were as bad as the reports promised.

As much as I wished to give up my search, I couldn't. Without claiming the much-needed coin from the job, Nomusa, Xaron, and I might soon find ourselves among the starving.

Xaron stirred and pointed. "There! By the Pillar. Is that him?"

I followed his direction, peering at the immense column of gray stone that rose high into the sky above. One of the remnants of an older civilization, the Pillars and the others like it scattered across Oedija made for convenient landmarks. I picked out a man standing near its base in bright red robes, a stark contrast from the browns surrounding him. Next to him stood a man half a head taller than everyone else.

A thin smile found my lips. Zotikos, the man we'd been searching for, and his bodyguard were those two men; I was sure of it.

Nomusa leaned forward. "Can you see who he's meeting with?"

I reached into my satchel and pulled out my peering glass.

Looking through it, I brought the man in red robes into focus. He was turned away from me, but his close-cropped, curly hair was the same as Zotikos's.

I lowered the glass and shook my head. "Too far to tell, and too many surround them. We'll have to move closer."

"Meeting by the Pillar." Xaron tutted. "You'd think criminals would know to be a little less obvious."

I shrugged. "I won't object to a straightforward venture for once."

"Don't speak too soon," Nomusa chided. "This job isn't over."

We made our slow way off the roof to the street below and endured the gibes of the orphans surrounding us. As our feet found the cobblestones, I muttered to Nomusa, "Is it just me, or are we getting too old for this?"

She drew me in with an arm around the waist. "You just need to practice Ixolo with me. Then you'll be as nimble as any street orphan."

"Or as naturally graceful as I." Xaron leaped the last several feet to the ground and stumbled as he landed.

I rolled my eyes. "Graceful as a three-legged mule. Hurry up."

As we pushed through the crowd, the stench of unwashed bodies filled my nose. From the dais, the oracle finished his story.

"Tyurn Sky-Sea knew we could not face Famine unarmed. So, giving all of his strength, he granted us his gift. Attuning the First Wardens to the Pyrthae, humanity gained the gift of magic. Wardens drew on the power of that spiritual realm and fought alongside the gods. Wielding the energetic elements like soldiers use swords and spears, they worked together to drive Famine and his horde from the world and, once again, bound him."

As he concluded, there was a spattering of applause, then silence — the quiet of anticipation. Soon, Despot Myron

Wreath, purported ruler of Oedija, would take the stage for his annual Radiance address. All around me, folk murmured their hopes for him. They dreamed of a year of plenty and quiet streets.

But Myron could do little for them. Even if he still possessed the influence of his forebears, nothing could prevent the hunger soon to come. No amount of trade with the other nations of the Four Realms could change the fact that our granaries were near empty and our fields fallow. Each nation had to watch out for themselves now.

It wasn't long before I glimpsed our quarry again through the crowd. Zotikos turned around for a moment, a scowl on his face. His guard, a tall, broad man who wore a yet deeper frown, stood nearby scanning the crowd. The smuggler turned back, gesturing at someone before him.

Xaron whistled. "That's a big man he brought."

"Not a problem for you, though." I cast him a sidelong glance.

He grinned. "Not if you let me off my leash."

"You're lucky we don't muzzle you, too." Nomusa grabbed his arm. "Come on. Let's get this over with."

2

OF SMUGGLERS AND DESPOTS

By all measures, Myron Wreath has proven to be a moderate and even-tempered man. Aware of his powers' bounds, he has rarely, if ever, strayed into perilous waters. In his twenty-two year reign, he has done much to preserve the traditions and state of the nation, and despite his efforts having a negligent effect on decreasing belief in the Eidola, he has done well in improving the commercial state of Oedija...

I find that few, if any, are opposed to his reign for many years to come.

- A Modern Account of the Wreaths; by Acadian Helene, Master Historian; 1170 SLP

We pressed forward, the crowd thinning as we neared. The bodyguard's forbidding glare was enough to make people think twice about coming close. Leaning around those in front of me, I caught a glimpse of Zotikos's contact. My mouth went dry.

The man was an honor, his caste clear from his shaved head and tin spiral earrings. But despite being of the servile class, he wore robes at least as rich as the merchant's. His dark green eyes met Zotikos's with the poise of a patrician, a jovial gleam in them. But though unusual, none of this was surprising. It wasn't our first run-in with Low Consul Feiyan's righthand man.

"Kako," Xaron breathed. "What's he doing here?"

I fought back a scowl. "What else? Dealing with smugglers is business as usual for Feiyan."

Nomusa shook her head. "We should have suspected she was behind this."

"She could just be an opportunistic buyer," I said sarcastically.

Nomusa raised an eyebrow. "Very likely, when he comes first thing to meet her righthand man after a long trip from the Bali highlands."

Xaron waved a hand. "Never mind that. Are we doing this or not?"

All three of us were nervous, that was plain. I couldn't help a wry grin. Nearly a decade in, and I still got butterflies before confrontations.

I glanced at the far-off dais. "Despot Myron's taking the stage. If he gives his usual performance, it should be a good distraction."

Confirming my words, the crowd roared as Despot Myron Wreath mounted the platform and waved regally to his people. At fifty years, he retained a broad frame, handsome features, and sharp eyes. He was a man you'd trust equally to lead an army and rein in a chamber full of bureaucrats — though, in truth, he did neither.

The Despot of Oedija boomed over the tumult. "My people! Thank you for this marvelous welcome!"

As a deafening wave of cheers swept over us, Xaron grinned at Nomusa and me and shouted, "Despot Myron, claiming the stage as usual!"

The cheers quieted, and the Ruling Wreath continued in his strong, rich voice. "We gather here to celebrate, as we do every year, the blessings that the Pyrthae grants us. The rains that fall from the heavens; the sun that warms and energizes; and, of course, our ancestors who take the form of pyr and move through and among us. Each one of us is touched by the radiance of the realm above." He gestured with a wide wave above him. "Let us never forget that."

A solemn murmur rippled through the crowd.

"Long, long ago," Myron continued, "our forebears encountered a catastrophe in the western lands. The Hunger War. The calamity was so profound that they deemed their lands too desolate to continue sowing. Thus, they abandoned them forever. A hard decision, indeed, and one that could have had terrible consequences. But they held to faith. With the Eidola lighting the way, they traveled the endless seas, braving starvation and storms for eleven full spans. Children grew languid and weak. Men and women faltered at the oars. But finally, they landed here, on Oedija's shores, and founded this great city. The Lighted Passage, as we now call it, was a great hardship to bear. But without our ancestors's courage, the prosperous Pearl of the Four Realms would never have existed."

There were some assents of approval, but joining them now was a susurrus of discontent. I didn't have to look far to know why. Though people were clad in their festival best, many of them were unwashed and underfed. Myron had overplayed his hand. Most did not feel the prosperity he claimed.

But the Despot seemed to understand their shifting mood. "I know we face trials now, many trials indeed. The gods and spirits of the land and sky have plagued us with pestilence and droughts, robbing us of our plentiful harvests. And Valem stirs, discontented, in the south, so that Avvad's fields are covered in ash, the rivers are muddied and polluted. The trade caravans that might alleviate Oedija's hunger encounter obstacles and delays. Yes, I know we have many trials to overcome."

As Myron paused, those who had protested were hushed with anticipation, waiting for his next words. *With hope,* I realized. They truly believed the Despot could say something that would change their situation. Desperate, they needed something to believe in and found none better than our nation's puppet ruler.

Myron's next words, however, were hard. "But turning to false religions is not the answer. Believing in false claims — in delusions — because you wish them to be true will do our future no favors."

The crowd was quickly becoming agitated now. Jeers and calls were hurled down at the dais. Laurel guards, with green leaves painted on their armor and carved into their helms, began to wade in at the edges of the crowd, spears and shields held at the ready. The less wise among the masses resisted, and spats broke out as guards dragged away the most vehement of the decriers.

I shared a look with Nomusa and Xaron. In my memory, unrest was unprecedented at Myron's addresses.

"But we need not dwell on our trials!" Myron boomed over the protests. "Today, we celebrate both the victories of the past and the present. And that is not all! For today, one of our own returns, who will one day wear the Evergreen Wreath in my stead. A day long from now, gods willing."

The crowd, who would have normally agreed, barely responded. Still, the Despot smiled benevolently up at us like we'd cried out his name.

"But I will let her speak for herself. My daughter, Asileia Wreath, future Despoina of Oedija!"

He swept his arm behind him, and his daughter came striding out from the eaves to join him. Asileia was a thin woman, taking after her mother, the daughter of a Qao Fu matriarch. She walked with such a sense of command that you could almost believe her an Oedijan ruler of old. As she strode forth, fine jewelry danced upon her and glittered brilliantly in the festival lights. She'd never had her father's sense of modesty when it came to demonstrating the inherited wealth of the royal family. But even more striking were the golden tatu that shone on her skin. At this distance, I couldn't tell if they were more extensive than when we'd last seen her. They gave her an otherworldly cast, making her seem like a pyr come into the flesh.

"That ought to be distraction enough," I noted to Xaron and Nomusa. "I'm going in. Wait for the signal."

Nomusa glanced at me. She knew that I spoke the reminder more for my sake than theirs. "We'll do our part. 'Thae's blessing, Aire."

I nodded and turned back to our quarries, who stared at the shimmering Asileia Wreath. Not giving myself another moment for doubt, I approached the trio.

The bodyguard spotted me immediately. I pretended to be peering toward the dais until I was within a dozen strides, then looked around with a smile. A smile wouldn't stop his fist from pounding me into the stones at the smuggler's command. But it might allow me a word or two first — all I needed.

Kako had followed the bodyguard's gaze. His face lit up as he gestured toward me. "Airene the Finch!" he shouted over Asileia's speech. "Excuse me, Zotikos, but here is an old friend come to visit. If I know her at all, I believe she'll have words for you as well."

"Kako," I greeted the honor stiffly as he approached. "How's your mistress?"

"Very well, thank you. Power suits her nicely." He gave me a coy smile.

I pointedly looked away.

Zotikos studied me with an open scowl. "An old friend, you say. What words do you have for me, girl?"

Little rankled me more than a man's casual scorn. My reply was cool and calm. "Many you won't wish to hear, Zotikos of Hull. And many you would not wish your wife to hear, either."

His lips curled in distaste. "A dirty pleb should speak no words to my wife. Leave us, wench. We have business to discuss."

His bodyguard turned toward me. My heart, already racing, began to gallop. But I continued to ignore the big man.

"As do we. If I were you, I'd send Feiyan's man away. You don't want an audience for what I'm about to say."

Kako watched with open amusement. "Never fear, my dear. I freely leave you to your fear-mongering. But remember the last time you meddled in Feiyan's business. I would think carefully before you interfere again."

With a subtle bow, the honor turned away and disappeared back into the crowd.

Relieved as I was to see Kako's back, the full attention of Zotikos and his henchman was no easier to bear. The merchant had reddened in the face as he turned back to me. But before he could speak, a collective gasp turned our heads.

"Yes!" Asileia was shouting. "The elder Eleven, the Eidola of old, have spoken to me. And as no other mortal has experienced, I have become—"

Her voice cut off as Despot Myron ripped Hilarion's hand away from her neck and slapped it to his own. "Thank you, Daughter," he said. As his low, powerful voice rolled over us, I could feel his rippling anger. "We are all happy to see you home."

Asileia stood for a moment, quivering with rage, then stalked off the dais.

Zotikos and his bodyguard turned back to me. "An ominous night for interruptions," he said coldly. "You spoil my business and threaten my wife. Who are you, Airene the Finch, and what do you wish to say?"

I didn't flinch. A Finch for nine years, I'd encountered more men like Zotikos than I cared to recount. And at the core of every one of them were the dark secrets they kept hidden from the world. Lies they whispered to themselves to obscure the truths that defined them.

But I knew how to unravel them.

"You've been keeping a secret, Zotikos. One that would break your family if it were revealed. Your wife might not care for honors, but I doubt she would excuse you… mishandling her handmaid during her evenings away." Despite the revulsion hollowing me, I pasted a knowing smile on my lips. "But it's up to you whether she hears of it or not."

The merchant's expression spasmed. His eyes darted from me to his impassive guard, then to the crowd around us.

"Liar!" he hissed, but the words caught in his throat. "It's all lies! You know nothing!"

"No doubt you wish to believe that. I, however, would not risk your reputation over a misplaced shipment from the Bali highlands."

Zotikos's eyes widened, then he gave a wild laugh. "Aha! So that's what this is about! You want a cut, do you? You think to threaten me so I'll just hand over the profits to you, you greedy strumpet? I know people, important people. I'll have you strung up for your slanderous words!"

I glanced at the bodyguard, who stared daggers into me, then pulled my gaze back to the smuggler. This was the critical moment. I had to hold firm. Swallowing hard, I prepared to lose a few teeth.

"That will not keep your family from falling apart, Zotikos. That will not keep business partners from looking at you twice and deals falling through. But all that can be prevented. Your secret will be safe with me. All you must do is return what you stole to those with whom you broke contract."

The river merchant stared at me balefully, his mouth pressed into a hard line. He was considering my offer. Soon, he would relent. He just needed one last twist of the knife.

"Think carefully, Zotikos. Everything you possess is on the line. Your dignity, your relationships, your fortunes — *everything*. And it can all be safe if you do the right thing."

I reached into my robes and seized the object concealed there. The bodyguard, no doubt suspecting a weapon, snaked his hand forward to grab my slender arm in a bruising grip. Pain raced through me, but I didn't struggle. I just had to wait a moment longer.

Xaron and Nomusa stepped into view behind the smuggler and his brute.

"I'd listen to her," Xaron said with a nonchalant air. "She won't let it rest until she's had her way."

"And you won't rest either," Nomusa said coldly. "This is the best way out for you, trust us."

Zotikos whirled. His bodyguard didn't release me as he eyed the newcomers warily.

"And who are you two?" the smuggler demanded.

I gestured toward them. "Zotikos, meet my fellow Finches. The other people who hold your fate in their hands."

"Finches?" His eyes narrowed. "Airene the Finch… Now I know why you sounded familiar. Filthy spies and thieves, the lot of you!"

"Can't dispute you there," Xaron said easily. "But it's hard to feel bad about it when we blackmail scum like you."

I could see we had him. If I had been alone, he might have forced down the fear of someone knowing his secret, assuring himself that his bodyguard could take care of it. But he couldn't stop three people from talking.

"Fine!" the river merchant snapped. "Fine. I'll give my investors their due. So long as you never speak of this to anyone." He eyed me shrewdly. "Which one of them put you up to this?"

I smiled thinly. "Best make sure you don't leave out anyone, just in case."

Zotikos bared his teeth in nearly a snarl, then gestured sharply to his bodyguard. The brute gave me one last bald glare, then released me and followed after his master.

Xaron grinned openly as he and Nomusa joined me. "That went well. As soon as you called us in with the lodestone, that is."

I rubbed at my prickling arm as my fingers brushed the concealed lodestone. Bonded through magnesis, one of the energetic elements, to a stone Xaron carried, each would move when the other was touched. It had been useful for faraway communication on many occasions, and served as a signal on this one.

"In the end," I conceded. "We'll have to follow up tomorrow evening to make sure he remembers what's at stake."

"I'd expect nothing less of the pig than to try and weasel his way out now." Nomusa stared at the retreating backs of the smuggler and his man, then turned her head aside with a small shake of disgust. "Come. There's a little of the festival left. We should give off this thankless work for a bit, find an untapped barrel, and celebrate."

I sighed, trying not to think of Zotikos's wife, and whether we did a greater injustice by keeping quiet or telling her. But it didn't matter. I wouldn't inform her of what scum her husband was unless Zotikos failed to deliver. A Finch was only as good as her word.

I followed after my companions to claim one last piece of Radiance.

3

CALL OF THE HORNS

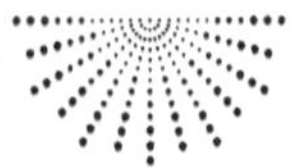

Oedija — o, Oedija — my home of contradictions
The Pearl of Civilization, yet fearful even of its
    jester
The advocates of freedom propped up on the backs of
    slaves
A people who rule themselves by choosing others to
    rule them
A religion that died when the gods
Abandoned us to the Tyrant Wardens...

- High Poetry of Lowly Things; by Hilarion the
    Second; 1085 SLP

S everal turns of the sandglass later, Nomusa, Xaron, and I stumbled back up the stairs of the derelict tower we called home. With wine-logged heads and sour stomachs, the climb to the top seemed never-ending.

As much for distraction as out of curiosity, I asked Nomusa, "Asileia truly said she was — what was it, 'the Hand of Clepsammia'?"

"So she claims. And supposedly, she has oracles following her around declaring the same thing."

"Two circles left," Xaron panted. "We're almost to Canopy."

"It's not that far," I chided him. "What happened to her governing the Peninsula?"

Nomusa shrugged. "How should I know? Myron made it seem like a good thing she'd returned. But he'd have to spin it that way."

"She was probably booted for burning her subjects alive," Xaron interjected.

I cast him a disdainful look. "Don't believe every rumor you hear. It's a long way from the Oedijan prefectures. Events are often inflated."

"But do you really doubt it? The woman mutilated herself. She cut off her ear markings and disavowed her mother's heritage. And now she's back when she's not supposed to be."

I shrugged. Being Qao Fu himself, Xaron was particularly offended that Asileia had severed the additional ear lobes of their people. It was typically a point of pride for the Qao Fu, and many — including Xaron — wore earrings through their ear markings. We didn't know why Asileia had removed hers, but it didn't much incline Xaron to like her.

We finally reached the top of the tower, the eleventh circle. The previous ten floors were filled with poor families or young men and women with nowhere else to go. At least in the loft atop it, we had the circle to ourselves. It was the best our bribes could afford. As Finches — hunters of secrets, misdeeds, or other knowledge that might turn a profit — we didn't have the most reliable income and couldn't risk trying for something more expensive.

Living on top of the tower was both a blessing and a curse. At the moment, with unsteady legs and a head already pounding from sour festival wine, I wondered what had possessed us to move here.

Yet as we pushed inside the door, Canopy was a welcome sight. Opposite the door, a great bay window, only a little cracked and grimy despite our negligence, afforded a stunning view of Oedija's cityscape. Along the right side, four small enclosures we'd fashioned into bedrooms, their ceilings open to the rest of the loft, huddled against each other. To the left lay the kitchen, cluttered with unwashed pots, and the pantry. I breathed in the faint stench of mildew and bird droppings, which wafted in from the finch cage on our balcony. The scents may not have been fair, but to me, they were the smell of home.

Saying their goodnights, Xaron and Nomusa closed themselves into their bedrooms. I wasn't ready for sleep yet. Despite my better judgment, I drew yet another cup of wine from the barrel that our last loftmate, Corin — who worked as a cartwoman rather than a Finch — had claimed for us, then moved to the bay window.

The festival lights glittered in the inner and outer demes of the city, as both inside and outside the wall the celebration continued. Bonfires, pyr lamps, and torches illuminated the city from below, while the green light of the radiant winds and the three moons, full as they were every Radiance, shone above. The gray Pillars rose ominously from the demes, the magic-forged columns shadowed specters in the darkness. Beyond the city wall, a gargantuan bonfire burned, so large I wondered for a moment if it were a city fire spreading.

But as I swirled my glass, my thoughts drifted. The sense of disquiet that had filled me of late, a cloud that followed wherever I went, rose in me once more. Amid the hunt earlier, it had dampened so I could almost forget about it. But it had always been there, simmering beneath the surface.

I feared to think what it meant.

Standing atop our derelict tower, staring over the glimmering city, I wondered what had come of my nine years of striving. Perhaps it had never been about the truth. Perhaps it was the power of it, of hunting down a story and claiming its essence for your own.

But the hunt could only thrill for so long. And it was hard to believe any of it mattered when, despite all the skills I had gathered, I still couldn't find my brother's murderer.

A sudden sound yanked me from my thoughts. It took me a moment to recognize it. Not since I was a child had I heard it, for it only sounded in the direst circumstances. It blared over the rooftops and poured into the reveling forums and silent alleys. It vibrated in my chest and shook all other thoughts away.

The shell horns of the Laurel Palace called over Oedija, solemn and forlorn.

Three warnings came by the horns. The first, for fire. The second, for war. And the third, for a death.

Fire was likely. With wood buildings common along the peripheries of the city, the bonfires of Radiance posed a grave danger if mismanaged. The fire that burned in deme Thys beyond the wall seemed a likely candidate.

War, beyond rare skirmishes, had not been known in recent history, not since the Concordance of the Four Realms. The Bali ishakas to the east quarreled among themselves. The Qao Fu jaitin to the northeast remained isolated, their power waning. The Avvadin Imperium to the south seemed content with conquering their southern neighbors along the Rift.

The horns sounded twice, then a third time. I had heard this call only once before. I'd been young then, and in my fear, I clutched to my father's robes and asked him if we were safe. He'd taken me into his arms and rocked me back and forth. *Three horns are nothing to fear, Little Songbird,* he'd murmured. *Three horns are nothing to fear.*

As the echo of the horns died away, the late festival-goers below pantomimed their distress. Some cried into their hands. Others clutched their heads and fell to their knees, heedless of the mud that caked the street. Some just stood staring up, as if asking the gods how this could happen.

I closed my eyes. The fading vibrations seemed to shake me awake after a troubling dream, filling in the gaps that had formed in me over the past two and a half years. The desire for knowledge ignited in me once more.

Three calls of the horns announced that Despot Myron Wreath, beloved monarch of Oedija, was dead.

Three horns made me remember what it was to be a Finch.

4

CHANGING WINDS

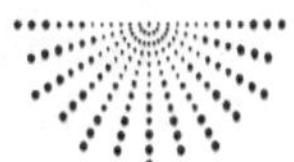

The Bali ishakas, a people of plateaus
Who succeed in only tearing each other down
Living in a land of plenty, yet never wealthy
They sit under thorny trees, hoping for wisdom
Like children, their Shakas squabble among
    themselves,
Never seeing the tiger prowling at their backs

- High Poetry of Lowly Things; by Hilarion the
    Second; 1085 SLP

In the turns after the shell horns blew, I flitted through the streets, dredging up every contact I knew. Some of the lights from the festival still glowed, but many had been extinguished. People had fled to their homes, waiting to see what would come in the wake of the Despot's death.

I could not have slept if I'd tried. I didn't know what was behind Myron's death or what it meant. But I knew enough. This represented change, more change than Oedija had seen in a century. And with change came opportunities for those who seized them.

25

Most of my contacts were missing, but a few were still around. I squeezed them for information, shelling out copper cullets and nickel magnes for whispers. I clung to every word. Yet for all my efforts, I learned nothing more substantial than the shimmering radiant winds. All agreed that Despot Myron had died within the Laurel Palace — but as to the cause, none could speak. Some claimed it to be a natural death. Others claimed assassination by Avvad, the neighboring empire to the south ever the object of suspicion. Still others believed Myron Wreath's own daughter to be responsible, since his untimely demise corresponded so closely with her return. But when I pushed for evidence or firsthand testimonials, my contacts became predictably coy.

Rumors of rumors — that was the best I could claim.

Gray dawn edged into the sky by the time I let off my search. Though I needed rest, I mostly stopped in order to reconvene with Xaron and Nomusa, who I assumed had left to dredge up whispers of their own. I'd bolted from Canopy without waiting for them, fire already coursing through my veins. I hoped that between the three of us, we could find a clear path forward.

Weary as my body was, my mind still turned. Inside me burned a thrill that I had not felt in a long time. It reminded me why I'd first become a Finch.

I slowly ascended the eleven circles of our derelict tower to Canopy. Reaching the door, I turned the handle. It was unlocked. Hesitating, I cracked it open and peered inside. A single pyr lamp lit the shadowed room. It was just enough to detect the silhouette sitting in a chair, a goblet held in its hand. Only when I saw the gleam of the figure's golden hair did I let out my breath.

Entering, I latched the door behind me and crossed the room. "Linos. What are you doing here? And don't tell me you've tapped our festival wine."

The boy glanced up from the chair with a grin, then took

another drink from his goblet. "Blame Nomusa — she let me in and told me to make myself comfortable. And you know this isn't my first taste, Sasa. You're not Pata. You know what I am."

"A scoundrel? I've known that since you were born." I held out my hand. "Give it here. You'll do whatever you please on the streets, but here, you don't drink."

My younger brother slowly gave over the goblet, his sneering smile telling me what he thought of my rules. As I took it, I glimpsed his hand in the pyr light. His knuckles were red and scraped. I quickly turned away and set down the goblet. My hand had begun shaking so that I thought it would spill.

When I had control of myself again, I turned back. Studying his face closer, I saw purple bruises beginning to form along his jaw.

"You've been fighting again," I said as calmly as I could.

His smile slipped away. "Someone was ruining our festival fun. I took care of it."

"And what about when someone takes care of you?"

Linos snorted and turned toward the bay window. "That won't happen."

I looked him up and down. His clothes were dirty and torn. It might have been excusable when he was eight-years-old, but at fifteen, he should have been past this mischief. As a man, it carried far direr consequences.

"Why did you come here, Linos?" I asked softly. "You should go home, clean up, put on a change of clothes. You reek, you know that?"

"And let Mother harp on me? I'd rather not. Besides, can't I visit my sister?"

"I don't like seeing you like this. You know that."

"Why? Because you think you can protect me?" His eyes were bright with drink, I saw now. "You should know better. I don't need anyone's protection."

I didn't try arguing. Quarreling with Linos had never worked before. "At least eat something. Knowing you, you've had nothing but wine all day."

"You're getting as sour as Mother. I didn't come here for a free meal, Sasa. I came on business. Or don't you want to know about the smuggler's markets?"

"I'm done with smugglers for the moment. Something else has my attention."

Linos raised an eyebrow. "And what's that?"

I hesitated. Despite his delinquency, I trusted my brother. He was the only member of my family whom I saw regularly. We even worked together on occasion, though I cringed at how he learned his information. But he was neither wise nor reliable. If there was someone behind the Despot's disappearance and they caught wind of my hunt, it could put the entire venture at risk.

I found myself speaking anyway. "I'm trying to figure out what happened to Myron Wreath last night."

He stared at me for a moment before a slow grin spread across his face. "You can't be serious."

I gave him a flat stare. "As serious as ever."

His smile faltered. "Sasa, that's crazy. Even for you."

"How? I'm a Finch. Parsing fact from rumor is what I do best."

"But not something like *this*. This is way beyond you."

I felt my temper rising. "You think I should abandon it."

"Of course!"

Something in his voice cooled my anger. There was real concern there, as well as something else. I searched my younger brother's face. What could cause him to worry? I didn't know he was capable of it.

As quickly as it had come, it was gone. Linos rose with a smile, though he didn't meet my eyes. "If you want to waste your time, far be it from me to stop you. Just let me know if you want to hear about the Valemish arks — I hear the contraband inside them is fascinating."

"Don't get in any more fights," I said to his back.

He flashed me one last smile over his shoulder, then slipped through the door.

Locking it behind him, I walked to the bay window and stared out over the pale cityscape. Did Linos know something that I didn't? I wondered if I should have pressed him for it. But pressure rarely worked with Linos; that he preferred living on the streets like a vagabond to living under Mother's rules was evidence of that. If he wanted me to know something, he'd tell me in his own time. More likely, it was his boyish arrogance at play.

I turned away from the window and entered my bedchamber, hoping for sleep that I doubted would come.

5

LOOSE ENDS

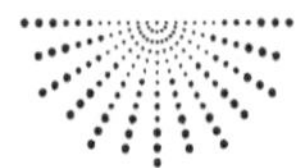

The Qao Fu jaitin, ever on the edge of ruin,
Skulking in caves like beasts hiding from hunters
Eating algae in place of bread and honey,
Too timid even to hunt down meat,
Too wise to enter the world at large...

- High Poetry of Lowly Things; by Hilarion the
*   Second; 1085 SLP*

I dreamed. Colors shifted within a fog, light refracting as if through glass. From that fog came a face, reptilian and malevolent. I looked up, and instead of the sky above me, the ground reflected back to me as if I stared at a mirror.

When I awoke, sunlight streamed in through the open ceiling. Groggy, I remembered the night's dream for a moment before all that had happened the night before returned to me.

Despot Myron was dead.

I sat bolt upright, heart pounding. From the noises outside my room, Nomusa and Xaron were up and about. Despite the late hour of the morning, evident from the bright sunlight on the ceiling, they were still here. Perhaps they'd been waiting to confer with me before they made a day of it.

Rising, I entered the main living space. Xaron had his feet kicked up on the back of our well-loved divan, idly playing with wisps of radiance between his fingers, weaving them in and out of each other and cursing as he broke the pattern. When we were alone, he didn't hide his greatest and most dangerous gift: that he was a warden, one of those touched by gods and given access to the energies of the Pyrthae. He was a fool ever to use it in my opinion. If discovered, he'd be hunted down and either killed or put into the Acadium, where he might as well be dead for all the freedom he'd be afforded.

Xaron looked up and flashed me a grin as I emerged, then narrowed his eyes again at the wisps of light twisting above his fingertips.

Nomusa was also before the window, moving smoothly from one form to the next in her people's martial art, Ixolo. Dressed in tight underwraps and glistening with sweat, she didn't even glance over at me.

An unpleasant realization slowly dawned on me.

When I hadn't shifted or spoken for a full minute, Xaron glanced at me again. "Something wrong?"

"What are you two doing here?" I tried to keep the edge of annoyance from my voice.

Nomusa and Xaron exchanged a look.

"Didn't I tell you?" he said to her smugly, then returned to his light weaving.

Nomusa just shook her head and continued her movements. She whipped herself into the air with a spin, then landed with splayed limbs like a prowling cat.

I finally found the words I'd been searching for. "You heard the horns. You know what's going on. But you're not out trying to find out anything. You're up here. *Practicing.*"

"And you were sleeping," Nomusa observed, barely out of breath despite her exertions.

The magic disappeared from Xaron's fingertips. "Look, Aire. The Despot's death is a shock and all that. But it isn't something we can do anything about."

"No?"

"No," Nomusa affirmed. "It's ridiculous even to consider investigating."

I looked from one to the other. The initial unpleasant surprise had faded, leaving me perplexed. "This is what we became Finches for. We'll never get another chance like this. How can you not want to know what's going on?"

"Many reasons." Xaron ticked them off on his hand. "One, it's dangerous. Two, it's pointless. Three, we're hungover."

"You're hungover," Nomusa corrected.

"There's just no profit to it," he continued, rising from the divan with a groan. "Besides, I have somewhere to be later, and I want to be fresh as a summer daisy."

"Again?" I said, exasperated. "And I assume you still won't tell us where you've been going this past season?"

"Perhaps a lady's house?" Nomusa asked, a smile quirking her lips.

"Perhaps," Xaron hedged as he strolled up to me and looked imploringly into my eyes. "Leave off this Myron business, Aire. No good can come of poking your nose into it. Besides, we have the Zotikos job to finish up."

"I'll leave off this job like you'll leave off channeling."

He chuckled. "Point taken."

I looked at him, then Nomusa. "I can't do this without you both. So, foolish as it is, I have to ask you to help."

Xaron hesitated, then dropped his gaze.

I sighed. I'd expected nothing less, but hoped for more. "I'll be back sometime later."

With that, I strode to the door, strapped on my sandals, and left.

I went slowly down the eleven circles of our tower, hoping one or both of my companions would come hurrying after me. But as I emerged from the tower onto the street, no one followed. I shook my head and started walking. Despite their lack of support, my resolve had not wavered. I would see what events had unfolded throughout the night. No matter their apathy.

I visited each of my contacts again as quickly as I could. Little had come in while I slept, but a few points of interest rose to the top.

Kyros Brighteyed, the Archmaster of the Acadium, and Tribune Vusumuzi, one of the highest officials of justice, had visited the Laurel Palace soon after the shell horns had blown. Theoretically, they hadn't yet left. It was particularly interesting because both were heavily involved with wardens and penning them in. It was also said that by way of the glowing gaze for which the Archmaster received his epithet, Kyros could see where channeling had recently occurred.

It could mean a warden had assassinated the Despot. Or one of the Imperium's bound pyrs, known as Silks, could be responsible. Or it could have nothing to do with channeling, and Vusumuzi and Kyros were just there to eliminate the chance that it did. Still, the implications were intriguing.

Feiyan, the Low Consul with whom I'd had misdealings in the past, had also visited the palace, but to confer with Asileia Wreath. Uneasily, I wondered what the Low Consul and the soon-to-be Despoina had to discuss. With those two women involved, it was best to assume the worst.

By two turns past noon, I'd gathered all the whispers I could, but still had no path forward. Still, I was committed to this hunt now. Now, I had to make sure Xaron and Nomusa were as well.

That meant tying up loose ends.

I found my way through Port to Maesos's shop. People had begun to return to the streets after a night spent in fear, and I walked past men and women peddling skewers of unknown meats from carts and stands, and traders spreading small trinkets from faraway places on rugs. Bali wood carvings from their trees rumored to grow as big around as Pillars and nearly as tall. Qao Fu silver workings with agate from their desert caves. Intricate bead workings and finely woven rugs from Avvad. All the Four Realms were present in Oedija. A Wreath might be dead, but life went on.

Arriving at the glassblower's door, I knocked and waited impatiently. Moments later, Maesos cautiously cracked open the door. Seeing me, a smile spread across his face, and he fully opened the door. "Airene! Glad to have one pleasant thing happen today. Don't be shy — come in!"

"I can only stay a moment," I warned him as I stepped inside the dark shop. The only light came from the glass pieces displayed on platforms across the room. It was Maesos's signature: incorporating pyrkin into his glassware in shifting designs that mesmerized his clientele. The old artisan had never had more success, though he did need to call in a Finch every once in a while to take care of problems that cropped up. Like a certain smuggler I'd stalked the day before.

"You heard the horns, of course," Maesos said as he wiped ashy hands on his dirty apron. As usual, his clothes were a mess and his hair singed. "Terrible thing. Myron Wreath always seemed a decent sort."

"Yes. I thought the same thing. Which is why his death is all the more surprising. Did you hear the Council declared it a natural death?"

"A natural death?" Maesos bellowed a laugh. "That old bull? I doubt it! What did they say he died of?"

"Foul humors of the heart. He's supposed to have dropped dead in the palace's banquet hall."

"A man of his size wouldn't let anyone stand in the way of his meal. I should know." He slapped his belly with a grin.

"That's actually what I wanted to talk about, more or less."

"Myron's gut?"

I gave him an indulgent smile. "About his unnatural death. This might be the job of a lifetime for me. If I prove it was an assassination and discover who was behind Myron's death..." I shook my head, unable to voice my hopes.

Maesos gave me a fond smile. "Oh, Airene. You haven't changed since you were a girl pretending to apprentice at my shop while you snuck around and took care of my competitors. That same fire still fills you after, what, ten years already?"

I grimaced at the memory. When, at my Calling, I had declared myself a Finch, I'd learned just how profitless naming yourself a Verifier of Truth was. Though I continued to believe myself a Finch incarnate, I had bowed to reality and become the clerk to a certain eccentric glassblower. Maesos, a recent widower then, had needed someone to attend to his accounts and the storefront while he devoted more time to his craft. Either he was desperate enough to take on a willful, inexperienced girl, or he saw something in me others did not, for he took me under his wing.

Though I'd lamented the necessity of helping the odd man and loathed the menial task of counting beads on an abacus, there was one place I truly excelled: undercutting Maesos's competitors. The glass smith finally became curious when his profits had doubled in the second season of my employment. When put to the question, I succumbed to his gentle urging and revealed the truth: that my evenings had been spent on excursions to the other glass shops in the surrounding demes, investigating their offerings for flaws, understanding their competitive advantages — and, where possible, digging up the dirty secrets of their practices.

Thus Maesos had become the first of my many clients.

"Ten years," I affirmed. "Ten long years."

The glass smith smiled. "If anyone deserves a break, it's

you. Follow this dream, then. But you don't need me to tell you that."

"No. But you can still help me. Did that rat Zotikos come by here today?"

Maesos frowned. "No. Should he have?"

I sighed. "Let's just say he was warned. I should follow through and ensure he delivers it, but..."

His eyes lit up with understanding. "Leave it for later, Airene. It's not immediate. I was eager to get my hands on those new strains of pyrkin because I had one to show you — a strain said to dampen a warden's channeling."

I raised an eyebrow. "And you believed whoever told you that?"

He smiled sheepishly and shrugged. "Ridiculous, I know. But after that warden Iela tried to kill you three years past..." He shook his head. "It was my fault you got mixed up in all that. I owe you something."

I tried not to remember the face of the woman he'd named. I'd seen it often enough in my dreams.

"You don't owe me anything," I said firmly. "But if you're alright waiting..."

"Yes, yes." He waved me toward the door. "Best get on with it. I know how you are when you catch wind of a mystery."

It was my turn to smile sheepishly. He knew me all too well.

TWO TURNS LATER, I found myself in a dirty back alley tavern.

The Ignorant Intellectual was far from my usual choice of drinking holes. Not only was it on the opposite side of the city in deme Bazaar, but its clientele were a rough sort. The place stank of cheap spirits and unclean patrons who hadn't made it to the chamberpots before heaving their guts. A goblet of wine rested before me, but I didn't dare drink from it, not trusting the dirty rag with which the bartender had wiped it. I suspected he'd sold me leftover festival wine. But then again, when I ordered "a chalice of unrequited intoxication," I wasn't looking for drink.

"You'll wear out your pretty teeth, grinding them like that."

I startled and looked around at the man standing next to me. "You know I hate when you do that."

Talan wore his usual half-smile as he slid down next to me. His dark, shoulder-length hair was barely restrained by a greasy leather strap. He wore a once cream-colored tunic underneath a sky-blue vest, and dark trousers tucked into worn boots. But cleanliness wasn't what I expected from the Guilder. One of the agents of Oedija's predominate crime syndicate, he had become a contact and a friend in the three years I'd known and worked with him.

He stole my goblet of wine and sniffed it, wrinkling his nose. "How does that barkeep ruin festival wine?"

"I assumed he would. But you know why I'm here."

"Yes, I suspect I do." He studied me critically. "But don't you think sniffing around the Despot's death is a bit extravagant, even for you?"

"Don't try to talk me out of it. I just want to know what you've heard."

His smirk didn't dissipate as he leaned back into the hard booth, hands folding behind his head. "I think you might require something more than talk. How about we take a walk instead?"

He rose smoothly and offered a hand to me. Perplexed, I took it and let him lead me out of the tavern.

"Where are we going?" I asked as we headed in the direction opposite from the way I'd come by.

The Guilder turned back with his usual half-smile. "Do you trust me?"

"Not in the slightest."

"Good." He turned and started down the alley.

Shaking my head, I followed.

After a series of back alleys, Talan finally stopped at the end of one opening into a forum. From the position of the Pillars looming above us, I knew we'd crossed from Bazaar into the neighboring deme Sandglass. The forum was laid out as a square, with a small moat separating a courtyard from the surrounding buildings, and delicate bridges crossing over. On the island formed by the canal stood a lonely edifice, a bluff, black pyramid barely illuminated by blazing braziers and twice as tall as the surrounding buildings.

"Interesting activities have been occurring here," Talan said softly. "Activities some might believe less than legal were they in a different line of work than myself."

"I assume you're referring to the arks? Linos mentioned something about smuggling items through them."

"Perhaps. More to the point, I refer to what I believe they harbor in the heart of the temples." His eyes bore into the dark stone as if he might see through it.

"And what's that?"

He flashed me a mischievous grin. "I can't tell you everything right away, can I? I know you, Airene. You're in this for the intrigue."

I smiled despite myself. "Come on, Talan. I'm in the middle of the biggest job of my career. I need to know if I'm wasting my time on more Avvadin conspiracies of yours."

The Guilder's smile slipped. "We'll find out soon enough. For you and I are going to investigate within."

I stared at him. "You're not serious."

He raised an eyebrow. "Am I not? Me, the most famous vault-breaker to come out of Erimis, isn't serious about breaking into a simple Valemish temple?"

"Yes. Because that same famed vault-breaker knows that a certain Finch isn't fond of house-breaks."

He cast me a wink. "We'll see who prevails."

I already knew. Since the last exception I'd made two years before, I'd held to my resolution. It'd be simple to resist this wild pyr chase as well.

I turned away. "Thanks for the brief diversion. But it's time to get back to the real work."

Talan halted me with a touch to my arm. His fingers burned with an inner fire, as they always did. I shivered, as I always did.

"Consider it," he implored.

As I met his eyes, they burned with something else, a fervor I couldn't understand. Even knowing his stories, his hate for the Valemish and Avvad was beyond what I could comprehend.

"I will," I lied, and I left him there in the dark alley.

6

CHANCE ENCOUNTERS

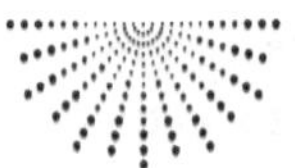

Avvad, oh mighty Imperium, warrior of the Four
    Realms
Volcanic Valem puffing up its backside
The leash of the Silks held in the hands of the Tefra
Priests too ugly to remove their masks
Fear, the yoke of its people, in the guise of belief
A cattle nation of conquerors the Kahin-Shah leads

  - High Poetry of Lowly Things; by Hilarion the
    Second; 1085 SLP

F ive long days passed.

I sat in a cafe by myself, sipping a cup of coffee, spirits low. Presumably, I waited for Xaron and Nomusa. Zipho, the owner of the cafe and a friend of ours, had a lead on a job for us and had asked us to meet at her cafe two turns past noon. After a morning of fruitless sniffing around, I'd arrived early and sat silently to drink my coffee.

I didn't want to abandon the hunt. I didn't want to consider other jobs. But with our purses rapidly lightening and food prices continuing to climb, I hardly had another choice. To make no mention of Nomusa and Xaron's continued resistance. Nomusa had tried bullying Maesos into letting us finish his job, but the loyal glassblower had stood firm even before her anger. Yet with the way things were going, I would have to track down Zotikos after all, if only for a little coin to continue my inquiries.

For five days, I'd scrambled for information. I'd tried to enter the Laurel Palace and been rebuffed. I'd tried to enter the Acadium to see Archmaster Kyros and the Tribunal to see Tribune Vusumuzi, but had been turned away at both gates. I'd thrown coins at hints of whispers and received less back.

The immediacy of the puzzle was rapidly dissipating. Myron had received a small, private funeral, at odds with the man who had always drawn a crowd. Plans for Asileia's Ascension were well underway and would commence the next day. Soon, she would be the Ruling Wreath. Whether or not she was behind her father's murder, I doubted she would be amenable to someone investigating it.

For all my efforts, I'd learned little. Feiyan had met with Asileia again and again, confirming my suspicions of a relationship between them. But what sort of relationship remained unclear. Valemish temples continued to be well-frequented, but whether the traffic was innocuous or not, I could not tell. Finally, whispers told of activity from within deme Thys. Xaron had said the Manifest had gathered a village there, and from what I heard, he wasn't wrong. Thousands of people were said to have set up in the encampments around the lake in the deme, and all were hoping for an impossible dream: to become attuned to the Pyrthae. But I didn't think a cult, even a growing cult lauding wardens, was likely to be behind killing Oedija's monarch.

I'd seen Talan yesterday during one of my long treks out for information. The Guilder had been less than empathetic and repeated his offer to accompany me into the heart of Sandglass's Valemish temple, pointing out I had no better leads. I found myself considering it before I returned to my senses. I wondered how desperate I'd be before I accepted, and feared I wasn't far off.

A quarter-turn after they were due to arrive, Nomusa and Xaron entered the cafe. I'd already finished my coffee.

"About time," I said drily as they approached my table.

"We're not that late," Nomusa objected. "And you can wait a little longer while we get drinks." She headed toward the bar that ran through the center of the room, behind which the portly Bali who owned the cafe, Zipho, bustled.

"Order mine too — you know what I like." Xaron sat down opposite me. "Learn anything interesting while you were out?"

I shrugged and recounted the day's learnings. "So not much," I summarized morosely.

He nodded with a sympathetic smile. For a moment, he looked as if he would say more. But he pressed his lips back together and remained silent.

"Let me guess," I said. "You think the hunt's dead in the water."

"I didn't say that. But I wouldn't be wrong if I had."

I shook my head. "I'm not done yet."

He shrugged and looked away.

An awkward silence fell. Despite my annoyance, I made a play at reconciliation. "And what did you do this morning?"

His gaze wandered to the ceiling. He didn't have to answer for me to know.

"Gone to your mysterious woman again?"

He finally met my eyes. "I've told you," he said with a touch of irritation, "it's not like that."

"Then what's it like? You haven't told us any details."

"I'll tell you. Eventually."

Nomusa approached the table and, seating herself, set Xaron's drink in front of him, a mug of coffee so sweetened with honey and milk as to be unrecognizable.

"What'd she say?" I asked.

"She was annoyingly vague." Nomusa took a sip of her coffee and made a face. "And distracted. I'd ask her for another drink if I thought it would be any better. You would think being the true Heir of our ishaka would count for more."

Normally, I would have rolled my eyes at Nomusa invoking her claim to royalty. Not that it was untrue. When she was a child, her father, Shaka of the Yorandu, had been killed with the rest of her family. Only her aunt and Nomusa had survived. Fearing for Nomusa's life, she had taken her to Oedija and cared for her until her death. Since then, Zipho, also of the Yorandu ishaka, had taken her under her wing and treated her in a uniquely Bali manner as both her rightful leader and an errant daughter.

But I was far from a joking mood. I couldn't think of who else Zipho would want us to meet other than a prospective client. With dread, I thought about how much harder it would be to drown out Nomusa and Xaron's objections to my fruitless pursuit when we had a paying job waiting in the wings.

She shrugged. "All I know is that we're meeting someone soon and were lucky they didn't arrive before us."

Just then, someone entered the cafe. All three of us looked around expectantly.

Xaron quickly turned back to the table, eyes wide. "Tribune," he muttered.

My heart hammered in my chest as I stared at the newcomer. The Bali man was dressed in the maroon robes of the Tribunal and stood scanning the cafe with a calm expression. His skin was dark and rich as newly rained earth. Though his robes hung thick about him, his thin face betrayed his spare frame. White gloves peeked out from beneath wide sleeves, and around his neck hung a bronze medallion composed of two half-circles connected by a thin lattice of silvery threads. The robes were sign enough of who he was, but the medallion legitimized his station as part of the Confessionary Tribunal, Oedija's judiciary branch of the government.

I leaned forward and spoke in a low voice. "That's not just any Tribune. That's Tribune Vusumuzi. He looked into Myron's death and is in charge of the Shepherds."

Zipho bustled over to the Tribune and made a big show of pouring him a drink, a performance at which Vusumuzi smiled politely.

"Did Zipho want us to meet *him*?" Nomusa whispered, incredulous.

My mouth had gone dry. This couldn't have come at a better time. After all my scrambling, here was someone with firsthand information on the murder. Why now, of all times, Zipho chose to introduce us was beyond me. But if the gods wanted to bless me with good luck, I wasn't going to object.

"They're coming," Xaron muttered as the pair approached. It took me a moment to understand the depth of his nervousness. Then it finally clicked. Tribune Vusumuzi, being in charge of the Shepherds, enforcers of the laws restricting wardens, would undoubtedly make a feral like Xaron uncomfortable.

The Tribune held a steaming cup as he stopped before our table. From behind his back, Zipho gestured impatiently for us to rise. We readily complied.

"Nomusa-sha," Zipho said, addressing Nomusa in the Bali manner, "please meet Tribune Yorandu Vusumuzi-sa. Honored Tribune, this is Eshalo Yorandu Nomusa-sha, true Heir to our ishaka."

Vusumuzi bowed and offered his arm. Nomusa gripped it at the forearm from above, while he gripped from below.

"Vusumuzi-sa," she said formally, "I am always delighted to meet a fellow of our ishaka. Have you been gone from it long? Zipho-ma has not given your family name."

"Please, call me Vusu, Nomusa-sha," the Tribune said as he withdrew his hand. "And as you may already suspect, I left our home a long time ago. The family I come from is no longer of consequence, as I am its last member." Though his words were firm, he smiled in a kindly manner.

"His tatu tell a different story," Zipho said conspiratorially. "He has only shown me once, but my eyes do not deceive. From the line of the old kings, he is."

I knew little of the history of the Bali chiefdoms, and nothing of the kingdom that had once united them. I glanced at the sleeves hiding his tatu. Nomusa's eyes showed she wished to see them as well but did not ask. Perhaps it would be considered rude.

"It is not entirely out of the realm of possibility," Vusu said with a smile. Then he turned to me. "And may I ask your name?"

That he addressed me directly threw me off balance for a moment. Typically, Bali spoke only to each other, even when others were present. Perhaps he had been so long in Oedija that he had adopted our manners.

"Airene," I said after a moment's pause. "Of Port."

He nodded slowly. "Very nice to meet you." He held out his palm face-up, and I hesitated before greeting him the Bali way. Even through his sleeve and glove, his skin felt feverishly warm. I withdrew quickly, studying him. Was he ill? It would explain his thinness. When I met his gaze, he smiled at me, and something about it seemed sad. It confused me, but I didn't let it show in my expression.

"And you?" Vusu said, looking past me to Xaron, who stood the farthest back of us all.

"Xaron of Port."

Vusu held out his hand, but Xaron looked aside as if distracted. Vusu let his arm drop but gave my friend a considering look. I wished Xaron had simply accepted the greeting. He risked drawing the Tribune's suspicion by not having done so.

Zipho watched the exchanges with more than a bit of her own puzzlement, but she quickly recovered her sheen of affability and turned to Nomusa. "I thought you all might be interested in talking."

With a nod, she returned to her counter to attend to the growing line of customers.

Vusu made no move to sit, so Nomusa, Xaron, and I remained standing. Silence fell as Vusu studied each of us. Despite the awkwardness, his gaze remained calm. I wondered what Zipho's reason for introducing us was. I didn't dare believe what I hoped for.

I broke the silence. "Tribune Vusumuzi, I'm sure you've been busy these past few days."

He smiled again. "No more than usual, I'm afraid. Myron's death is just the latest trial."

It seemed a flippant dismissal of the momentous event. Could Vusu not suspect anything of it? Could it be a natural death after all? My stomach sank.

Desperate to keep my hopes afloat, I said, "I would think the Despot's death is a greater challenge than most."

Vusu continued to wear his slight smile. "It is a piece falling on a board full of pieces, Airene of Port. But other designs continue forward."

"You see this as a game, then. I wonder who the players are."

The Tribune's eyes crinkled. "No one surprising for you if I'm not mistaken. Yes, I've heard of you three before. Finches, after the old Order of Verifiers."

I tried to repress a wince. Our work wasn't exactly illegal, but it couldn't be called sanctioned by the law either. And Xaron's abilities had sometimes been key to our success. Perhaps a pattern would be apparent to one who worked closely with wardens like Vusu.

"Yes," I replied shortly.

"Do not fear. I have no wish to interfere with your work. In fact, I believe it a worthier path than most. After all, at its heart is the pursuit of truth. And truth should always be unveiled, lest we all suffer the consequences of secrecy."

The Tribune was not at all what I'd expected. I wondered what Nomusa and Xaron made of him. "I appreciate you saying that. We try to uphold the Verifiers' mission as much as we can."

"And from what I've heard, you've done well."

I nodded, unsure of what else to say. I knew where I wanted to turn the conversation, but considering the Tribune's earlier dismissal of my inquiry, I didn't think I'd have much luck.

Vusu glanced at the sandglass Zipho had mounted on one wall, which told the time as two-and-a-half turns after noon.

"I fear I must go." He looked to each of us in turn, and I thought his gaze lingered uncomfortably on Xaron. "It was a pleasure meeting you, Airene, Nomusa-sha, Xaron. Do stop by my solar soon. I would like to speak further. Perhaps your talents might be useful in these tumultuous times."

Stunned, I muttered words of thanks, then each of us bowed. The Tribune nodded his acknowledgment and turned away, setting his mug on the counter untouched. Waving his farewell to Zipho, he turned out of the cafe.

A moment later, Zipho bustled up next to Nomusa, staring at the closing door. "That man! Half the time he comes in and forgets to eat or drink. No wonder he's withering away!"

Nomusa drew her close. "Zipho-ma, why did you introduce us to the Tribune? And don't think to play coy with me anymore!"

The cafe owner huffed. "I do not play coy, Nomusa-sha! A Tribune is a good man to know, is he not? Vusumuzi-sa has come here for some time, on and off. I would not have asked him to meet you, as I did not want to overstep my relationship with him."

Nomusa bowed her head in thanks.

"But then he asked about you," Zipho continued.

"He initiated this?" I interjected, forgetting myself.

Both Nomusa and Zipho scowled at me.

"Yes," Zipho replied stiffly, though she looked at Nomusa. "He asked about you two days ago. I was vague, but when he continued to be interested, I invited him here."

"You should have told us more directly," Nomusa rebuked her. "What if he were after us?"

Zipho scoffed. "Vusumuzi-sa is a good man."

"He's a Tribune. Still, I thank you. He could be a good man to know."

Making our pardons, we left Zipho's. I burned to ask what their impressions were of the Tribune, but I couldn't do it now, not out in the open. Vusu had known of us. Gratifying as that was, it was worrisome. We would not stand up to the scrutiny of the Tribunal.

But even so, we'd talked to the Tribune, and he wanted to speak further. It was another lead if I pursued it with patience. A man of contradictions such as Vusu was not to be trifled with lightly. But even with the risks, I would approach him. I couldn't stop now.

I halted abruptly in the street. Xaron and Nomusa turned back.

"Hunting again?" Nomusa asked in a neutral voice.

"Now?" Xaron objected. "We have to discuss what just happened."

"I have to know more if I'm going to speak further with the Tribune." I said it off-hand as if it were a given.

They stared at me, speechless.

"He was there," I continued hurriedly. "He saw the scene of Myron's death, and likely his body. If anyone would know if it was murder or not, it's him." I met each of their gazes.

"Tomorrow I mean to go to his solar and ask him about it. And I mean to know as much as I can at that time."

Nomusa laughed scornfully and began walking away. Xaron lingered a moment, looking helplessly at me. "Good luck," he said, then followed after her.

As I watched them leave, loneliness settled in again. The three of us had usually worked together on inquiries. I doubted I could have remained a Finch for so long without them. But still, I couldn't give this up because they would not join in. I had to believe that once they saw evidence of a conspiracy, they'd cave. They would come around in the end.

Someone grabbed my arm.

I startled and spun away, disoriented. Everything came into clear focus as I recognized the honor grinning at me, his hand still extended from touching me. Kako.

"You," I hissed. Fear, cold and clammy, spread inside me.

"Me," Kako agreed easily. "Had you expected someone else?"

"What do you want?"

"You know what I want. Or should I say, what my mistress wants."

Whispers went both ways. Feiyan must have heard I'd been inquiring after her. She was the hawk watching for ripples on a pond, ready to dive at the first sign of prey — only she had a hundred eyes watching for her. I had been careless.

And carelessness could deliver Xaron straight into the Shepherds' hands.

"We had an agreement," Kako said, his tone pleasant, his eyes anything but. "You were not to investigate anything related to my mistress. In return, we would leave be your... secret."

Fear chilled me. I knew the secret he referred to. As a result of the incident three years ago when I'd narrowly avoided dying, Feiyan had gathered that either Xaron or

Nomusa was a warden. Though she didn't know which of them was, I knew it would do little to protect any of us if Shepherds came knocking at Canopy's door.

Though I needed to appease him, I could give no more than a perfunctory bow. "I apologize. It was not your mistress I've been looking into. It's the woman she's been seen with."

The honor shook his head with a knowing smile. "No, no, Airene of Port. Do not attempt to deceive me with such thin lies. You knew precisely what you sniffed after. Yet, like a hungry mongrel, you could not help yourself. I understand this. We all have desires burning inside us, waiting for the opportune moment to sate them."

His gaze had gained an uncomfortable edge. I looked aside. "I will avoid her. You have my word."

The honor took a step closer. "And you will avoid whispers of Asileia Wreath as well," he said in a low voice. "Understood?"

"Yes."

He leaned back, his smile renewed. "Good. Now may you have a pleasant, uneventful day. Can't have too much normalcy in times like these."

He gave a mock bow as he spun off into the crowd. I watched the strange honor as he disappeared out of sight.

I turned and walked quickly toward Canopy. No doubt Feiyan would keep eyes on me still. I would be able to learn nothing more today. But no matter what I'd told Kako, I would not stop. That Feiyan protected Asileia was further confirmation that something was amiss here. I would have to step more carefully and speak more softly and continue on. Despite the risks.

Though I wondered what this hunt would cost me.

7

FINCH IN THE RAIN

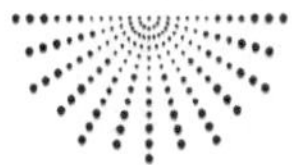

Though the Wreaths were reinstated as the monarchs of Oedija, true power was reserved for the members of the People's Conclave. Yet one hundred and twenty-one Servants were far too many to act quickly in emergent situations. Thus the Demos Council was formed, eleven Low Consuls each elected through the support of ten fellow Servants. These Low Consuls have, in dire times, wielded supreme power. However, oftentimes the eleventh seat has lain undecided, disagreements remaining between the Servants who would determine it. Thus the Archon, representative of the Wreath in the Conclave, has acted as the deciding vote in tied decisions, and has brought back some measure of power to the Laurel Palace.

- Oedija: A History; by Acadian Helene, Master Historian; 1167 SLP

Nomusa and Xaron were surprised to see me return shortly after them. But as they sensed my mood, neither commented on it. The afternoon wound on and evening settled in, and soon, our usual routines found us.

Despite the impending famine, neither of my companions

seemed avid to pursue another job. Nomusa eventually went out again, purportedly to stir up some leads, but I knew it was as likely she'd wind up in a tavern on the arm of a handsome man. Xaron, meanwhile, reclined on the divan and practiced his channeling.

Stuck inside for the day, I pretended to read the book open before me, *Tales of the Desolate.* A book of Bali tales pressed upon me by Nomusa when the Manifest cult started to rise in Oedija, it recounted legends surrounding the Zakale people, who, following twin warden brothers named Yama and Lophe, nearly conquered the whole of the Bali highlands. When they failed, the rest of the ishakas exacted vengeance on them, expunging every man, woman, and child from existence, even to the name, for the Zakale became known as the Unnamed afterward. What Nomusa found fascinating was just as a serpent god had been at the center of the Zakale cult, so was a wyvern for the Manifest. Though if it was for the Manifest a god or a mere symbol, neither of us knew.

But my attention wandered from the pages. What to do about Feiyan was beyond me. I couldn't continue to ply my contacts without her knowing. I didn't know who was reporting on me, or where she had eyes posted. Until I had a solution, I couldn't continue to investigate.

All the more infuriating because now I was surer than ever that there was actually something to investigate.

The door to Canopy roused me from my brooding thoughts. Corin, the last of our loftmates, entered and wearily bent to unstrap her sandals, no mean feat with her legs caked in mud. As a cartwoman, she ran back and forth along Oedija's streets, transporting those who could afford not to walk. She was one of the few women to take on such a laborious profession, but was built well for it. Outlanders, as the natives of the islands to the far northwest were called, were known for their strength and tall stature. Corin, however, was a force unto herself, both in body and mind. Working day and night, she sought to raise enough money to bring her sister, Kari, over to Oedija. Corin was a woman of few words, but as far as I understood, Kari was persecuted for some reason, and might be safer in Oedija. But in the two years Corin had been living in Canopy, she had not raised enough money to bring her over.

We greeted each other, but the cartwoman quickly retired to her room. I tried to return to my reading, yet found myself distracted by Xaron's channeling. Channeling ice, I'd learned from him, was no mean feat. It involved manipulating one of the elements, radiance, in an inverse manner. But it was from whom he'd learned it that irked me.

Nearly three years ago, a feral warden named Iela, who'd had a propensity for channeling ice, had come into our awareness after killing a patrician. When we had pursued her, she'd singled me out, and by a threat to my family, lured me from Canopy. Just before she was going to kill me, she'd boasted of her master experimenting on and killing my older brother, Thero, years before. Talan had saved me, but it was I who had killed her.

I shivered at the memory of plunging the knife into her neck. My stomach turned.

"Airene?"

I met Xaron's gaze, but my eyes flickered to the icicle he had willed into being. "I'm fine," I lied.

His eyes followed mine, then widened. In a moment, the icicle dissipated into shimmering mist. "'Thae below, Airene. I didn't even think about… well, you know."

"You shouldn't have to." I tried for a smile.

From his expression, I knew I'd failed. Xaron studied me as he leaned back into the divan, but he said nothing.

As much to escape the memories as to fill the silence, I found myself speaking. "Sometimes, I'm jealous of you."

He laughed. "I'm sure you are."

"No, really. When I was little, I wanted nothing more than to be a warden."

"Truly?"

I nodded. "For years, I pestered my mother and father, begging them to tell me why I wasn't attuned, and how people received the blessing of a god to become so. I wanted to know all about the Pyrthae and how wardens channeled its energy, and how it felt to work magic. Of course, they didn't have answers for me. I asked about it at our local temple, but the oracle knew little, and the few paltry books in its library held more myth than fact."

He smiled smugly. "They're writing about it secondhand. Of course they wouldn't know." His grin faltered. "It's funny. I was just the opposite of you when I was young. I hated that I was a warden."

That was hard to imagine. I couldn't picture Xaron not being a warden. It was too integral to who he was. "Really? Why?"

"My mother. And the extent of my… gift." He paused for a long moment. "My parents fled the Wumofu because of the Matriarchs' restrictions on channeling. My mother wished to utilize an energetic element not sanctioned for use within the jaitin, one based on formulae, and the Matriarchs refused her request to pursue them. But Mother's not one to take no for an answer. There's no hiding something like that among the Qao Fu caves, so we came to Oedija. For a while, she practiced in secret, despite the risk of death hanging over her and Father. She even became famous in some circles for her powerful distillations, though obviously no one knew she channeled to create them."

"How did that work? I thought wardens utilized energy, not formulae."

Xaron shrugged. "From what she said, distillations *do* have energy, just like fire and force. And because of this, she was able to use them as mediums for channeling incredible effects."

I shook my head. "I'll take your word for it. Still, that doesn't seem so bad a home to grow up in."

"Everything was different for me. Before I was born, Mother had an accident. An experiment had gone poorly, and she'd burned herself up both arms and across her torso. It changed her, my father says. From then on, she's been in pain. She gave up her concoctions and stopped using her powers. And she didn't want the same thing to happen to me. She decided playing with the elements was bound to burn you sooner or later."

"So no channeling."

"No channeling around her," he amended with a slight smile. "She tried not to let me start, but that didn't sit well with a curious child like me, especially not when my attunement was so strong."

My gaze wandered to his hands. Xaron had ten shifts, seen in the faint, ever-moving patterns along his fingertips. It meant he was as powerful a warden as they came. Such a strong attunement only emerged once a generation, even in a city the size of Oedija, at least according to what Xaron had told me. Not that he had much opportunity to use it.

"What does it feel like?" I asked, staring at his hands. "When you're channeling?"

He didn't answer, but shuffled a hand in his tunic and produced two copper cullets and three nickel magnes on the tips of his fingers. His brow creasing, he stared at them like a taskmaster at a tested pupil. After a moment, the coins began to float, lifting a cubit away before settling to hover a few inches above his fingertips.

It seemed a mere parlor trick, but I knew it was far more. It was access to a world parallel to our own, a plane beyond my understanding. The Pyrthae was said to be composed of the energetic elements, and home to pyr and the gods. I didn't know that I believed in spirits and divine beings, but it was hard to deny the existence of the Pyrthae when Xaron could access its power.

"It's like undamming a stream," he said softly, eyes watching the coins. "You always feel it there, pushing, almost pleading to be woven and formed."

"Where does it push?"

"Everywhere. But it starts here." He used his free hand to indicate his torso.

"The locus." The point through which wardens drew the Pyrthae's power. The drawings I'd seen in the temple library showed a man with his limbs splayed and a circle drawn around him, with the locus indicated at the middle point. The exact center of a human being.

Xaron nodded. "You have to dam it consciously at first, but it becomes second-nature."

"Sounds exhausting. I never knew you had to maintain it. Is that why you're constantly itching to channel?"

"Not exactly. If you could feel it, you'd know why. It's invigorating, sensing the power rush through you. Intoxicating."

"No wonder you can't control yourself," I teased.

He grinned sheepishly. "Exactly."

"Is there one element that is more invigorating than the others?"

"Yes and no. Each element has a unique feel. Radiance makes you warm and light-headed. Kinesis is the opposite — you become grounded in the physical and feel like you can do anything. Magnesis is subtler. There is a humming that flows through you, soothing and stirring at the same time." He smiled — from the humming of magnesis in him at that very moment, I imagined. "The effect is greater if you channel more, or if you don't know how to direct the energy. When I was young and first channeled, the energy didn't know where to go, and it filled all of me so I thought I would burst. Now, the flow knows: straight to the fingers and toes."

I shook my head. Strange that the most delicate parts of the human body could control so much power. "So you let it stream in and then… what?"

"You form it." He tapped his head with his free hand. "With your focus. What we call your mental energy."

"And that's it?"

He flashed me a wry grin. "In a sense. But it takes years of practice to channel reliably. I failed to control even kinesis for years, which usually comes easiest to people. The things I managed were by accident, like when my father woke me and I sent him flying across the room like he were a doll. But it's like music. You can hear how a song is supposed to go long before you can play it. And even people who have no training can feel the music, and know when it's right and wrong."

I stared at the gaps above his fingers, straining to see what held the coins up. But it was like the weight of the Pyrthae, ever pushing down on the air and us — a force you could feel, but couldn't see. I sat back, disappointed.

He saw and laughed. "Trying to see what causes magnesis is like trying to see how a singer sings. You can't see the mechanism. And what's more, you lack the faculties to emulate the effect."

I arched an eyebrow at him. "Someone's sounding scholarly today."

He blanched, then muttered, "You asked, didn't you?"

I studied him as he looked aside. It was a strange reaction to an innocent statement. Seeing nothing else for it, I shifted course. "So you just felt the energy pushing on your dam one day?"

He seemed to recover. "Well," he said, laughing so that the coins wobbled, "there wasn't a dam at first. To be honest, it's like wetting the bed when you're young — your body has to learn to prevent it. You build that self-control, that limit." He patted his navel. "And eventually, with the right training, it's only there when you need it."

I fished a coin from my purse and threw it, trying to take down one of his hovering coins. But even though it connected, the coin drifted back into place. Xaron had such a look of satisfaction I couldn't help but reach out and swat them away.

"Hey!" He laughed and rose to retrieve the coins.

Smiling, my eyes wandered by habit to the finch cage on the balcony. A drizzle had started outside, and the cage was indistinct, but I could just detect a finch pecking from the seed basket. On its leg, a bedraggled message flapped in the wind.

Xaron followed my gaze. "A finch?"

I was already rising. "I'll go see what it says."

Excitement bubbled up in me as I exited into the chill night and took the new arrival in hand. He shivered, and I cooed softly to him as I untied the message, then put him in the cage with the others until it was time to send him back.

Retreating inside, I squinted to make out the smudged lettering:

The Wolf is watching.

The note was unsigned. I stared at the script, trying to pry out more from those four words and understand what they meant, to make no mention of who had sent them. The script looked vaguely familiar, but wasn't immediately recognizable.

Xaron approached to examine it over my shoulder. "What's it say? I can't make it out."

"'The Wolf is watching.'"

"From who?"

"Don't know."

He stepped back, brow creased in thought. "Who have you sent queries to lately? Who might need to respond with a cryptic message, sending a bird out on the worst night for it? Who's in danger?"

His questions sieved my contacts until I recognized the floral script. "Nikias."

"The new Archon's steward?"

"The very same."

"I suppose he might know what's going on. But strange that he feels in danger."

A smile had found my lips. "Not so strange if you assume one thing."

Xaron groaned. "Let me guess. That the Despot was murdered."

"It makes the most sense. This afternoon—" I cut off mid-sentence, having been on the verge of telling about my earlier encounter with Kako. But with the inquiry gaining momentum and Xaron finally showing interest, I didn't want to undermine it now. "This afternoon I learned that Feiyan has been meeting with Asileia a lot recently."

He raised an eyebrow. "I thought you'd already told us that."

"I heard it again, which is significant enough," I lied. "And what do you think Vusumuzi wants with us? Why seek us out now, when he must have heard we were Finches from Zipho a long time ago?"

"What are you getting at?"

I held up the message. "This isn't an ordinary message. It's short, unsigned, and in a code we don't have the cipher for. And it came in the rain — not a good time for finches to fly, but the best time for a bird to pass unseen. And the words — 'The Wolf is watching.' If this came from Nikias, that means someone is watching from inside the Laurel Palace — our Wolf, whoever that is."

"Not necessarily from within. They could be watching outside."

I shook my head. "He wouldn't be worried about interception if they were outside. It'd be simple enough to sneak out a bird."

Xaron shrugged. "Fair enough. So who is the Wolf?"

I thought for a moment. "If we narrow it down to people within the Laurel Palace, that makes it easier to guess. Asileia is the most obvious choice, but I wouldn't describe her as a wolf."

"Maybe that's the point. I wouldn't necessarily be specific about the person I was accusing if I were sneaking out a message."

"But it wouldn't make for much of a code then, would it? I think it has to cue someone in particular."

"What about one of her oracles? Or maybe Feiyan, since she's there so often now? She has some wolfishness to her."

"It could be any of them. Or it could be Jaxas, or First Laurel Lykos, or a hundred other people we don't know about. But I know one thing. If someone doesn't want word getting out from the palace, it tells us there's something more going on." I cocked a smile at Xaron. "You don't cover up an accident."

Finally, I saw it in his eyes. He believed. And he was curious, too, if Myron was murdered.

"Fine." Xaron exhaled noisily and looked out the bay window. "So how do we start narrowing down who it could be?"

I followed his gaze and stared out over Oedija, thinking. With the Festival of Radiance ended, the view had dimmed. Yet between the green radiant winds and the moons, a soft light still blanketed the rooftops.

Before I could answer, a knock came at the door. Three quick raps — a familiar signal.

Xaron cocked an eyebrow. "An appropriate time for your brother to visit. In the middle of the night while we discuss conspiracies against the realm."

I gave him a flat look, then crossed the loft to open the

door. Linos sported his usual tousled, blond hair and soiled clothes. But instead of a confident smirk, he wore a serious expression. Despite the worry that rose in me, I knew I had to keep the conversation light. Linos was flighty. If something were wrong, I couldn't risk scaring him off.

"Back already?" I observed drily. "Two visits in half a span. I'd almost think you miss me."

"No such chance." His smile was quick and nervous. "Purely here on business."

"Business that I'll want no part of, I'm guessing."

He seemed to sense my true suspicions. "I'm not in trouble. I have information I think you'll want. Are you going to let me in?"

I stepped aside slowly, watching him as he entered. He had a slight limp to his step and shadows under his eyes, but seemed not much the worse for wear. Closing the door behind him, I drew him into a hug.

"Do you have to?" he complained as he extricated himself.

"I'm your Sasa, aren't I?" I grinned at his uncomfortable glance at Xaron. "Don't worry. He knows you're my Little Lion."

"I don't know why I help you," he muttered. "You want to hear this or not?"

"Let's have it. What do you have that could possibly intrigue me?"

Despite my light tone, apprehension filled me. His eyes flickered to the door before settling back on me.

His voice was lower when he spoke. "You're still looking into what happened with the Despot, right?"

My attention perked up. "Yes."

"Have you had any leads?"

I considered how truthfully to answer that. "Some. But nothing too promising."

"Then you haven't heard the First Laurel will be visiting the Valemish temple in Sandglass tonight?"

My heart began to pound. "Where did you hear that?"

His eyes were bright with excitement, but he shrugged. "I was hanging around the palace and overheard some guards talking about it."

I considered it. First Laurel Lykos was head of the Laurel Palace guard. If he was out visiting a Valemish temple in the middle of the night, I had to know why.

"When did you hear this?"

"A few turns ago? I came here as soon as I could."

"And he's going tonight?"

"Not long after dark falls, from what I heard."

I considered it. "What are you doing at the temple, Lykos?" I muttered. As I said his name, a realization jolted me. "'Thae below. The Wolf."

Linos stared at me. "Alright there, Sasa?"

I shook my head. "Never mind. Thanks for the tip. You don't know how much it means to me."

He barked a laugh, louder than normal. "You've done more than enough favors for me. Call us even."

"I wouldn't go that far. I'll be following up on that now. I'd offer for you to stay, but I know how you like our wine…"

"No, that's alright." He glanced behind me toward the bay window. "Actually, there was one other thing."

Impatience fluttered inside me. "What is it?"

"I might be going away for a while. A span, maybe." He didn't meet my eyes.

The thrill of the hunt faltered, and the usual worry edged in. "Why so long? Mother will throw a fit."

"Nah, she won't. I'm hardly there anymore." He lowered his gaze to the floor. "I just didn't want you to worry if, you know, you tried finding me."

I opened my mouth, then closed it. Linos didn't like when I worried about him, saying it reminded him too much of our mother. Instead, I contented myself with, "Thank you for telling me."

He nodded, then abruptly turned toward the door. As he opened it, he hesitated at the threshold. "Take care, Sasa."

"You too, Little Lion."

He nodded, then closed the door.

Before it clicked shut, I'd turned back toward Xaron. I had to believe Linos could take of himself. Besides, I had a job to pursue.

"You heard all that?" I said as I walked back to where he reclined on the divan.

He studied me. "I did. But I don't understand your conclusion. How do you know Lykos is the Wolf?"

"It might have been enough that he's watchful and head of the 'pack' of laurel guards. But I also remembered from my schooling days that Lykos means 'wolf' in the Lighted-tongue."

Xaron laughed and stood. "Simple as that! The things I never could have known. Figures a stuffy old man like Nikias would use the old Oedijan speech as a cipher."

"No time to waste; we have to go." I went to the door and began strapping on my sandals.

His smile faded. "I suppose so. But what about Nomusa?"

"No time to find which tavern she wound up at. Are you coming or not?"

Xaron groaned, then went to find his own sandals. "You'll get me killed one day."

I smiled grimly. Considering what we were about to do, I could only hope it wouldn't be today.

8

TEMPLE'S HEART

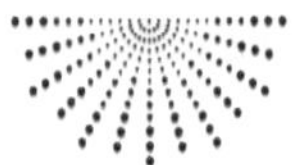

Father, chain me to your song
Beat my heart to your bloody march
Subjugate my straying will
Dominate my fleeting heart
Harden my purpose with your forge
Burn away my feeble remorse

I am yours, heart and spirit
I am yours, body and soul
Burn me to cinders in your fire
Scatter me, ashes among the coals

- Prayer to Valem, origin unknown

Two turns later, Xaron and I found ourselves entering the Ignorant Intellectual. With the night growing long, it was nearly deserted. A pair of drunks argued loudly in one corner, and a few others were scattered across the room in various stages of stupor. It was the last place I wanted to be, with the first real lead on my investigation quickly slipping through my hands. But even as I fidgeted with the strap of my satchel, I knew it was necessary.

When breaking into a Valemish temple, it paid to have a professional.

Talan took his time, half a turn passing before the Guilder emerged through the tavern door. His hair was untidier even than usual, and I wondered if I'd finally caught him sleeping.

"A later call than I've come to expect from you," he observed with a raised eyebrow. "What's the hurry?"

"We'll tell you on the way."

Ushering him out of the tavern, I set our course for Sand-glass as I filled him in. He listened in silence until I finished, then observed, "Your brother is remarkably well-informed."

I glanced at him, but the night hid his expression. "What does that mean?"

"Nothing more than what I said. It was wise of you to call me. I assume you've never been to a Valemish sanctum before?"

"Never had reason to. Is that where Lykos will go?"

"More than likely. Depends on what he's after. But I suppose we'll find that out soon." With an enigmatic smile, he gestured us forward.

As we reached the temple forum, I peered out. The forum felt ominous with its stillness. All the bustle of daytime was gone, leaving the black igneous temple to loom alone in the night. The braziers mounted around its base only succeeded in casting flickering shadows along its dark sides. Ascending the stairs in secret to reach its single entrance — and exit — would be an impossible task. I suddenly saw the genius of its architecture. A structure of stone with only one way in or out had to be inconvenient, but it could act as a fortress if need be. My stomach churned.

Talan touched my arm lightly. "Men approach the temple."

I saw them almost as soon as he did, three figures crossing the small bridge over the moat. Their armor gleamed with the light of the braziers, but I couldn't see if the green leaves of the Laurel Palace were painted upon them. Yet from the shoulders of the middle man, a short cape whipped back and forth, throwing shadows across the courtyard with each step. I sent Linos a silent thanks. Only First Laurel Lykos, head of the guards of the Laurel Palace, would wear such a cape.

The three men paused in front of the temple, then climbed the stairs. At the top, Lykos hammered on the door, but waited no more than a moment before he pushed his way in. One guard followed him, while the other closed the door and took post outside.

Xaron cursed softly. "How are we supposed to sneak past now? We should have gone immediately."

Talan's smile didn't falter as he nodded at my satchel. "I think our lady Finch has something in mind."

"I do." Heart pounding, I reached inside the satchel and drew out two masks and medallions.

Xaron leaned forward, wide-eyed. "Tell me those aren't what I think they are."

Talan cupped one of the medallions, studying it. "I believe they are." He looked up slyly as he released it. "Tribunal medallions. Or at least, they're supposed to be."

"They're good enough forgeries to pass a cursory inspection." I held out a mask to Talan. "Up to you if you trust me."

Xaron looked outraged. "You two are entering without me?"

I winced. "Sorry, Xaron. But I only have two sets, and Talan needs to show me the way through."

"Let me go in your place then. As much as I'd hate to spend more time with him than I have to, I'm a house-breaker. This is what I do."

"No. I have to go. I need to see and hear exactly what they say. You know how I work."

"You seemed happy enough to let me risk my neck for other jobs," Xaron muttered as he slumped back against the wall.

Talan was turning the mask over in his hand, a tapestry of orange and yellow and shaped as a finch's face. "You kept these from the previous Carnival of Veils, didn't you?"

I shrugged. "Possibly."

"A bit strange for a Tribune to wear these in the season opposite the festival. You believe the guard will let us pass without showing our faces?"

"He'll have no choice. We outrank him."

He slipped the medallion over his neck. "This is an even more foolish disguise than the last time I broke into a temple."

"You've told me about that time, and I'm fairly certain this is better than entering a haunted vault as acolytes to dance away daemons."

He grinned. "Now that you mention it, you're right. That was far stupider."

I slipped on my own medallion and felt the weighty iron settle under my chiton. With any luck, just telling the guard we were Tribunes would admit us. After all, as a man of the Laurel Palace, he had no right to bar anyone from entrance to the temple. But it paid to be prepared.

Xaron put a hand on my arm as I started to strap the mask on. "Aire," he said urgently, "please. This is rash even for you."

I gently pried his fingers away. "I have to do this, Xaron. I have to find out what Lykos is up to."

He looked far from convinced, but he backed away, frowning, his eyes tight with worry.

"Besides," I continued, "you have to keep me safe. You still have your lodestone?"

He nodded glumly. "You want me to keep watch, don't you? To warn you if the guard comes after you."

"You stole the words from my lips. Can you do it?"

"You know I will." He pulled me into a quick embrace. "Be careful."

"I will."

Turning away, I adjusted my mask to sit more comfortably. The eye slits were narrow, and I couldn't see as much as I preferred. I'd just have to make do.

"You ready?" I said to Talan.

He'd also donned his mask, but I could see his eyes crinkling in a smile behind it. "A Guilder is always ready for trouble."

Xaron suddenly reached out and gripped Talan's arm. "Keep her safe, rogue," he said in a low, rough voice.

"I will." Talan met Xaron's gaze until he withdrew his hand.

"And I'll protect both of us," I said sarcastically. "Now come on before you two start hugging."

Talan and I stepped out from the alley and walked toward the bridge. Crossing the moat, we entered into the flickering light of the forum's braziers. The guard noticed us immediately, his head following our approach like a hound to the movements of a squirrel. My breath came shallow and my heart was loud in my ears as we approached the temple.

When we were twenty paces away, he cried, "Halt! Who goes there?"

Talan and I didn't break pace. By unspoken agreement, we reached the stairs and mounted them on either side.

"Halt, I say!" the guard commanded again, the edge of his voice growing sharper. "No one without the proper authority—"

"Does this suffice as 'the proper authority'?" I drew out my Tribune medallion and brought it into the light.

The guard's expression spasmed. His eyes darted from the medallion to my masked face and back. But though he looked uncertain, he didn't move aside.

"Pardon me, Tribunes," he said, eyes sliding between us. "But you're not dressed as usual. And why wear Carnival of Veils masks?"

"Why indeed would men go about in disguise?" Talan said drily. "We did not wish to be recognized, fool."

The laurel guard's jaw clenched. "Listen. I know you two can go wherever you please. But I've got orders to keep everyone out. If you would just wait half a turn or so, everyone can—"

I ignored him and moved forward, gripping the door handle behind him. The guard stepped into my way, preventing me from opening it. I met his eyes through the mask's eye slits and didn't look away. I willed him to believe the lie, willed myself to believe it.

Whatever he saw made him flinch and step aside. Repressing a sigh of relief, I walked forward and pulled open the door. "Tell no one of this," I warned. "Including your First Laurel."

With one last glare at the guard, Talan and I slipped through the door and pulled it shut behind.

My eyes took a moment to adjust to the gloomy interior. The sparse, square chamber was lit by flickering torches, and held nothing more than an offering tray in the same black stone as the rest of the temple. Three hallways branched out before us. The dark, igneous rock closed in on all sides, making them look like tunnels into the heart of a volcano. If only it could be as warm. I shivered in the cave-like chill, drawing my arms close around me.

Talan's warm touch on my arm was a welcome change. "We'd best move quickly."

I tried recalling what I knew of Valemish temples from my few past visits. "The middle passage should lead to the altar chamber, right?"

Talan nodded. "If the First Laurel wished to speak to the Kul of this temple, that would be the path he followed."

I knew little of the Valemish, but enough to know a Kul was the head priest of a temple, like an oracle for Eidolan sanctuaries. "Then that's the way we'll go," I decided.

We set off down the hallway. The corridor soon turned into a stairwell with barely enough room for two astride. At the end of the stairs, which went far enough down to take us below the level of the street, more passages and rooms branched off from the main hall. Keeping straight, the ceiling and walls began slowly widening, and ahead I could see the edges of lit braziers illuminating what looked to be a large, open room. The altar chamber neared. My heart, already beating hard, began to race.

When we were a short distance from the entrance, I stopped Talan with a touch. Voices echoed faintly from the chamber ahead.

"Is there a better way to sneak in?" I whispered to him.

He shook his head. "One entrance, open to the rest of the altar chamber. If they're in there, they'll see us enter. But if they're in the sanctum beyond it, we'll still be safe."

I weighed the risks in my head, then nodded. What was one more risk at this point?

We started moving forward again, slower now. Every creak of my sandals made me cringe. We stopped five paces from the entrance to listen again. The voices echoed across the chamber, which I could tell was large and cavernous. The words were still indistinct and soft. They had to be in the sanctum.

Talan was already moving past me, and I followed him through the wide archway. For a moment, all I could do was stare.

The altar chamber's ceiling rose high above, its heights lost in the darkness. Stained glass windows lined the walls sixty cubits up, backlit with torches and illustrating people and stories in vivid color. The stone pews encircling the center altar were austere, while the figures etched into the floor were carefully wrought. The plateau on which the altar rose was carved with figures reaching up, their bodies mangled, their faces contorted with pain. A ring of black coals around its base told of fires lit there many times before.

But all this was ornamentation next to the depiction of their god. Slowly, I recognized the patterns on the floor drawing a man's face half-morphed into a lizard, scowling up at those who dared to tread on him. Valem, ever watching from the Underearth he ruled, always demanded obedience from his followers.

I had moments to take it in before Talan pulled me toward the center of the chamber to crouch behind the altar's plateau. The voices echoed louder here, and I could just make out their words. I shared a nervous look with Talan and leaned around the stone to listen.

"Don't lie to me," a man's voice commanded, sharp and hoarse.

"Of course I won't," a second man said smoothly. "Everything I have claimed is the truth, or may Valem burn me where I stand."

I guessed the first man was Lykos, and the second the Kul. The priest's voice was deeper and full of velvet tones; I could imagine him preaching before a congregation. The First Laurel had the tone and directness of a soldier.

After a moment of silence, Lykos's harsh voice came again. "Let me ask a different way. I am not a Tribune. I am not responsible for punishing traitors conspiring with foreign enemies. I am here for one thing: the protection of the Wreaths."

"A concern we all share, most wholeheartedly, I assure you."

"Play your games and speak your false words, priest. But continue this farce, and you will find undermining the Despot's rule to be costly."

"The Despot's rule? But surely you mean the Despoina —
is her Ascension not on the morrow?"

Lykos didn't immediately answer. "Of course," the First
Laurel spoke again, voice tight with anger. "But it won't be in
her name that the Tribunal comes here tomorrow morn."

Sandals shuffled on stone; metal rubbed and rattled.
Lykos and his guard were leaving, and after revealing so
little. Yet all the same, I took Talan's arm to pull him away.

Talan resisted, nodding toward the voices, expression
disguised behind his finch mask. Blood hammered in my ears,
but curiosity won out. I held my breath and listened again.

"Now wait, my good First Laurel. There's no need for
this."

The footsteps ceased. "Tell me what you know," Lykos
said, voice echoing louder. He had entered into the altar
chamber. Fear prickled down my spine, but I remained next
to Talan, pressing closer to the pained stone faces.

"Tell me," the First Laurel's voice snapped like a riding
crop. "All of it."

"It is nothing more than revenue, good First Laurel, to
support those who need it most," the Kul said, his voice
pitched higher. "Why would we kill the venerable Myron? It
can only destabilize the currency and commerce. Bad for
business, wouldn't you say?"

Footsteps sounded again, and I flinched until I realized
they were headed away from us. Talan's hand found my arm,
hot with Pyrthaen energy, steadying and reassuring.

Lykos spoke so softly I could barely hear. "And what are
you bringing into our city, priest? What is in those arks?"

"My good First Laurel, I am not at liberty to say. That is
most sacred business—"

"I have seen the masks. Do not put me off with talk of
sanctity. If you think I could believe you innocent, you are a
fool."

Something twitched against my leg. Biting back a startled yell, I thrust my hand against it. As it settled over a smooth, round object, I remembered. *The lodestone.* Xaron was sending the signal.

"The guard is coming," I hissed to Talan.

"If he just entered, then we still have time. Listen."

"Very well," the Kul was saying, his voice simmering with anger. "Masks and robes are interred within, holy objects to us."

"The masks of the Tefra are far from holy things."

My breath caught. The Tefra, priestly wardens who fanatically served both their god and their nation, were responsible for the Avvadin Imperium's widespread military success. Silks, the pyrs they enslaved, were relentless in battle and impossible to kill.

I didn't like to think what it meant if Tefra had come to Oedija.

"And what about the robes?" Lykos continued.

"Garments for priests to wear," the Kul replied bitingly.

"Do not toy with me, priest. I tire of this farce. Show me one of these arks."

"Admit you into the sanctum's heart?" Outrage limned the priest's words. "Already you have defiled this temple. I cannot allow—"

"You do not dictate what you allow!" Lykos's voice cracked like a whip, silencing the Kul. "Show me to this ark, or I will find another priest without a wish to be wrapped in chains."

"Valem will burn you," the priest promised darkly. "This way."

Their footsteps faded as they entered deeper into the sanctum. I pulled at Talan's sleeve, but he was already rising. We walked on quick, quiet feet back the way we'd come and into the flickering light of the corridor. No sooner had we reached the entrance, however, than did we see a figure striding down the stairs.

Talan and I pulled back and locked eyes across the doorway. My mind grasped for what to do. The only way to flee was further into the temple, but I doubted we'd find refuge in the sanctum. Eventually, Lykos and his guards would find us. Not knowing what else to do, I pulled up my chiton and found the hilt of my dagger, then pulled it free.

Talan watched me. When I met his eyes, he shook his head, then motioned for me to back away. His eyes were flat and cold behind his mask.

I knew then what he intended. I didn't move, but shook my head sharply.

He pressed his lips tightly together, but curtly nodded, then motioned me back once more.

This time, I complied with relief. There was no avoiding conflict now, but at least the guard wouldn't die. I hoped.

The laurel guard stepped through the doorway moments later, sword bared. He almost walked past Talan, then startled and whirled toward him, raising his sword. "Back!" he barked. "And step into the light!"

Talan motioned with his hand. The sword in the guard's hand suddenly acquired a life of its own, spinning then slamming into the man's helmet with a dull ring.

The guard stumbled back. "Tyurn's balls!" he growled, staring at the sword, now floating in the air where he'd gripped it. "How—?"

"It will all be a dream soon," Talan reassured him, then flicked his wrist. The sword struck forward, the flat of it again connecting with the surprised guard's helmet with a loud ring. This time, the man fell to his knees and swayed, disoriented.

"Damn you," the laurel guard said thickly.

Talan stepped forward and, taking the sword in his hands,

swung it at his head a third time. Finally, the soldier folded over and didn't rise.

I let out the breath I'd been holding and stepped forward, wincing as I stared down at the prone guard. His face was slack, and a trickle of blood ran down his cheek. "He'll live?"

"Hard to know with three blows to the skull." Talan set the sword down next to the guard's hand, positioned as if it had fallen from his grasp. "I'm more concerned that he'll remember a warden put him down."

"Maybe he'll think it was a dream." I flashed Talan a weak smile. "Come on. We'd best get out of here."

9

EYES IN THE DARK

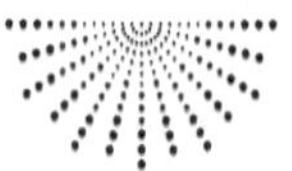

Six demes lay inside the city
Four lay outside
Six sheltered by thick walls
Four left out to dry

Six, the inner city demes:
Iris, center of the eye
Sandglass, counters of the coins
Bazaar, bustling marketplace
Gate, entrance to the rest
Hull, site of old ship moored
Port, sea-trade near and far

Four, the outer city demes:
Brinecoast, salt stacks 'long the shore
Thys, lake large and vast
Riverport, trade up the Walano
Drifts, mix of mud and mines

All the demes are Oedija,
All the demes make up one.

And with the Conclave and the Wreaths,
The demes number eleven.

- Children's song; origin unknown

Gathering Xaron on our way out of the temple, we headed toward one of Talan's nearby hideouts. The walk was quiet, all of us watching for signs of pursuit or city guard patrols. If they held us for questioning, Lykos would as good as have us.

To stay out of sight, Talan led us through alleys and back-ways and over rooftops so even I had difficulty keeping track of our path. It was tense, laborious work, and by the time Talan stopped, I was panting, pain needling my sides.

I eyed the small, wooden door we'd stopped in front of, which was set into the corner of a moss-covered tenement building. "This is the place?"

He smirked. "Not up to your standards?"

"As much as I expected from *you*," Xaron muttered.

Talan opened the door, and after Xaron and I exchanged a skeptical look, we followed him inside. It was, if possible, even drearier within. The room was so small I could almost touch opposite walls. Rubble and dirt had accumulated in the corners, and a suspicious black mold grew on the planks. A musty scent hung heavy in the air. All that occupied it was a narrow cot and a lidded pot that assumedly contained pyrkin. Closing the door behind us, Talan confirmed my suspicions when he opened the pot, and a soft green light like sunlit moss filled the room.

I wanted to sink onto the cot and rest, but I wasn't about to risk it. "We're safe here? Except from lice, that is."

Talan didn't share my qualms, but sat down on the cot, perfectly at home in his grubby clothes. "Perhaps, if we went unobserved. Either way, we should stay here for the night.

We'll find out by the morning whether or not we escaped attention."

"Stay here until morning?" Xaron exclaimed. "You have to be kidding."

Talan donned a mocking smile. "For you I am."

I blushed, but if there were hidden intent in Talan's statement, I chose to ignore it. "Don't you have a secret tunnel we can escape through?" I suggested sarcastically. "I thought the Underguild had a network all across Oedija. "

"They do. But my hiding holes aren't connected. That would ruin the whole point of having places to tuck away."

"You could have at least kept them up."

He raised an eyebrow. "I have over a dozen such hideouts. And I can't hire an honor to clean them. Far more important that my shirts aren't in one place than that they're clean."

"Ah, yes. One of the lessons from your famous heist." I cringed as I leaned against the wall. "A shame you didn't also learn not to gamble, or to mess about in Valemish business."

A smile curved his lips. "I'm a slow learner."

"I don't want to stay here longer than I have to," Xaron interjected. "What did you two learn in there anyway?"

"Lykos is suspicious of the Valemish," Talan said, his eyes closed.

"Or wants to make it seem so," I pointed out.

"It wasn't a show. If it were, they would not have come in the dead of night."

"Unless someone were trying to make his investigation look legitimate to cover his own tracks."

Xaron stared at me with a creased brow. "Can you two start at the beginning? What *actually* happened in there?"

I sighed, then briefly recounted what we'd witnessed. By the time I finished, Xaron's eyes were wide. "I suppose it means Myron was murdered, doesn't it?"

I hid a smile. "Probably. Though it could be unrelated, the timing is too suspicious. And what other reason would the head of the laurel guard have to investigate the Valemish? He isn't in charge of the safety of the demotism, only of the Wreaths and the Laurel Palace."

"Perhaps because war with Avvad endangers us all." Talan's eyes were slitted open, gleaming in the green light.

Xaron looked thoughtful. "So the masks, the robes… Does it mean Avvad is invading? That Tefra are coming to Oedija?"

"Perhaps they're already here," Talan said darkly.

I shook my head. "If they are, they've been keeping a low profile. No one has spoken of Tefra masks or priests with burned faces. But that's beside the point. Lykos is charged with the safety of the Wreaths. It's far more likely his investigation of the Valemish has to do directly with justice for Myron's murder."

"If he *was* murdered," Talan said with a smile.

"Why would Lykos suspect the Valemish?" Xaron wondered aloud.

Talan rose on an elbow. "The Valemish are an arm of Avvad, no matter how much they might plead otherwise. If the Molten God's priests are at work, it is at the behest of the Kahin-Shah."

"But the Kahin-Shah has seemed content with conquering the Riven Lands up till now," Xaron pointed out.

Talan shook his head. "Burak Aasjuqal is never content. It is a matter of when, not if, he turns to conquer the Four Realms."

"But the Kahin-Shah has not done so because trade and peace are profitable," I said. "That hasn't changed. So if Avvad is behind this, why now? I think we should look at who else might have profited greater."

Talan and Xaron looked at me expectantly. I smiled. They knew me well enough to sense a forthcoming proposal.

"Myron Wreath was well-loved, but he had little actual power. His death has caused unease in the city, but it hasn't destabilized the government and gained any advantage for

Avvad commercially. If anything, it disadvantages Avvad in the short-run. There is, however, one person who greatly benefits from Myron's death."

"Does she happen to be holding her Ascension tomorrow?" Xaron piped in.

"Asileia Wreath does benefit, and is certainly mad enough," Talan said. "But that, too, serves the Kahin-Shah's purposes. If Oedija is unstable, then it makes it all the easier to conquer."

We sat in silence for several long moments. Hunger gripping the city was bad enough. Now it seemed Oedija was dry kindling, ready to set aflame at the first spark.

Xaron spoke into the lull. "There could be a third party that benefits."

Talan and I both looked to him. "Who?" I asked, brow furrowed.

He looked almost sheepish. "The Manifest."

"The serpent cult in Thys? They may be gaining followers lately, but I doubt that qualifies them for insurrection."

Xaron shook his head. "I don't know about that. Their compound has been growing more of late, and their Seekers, as they call them, become more zealous by the day. Their leaders, the Visage of the Wyvern and the Dishonored, speak of revolution, of empowering the common man and woman, of overthrowing those who would keep them down. They have a base of operations in the Wyvern's Claw, the amphitheater off the lake. And they have dangerous ideas about wardens, even by my standards." He shrugged. "You know I think magic shouldn't be outlawed and punished. But they… they think it should be unbridled."

Talan watched him through narrowed eyes. "You seem to know an awful lot about the Manifest."

Xaron shrugged and smiled, but the smile seemed strained. "You hear things."

I stared at him, wondering, but let the odd moment pass. "If it's the Manifest, this investigation of Lykos's is moot."

"As it would be if Asileia is to blame," Xaron countered.

I shook my head. "Not if it's deliberate deception. Think about it. If Asileia were responsible, she would need to pin it on someone else. Who better than Avvad?"

Talan leaned up against the wall. "So you're proposing that Asileia killed her father and is covering it up by setting Lykos on a false trail."

"Or they're in collaboration together, along with Feiyan. More likely than not, Feiyan is behind the deception. It's always been her forte."

Talan shrugged. "It's possible. But I think this the lesser of the two mysteries now. Perhaps these Tefra masks mean something else. Perhaps they seek to force the wardens of Oedija to join their ranks."

"Force them?" Xaron narrowed his eyes. "How could they do that?"

Talan met Xaron's gaze. "Considering we prefer not to speak, I haven't told you of my life in Erimis and the things I've seen." He glanced at me. "You remember the Damask Esir?"

"Of course. Elite soldiers controlled by pyr to serve the Kahin-Shah."

"The one Damask Esir I knew was also a warden."

Fear slowly rose in me at the thought. It meant Xaron was susceptible to being controlled by Avvad. Even Talan was vulnerable.

Xaron sighed. "Just what I needed — another thing to stop me from sleeping at night."

"You don't have any trouble sleeping — I've heard your snoring." I pushed away from the wall. "Speaking of sleeping, I suppose we'd best all grab a few turns' rest before the sun rises."

Xaron rose and stretched with a great yawn. "Good. I was just about to fall asleep where I stood."

Talan rose from the cot as we made our way to the door. Opening it, I stepped out into the night and scanned the area. Shadowy figures lingered in an alley opposite of us, but I doubted they were laurel guards or city watch as they slinked away.

I could tell Talan was uneasy as he stepped up next to me and watched the alley where the figures had disappeared. "Are you sure you shouldn't stay?" he asked in a low voice.

"I'm sure."

He shook his head. "Have it your way. But remember there are more dangers than Lykos in the city, especially now."

"We will." I took his hand and pressed it. "Thank you. You're always there when I need you."

Talan flashed me a small smile. Releasing my hand, his eyes flickered to Xaron, and he nodded at him.

I turned to Xaron, who didn't bother hiding his smirk.

"You sure you want to leave?" he muttered to me as we walked away.

I rolled my eyes and didn't bother to respond.

A DRIZZLING rain fell on our way back, both a blessing and a curse for travel. Rain hid us from the city guard and drove them to take shelter. But rain was also miserable when we had a two-turn walk through the dark city streets.

We made it back to Crossing with little incident. It was only as we turned onto our street that a shadow materialized from an alley. I grabbed Xaron's arm and hissed, "Ahead!"

Xaron flinched and raised his hands, preparing to channel.

But when the face came into the light of the pyr lamps

mounted on the corner, I relaxed. "You could have just walked with us, you know."

Talan stepped from the darkness. "I need to speak with you. Alone."

"Here we go," Xaron muttered under his breath.

Ignoring him, I studied the Guilder. His brow was drawn, and he wore no hint of his usual smile. "I'll meet you inside, Xaron."

"I'm sure you will." Xaron cast one last droll look back before disappearing inside the tower.

Talan motioned me toward the eaves of the tower door. I huddled next to him. "What is it?"

He leaned close, his voice soft. "You were watched on your way home."

Fear trickled down my spine. "Where? I didn't see eyes in the rafters."

"They were there all the same. I plucked those that I happened across, but I'm sure there were more."

I felt dizzy. "How do you know they watched me?"

"They tailed you across the whole of Iris. I did not intercede needlessly, I assure you."

"Thank you. You shouldn't have followed me, though. You have better things to do than protecting me."

A smile tugged at the corner of his lips. "But you need so much protection."

I flushed. "You can't always keep me safe. One night won't make a difference in the long run."

"This night could have." He paused. "Besides. I couldn't sleep in that room. It's horrible and smells like a cave."

I laughed softly. "Yes. It does."

Talan reached forward and took my wrist in his hand, his fingers brushing warm against my skin. "Is there someone who might have reason to watch you, Airene? Someone alerted to your hunt?"

I sighed and pulled my wrist away. The truth wouldn't

stay buried forever. And it would be a relief to tell someone. "Feiyan," I admitted. "She sent Kako to threaten me yesterday."

Talan's eyes went as hard as flint. "Threatened you how?"

"Remember how she suspects Nomusa or Xaron of being a warden? Kako said she'd set the Shepherds on them if..." I sighed. "If I didn't stop investigating Myron's death."

"So that's why you believe Asileia to be behind it." Talan gathered a considering look. "It's a dangerous game you play."

"No more than you gamble everyday by being a Guilder."

"True," he acknowledged easily. "But I'm a warden and much more capable of protecting myself than you. And it is my own life I gamble with, not others."

I wanted to argue, but he was right. Guilt churned in my gut. "What else can I do, Talan? I have to follow this hunt to its end."

"Why? Why not leave it and keep yourself safe?"

"And let Feiyan win? And let Myron's murder be covered up by lies?" I shook my head. "You know I can't do that."

Talan wore a half-smile again. "And you're sure those are the reasons you're doing this?"

"What's that supposed to mean?"

"You know my story, Airene. I have held nothing back from you. You know I have seen my share of desperate people." He paused, eyes flickering back and forth between mine. "No hunt is worth your life."

I turned my head aside, unable to meet his gaze. It hurt to know what he thought of me — some poor, desperate woman clinging to an invented purpose because she had no other. It didn't help that I wondered if he was right.

As much out of need as to escape my thoughts, I found myself speaking. "Can I ask you a favor?"

"Of course."

"When Linos gave me the tip earlier about Lykos, he also told me he'd go missing for a while. He told me not to come looking for him, but with everything going on, I can't help but worry." I met his gaze. "I won't be breaking my promise, though, if you're the one who looks after him."

He nodded. "He's young, but he doesn't completely lack sense. I will find and watch over him all the same." He gave me an odd look. "But he isn't the one I was concerned about."

I sighed. "I'll think about what you said. That's as much as I can promise."

Talan took my hand, and I pressed his in return. Without a word, he released his grasp and turned away. I watched him disappear down an alley and lingered a moment longer before shaking my head and making my way inside.

As soon as I entered Canopy, Xaron and Nomusa turned toward me from near the bay window, nearly silhouettes in the dim light of the loft. I raised an eyebrow as I approached them. "Trying to spy on me?"

"Why'd you have to stand next to the tower?" Xaron complained.

Nomusa wasn't smiling. She had shadows under her eyes, accentuated by the low light. I wondered if she'd slept that night.

"Xaron had just started to fill me in on what you two were up to with Talan," she said, her words picked carefully. "Care to elaborate?"

Tired, hungry, and paranoid as I was, it took all my self-control not to snap at her. Instead, I took a breath and explained what had happened. Guilty as I felt, I held back my last conversation with Talan. I wasn't ready to risk the job yet by telling them about Feiyan's threats.

"You could have been killed," was all Nomusa said when I finished.

"But we weren't. And now we have further leads."

"Not much. What did you learn? That the First Laurel is investigating the Despot's murder? Hardly surprising. And can you really know what the Valemish are up to from this one conversation?"

I shook my head. Why Nomusa had such resistance to the inquiry, I couldn't explain. When we'd first become Finches, we'd dreamed of an opportunity like this. It seemed that those days were gone.

I stretched and yawned. "Time for bed. See you both tomorrow."

I rose and headed for my room. Before I could enter, Nomusa approached and folded me into an embrace. Surprised, I relented. Touch was common for her, but considering her stance toward the job, I hadn't expected any hugs forthcoming.

"I know I haven't been cooperative," she said softly in my ear. "And I can't say I agree with your inquiry. But... I've lost family twice, Aire. I don't want to lose you, too."

All of my pent-up annoyance with her suddenly dissipated. I held her tighter. "We've always taken risks, Nomu. Yes, these are greater than before. But I'd be denying the very thing I'm meant for if I didn't look into this."

Nomusa didn't answer for a long moment. "I know. But can you at least not take such foolish risks?"

I gently extricated myself from her. "We'll see."

She turned her gaze aside. We both heard the lie in the words.

10

ASCENSION

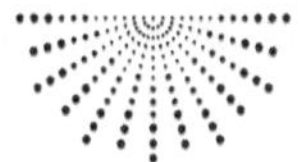

Asileia Wreath, unlike her father, has never seemed aware that the Despoina would have any limits to her authority. In this, she is like Zalfene Wreath, who, generations before, built the Half Wall and nearly began a war with Avvad. Reports of her activities as governor of the Oedijan peninsula are preliminary, but Asileia appears to use autocratic methods to enact laws with little consultation from her subjects, nor even agreement among the landed patricians...

Should she fail to learn wisdom, I fear for our nation when Asileia wears the Evergreen Wreath.

- A Modern Account of the Wreaths; by Acadian Helene, Master Historian; 1170 SLP

A bird awaited me when I woke.

Rising before Nomusa and Xaron — though after Corin — I went to the balcony, as was my habit. There waited an unfamiliar finch, impatiently hopping back and forth. Heart pounding, I took up the messenger bird and unwound the scroll from its leg. It bore no distinguishable seal, but I suspected who it was from as soon as I began reading.

My Honeycomb,

I have left you forlorn for far too long. We must be reunited, and at once, or I fear I shall expire from want. I miss the sweet nectar of your kiss; life here is far too bitter and growing more so every day.

Meet me at the place where, if I were so blessed to be the Wreath, I might first lay eyes upon you, and at the time this evening that she might least observe it.

Forever longing for your flower,
Your Aimless Bumblebee

I smiled at the floral, love-sick language. It was at odds with the stiff, formal man I knew Nikias to be, but Jaxas Wreath's steward was a surprising man. When it came to his own master, he was loyal to the bone. For all other matters in the Laurel Palace, however, his tongue was alarmingly loose.

On the whole, the message seemed thin on information and thick with alarm. If Nikias felt threatened, it didn't bode well for his continuing to provide information. Still, if he wanted to meet, that would have to be enough.

Xaron appeared in the balcony doorway and scowled at the dreary sky. "Any news?" he asked.

"Nikias sent another finch. He wants to meet."

His expression brightened. "Truly? When?"

"Tonight, if I'm reading the message correctly. In Forum Demos during Asileia's Ascension. Here, read it yourself."

Accepting the message, Xaron glanced it over and made a face. "Has he never written a love letter before? Laid it on a bit thick to be believable."

"And made it too obvious — I was quick to decipher it, and I'm sure others would be as well. Still, I don't see what choice we have but to meet him."

He handed me back the message. "How about *not* meeting him?"

I raised an eyebrow at him, then looked him up and down, noticing for the first time he was fully dressed. "Where are you headed?"

He gave me an uncertain smile. "Visiting my parents. Their health isn't well."

I snorted, knowing the lie for what it was. Though it did hurt that he didn't tell me where he went these mornings. "Very well. Keep your secrets."

"I'll see you tonight. Meet at Zipho's first? Four turns past noon?"

"Fine. See you then."

Once he'd left and the finch was sent, I returned inside. A thought occurred to me, one that made me sweat. If we met Nikias tonight, he'd expect to be paid. The steward wasn't a cheap informant. Most of my eyes and ears around the city took copper and nickel for payment. Nikias accepted nothing less than silver, and a hefty amount at that.

I chewed my lip as my eyes slid to the loose stone in the kitchen wall where we kept our shared Finch money, which comprised half of what we earned. I knew as well as Xaron and Nomusa how much was left there: thirty-three silver scions, fifty-nine nickel magnes, and a smattering of copper cullets. The steward likely wouldn't take less than fifteen scions. Considering the times, it was foolish to spend half of our money on one whisper.

Yet I knew what I would do. No matter how under-handed it seemed, this would be best for all of us. Discovering the Despot's murderer would bring more wealth than any of us would be able to spend.

The ring of rationalization was loud in my ears.

I slipped the false stone from the wall and set it softly on the floor. Glancing over my shoulder to make sure Nomusa's door was still closed, I took out the silver, a full fifteen pieces, and silently stashed them in my private purse, quieting them with slips of cloth between each coin. Replacing the stone, I swept away the dust from the floor below the cache.

As I rose, I heard the creak of an opening door. My heart caught in my throat. I sidestepped closer to the pantry and began pulling down food.

I glanced back as Nomusa emerged from her room. "Morning," I said with false cheeriness.

"Morning," she replied, walking toward me. "I'm starving."

"You always wake starving." My teasing sounded over-done to my own ears, my voice unnaturally high-pitched. I hoped Nomusa wouldn't notice.

She smiled blearily at me. "Ixolo burns fuel." She looked me up and down. "Leaving already?"

"I want to know what Oedija whispers before the Ascension tonight. Though Xaron beat both of us out, if you can believe it."

She pulled out bread from the pantry and began cutting it. "To his usual mysterious spot, is it?"

"So it seems."

I needed to leave. It somehow seemed the silver would give me away the longer I stayed. "We're meeting at Zipho's four turns after noon for the Ascension. I'll see you there?"

"Sure." Nomusa nodded at my hand. "But aren't you going to eat that mango first?"

I looked down at my hand. I hadn't even noticed what I'd grabbed. Letting out a nervous laugh, I replaced it on the shelf. "I'm not as hungry as I thought. See you later."

Nomusa watched me strangely as I headed toward the door. "Till then."

I put on a strained smile and turned away. Only as I exited did I remember I hadn't mentioned Nikias. But with my stomach turning, I didn't turn back, but fled down the stairs.

~

As promised, Nomusa, Xaron, and I met at Zipho's that afternoon. With guilt still coursing strong through me, and the mystery of Xaron's morning between us, it made for awkward conversation over coffee.

We made small talk as we pushed on to Forum Demos. Nomusa told us of her night, which consisted of a handsome man in a tavern who claimed to be a laurel guard. I smiled in response while my mind wandered. I had only just realized I'd have to pay Nikias in front of them, and I didn't have the first clue as to how I'd pull it off.

"Are we meeting Nikias first?" Xaron asked suddenly.

Startled from my thoughts, I guiltily looked at Nomusa. She wore a frown. "No one told me we were meeting Nikias," she said slowly.

Xaron glanced at me. "You didn't mention it this morning?"

"It slipped my mind," I lied.

An awkward silence fell between us.

"You may as well tell me about it now," Nomusa said flatly. "What did the message say?"

Xaron recounted the missive and my conclusions about what it meant. "We don't know exactly where he intends to meet, but I'm sure we'll sort it out."

"Do you have the message? I want to see the exact wording."

Silently, I handed it to her. Apprehension built inside me as she read. Sooner or later, her mind would turn to payment. I didn't know what I'd say if she asked about it.

"*Meet me at the place where, if I were so blessed to be the Wreath, I might first lay eyes upon you, and at the time this evening that she might least observe it,*" she read aloud. "He has a fondness for convoluted riddles, doesn't he? At least its meaning is obvious."

"Is it?" I asked, curious. "Where exactly is it?"

"The Pillar. It rises right before the dais. Impossible to miss."

Xaron groaned. "Not the Pillar again. A bad cipher and a poor meeting place... I'm beginning to question this whole venture."

"As am I," Nomusa said wryly.

I looked away, having nothing to say in response.

When we were still a mile away from Forum Demos, the crowds thickened. Sweat and the stench of humanity permeated the air. I kept one hand on my purse and a wary watch. No one celebrated ceremonies as much as cutpurses, and I wasn't about to line some urchin's pockets.

We passed the gated Acadium, its campus of towers the last landmark before the forum, and a welcome sight after our long, uncomfortable march. Seeing it made me wish again that I could have one conversation with Archmaster Kyros and hear what he knew of the Despot's death. At least I would soon speak to Tribune Vusumuzi. I'd learn what I needed, so long as I could find the patience to tease it out.

As we drew close to Forum Demos, a palpable excitement grew in the air, electrifying the shouts and hurrying our steps. To my surprise, I found that I'd caught it as well. Though a leaden weight still lingered in my stomach, my spirits lifted bit by bit. The sun began to set, and the glow of lights from Forum Demos appeared ahead. Pyr lamps, braziers, oil lanterns, even candles were suspended above the streets, a path of stars to light our way.

Then we reached Forum Demos itself, the sprawling half-mile of amphitheater packed full of people for the second time in a span. We made our way directly toward the Pillar. My anxiety increased with every step. Would I be able to slip the silver to Nikias? I didn't dare think of the ethics of it lest I lose my nerve.

As we reached the Pillar, I scanned the crowd for the

steward, but he was just one in a sea of humanity. Xaron, a few inches taller than I was, rose on his toes, but fared no better. Nomusa was half-hearted in her search, her scowl deepening with every new person who shoved against her.

Finally, I saw him. I'd only met him a few times before, but I recognized the squinting eyes set in the scrunched face looking back and forth. Finely trimmed gray whiskers lined his jaw, and even in the midst of the crowd, he stood erect and proud in his patrician finery.

I pressed toward him without alerting Xaron and Nomusa. A desperate idea had occurred to me. I just had to hope the steward would comply.

Nikias turned and noticed me, then stood and waited. He didn't acknowledge me, for which I was thankful. No doubt both of us wished to escape as much notice as possible.

Nearing him, I withdrew the purse of silver from inside my chiton's pocket and clutched it tightly in my hand. As soon as I stood before him, I thrust it toward him.

The steward reflexively stepped back. "What is that?" he demanded, shouting to be heard.

"Take it!" I hissed, pressing it into his hand. "I'm paying in advance!" A glance over my shoulder showed Xaron and Nomusa heading our way.

Nikias's ample eyebrows drew down, but he accepted the purse and secreted it beneath his many-layered robes.

Just then, my companions joined us. "Nikias!" Xaron greeted him. "Good to see you! You should have told us you were such a stunning poet!"

The steward scowled. "As much as I would love to bandy words, I must return to my master's side soon."

My mouth felt dry as I leaned close, my companions leaning with me. "Tell us what you know of the Despot," I said as loud as I dared.

Nikias nodded sharply. "The official story is he died of

foul humors of the heart due to the rich foods of the festival. But the honors tell another story."

"Go on."

Nikias spoke so low I could barely hear. "The Despot was murdered in his own rooms. Pushed from his balcony by the look of it."

"Pushed from his balcony?" I frowned. "How do you know? Was his body found below?"

Nikias's whiskers bristled as he leaned away. "No body has been found that I've heard of. But the Despot was gone without a trace! Not a spot of blood on the carpets, nor bed sheets, nor walls. The only thing out of sorts was that his balcony door was ajar, and a spattering of mud lay on the stone."

I glanced at the others. Xaron wore a skeptical look, while Nomusa seemed thoughtful. Turning back to Nikias, I asked, "How can we be sure he didn't disappear somehow? Perhaps he was kidnapped."

Nikias looked to the sky as if seeking consolation from the gods. "No one saw him leave, no one, out of the entire Laurel Palace. There's only one door to Myron's old chambers. He entered that night and never left."

"But someone else must have entered as well," Xaron objected. "Or are you saying the old boar threw himself to the rocks?"

Nikias ignored him. "There is more. An honor overheard the guards afterward. One said he heard arguing from inside, then a roar like a blazing forge. He and his fellow tried to enter but found it bolted from within. It was only after the First Laurel had arrived that they broke it open and found nothing inside."

The First Laurel had been the first to arrive. That cast a new light on Lykos. I'd assumed him innocent. Either there had been no other evidence on the scene, or he had disposed of it before others arrived. The roar could be explained by a tricky bit of chemistry or an enchanted object. Pyrthaen-lit braziers, for example, had a tendency to blaze up on occasion.

Or, of course, it could be from the magic of a rogue warden.

"Safe to say there were two people in that room," Xaron reasoned. "Unless the Despot was as crazy as his daughter."

"And if they had a way in," Nomusa interjected, "they would have had a way to secret out the Despot."

"It's impossible!" Nikias protested. "There are no secret passages to that room, I can assure you of that. And the balcony is as inaccessible. Not only is it watched by a dozen guards from a dozen different angles, and lit as brightly as the moons, but it is set over a sheer, slick cliff. Not even the most dexterous of gymnasts could manage it."

"Perhaps they didn't enter," I said, a thought coming to me. "Perhaps they hid in the room until the Despot returned."

"And then went where?" Nikias pressed. "Did they leap after their dark deed was finished?" He sniffed. "I hardly think even the most dedicated assassin would commit to that."

I shared a look with Xaron, and he shrugged. Nomusa seemed to have spoken her piece and remained silent as well.

"Is there anything more?" I asked Nikias. "What about Asileia Wreath? And Lykos — what has he been up to?"

"One at a time," he said irritably, eyes darting this way and that. "The palace has felt like the air before a storm, to borrow my master's words. People move with caution and speak softly, especially around our soon-to-be Despoina. As for her, I've seen with my own eyes that she has truly been touched by malevolent pyr."

It was hardly surprising to hear. Yet I couldn't let others draw conclusions for me. Too often in the past had others' assumptions led me astray. "What signs has she shown?"

"What hasn't she? She surrounds herself with those backwater oracles, who prattle in her ear that she's the 'Hand of Clepsammia' and other such rubbish. She speaks to herself in front of others. She sees things that are not there, while other times she's blind to people standing directly before her. But most of all..." Nikias hesitated.

"Don't stay silent now," I coaxed him.

His jaw flexed. "I cannot say more. It would betray my master's confidences, and that I would not do for silver or gold."

I leaned back, disappointed. He had given much already, but this seemed to be the crucial bit. What had Jaxas, Nikias's master, told him that was so important? It might be the key to knowing if Asileia was guilty or innocent.

"Then at least speak of the First Laurel," I pressed. "What has he done since the Despot's death?"

"How can I tell? He's hardly been in the palace. But others have said he's looking into the Despot's death, and Lykos has never given me reason to believe otherwise. I would not suspect him in your little game."

I nodded. It didn't exonerate him, but it was good to know Nikias's opinion.

Nikias glanced back toward the dais. "I must return. I cannot promise to speak again. The way things are looking under the Despoina, information may cost my life next time."

"Then you'd best avoid paying," I said with a forced smile. "Thank you as always, Nikias. May the Eidola watch over you."

"I had better pray someone will," the informant muttered as he turned and stalked through the unwashed crowd, shoulders raised like an alley mongrel.

"How much of that was lying at his master's behest?" Xaron murmured in my ear as we watched the steward disappear into the crowd.

I shrugged, glad that neither of my companions had inquired into the seeming lack of payment to Nikias. "You'll drive yourself madder than Asileia worrying about the truth. All we have to worry about is what fits."

"What *does* fit?" He ran a hand through his hair. "I still feel as if we've not discovered anything conclusive."

"We can discuss this later," Nomusa broke in. "Let's go to our usual perch."

We pushed back up through the crowd to the buildings lining the back of the forum, then clambered up the crates to the roof above, ignoring once more the jeering of the orphans. No sooner had we sat than an unnaturally amplified voice cut through the crowd.

"Hark!" Hilarion's high-pitched voice called. "Make way for our beloved Wreath!"

The procession streamed through the crowd like a great snake. Rank upon rank of trumpeters, dancers, and polished city watchmen marched through Forum Demos toward the dais.

After the common paraders came the foremost of Oedijan officials: the Servants of the People's Conclave. Signifying their connection to the people, they walked on foot, though their flawless, flowing robes sewn with an abundance of cloth and pinned with gems and silver spoiled the effect.

Behind the Servants walked the Low Consuls, the supreme leaders who ruled through the Conclave. As I spotted Feiyan walking among them, her chin held up proudly, I sent up a small prayer that she would trip over the hem of her robes. To my dismay, no gods or pyr paid me heed, and the snake of a woman passed by unimpeded.

Next came the Tribunes, swathed in burgundy robes, with the Shepherds walking among them. In aqua cowls and manacles hanging from their wrists and ankles, the warden enforcers of the Confessional Tribunal kept their gazes forward and held themselves in an unnaturally stiff manner. My stomach twisted upon seeing them, as it always did.

There was something strange about Shepherds that I'd never quite been able to put my finger on.

The Acadians followed the Tribunes and Shepherds, Archmaster Kyros Brighteyed at their head. His telltale eyes could be seen glimmering even from this distance. After the Acadians rode the five Stratechons, elected leaders of the city watch and the militia taxoi when needed.

Finally, the royal palanquin passed by. Eight honors contorted their bodies to bear our new Despoina down the steps to the dais. Before her rode Hilarion, the middle-aged, warden jester looking distinctly uncomfortable atop his humorously small mule. His sackcloth clothing no doubt made his situation all the worse. A mocking crown of golden wheat was twined about his mostly bald pate. With the piteous sight he made, I could almost understand people becoming dismissive of wardens' powers, as Hilarion was meant to do.

Coming behind them rode Lykos, making for a stark contrast. He peered about with his wolfish eyes from atop a fine chestnut, polished bronze armor shining.

As the last of the parade followed, the Despoina was carried up to the brilliantly illuminated dais, and the canopy of her palanquin was pulled back. The gathered crowd collectively gasped — how godly she appeared! Her skin had been rubbed with golden pyrkin, and with her chiton cut to leave both breasts exposed, there was plenty of skin to glow. Had she been anyone but our Despoina-to-be, she would have been derided as a whore. But Asileia's nakedness cast an aura of power. She appeared brighter than the three moons and more wondrous than the radiant winds. I suspected she basked in all her contrived glory.

"I don't think Myron glowed like the sun during his Ascension," I said to Xaron and Nomusa.

"Myron wasn't mad," Nomusa surmised.

Hilarion's high tenor broke through the babbling of the

audience once again. "Hail!" he called. "Hail, one and all! The Low Consuls of our nation!"

The ten Low Consuls of the Conclave processed to the front of the dais to stand beside the Despoina-to-be, looking like frail, mortal creatures next to a radiant goddess. One by one, Hilarion pressed his fingers to their throats, and each said their piece to muted effects from the crowd. True rulers of Oedija or not, the common people were not here for their speeches.

After they'd finished, High Tribune Photina stepped forward. Held aloft in her hands was the Evergreen Wreath. The crown was said to have been worn by the first Despot six hundred years before, and was still as vibrant a green as the day it was woven. The crowd rose in a sudden roar of cheers — and jeers, unless my ears were mistaken. My interest piqued, I fished out my peering glass and adjusted it to watch the proceedings.

Hilarion pressed his fingers to Asileia's golden throat as she stepped forward. "People of Oedija," her commanding alto boomed. "The demos of our demotism. I welcome you, and welcome your worship."

There was pocketed applause, but more loudly rose the murmurs.

"That wasn't what they expected, I'll warrant," Xaron muttered. "The mad hag."

"We gather here not just for ceremony," Asileia continued. "We gather not just because tradition demands it. We gather to witness the passing of this nation's leadership, and to witness a change more profound than the switching of the seasons. We gather to witness my donning of the Wreath."

This was something the people could get behind, and they started clapping. But true to her manner, Leia barreled through with barely a pause.

"Some claim I am to be a mere figurehead, as my father was, and his father was, and his mother before that. Little more than a statue on a throne." Her voice rose in anger. "Some claim that I will be meek as a lamb, shepherded by a band of old fools."

Murmurs gave a bubbling undercurrent to the speech. Something was stirring, though I couldn't tell precisely what.

"They are wrong!" The Despoina's voice crashed like cymbals in my ears. "And they will be shown to be wrong! This is my promise to you: change is coming. And it is coming tonight."

The bubbling became a swelling river, protests and assents sounding in equal measures. I shared a worried look with Nomusa and Xaron. None of us moved. If something were to happen, we had to be present for it.

"We are weak," Asileia sneered. "We bow under famine and hunger. Our army is little more than children playing with toys. We cower before another nation as if we were already their slaves. But we will cower no longer. I bow before no one. *No one!*"

People began crying out now, the noise reaching a zenith. I couldn't tell if protest or approval was winning out. Even still, the Despoina's voice crashed over them, like thunder over stormy seas.

"I am the Eidola's chosen, the Hand of Clepsammia! The oracles have spoken of my coming! And I will lead our nation to the glory it was fated to seize!"

And with that, a hush stole over the crowd. For some, it was heresy. For others, it was hopelessly grandiose. I knew it now to be mere madness.

Then, through the peering glass, I saw Asileia suddenly jerk back from Hilarion, her mouth parted in a scream. It echoed through the forum, then abruptly cut to a normal pitch. Heart pounding, I pieced the scene together from glimpses.

The Despoina, her robes engulfed in hungry flames, stumbling across the dais.

The Low Consuls scattering and scrambling to flee the platform.

Hilarion, still standing where the Despoina had left him, staring in horror at his hand.

"Kill him! Kill him!" Her scream echoed thinly up the forum. Focusing my glass on Asileia, I saw she pointed at someone. As I followed the line of her finger, I glimpsed Hilarion as a sword whipped a red line across his neck. The jester crumpled to the ground. But the attacker wasn't finished yet. The sword bit into the back of Hilarion's neck, spraying blood across the stage, and a third time as the sword pierced through his back.

I watched through my glass, trying to steady my shaking hands, as I identified the assailant. Lykos, gleaming armor spattered with blood, withdrew his blade and scanned the swell of faces as if searching for more victims. All the while, Shepherds swarmed the stage.

Asileia Wreath still screamed as honors rushed up to her and swung rags to dampen the flames licking across her golden skin. The noise of the crowd drowned out her words. I saw someone kneel by the dead body of Hilarion — Kyros Brighteyed, his gaze as hard as Lykos's had been.

"Great ancestors protect us all," Xaron muttered as he gripped my arm. "Did that just happen?"

I was too preoccupied to answer. As shock slipped away, suspicion replaced it. I panned my peering glass across the stage, studying the scene.

"Airene, we have to leave," Nomusa said, taking my other arm. "It isn't safe here."

I sighed and lowered the glass, then followed them off the rooftop to the chaotic streets below.

JAXAS

Jaxas stood just beyond the doorway, head turned aside. From the corner of his eye, he could see the room lay in disarray. Mirror glass glittered across the carpeted floor. Curtains had been ripped down and torn apart. Pillow feathers were strewn about the bed.

She stood in the midst of the chaos, the goddess calm again after the storm. The Despoina had returned to her right mind.

"Leia?" Jaxas inquired cautiously. He didn't look at her. "Are you sure you wouldn't like me to call back the surgeon?"

A turn before, her skin had been reddened and boiled by the lancing flames of the late Hilarion. But Kallias the Sculptor had done his job well. As she stood naked in the middle of the room, he could see the Acadian surgeon had returned her flesh to its ashy bronze.

If only he could restore all she had lost.

"Leia?" he called softly once more.

"It is not the first time I've burned, Archon Jaxas." She distanced him with the new title she'd granted him. "You have not forgotten my mother's gift to me, have you?"

He had tried to forget many times, but Leia had never let

him. She despised him for how he saw the best in her. Or how he imagined it.

"That disgusting skin hanging from my ears," she continued, merciless, though she seemed to be speaking to herself. "And she thought I would keep it — hah!"

Jaxas tried again to lead the conversation away. "You look well, but if it hurts too much to put on your robes, I can call the honors back—"

"You do not need to coddle me, Jaxas. Just because my father is dead does not mean I cannot take care of myself." She laughed mirthlessly.

"Then perhaps you will dismiss me."

"Come closer — I cannot hear you from over there."

He could feel her mocking smile, but it was his Despoina's explicit command. As little as he wanted to, he turned to the room and faced her. He had seen his cousin naked before, and not only as children, for their bathing times sometimes coincided. But never had she displayed herself like this before him. He took two obliging steps forward and halted.

Her lips curled. "Closer."

He took another step.

She laughed aloud at him again. "You always were skittish." Now she approached him, coming close enough to touch. She held herself tall and erect, as if her nudity were armor, as if the shame it spread through Jaxas were something to be proud of.

Leaning closer, she spoke in his ear, breath tickling his neck. "I know he's dead. Even though there was no body, I know it. Would you like to know how?"

He said nothing, dreading her words.

"Because, dear cousin, I killed him."

Jaxas stepped back, his heart racing. "You don't mean that," he said as calmly as he could manage. "You can't. I sat with you that night in your father's solar."

"Not with all of me." She smiled at his shock, his fear, his loathing. "I am the Eidola's chosen. The Hand of Clepsammia moves her spirit as readily as a pyr between the Pyrthae and the world of flesh. I killed him, if not with my worldly hands, than with my immortal ones."

"Leia, don't say such things. You're not in your right mind."

She laughed, and before its harsh sound, he couldn't bear to stay a moment longer. He turned from her chambers and fled.

Down the hall from her doors, he pressed himself against the cold stone. Her laughter had cut off as abruptly as it had come. No doubt she had lapsed back into one of her stupors — her visions, as she called them.

Jaxas closed his eyes and tried to still his spinning head. He didn't believe it. He couldn't. Not of her. But he'd heard it from her own lips. She believed she had killed him. Was delighted she had. Even if she hadn't done it, wasn't that bad enough?

He continued to flee, his footsteps falling faster and faster. His eyes burned, but he wiped away the few tears that came until his eyes were dry. This was the sign he'd been waiting so long for, he told himself. It was an impossible task before him, but he could not flinch from it any longer. She had shown too much of herself now. He could no longer tell himself that somewhere in her, beyond the cruel desires and feelings, there was some good part of her that would rise above the rest.

He came to an abrupt halt before a tall window that looked out over the bay. The night had hidden much of the sea from view, but in the crests of the waves, pyrkin came alive in green washes. He had always treasured living in the seaside palace. The orphaned cousin taken in at eight when his parents died of plague, he'd always known he was lucky to even be alive, much less be surrounded by plenty. Myron had cared for him as a father for a son, steady even when his wife succumbed to the same disease. And Asileia, having lost her mother, bonded close to Jaxas in her grief.

The peaceful sounds drifting up the cliffside could not calm him now. Asileia was not the girl he'd grown up with. To continue loving her, she who had once been a sister to him, would be living a lie.

Yet doubt haunted him. Even knowing what she was, even knowing what she believed herself capable of, he didn't know that he would be able to do what needed to be done. For the good of all. Eidola above, for Asileia's own sake.

Jaxas stared out over the quiet ocean, seeing little and understanding less.

11

THE AUGUR

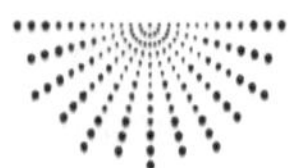

Master Eltris says there are many things to be seen in birds. She says they are attuned to the Pyrthae in ways that humans are not. All of us contain the energetic elements within us — radiance, kinesis, magnesis, and the like — but many animals possess these to a greater degree than we, and birds most of all. Master Eltris claims that birds are able to fly high among the cold winds because of a natural attunement to radiance and kinesis. And they navigate by magnesis, reading the magnetic fields that encompass Telae the way we would read a map.

In whisper finches, the Master Augur says, the most important of the energetic elements is present. It is this element that we humans possess that allows us to think in our heightened capacity, and to force our will on the world. Quintessence, she calls it, though she cannot tell me any more of it than that. If I ask, she quickly grows cross.

But I do not wish to study birds. I believe her to be a daft, wool-eared woman. Even if I did like her, I fear I have ruined my chances to become a master by being placed under her tutelage. Archmaster Kyros does not appear to care for her either. I am sure she would not be Master Augur had she not already long held the position. It's said she's as old as most of the buildings in the

Acadium, even if she doesn't look it. I believe it when she talks sometimes, of things people shouldn't know of. The look she gets in her eye frightens me.

- Diary of an Acadian pupil, name and date unknown

I t was well after dark when we reached our derelict tower and wearily climbed to the top. Once there, we gathered the last of the scraps in our household and made a meager meal, complete with goblets filled with the dregs of festival wine.

"Alright," Xaron said, collapsing into the old armchair and ripping off a bite of dried sausage. "What happened back there?"

I barely tasted the food I ate. "It's more proof that Asileia killed her father."

"How?" Nomusa demanded. "The Despoina was attacked by a warden. How else could those flames begin so suddenly?"

"Unless it was a performance. You couldn't see Hilarion's expression before Lykos cut him down. He stared at his hand like it had betrayed him."

"Perhaps it was an accident," Nomusa suggested.

Xaron shrugged. "Such things can happen even with an experienced warden. But one thing I do know is that Hilarion wasn't trying to kill her. His fingers were pressed to her throat. It would have been simple to do, if stupid, considering the forum was full of witnesses."

"Unless someone was trying to make a point," I murmured. "The Manifest… didn't you say they're for liberating wardens?"

Xaron's brow creased. "Yes. But didn't we just establish that Hilarion wasn't trying to kill her?"

"I still agree with that. But would it be possible that someone was framing him?"

"Shepherds were around the dais," Nomusa noted.

Xaron shook his head. "No Shepherds were close enough or at the right angle. It had to have been someone within a dozen feet, and even then they'd have to be a powerful warden." He paused, his eyes going wide. "Oh, Tyurn's tits…"

"What is it?"

Xaron looked between us, then sighed. "You know how I've been leaving most mornings for the past several months?"

"Hard to miss," I said drily.

"Well, I suppose I now have to tell you what I've been up to… and it wasn't visiting my parents, or seeing a special woman. I've been — well, receiving lessons from an Acadian."

Silence filled Canopy.

Nomusa recovered before I did. "You're even stupider than I thought."

He smiled sheepishly. "I'm sure that's not altogether surprising."

I was far from amused. "How could you, Xaron? If you're caught, you could be confined there for the rest of your life — if the Shepherds don't decide to kill you instead."

"I know the risks. I know it's a foolish thing to do. But it's all a long story. What's important is that in my time in the Acadium, I've learned a lot about another warden who was on stage with Asileia, one powerful enough to channel radiance at a great distance before it burst into flame. And one who might have the motivation to frame Hilarion."

It took all my self-control to rein in my impatience. "You've just told us you've been a fool for the past season. Now you're holding out on us. Who else could have done it?"

Nomusa's eyes widened. "Kyros Brighteyed. That's who you mean, isn't it?"

Xaron nodded. "I've heard things spoken about him, but I didn't know what to make of them. That he comes and goes at strange turns of the night. That he has become increasingly vocal about the need for Acadians to step up their role within Oedija. Even that he's been training Acadians to fight."

Fear struck through me, quick and cold. "To fight? What does he want, to become one of the Tyrant Wardens of old?"

"Or maybe he's the leader of the Manifest," Nomusa said darkly.

Xaron shrugged helplessly. "I can't say for sure. But Eltris can probably tell us more."

Nomusa and I shared a look. "Who is Eltris?" she inquired.

"She's, well, my mentor, I suppose."

"Mentor for channeling?" I guessed.

He nodded. "My mother never taught me anything beyond dampening my gift. I'm *shur*, a ten-shift warden, yet Eltris has shown me just how little I know." He lowered his gaze. "It may seem wrong to you. 'Thae above, it felt wrong to me at first. But learning about channeling can be for good as well as evil."

I didn't look at him, not wanting him to see the fear in my eyes. "Let's assume that Kyros did set up Hilarion. What would he gain from it? This can only incite anger against wardens."

"But if he's part of the Manifest, that may serve him well," Nomusa said thoughtfully. "People clearly support the cult's ideas. If he inflames relations between wardens and the demotism, it could propel their movement further."

"I have an idea." Xaron stood and stretched. "How about we go visit Eltris tomorrow morning. She can tell us more about Kyros, and I can stop feeling guilty about lying to you."

I hesitated. On the one hand, I didn't have a better explanation for what had happened at the Ascension. But I found it hard to accept that the Archmaster was leading an insurrection of wardens. It didn't explain what was happening with Asileia and Feiyan, nor with the Valemish. And I still found the Manifest the least of the threats that faced us.

Cults were fragile, and surely all the more so with wardens involved.

"It seems risky to gossip about Kyros in his own domain," I hedged. "How can you be sure we won't be watched?"

"Eltris has mouthed off about him this long. I'm sure we'll be fine."

I looked at Nomusa, who shrugged. "May as well," she said. "We might find out something."

I sighed. If it could bring me closer to the Archmaster, one of the few who had seen the scene of Myron's disappearance, then I had to at least try. "We'll go then. But afterward, we stop by the Tribunal to speak to Vusu. It's past time we heard what he said."

Xaron looked uneasy. "You two can go. I'll pass. That Tribune makes my skin crawl."

I nodded with understanding. The branch of the demotism that backed the Shepherds wouldn't be a comfortable place for Xaron to enter.

"We have a long day tomorrow," Nomusa said, rising. "And you two didn't rest much last night. Let's try to sleep the night through for once?"

My heart was light as I went to my bed. Despite everything that had happened, I found a smile tugging at my lips. Perhaps they didn't know it, but both of them were finally on board with my hunt.

Things were starting to look up.

I woke to the taste of blood.

I turned onto my side and spat in my washing dish. Working my swollen tongue around my mouth, I suspected I'd bitten it during the night. I groaned and sat up.

The dream slowly came back to me.

An endless, red ocean had surrounded me. The viscous

liquid clung to me as I broke the surface, but I'd enjoyed the feeling of being coated in it. It felt like having a second skin under which I could not be harmed.

Next to me, a man rose from the sea. I turned to him, smiling. But before I could see his face, I'd awoken.

I rubbed the dream-crust from my eyes, the logic of the images unraveling. I recognized it now as a scene stolen from the book Nomusa had lent me, *Tales of the Desolate*. Yama and Lophe and their Unnamed ishaka had conquered their neighbors and Nomusa's ancestors, the Yorandu. For some unexplained ritual, they had begun slaughtering their prisoners. The Twins had hung up the bodies as they slit their throats, draining them of blood into a large pit. Then they were said to have bathed in it. All in the name of their Serpent God.

I shook my head and rose from bed. Eidola above, I had to return that book of myths to Nomusa, or it seemed I'd go crazy.

Xaron and Nomusa rose soon after. As he usually did, Xaron made straight for the pantry and groaned. "No food."

"No time for that," I said impatiently. "We can get something on the way."

"Our money won't last long on stall food," Nomusa pointed out. "Especially since we're not taking paying jobs."

"We still need food!" Xaron objected. "Can't we get some on the way?"

"Fine. I'll draw a silver from the fund." Nomusa headed toward the loose stone in the wall.

My stomach lurched. "I'll get it!" I lunged from across the room, reaching the stone before her and pulling it out.

I could feel Nomusa staring at my back. "I didn't know you were so eager to buy groceries."

I kept the bag containing our stash as much out of sight as possible. "Someone has to keep a leash on Xaron."

He laughed. "It's true. I'd eat us out of this tower if I could."

Nomusa didn't say anything. The coin withdrawn, I tied up the bag again and replaced the stone, then stood and turned. "Ready?" I asked lightly.

Nomusa gave me a studying look, then nodded. As Xaron and I followed her out the door, I repressed a sigh of relief. For now, my lie remained undetected.

I doubted the reprieve would last long.

IT WAS ONLY a turn before noon by the time we arrived at the Acadium. As we approached the gates, Nomusa and I slowed, uncertain before the scrutiny of the guards. Xaron, however, urged us forward to the small gatehouse, where little more than his name had the gates swinging open. Masking my surprise, I followed him up the stone pathway to the buildings on the hill above.

My curiosity soared as I stared at the campus around me. The Acadium had been carved out slowly over the past century, the Conclave allotting bits and pieces as the years wore on and its population of wardens and scholars grew. As a result of this incremental development, the buildings demonstrated a clashing variety of architectures. The central forum at the top of the hill was a prime example, with what might have been a patrician's manor facing an adobe house barely fit to be a bakery. From our vantage point, I could see the campus continued in every direction in a similarly mismatched fashion, all the way to the far end, where a black tower rose high into the clear sky, only eclipsed in height by the gray Pillar before it. It had to be at least twice the height of our own derelict tower. I wondered if it, like the Conclave's dome and the Pillars, were relics from the Lighted years of Oedija, when wardens were revered rather than penned up like caged bears.

"The Archmaster's tower," Xaron said when he caught Nomusa and I staring. "You can see how someone would think themselves above others from up there."

Xaron led us past the forum and down the other side of the hill. We followed the paved road that wound through the campus for a while, glimpsing the numerous inhabitants of the Acadium. Acadians wore robes of gray, brown, and black, and distinguished themselves by colorful stoles indicating their discipline of study. Pupils were afforded no stoles, but hurried about in even more meager clothes to their tasks. Honors, too, walked the road, as well as a few common folk — laborers and merchants, by the look of them.

When we had gone halfway to Kyros's tower, Xaron turned off the main road into an alley with an uneven dirt path. Walking a little ways in, the buildings began to look increasingly desolate. Windows were boarded up. Debris lay scattered before doors. In the corners, wood rotted and stone had worn away. Peeking above the forgotten buildings was a squat stone tower, like a bent, old man among his starving grandchildren. It was before its gray, weathered door that Xaron stopped.

"Is this where she lives?" I asked in a low voice.

He nodded, then let out a long breath. "Brace yourselves."

As Nomusa and I exchanged a look, Xaron knocked twice. Several long moments passed. I glanced at Xaron, but he made no move to touch it again.

"Is she coming?" Nomusa asked drily.

No sooner had she spoken than the door cracked open. A pair of startling yellow eyes peered out from behind wisps of curly gray hair.

"Not today," the woman within said. "And not with them." She started closing the door.

"But—" Xaron objected.

"Not. Today." The door rapped shut.

Xaron stared at it in disbelief for a moment, then looked around sheepishly. "She gets like this. But usually, if I try again—"

"*Not. Today,*" Eltris repeated through the door.

"Friendly, isn't she?" Nomusa noted in a low voice.

"You may want to keep that to yourself," Xaron spoke aloud. "She has eerily keen hearing."

I stared at the door, wondering at the amber eyes behind it. "You've told us her name, but we know next to nothing of this Eltris."

Xaron shrugged. "Eltris is Eltris. She's the Master Augur in title, but no one pays much attention to her order." He glanced at the door again, and his eyes suddenly lit up, a wicked grin spreading across his face. "You see," he said loudly, "augury isn't a legitimate Pyrthaen discipline like the others here at the Acadium. It's not rigorous or really all that useful—"

The door opened again to reveal an old woman, bent and scowling like a forest crone. A frumpy, brown robe fell past her feet, battered pins barely holding it together. Master Augur Eltris glared at each of us, her frown deepening with each passing moment.

"If you must antagonize me," she said, disgust dripping from her words, "you'd best do it in here."

As Xaron followed her into the tower, he didn't bother to suppress a grin. I looked at Nomusa.

"We're already here," Nomusa said without enthusiasm. "May as well hear what the crone has to say."

"Xaron said she has good hearing," I reminded her before entering through the decrepit doorway.

It was dark within. The tower's arrow slits were boarded up, and the walls were lazily smeared with yellow pyrkin. A mess of books, papers, broken pens, and other implements sought to trip us with every step. Nomusa's mouth tightened as she looked over the mess. She had never been able to tolerate clutter.

Eltris stood at the base of a staircase that wound around the edge of the room. Her eyes caught the light, making them gleam like a cat's.

"Why are they here?" she demanded of Xaron.

"We need to talk to you, master. About Kyros."

I wondered if I even knew Xaron. There hadn't been a shred of sarcasm in his voice when he'd said "master."

The frumpy woman snorted. "I'm not a gossip. Their curiosity is not my concern."

"It should be," Xaron pressed. "If Kyros has been—"

"Can they channel?" She glanced at Nomusa, then stared at me for a long moment. Her eyes seemed to flash, but when I blinked, only the pyrkin light gleamed in them.

"No," she continued. "As I suspected. Scoria, the both of them."

"Scoria?" I asked.

Eltris snorted. "Those who can't channel are scoria."

I wondered if I should feel insulted. Before I could decide, the augur turned away to ascend the stairs. "If you are finished with this," she called over her shoulder, "we will attend to your training."

Xaron looked pleadingly at Nomusa and me before climbing the stairs himself. I was curious enough that I clambered up after him, though Nomusa looked more annoyed than before as she followed.

The second circle of the tower emerged in a wash of flickering light. The air hung hot and heavy, no doubt from the braziers lining the edge of the room and illuminating it in lieu of the boarded up windows. Their flames blazed too brightly to be natural. I stared at them, curious why I'd never seen such Pyrthaen creations before. The rest of the room was empty except for a large rug, faded and pilled, that ran the length and width of the tower.

Whistling suddenly filled the air. I looked up and saw a couple dozen finches in the eaves. To my amazement, I thought I detected the blue breast of a whisper finch among the mix, but I couldn't be sure. How an Acadian could afford one was beyond me. From all I'd heard, one could purchase a modest estate with the price such a rare bird would fetch.

Eltris had hobbled over to the far end of the carpet and stood facing us. Noticing me watching her birds, she nodded up at them. "My assistants."

I kept a straight face. "Their singing is lovely."

She snorted and turned her gaze to Xaron. "If you wanted to show off in front of these girls, you chose the wrong way. I'll put you on your back if I see one lapse of concentration."

"Yes, master." He took up a position opposite of the augur, closed his eyes, and rolled his shoulders, visibly relaxing his body.

I watched, bemused, as they proceeded to move slowly and deliberately, breathing deeply through their noses. All was silent except for the calling of the birds overhead. Nomusa had shed her look of annoyance and was watching with growing interest. "Not unlike Ixolo," she whispered to me.

"No talking," Eltris said without opening her eyes.

Nomusa frowned again, but she said nothing more.

After they performed the breathing exercises and move-ments for a quarter turn, the true training began. Eltris's first demand was that Xaron channel a radiant ray that she couldn't break. Setting his hands forward and screwing up his eyes, he attempted to do just that, projecting a beam of light toward Eltris. Before it reached the opposite side of the tower, however, the beam fractured and fell apart. I winced. Eltris hadn't even been looking when she dismantled his channeling, instead cooing softly to a bird that had alighted on her finger.

Xaron gritted his teeth and tried again. Twice more he

shot the radiant ray at his teacher, and twice more she broke it apart. After his ray shattered a sixth time, Xaron threw up his hands. "Show me how to do it already!"

"You know how," Eltris snapped. "Knowledge is not enough. You must apply what you know."

"I don't know what to apply," he muttered sulkily.

I exchanged a glance with Nomusa. Xaron was as talented of a warden as I knew, yet Eltris countered his channeling with seemingly little effort. I wondered with no small amount of trepidation how powerful she must be.

Eltris sighed. "You think of channeling as ten separate streams, one for each of your shifts."

"I don't," he protested. "Not exactly. I have to weave the ten streams into one—"

"No. It is one channel, from when you draw it in through your locus to when you channel it through your fingers. One, all the way through." She nodded. "Keep the stream as one, and no one will be able to break it apart."

"Alright," Xaron said dubiously.

Once again, he raised his hands, and after a moment, channeled radiance. This time, the ray nearly reached Eltris before it spun apart.

"Better," she said grudgingly. "Try again."

By the time they had finished, the ray had touched Eltris twice. A smile tugged at the augur's lips for a moment, but it was gone as she moved to the next task. "Now we will switch, and you will break my channeling."

"I thought you said no one would be able to break my stream if I thought of it as one," Xaron objected.

The augur's expression soured. "That is for radiance. Now we are channeling kinesis."

"Ah, right." He glanced over at us. "Kinesis takes a form that is easily dispersed for those who know how. It lacks the natural integrity of radiance."

"You have the knowledge," Eltris said, a hint of approval in her tone. "Now apply it."

Without hesitation, the augur thrust out her hands. Around them, the air rippled, and pure force barreled across the room toward Xaron.

He didn't dodge out of the way, but tried his best to shred the wave. Though whatever he did seemed to lessen the impact, the wave still sent him sprawling, the old carpet doing little to cushion his fall. I stifled my laughter once again, and Nomusa struggled to do the same.

Xaron shot us dirty looks, but wordlessly returned to his feet and readied his stance. Eltris gave him no time to prepare before shooting the next wave over.

Again and again, Xaron was knocked down by his teacher. When Eltris was satisfied that Xaron wouldn't master kinetic shredding that day, she moved onto magnesis. "This should be simple enough for you. Raise the lodestone."

Xaron, beaten and bruised, started to smile. But from the smile creeping onto his master's lips, I had a feeling he'd have just as little success here as before. Xaron extended one hand and furrowed his brow at the small, black stone six paces before him. But instead of it rising into the air, it stayed where it was.

He dropped his hand. "You're stopping it!"

Eltris smirked openly and held up her hands. "You cannot disperse or shred magnesis. What, then, could I have done?"

"You—" Sweat beaded on his forehead, and he wiped it away distractedly. "You created a pull in the opposite direction. A like or greater field to counteract my own."

"Very good. Now, how do you undo my efforts?"

"Creating a pull greater than your own…"

I kept in a snort. That option didn't seem likely.

His eyes fell on the stone. "Or… I move your anchor."

The carpet suddenly rippled as something shot under it toward Xaron. He leaped out of the way just as it sailed out from underneath to clatter against the wall. A sheet of metal, I saw it was when it finally settled.

Eltris was frowning. "You could have pulled it more gently and spared my wall."

"Sorry." Xaron ran a hand through his hair, pulling it from its tail to fall about his face, as he grinned shamefacedly.

Eltris glanced over at Nomusa and me for a moment, then looked away. "Perhaps that is enough for today."

Xaron's expression fell. "Master, if I could...?"

"Quickly," the augur snapped.

"Perhaps we could make one more attempt at sparks," he rushed to say. "Since I seem to have the best feel for magnesis."

"Yes, you do seem inclined that way..." She nodded sharply. "We will make three attempts. Do you remember the positions from before?"

He nodded as eagerly as a child offered a honey-stick, then held up his hands less than a foot apart. His brow drew down, and his eyes focused on the air between them.

"Good," Eltris said after a few moments. "Your magnetic field is stable. Now expand it."

His jaw clenched, Xaron slowly drew his hands apart. After a moment though, he threw his hands up and hissed in frustration. I guessed that he'd let the magnetic field lapse, though my "scoria" eyes could see nothing of his magic.

Eltris's frown deepened. "Again."

This time, she held to the task so long that even I started to grow restless. When Xaron finally managed to sustain the magnetic field with his arms spread nearly as wide as they could go, I thought we were in the clear. But Eltris took him one step further.

"Place one end of it on this iron ore," she commanded, tossing him a grey-veined chunk of rock.

Xaron, a field assumedly still sustained between his hands, kneeled and placed one hand on the ore. After a few moments, he lifted it away and stood, grinning. I couldn't see it, but from the way he only held up one hand toward the ore, I guessed he now sustained the field between his hand and the rock.

Eltris allowed him a brief smile. "Good. Now kneel down again. You will need to make the field as strong as possible if you're to form a path."

"Right," Xaron said as he obeyed. Sweat dripped down his brow as he stared at the air between his hand and the piece of ore. I wondered if he could see the magnetic forces that lay between. A pang of envy went through me. I never much enjoyed the reminder of all I missed out on experiencing because I wasn't a warden.

"The air must be transformed into plasma for lightning to follow the path." Eltris walked to the cluttered perimeter of the room and withdrew from a pile of debris another piece of ore. Holding it in one hand, she placed her other hand on it and drew it back as suddenly as if she were drawing a bowstring. I jumped as sparks crackled between them, my heart thumping in surprise.

Eltris glanced over with a mean glint to her eyes. "Is this the show you came for?" she taunted Nomusa and me.

I didn't respond, but shared a rebellious look with Nomusa. Though, I was honest, the augur was not far wrong.

The frumpy tutor turned back to her mentee. "You saw how I did it?"

Xaron nodded, then reached out to pick up the ore.

"Don't hold it," Eltris snapped, and Xaron dropped the stone and jumped back. "If you don't know how to redistribute the energy, you'll shock yourself. Leave it on the ground for now."

He nodded, then kneeled to form his field again. We waited while he stared at the ore, his hand hovering above it. Another quarter-turn passed. As fascinating as channeling was, this practice session was becoming tedious. I started to pace, my mind falling away from the sights before me to mull over my inquiry into the Despot's killer. When would we speak of Kyros Brighteyed? I didn't want this trip to end up a waste of time.

Though I wasn't watching directly, I still noticed when Xaron produced a spark. A bright flash filled the room, and Xaron yelped and leaped back, staring at his hand. The Master Augur threw back her head and laughed.

"We'll make a warden of you yet!" she declared.

Xaron's grin was as wide as I'd ever seen it.

The smile died on Eltris's lips, though, as her eyes swept over Nomusa and me. "Why did you ask after Kyros?"

Caught off-guard, I searched for a response. Xaron's tongue was looser.

"We're hunting for the Despot's killer," he said, "and have a suspicion that—"

"Xaron!" Nomusa and I hissed together.

He looked between us. "We can trust her," he objected. "She knows far more damning things about me than this."

I bit back words that would have to be saved for later. For now, I had to try to salvage the mess Xaron had made. "It's true that we're curious about Myron Wreath's death," I said evenly. "And we know the Archmaster saw his rooms the night he was killed."

Eltris's eyes were sharp as a hawk's as she stared at me. "That might be true. But why ask me about rumors concerning Kyros?"

Xaron opened his mouth, but at my glare, he closed it again. Nomusa answered instead. "Better to know the man before we approach him."

The augur walked across the old, fraying carpet to stop a dozen paces away from us. "Tribune Vusumuzi also visited the Despot's chambers, it is said. Why not pay him a visit?"

I narrowed my eyes. It had to be a deflection from talking

about Kyros, yet it was eerie how close it came to foretelling our plans. "Perhaps we intend to," I supplied.

Eltris looked at Xaron, studying him. I hid a wince, hoping he would stay strong beneath her gaze.

He cleared his throat. "So, master. Could you tell them what you've told me about Kyros?"

A mirthless smile spread across her lips as her gaze turned back to us. "I suppose I could. That's why you two came, after all. To hear the Archmaster has begun training wardens to use their gifts."

My pulse quickened. "Xaron did hint at it," I said, trying not to betray my excitement. "So it's true? He's teaching Acadians to fight?"

"Yes. Just as I'm teaching Xaron to."

I pursed my lips at that. This was all so that Xaron could fight? But it was a mystery for another time. "How long has he been doing so? And how many?"

"How should I know? I'm an old crone who stays in her tower all day. But I've heard the rumors since a full season ago."

"Why now?" Nomusa demanded. "He's been Archmaster for years. Has he been training Acadians from the beginning, or did something else bring it on?"

"Why did a drought strike this harvest when the past decade has been bountiful? Why is the Demos Council in a tighter deadlock than it ever has been before? Why did Asileia Wreath catch fire in the middle of her Ascension?" Eltris wore a grim smile. "The city is full of unanswerable riddles."

Uneasiness spread through me as I contemplated the augur. Despite what she claimed, she seemed to know far more than a recluse in a tower should. I wondered how much we could trust any of what she said.

"Can you tell us nothing more of Archmaster Kyros, master?" Xaron pleaded.

Eltris turned her head aside. "That will be all for our lessons today. It may be some time before I am ready for our next one. You may check in three days if I am ready."

Xaron's expression crumpled, but he gave a small bow. "Yes, master. I will come back then."

As Xaron led us out of Eltris's tower, I cast one last look back at the augur, but her gaze was turned aside. Yet I had the uncomfortable feeling of her eyes on our backs as we descended the tower stairs into the gloom below.

12

WITH EVERY GOOD TURN

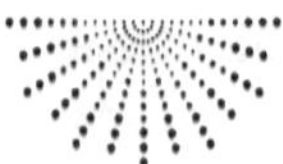

*HIGH TRIBUNE: Why have you come before us
    today, Verifier Jaxale?*
*VERIFIER: My reason is plain, High Tribune, yet it
    requires foundation to explain.*
*HIGH TRIBUNE: Go on then. We do not have
    all day.*
*VERIFIER: The Confessionary Tribunal was estab-
    lished as the sister branch of the Order of Veri-
    fiers, was it not? To accept the cases brought
    before it by both Finches and common citizens
    alike, and distribute justice as its Tribunes found
    wise?*
*HIGH TRIBUNE: Yes, in large part, that is our aim.
    But ours is the parent order, not the sister. We
    are not equals.*
*VERIFIER: Your words make many things clear. For
    often have I brought whispers that form a clear
    picture of corruption and yet been ignored. That
    you believe it your right to do so is, as I under-
    stand the Charters, a deviation from your
    mission.*

*HIGH TRIBUNE: Fortunately, that is for the
    Conclave to decide, not you. That is all, Verifier.
    Do not return unless you have something for me
    to consider. I do not appreciate my time being
    wasted.*

*- Verifier Jaxale before High Tribune Krynollon;
    1067 SLP*

After we navigated the mess of Eltris's tower and made it back into daylight, Nomusa exhaled. "What an insufferable hag."

"She can probably still hear you," Xaron pointed out. Despite his ultimate success during the training session, he seemed almost morose now.

I leaned closer and whispered, "We'll have to talk more about her later. For now, it's past time that we paid Vusu a visit."

Xaron shook his head. "I'll pass."

"Maybe you can ask around and see what people are saying about the Ascension."

He acquiesced with a nod.

"I'd ask you to buy food on your way back," Nomusa said. "But knowing you, it'd be all candied meat, and gone by the time you returned home."

"Can't fault you there." He smiled, recovering a bit of his old humor. "I'll gather whispers then. When will you be back at Canopy?"

"This evening, most likely," I said. "I might do some poking around myself after our meeting."

Nomusa shrugged. "The same for me. I need to check in on work that will actually make us money."

I gave her a small smile, choosing not to take it as a gibe.

"Then we'll have story time around the hearth." Xaron nodded toward the gate. "Now let's get out of here. No matter how many times I visit, this place still gives me the creeps."

~

WE PARTED ways outside of the Acadium. For a time, I listened to the bustling stall owners calling out their goods and services as I thought over the augur's words.

"Does she know more than she's letting on?" I wondered aloud. "Or does she think she knows more than she does?"

"Your guess is as good as mine. What worries me more is her influence over Xaron."

I chewed my lip. "He would have told her anything she'd asked about if we hadn't stopped him."

"And he calls her 'master.'" Nomusa shook her head. "I don't see what we can do. But it makes me uneasy."

"One thing at a time, I suppose. We can figure it out after we meet with Vusu."

Not long after, we arrived at the Tribunal. Located in deme Iris halfway between the Conclave and the Laurel Palace, the Confessionary Tribunal was housed in a building with a white dome. Mirroring the symbol of their order, the dome was separated into two halves by a hand-width crack. Not nearly as large or grand as the Conclave, it still had an impressive number of wings extending out from the main body. Formerly an Eidolan temple, deific statues of patina-painted bronze and moss-covered marble remained scattered across the courtyard.

Queasy with anticipation, I approached one of the guards at the gate, a young man with dark, handsome eyes, with Nomusa following close behind. "We're here to see Tribune Vusumuzi," I told him.

He looked me over, then his eyes flickered to Nomusa. "Airene of Zipho's?" he addressed me.

I would have smiled at the moniker had I not been stunned to be greeted by name. "That's me."

"Right this way. Your friend may enter as well."

I repressed a cringe, knowing how Nomusa would take the unintended slight. A glance her way showed she already wore a cold expression. Not an auspicious beginning to a difficult conversation.

Opening the gates, the guard led us between the rows of laurel trees and ferns to doors of plated gold, an extravagance that even the Laurel Palace didn't boast. Inside, the building shimmered with gold and white pyr lamps and pyrkin spread in designs on the walls. Above us, the Eidola had been painstakingly painted and preserved. Tyurn Sky-Sea stood in the center of the fresco, his tell-tale shimmering cloak waving behind him, leaving the rest of his muscled figure bare. The other two of the Foremost — his wife, Yena Third-Eye, and their son, Caradon Night-Veil — curled along the sides of the dome around him, while the Resolute Seven were crowded around the edges. I picked out Clepsammia, her sandglass held in the palm of her hand and a bemused smile on her lips. Behind the rest of the Eidolan gods loomed the Jealous One, Odaon the Sun, burning with his hatred for the living.

The young guard led us across the room to a female clerk sitting behind a desk. "Pelagia will help you," the guard said, and with a small bow, he departed.

The clerk looked a bit older than Nomusa and me, and wore spectacles perched on the tip of her nose. As she studied us, the skin above her nose pinched in well-defined creases. "What do you need?" she asked bluntly.

"Hello," I said pleasantly. "We're here to see Tribune Vusumuzi."

Pelagia's expression didn't shift. "He told me to expect you."

I glanced at Nomusa. It was as if Vusu had expected us that very afternoon.

The clerk's eyes slid to Nomusa. "I don't know who you are."

"She and I work together," I said hastily as Nomusa's expression blackened. "The Tribune will be delighted to see her as well."

Pelagia sniffed. "We'll see about that, won't we?" she said, rising. "Follow me."

The clerk led us down the halls in silence, clutching a stack of papers to her chest. When we'd passed nearly a dozen doors, she stopped and gestured to an entrance much like the others. "He'll be in there. Knock before you enter."

I nodded. "Thank you."

The clerk gave us a strange look, then briskly walked back down the hall. When she was out of earshot, I turned to Nomusa. "What was that about?"

"Vusu must agree with the change in regime in my isha-ka," Nomusa said, her tone flat.

I shook my head. "You're jumping to conclusions. Maybe he's just lived too long in Oedija. He is rather old. Or maybe he's just ornery."

A faint smile graced Nomusa's lips, but it quickly disap-peared. "I shouldn't have come."

"No, this is best. Between the two of us, we'll get the answers we need."

She inclined her head, which was all I could hope for at this point. Bracing myself, I knocked.

"Come in," Vusu called from within.

I took a breath and opened the door. The solar was as underwhelming as the door, cramped and small for one with such authority as the Tribune. It had no windows, but was lit by a number of pyr lamps mounted on the walls. Likely it had been a priest's quarters back when it was an Eidolan temple. Opposite the entrance, a birdcage housed a white and black finch, a gently glowing blue patch nestled underneath its beak. I stared at it. What were the odds that I would see two whisper finches in one day?

"Fascinating, is she not?" Vusu rose from a small desk in the far corner. He smiled as he walked over and reached a finger through the bars to stroke the bird's feathers. "Disela is her name."

"Disela," I echoed, stepping closer to the cage. "What does it mean?"

The Tribune hesitated, then said softly, "Remembrance."

"Remembrance," the whisper finch repeated loudly. I stared in wonder. The bird hadn't stumbled over its pronunciation, but spoken it as clearly as any native Oedijan.

An uncomfortable silence fell over the room. Nomusa, standing near the doorway, still hadn't said a word. I looked about Vusu's solar as I thought of how to begin the conversation. The walls were bare save for one arras, a depiction of a dragon with its mouth gaping open. I recognized it at once: Famine, the daemon god, trapped inside his mask, as some of the myths claimed he had met his end.

I nodded at the banner. "A rather ominous hanging to stare at all day."

Vusu smiled faintly as he glanced at it. "I find it a good reminder. That there are threats lurking just beyond our awareness, waiting to consume our good works, should we let them."

Again, the strange answer put me at a loss for words. Nomusa was no help. Vusu at least looked at her now, but he still offered her no words.

Finally, he moved and drew two chairs out opposite to the one at his desk. "Please, sit," he said, gesturing toward them.

Once we were seated, he sat as well, maintaining an upright posture. "Nomusa-sha," he finally acknowledged her.

That he used her royal honorific seemed a good sign. "I hope you're keeping well."

"Well enough." Her reply was far from warm.

He nodded politely, not seeming to notice. "But I suppose we are all busy these days. You saw what occurred at the Ascension?"

"Yes," I said. "A horrifying thing for Hilarion to attack the Despoina."

Vusu eyed me carefully. "You need not uphold pretenses around me, Airene. Unless you truly believe it was Hilarion who attacked Asileia."

My pulse quickened. Sensing an opportunity, I took a gamble. "No, I don't suppose we do. Nomusa and I believe someone framed him."

The Tribune smiled. "As shrewd as I'd hoped. I'm glad you stopped by my solar today."

"And why is that?" Nomusa asked flatly.

Vusu met her gaze. "Because, Nomusa-sha, things are stirring within this city that need to be uncovered. Things I had believed impossible until recent years." He paused to rub the bridge of his nose. "Forgive me. It has been a taxing span."

"No apology needed." I leaned forward. "What exactly are you referring to?"

"One particular issue. A recent matter that is on many of our minds."

I forced myself to remain still, waiting, hoping.

He looked at me, his dark eyes seeming like great chasms for a moment. "The death of the Despot was no accident," he said quietly. "And I mean to find out who is responsible."

My breath caught, though I tried not to let it show. "I suspected as much," I said as calmly as I could manage. "As it so happens, we've already been looking into it, to the extent of our reach. Though all we've had to go by were rumors and conjecture."

"Then we ought to rectify that." The Tribune smiled

slightly. "Reach will no longer be a concern for you. Tribunes find very few barriers in their investigations. With my sanction, you will not struggle to gain an audience with anyone. But first, you will need a symbol for your new office."

My mind raced over the words, hearing but not comprehending.

Vusu reached behind him and opened a drawer. From it, he withdrew a dull, metal chain with a medallion swinging from the end of it. A symbol of two half-circles stared back at me, but unlike the Tribunal's symbol, they faced away from each other. Atop them, a chevron pointed toward the heavens so that the symbol resembled a bird.

"Is that…?" I started to ask, stunned.

"The symbol of the Order of Verifiers," Vusu confirmed. His eyes flickered to Nomusa, but he held the medallion out to me. "I cannot bestow a Tribune's medallion upon you, but this ought to work just as well. And it suits you, does it not?"

I took it slowly, cradling the heavy iron in my hand. The back of the medallion was uneven and rough. I ran my fingers along it. "Will people recognize it? It's been so long."

"I've sent missives to those whom it should concern, instructing that you should be able to go anywhere I would and speak to whomever I may. This includes the Conclave, the Laurel Palace, the Acadium, and anywhere else you might see fit."

I ran my fingers along the symbol, unable to believe what Vusu was telling me. A lingering question cast it all in doubt. "But… why would you trust me with this? Trust us," I amended quickly, hoping Nomusa hadn't noticed my misspeak. "This is only the second time we've met."

"Yes," he said, smiling gently. "But I know you better than that. The reputation you and your companions have managed to gather is quite the achievement for ones so young. I spoke to some of these former clients of yours, including Zipho, of course."

We'd only performed minor tasks for Zipho — cafes were in a less predatory line of work than some businesses — but it didn't surprise me to hear Zipho recommending us, if only for Nomusa's sake. Yet Vusu's trust still seemed premature.

I gently placed the medallion in my lap. "I am grateful, Vusu. But it's still somewhat hard for me to believe. This… it's exactly what we've been waiting for."

"I know. And, unless I'm mistaken, you are exactly what I've been waiting for."

"You," the whisper finch suddenly said from behind, "are exactly what I've been waiting for."

I startled and looked around at the bird, then glanced at Nomusa. She did not look as pleased, but stared stoically back at me. Inwardly, I sighed. It likely meant objections were forthcoming.

Looking back to Vusu, I asked, "Does Disela always do that?"

"Often enough that I spill my drink at least once a day. The honors are becoming terribly cross with me." He gestured to the medallion. "I hope this brings you aid enough. If you find any door still barred, come to me, and we will sort it out. Or come by for any other reason — you are always welcome."

It was a generous offer. I nodded politely, unsure of what else to say.

He began to rise, then hesitated and settled back down. "There is one more thing. You have no doubt heard of the Despoina's latest actions? Among the embassies?"

A flush gathered at my neck. Here he was entrusting us with a Verifier medallion, and we were already behind on events. I cursed Xaron silently for holding us up in the Acadium that morning. "I don't believe so," I said neutrally.

"It has only just occurred. Asileia Wreath has seen it fit to insult, threaten, and expel half the dignitaries among the embassies. The Qao Fu, the Bali, even Avvad have been subjected to her capricious moods."

"An eventful first day as Despoina," I noted.

"Indeed. Yet her demands of the Avvadin envoy are worse still. She says if the Kahin-Shah does not pay tribute, Oedija must respond with force."

Threats against Avvad. The sheer idiocy of such an act defied my comprehension. I clutched the Verifier medallion and stared at the floor, wondering how long our fragile city could withstand Asileia's whims.

"If I may make a suggestion for your first line of investigation," Vusu interrupted my thoughts. "Our new Archon, Jaxas Wreath, may be of assistance to you. I have spoken with him on several occasions, but I have the sense he has more to tell regarding his cousin's recent behavior."

Yet another point of intrigue. I nodded, and as he rose, I rose with him. Nomusa followed more slowly.

"I cannot thank you enough," I murmured. "I'll let you know as soon as I find out more."

"Do," he said with a smile, then bowed his head to his work as we left his solar.

Despite our earlier plans, Nomusa and I both returned to Canopy.

"He gave us a Verifier medallion." I'd said it half a dozen times, ran my hands over it constantly on the walk through Oedija, but it still didn't feel real. The medallion I wore on my neck was the same as the Finches of old had worn. I'd nearly attained what I'd always wished for, but never dreamed possible. To be a Verifier not just in mimicry, but in actuality.

And it had all but fallen in my lap.

"He gave *you* the medallion," Nomusa observed flatly.

I couldn't let her wounded pride fester. "I know he slighted you. I know it's strange the way he gave it to us. But just think for a moment. Think about what this can give us access to. You heard what he said. The Acadium, without Xaron needing permission from that strange augur."

"And I was so eager to return."

I ignored her sarcasm. "The Conclave, maybe even while it's in session."

"How intriguing, listening to a bunch of old fools prattle on about politics."

I knew she didn't want to hear it, but I couldn't contain myself. "Even the Laurel Palace. 'Thae above, we're supposed to go speak with the Archon himself."

Nomusa leaned in close. "Listen to me," she hissed. "You're not using your head. Look at this, *truly* look at it, and tell me you don't find the whole situation suspicious."

"Yes, it's unusual," I said with annoyance. "But it's simple to explain. The Tribune is looking into the Despot's death and has heard good things about our reputation. Why wouldn't he want our assistance?"

"For exactly the reason you stated in his solar. He doesn't know us."

"But he knows people who do. We don't always know the people we work with. Remember the first time we worked with Talan? We didn't know the first thing about him, but that turned out well in the end."

Nomusa shook her head. "You're still missing the flaws in your reasoning."

"And you're speaking from a bruised ego rather than logic," I snapped. "What other possible reason could Vusu have for giving us access? And how could it benefit him other than exactly as it seems?"

She fell quiet, though not in submission. She often withdrew when she was losing an argument. I snorted in disgust. We continued our long walk home in silence.

For a while, I brooded on Nomusa's stubbornness and the truth of her points. But slowly, unable to make sense of the windfall myself, I decided to accept it and think rather of the opportunities Vusu had just afforded us. We'd go to Jaxas first, if only to honor Vusu's suggestion. Then I had more than half a mind to look further into Kyros. Confirming our suspicions regarding his role during the Ascension would go a long way toward unraveling the conspiracy.

My plans had begun to circle by the time we reached Canopy. Letting Nomusa ascend before me, I debated how soon I could reasonably use the medallion. Would his messages be received today? Or would tomorrow be the earliest I could test it? My impatience was winning the argument, but I forced myself to keep climbing. First, we had to check in with Xaron.

As we ascended the last circle of the tower and came before our door, Nomusa stopped abruptly. "*Faresh*," she muttered.

Her tone instantly drew me from my thoughts. "What?" I asked, trying to look around her.

She leaned out of the way, and I stared. The lock to our door had been broken and now hung among splintered wood.

"It would be wiser not to enter," she murmured.

"And never return home?" I swallowed. "Whoever did this did it explicitly. It's a warning, not a trap." I had a bad feeling I knew who the warning was from, too.

After a moment's hesitation, Nomusa nodded and cautiously pressed the door open. We stepped inside.

My stomach twisted into knots as I took in the destruction. The legs of the tables ripped off. Shelves torn from the pantry. The divan shredded and fractured in half. Dishes lay shattered on the floor, clay shards joining the glass from the broken bay window. The wind whistled into Canopy, cold and incessant.

Xaron, alone among the wreckage, spun at our entrance, hands raised. I flinched, half-expecting flames to erupt from his hands, but he quickly lowered them again.

"Sorry," he said with a nervous laugh. He gestured to the wreckage about him. "I'm a bit jumpy."

Nomusa stepped carefully over the broken bits across the boards. "What happened?"

"It was already like this when I returned. Whoever it was had it in for us, though, didn't they?" He gestured to the kitchen.

I instantly saw what he meant. "Our savings."

He nodded. "Gone. I checked."

"Our personal stashes as well?" Nomusa demanded.

Xaron shrugged. "I only checked mine, but it was also taken."

Nomusa stalked over to her room and disappeared within.

I stared over it all, rooted to my spot by the door. Part of me had known something like this would happen. Yet I hadn't warned either of them. I hadn't let them decide for themselves if what I did was worth the risk. And Corin — she'd return to a ruined house, and all the savings she'd accumulated would be gone. What would she do, with everything she'd earned to bring her sister to Oedija dissipated?

"Airene?" Xaron asked, approaching from across the loft. Nomusa had emerged from her room, her deepened scowl confirming that her savings were gone as well.

I took a steadying breath, for the little good it did me. It was past time to end the lies.

"I have something to tell you both..."

13

MARKS

The Eidola, the gods of our people, number eleven in total, a number many hold to be holy — or among gamblers, lucky.

Foremost among the Eidola are three:

Tyurn Sky-Sea, World-Father and seed of the gods;

Yena Third-Eye, the World-Father's wife and the watcher of all things, of which she whispers into her husband's ear;

And Caradon Night-Veil, their eldest son, and the one who brings night to shield us from the day.

- The Traditions of the Eleven: Eidolan worship in the demotism of Oedija; by Oracle Iason of deme Iris; 1164 SLP

Nomusa left immediately after my confession, slamming the door behind her. With the latch broken, it swung uselessly back open. I stared after her. Perhaps I should have been more open before. Perhaps I should have told them all from the start. But would I have done differently, even now? I wasn't sure I wanted to know that answer.

Xaron remained in Canopy, staring out the bay window. After a long silence, he turned and met my gaze. I searched his face, but for once, his feelings were hidden from me.

Then he smiled slightly, which only served to reveal the sadness behind his eyes. "Let's get some food. I have enough coin for us to eat tonight at least."

"Alright," I agreed. He held back his true feelings, and I didn't enjoy the suspense. But he had the right to respond in his own time.

The day was turning golden as the sun fell behind the sea, and the buildings cast long shadows over the street as we exited the tower. "Can we pick up sweetmeats?" he asked hopefully.

I waved a hand. "If you want to eat like a child, that's your business. Either way, I'll pay for your meal. I owe you that much."

"You owe me at least ten silvers, actually."

His tone was teasing, but I still winced.

I bought our meals and was scandalized by the expense. The price was half again as expensive as it had been the last time I'd bought stall meat. With no savings and no paying jobs, I wasn't sure even the substantial progress we'd made on the Despot job would be enough to keep us from going hungry.

I returned, dejected, to the tower stoop to sit and eat with Xaron. After licking his first skewer clean, he finally spoke. "Why didn't you just tell us?"

I bit back the defensive words that first sprang to mind and instead responded as honestly as I could. "I thought you would stop the hunt."

"Really? Why?"

"You and Nomusa seemed hesitant. I thought you believed it a fool's errand."

Xaron laughed. "Most of what we do are fool's errands. Sure, this one is riskier than most. But that doesn't mean I wouldn't have supported you. You know that I suspected you'd paid Nikias Canopy funds without telling us? I knew that pompous weasel didn't tattle for free."

I hid my wince by chewing through another bite of goat. "You know how you've been distracted lately, and spending more and more time at the Acadium? I think I took that to mean you weren't invested in the hunt. That you didn't approve of it." I shrugged. "I guess I jumped to conclusions."

"I can understand that, and you should know I didn't intend it. But the rest..." He shook his head and studied the cobblestones. "Feiyan's threat was toward me, Airene, even though she doesn't yet realize it. I know it's affected all of us, but what she said nearly three years ago — that's aimed at me. I've seen what the Shepherds can do. Even with the training I've had so far, no way could I beat one if she set them on me."

I rested my hand on his arm. "It won't come to that."

He raised his gaze to meet mine. "How can you promise that? You won't give up the job."

His words wrenched a knife through my heart. I feared to speak. There was only one truth I could offer him, and it wasn't what he needed to hear.

He looked aside. "I'm not trying to guilt you; really, I'm not. In fact... I think you should keep going."

Hope and guilt twined together in my gut. "Truly?"

"It's the right thing to do. If the Despot really was murdered, he deserves justice." He flashed a smirk worthy of Talan. "And that's what we Finches deliver, isn't it?"

I squeezed his arm. "Xaron... Are you sure?"

He took my hand and pressed it in return. "I'm sure. Just one thing. Don't lie to me again. Please."

I bowed my head. "I promise."

We sat for a few moments holding hands in companionable, if guilty, silence.

"Do you want to go out tonight? And use that new medallion, I mean."

I glanced up and down the street. "I do, if only to listen

around to the whispers on the street. Speaking of which, we never talked about if you learned anything."

"Oh, right." He slurped the juices off of his fingers, grinning when he noticed my grimace. "Can't waste the best part! Did you hear what the Despoina did to the Avvad diplomat?"

"Vusu told us," I admitted.

"Oh," Xaron said, deflated. "That's the biggest piece. But if you want the smaller details, I—"

"A strange sight," a voice said from next to us. "Airene of Port, relaxing before an inquiry has been pursued to its bitter end."

I'd halfway risen before I recognized who it was. Talan leaned against the tower wearing his usual half-smile, yet he was transformed in every other respect. His clothes were clean and tailored, though still in an Avvadin style of trousers, tunic, and jacket. His hair was free of sweat and oils and neatly pulled back in a tail. Gone was the greasy Guilder, replaced by an Avvadin man who could almost pass as respectable.

I sighed in relief. "You scared me. What are you doing here?"

"What *are* you doing here?" Xaron muttered.

Talan ignored him. "I have news. Uncertain news, to be sure, but as he's your brother..."

My gut wrenched. "Linos."

Xaron looked between us. "What's happened to Linos?"

Talan's gaze rested on me. "My orphans have seen him among the Seekers."

I blinked. "He's mixing with the Manifest?"

"More than that. He appears to have joined them."

My mind spun, trying to understand his revelation. Linos wasn't a fanatic. He longed for freedom and independence. Why he would surrender that to join a cult was more than I could comprehend.

Yet one thing at least was clear: I had to go after him.

"Explain on the way," I said to Talan.

He raised an eyebrow. "The Manifest compound is a poor place for a late-night visit."

I gave him a flat stare. "Whether or not he's there willingly, I need to go to him. I've already lost one brother. I don't intend to lose another."

Talan studied me for a moment before he nodded. "Your boldness never ceases to amaze me, Airene the Finch." He returned me a mocking bow. "Of course, I will come at your behest."

A fraction of the tension left my shoulders. "Thank you," I murmured. "Really."

He waved off my words, his eyes never leaving mine.

Xaron stepped forward. "I'm coming too."

We both looked at him. "I think not," Talan said calmly.

Xaron rounded on him. "And you believe you can stop me?" He shook his head. "If Linos is in trouble, I don't mean to stand by. 'Thae above, I'm the best house-breaker in Oedija."

Talan's mouth twitched. "You do believe that's true, don't you?"

Xaron scowled, and I rested a hand on his arm. "Thank you," I said, trying to instill all the gratitude I felt into the words. "Especially now of all times."

The frown broke into an embarrassed smile. "Of course I'll help, Aire. Nothing's changed between us. Besides, he's your little brother."

My little brother. Guilt poured afresh through me. Linos had told me he was going away. He'd told me not to worry. I should have read the sign for what it was. I should have protected my little brother, even from himself. Especially from himself.

"No point in wasting time," Talan said, turning on his heels. Xaron and I followed behind.

Deme Thys was a long way from Port, on the north side

of Oedija beyond the city walls. It gave Talan ample time to explain what he'd learned of Linos.

"They saw him at one of the Manifest's gatherings," he began.

"They. Multiple orphans spotted him? But there are supposed to be thousands of Seekers."

"There are. But Linos was easy to spot, considering he was up on the stage of the Wyvern's Claw."

"The Wyvern's Claw," I repeated. My father had taken me to it once, more than a decade ago, before it had stopped hosting plays.

"The old, wooden amphitheater north of Lake Thys," Talan explained, taking my words for a question. "They think the name makes the rickety thing grander."

I dreaded my next question, but Xaron had no such qualms. "What was he doing on stage?"

Talan took a long moment to answer. "My orphans aren't precise with details, especially not speeches. But it sounded like he was being held up. As an example."

"I can't imagine Linos as much of an exemplar," I said with a thin smile. "Did he look well?"

"Hard to say. He wore gray robes, and did what the Visage commanded him to." Talan glanced at me, his expression hard to read in the dimming light of the evening. "But you know what the Manifest claim. That they can make wardens of ordinary folk."

"You don't believe that," I said, aghast.

"Of course not. But there are many things that wardens can do beyond what Xaron has displayed. Worse things. Take the Damask Esir."

"The elite soldiers of Avvad? What do they have to do with this?"

"They're not just elite soldiers, Airene, as you should know. They're disciplined and loyal to the death. Because they've been made to be by the priests of Valem. The Tefra yoked their minds to serve the Kahin-Shah, and in doing so, took away all will of their own."

His words filled me with foreboding. Despite myself, I pictured Linos in a cell, shadows standing around him. What had been done to him that he would obey anyone's commands? The boy I knew took orders from no one.

I lengthened my stride. "Then we have no time to lose."

Even as we increased our pace, darkness had fallen by the time we reached the northern city gate. Despite the turmoil following Myron's death, peacetime practices were still being followed, which meant the gates were open day and night between the inner and outer demes. The guards watched us with evident interest as we passed through, but perhaps it was because we were the only ones crossing at that time. I hoped so. The less we were observed this night, the better.

Once outside the walls, Talan told us the plan he'd concocted. It was straightforward and simple. Since the Manifest movement had recently inflated beyond any hopes of regulation, the entrances to its compound were loosely monitored. Entering would be little more than a matter of walking in.

Yet as we approached the compound, it became apparent we'd been misinformed. Tall wooden fences, nearly twice as tall as myself, extended in either direction, with torches mounted at regular intervals. There was no gate, only an opening in the wall, yet that entrance was guarded by no fewer than four Seekers, their faces cast in shadow. As we were within reach of the torchlight, I guessed they'd already spotted us.

Xaron leaned in close. "I could easily vault over that wall, as could he." He nodded toward Talan. "You, however, are a different story. You still want to go through the gate?"

"We all go through the gate. They've likely seen us by now, so it would look suspicious for us to stray." I plotted fast. "We're three people looking to become Seekers. We couldn't sneak away from our homes until nightfall without being immediately noticed. We all work at a glass shop." It was the trade I knew best from my early years in Maesos's employment.

"Fine," Talan said. "But I assure you both, there's nothing to fear. They are welcoming as far as cultists go, so long as you know what to say."

"And you have much experience with cultists?" I inquired with a raised eyebrow.

He gave me a sly smile. "More than you might think."

As we approached, one of the guards called out to us. "May the One grace you! Who of our brothers and sisters approaches so late at night?"

"May the One not pass over you," Talan replied. "We are three of those who have been lost among the Unknowing."

We walked up to the gate, stopping a dozen paces away. I shifted my feet nervously, hand itching to grasp the knife hidden beneath my chiton. I'd killed one person before and had no desire to do it again. Yet approaching the cultists at this hour put me on edge, in no small part because they stood between me and my brother.

"You speak as Seeker," another of the guards spoke, a man with a gentle voice. "Yet you lack the mark. I cannot allow you to pass without questions." The man nodded at Xaron and I. "You two. Are you initiated as well?"

I hesitated, unsure of the best thing to say.

"No, they are not," Talan spoke for us. "I apologize, but I told them it would be best that they let me speak. I did not want to offend my brethren without need."

"You need not fear that," the same guard as before responded. "We welcome all Seekers to see the Truth for themselves. But would it not have been better to come during the day? Storms are gathering on the horizon, and red men walk the streets come darkness."

His words incited a burning curiosity in me, but I didn't

dare ask after them. Instead, I gave a bow and spoke, judging that they wanted to hear from more than Talan. "I apologize as well, good guards. We are but newly fled from our employer, a glass smith down in Port, and could only find the opportunity to come unnoticed during the night. Our friend was kind enough to wait to escort us. We understand it is difficult to admit us at such a turn of the night, but we have nowhere else to go. If you admit us now, I assure you, we will be as devoted as any of our new brethren."

There was a pause of appraisal before the cultist said softly, "A curious profession to produce someone with so honeyed a tongue."

Fear tightened in my gut.

Then the Seeker shrugged. "But who am I to question a woman's pretty words? We welcome all who seek the Truth here. And the seeking does not wait for the sun." At a nod, the shadows stepped aside and turned to form a tunnel for our passage. As they turned, the firelight finally illuminated their faces.

For a moment, the world seemed cast in glass. I stared at the patterns that played along their skin, violet lines spider-webbing around their eyes, cascading out like ripples in a still pond. This was the first Seeker I'd seen, yet I knew that pattern. Fourteen long years ago, I had seen it inked onto a face I knew well, and had not seen it since. Now the pattern suddenly appeared before me again.

"Jaxale."

I felt a tugging at my arm, and noticed Talan there, a shadow across his face hiding his expression.

"Jaxale," he repeated, "are you ready to go?"

Slowly, I understood his attempt to hide my identity. I nodded mutely. He and Xaron led me forward, between the faces imprinted with the tatu of my long-dead brother.

"May you find what you seek," the cultist said, "and the One not pass over you. There is a gathering two nights hence, Seekers. If the One wills it, perhaps we will see you there."

"If the One wills it," Talan responded, then quickly pulled me through the gate.

I hardly knew myself as we walked through the Manifest compound. I couldn't make sense of what I'd seen. The compound, cast in a darkness alleviated by intermittent pyr lamps, only added to my confusion. What did this place have to do with Thero's death? What was the connection across fourteen years?

I let Talan lead me along the street, packed dirt wide enough for two carts to pass abreast. Shadowed tents lined either side, as similar to one another as stones in a river. Some few people moved along the road with us, but I heard many rustling within their makeshift homes, settling in as they lay down to sleep.

After a time, the tents lining our right were replaced by a series of shops, dissimilar from the tents only in that they stood taller than the squat homes and had wide entrances that were draped closed at the late hour. They did not look well-secured; it wouldn't take a determined thief to steal their wares. Further to our right and down a hill, I saw the dark canopy of a strip of forest. Beyond that, by the shore of Lake Thys, rose the Wyvern's Claw, two hundred cubits high, seeming a shadowy mountain in the darkness. The long talons, curved spires of wood that rose well above the last of the viewing platforms, were silhouetted against the moons. Even at this hour, torches burned along its walls, a risky venture near all that wood.

My two friends directed me down the road. Though I saw my surroundings, my thoughts circled around the Seeker tatu. One memory rose above the miasma of the others. Iela, the feral warden I had long ago killed in self-defense, had claimed her master was behind Thero's murder those fourteen years ago. She'd described the strange pattern of tatu on his face, the same as I'd seen on the Seekers' faces tonight. But what did it mean? That her master had been at his experiments for the past decade and a half? Or longer? But with what aim? And did it mean this master was also the architect behind the Manifest?

We went further into the compound before Talan directed us into a shadowed alley, where he and Xaron gently settled me down onto the wet ground. I sat, heedless of the mud that caked my chiton and soaked through my underwraps.

"Airene," Xaron said worriedly, "what's going on? You froze back there. And you haven't spoken since we entered."

Talan pressed my hand. "Airene," he said in a low voice, "did you notice something I did not?"

I worked my tongue around my dry mouth. "Thero."

Xaron's brow creased. "Your brother? What does he have to do with this?"

I kept my eyes on the ground. My vision was full of memories. "We found him after he'd been gone for three days. The guard pulled him from a moat. Another few minutes, and he might have been flushed out to sea. His features were bloated and purpled, so much so that I almost didn't recognize him. But there was still enough of his face to see the pattern inked into it. The same tatu those Seekers wear."

"Are you saying he was part of the Manifest? But he died fourteen years ago. The Manifest have only been around for a few months." Xaron paused, his brow creasing. "Haven't they?"

"I don't know."

Talan shook his head. "Perhaps we should not be here until we know more about who and what we face."

I rose to my feet. "No. We can't turn back now. Not only would it seem suspicious to the guards, but... I need to know. I need to find out what this means." I met each of their eyes in turn, and saw the same concern reflected in both their expressions. "I need to find Linos before the same thing happens to him as happened to Thero."

I didn't need to say anything further. Talan nodded, and Xaron followed suit.

"Come," Talan said, then turned back toward the street.

I drew in a deep breath and followed. "I'm coming," I murmured to my brother's faraway ears. I just hoped I wasn't too late.

14

SEEKERS

Next of the Eidola come the Resolute Seven:
Lavvash, goddess of thunders and the passions;
Hinaron, god of the humors and health;
Saxeus, god of the seas and storms;
Nadalene, goddess of the forests and growing things;
Mandeia, goddess of psyche and spirit;
Cendaur, god of beasts and birds;
And Clepsammia, goddess of time and fate.
Last is the Jealous One, Odaon, who is mounted in the sky as the burning sun, longing to destroy all from his lonely, high place, but is only able to bring life to the world.

- The Traditions of the Eleven: Eidolan worship in the demotism of Oedija; by Oracle Iason of deme Iris; 1164 SLP

As we reemerged onto the main road of the Manifest compound, I leaned toward Talan. "Where do we seek Linos first?"

He scanned the area around us, ensuring no one was close enough to hear. "The Wyvern's Claw. The place where their largest gatherings are held."

"Why there?" Xaron asked. "There won't be any gather-ings at this time of night."

"From what I've heard, the most valuable members have their quarters within the amphitheater, including the Dishonored and the Visage of the Wyvern. If Linos is impor-tant enough to parade on stage, then he's certainly important enough to hold back there."

"And we're just supposed to rely on your intuition," Xaron said sarcastically.

"Enough, Xaron," I snapped. "Talan hasn't led us wrong before. I trust his information and so should you."

Xaron's mouth worked for a moment, then pressed into a firm line.

We walked in silence toward the amphitheater. Contin-uing along the street until we reached the beginning of the path down the hill, we saw four more Seeker guards standing watch. Talan only just pulled us back into the shadows before they glanced our way.

"We must cross down the hill off the path. Step carefully. The terrain is slick and steep, and we can bring no lights. Especially not summoned ones." He glanced at Xaron at this last statement.

"I wouldn't do that," Xaron muttered.

I suppressed a sigh. "Let's go then."

The thin light from the moons and the shifting radiant winds helped us see as we approached the hill and began to pick our way down. But with the tent shops looming behind and thick foliage overhead, the paltry light was soon choked out, throwing us into near complete darkness. I could barely see my companions as we slipped and slid down the hill. Already caked with mud, I didn't bother trying to stay clean. My hands were scraped and cold, my sandaled feet much the same.

Halfway down, I grew tired of my chiton snagging on

every stone and root, so I pulled it off and tucked it under a tree. "We'll return for it?" I asked Talan.

He nodded. "Best to leave no trace of our passage."

"Just a little further," Xaron muttered.

I followed his gaze to the Wyvern's Claw, no higher than a hundred paces past the tree line. Now level with the base of it, it loomed more than ever. It was a wonder that such a large building could be overtaken by a cult with so little protest from the Conclave. True, it had been in disrepair and infrequently used to host dramas or other public events in recent years. But now, I wondered what influence they possessed to be able to maintain such a claim.

We ghosted through the forest to the edge of the trees, then at a signal from Talan, we stole across the open ground. There was only one entrance to the Claw that Talan had been able to detect, the wide gate in front. No fewer than eight Seeker guards stood watch by it. Even though many of them were focused at the moment on a game of tiles, there were still more than enough of them to cause a racket if attacked.

Huddling next to the wall in one of the pools of shadow between the mounted torches, I gathered Talan and Xaron close. "Any ideas?"

Talan pointed up. "Were I on my own, I would enter there."

I followed his gaze and saw that thirty cubits above, the wall was shorter as it rose to its full height at the top of the stands. My mind boggled at the feat. "Thirty cubits? Is that possible, even for you?"

"It's definitely possible," Xaron declared. "I've nearly leaped that before."

"Have you?" Talan remarked drily,

"It doesn't matter," I cut in. "I can't get up that way, so we need a new plan."

Talan looked thoughtful for a moment. "Perhaps you could stay out here," he suggested quietly.

"Absolutely not." I'd wondered when one of them would suggest it. "He's my brother, and I've let him get caught up in this mess. I won't abandon him now."

"Even if it means endangering him further?" Talan shook his head. "Airene, I understand what it is like to leave your task in another's hands. But I assure you, I will do everything in my power to recover Linos."

"We both will," Xaron interjected.

I set my jaw. "There has to be a way. Just give me a moment to think of it."

"Every moment we wait is another moment we might be discovered," Talan pressed.

I swallowed down a sharp reply and said instead, "What if I show them the Finch medallion?"

Xaron blanched. "You've only just received it, Airene. You haven't checked if anyone has acknowledged it yet."

"They won't recognize it here." Talan's eyes were filled with pity, but his words were assured and cool.

I knew they were right, yet I found myself shaking my head. "I'm going," I repeated. "So instead of thinking up objections, help me figure out how I'm getting up there."

Talan and Xaron exchanged looks. I wondered if this would be the one issue that united them. But Talan glanced back at me and shrugged. "All we need is rope."

"And do you have one hiding in your trousers?" Xaron asked sarcastically.

"No. But the docks along Lake Thys should have plenty."

Relief flooded me. Despite my bold words, I hadn't been sure I would actually be able to enter. "Let's go retrieve one then."

"You stay. You'll only slow me down." With a slight smile, Talan turned and loped silently into the darkness.

Xaron and I stood waiting. The night air was chill here near the lake, and I shivered.

"He'll be alright, Linos," Xaron murmured. "He's a tough kid. Way tougher than I was at his age."

"He's probably still tougher than you." I managed a smile.

Xaron flashed me a tempered grin. "True. It's never been my strong suit."

We lapsed into silence, listening anxiously for any sound of movement. The last thing we wanted was for an errant patrol to find us.

When footsteps approached, we both tensed. It seemed too soon for Talan to return. Yet as the firelight revealed his lilting smile from the gloom, I breathed a sigh of relief.

He hefted the rope in hand. "There will be a disappointed captain at the docks, but we have our rope. Careful, though. It's slick with moss."

"Sure. You're certain you two can get up there?"

Xaron chuckled as he turned to face the wall. "I suppose you'll just have to see, won't you?"

Talan inclined his head, then gestured to the stands rising above. "Perhaps you can show me how it's done."

"I will," Xaron declared.

Crouching low and placing his hands on the ground, he heaved himself up into the air. The speed with which he ascended was astonishing. My jaw drifted open as I craned my head back to watch him jump not only to the lip of the stands but just over it, then disappear out of sight to land with a light thump.

"He's powerful," Talan admitted, "but he lacks refinement. And wisdom."

"Two things you have plenty of," I said sarcastically.

He smiled lopsidedly. "I'll throw down the rope once I have it secured." Without another word, he turned and, with less effort and more finesse, followed Xaron up.

I waited anxiously, peering at the dim ledge above. Soft scuffles echoed down. Just when I wondered if I should call up to them, something moved above, and the rope fell down with a hiss to swing before me.

Wasting no time, I grabbed it and began to climb. As Talan had warned, the rope was slick with moss, but it afforded just enough grip. I braced my feet against the wall and hauled myself up, hand over hand. My arms, unaccustomed to such work, began to burn halfway up, but I soon reached the top of the wall, where Xaron and Talan helped me over.

As I kneeled and shook out my arms, Talan hauled up the rope and coiled it. "Can't leave it around," he whispered, then held it out. "Take it. Just in case."

I accepted it, wondering uneasily what scenario he was planning for. Around the bend of the stairs, I could see the glow of the sentries' fire at the entrance. From the laughter that echoed up to us, they hadn't detected anything amiss. But all it would take was one mishap to bring them running.

"No point in waiting around," Xaron muttered, glancing down the stairs. "Which way?"

Talan pushed past him to the dark corridor beyond. "Only one way to go, unless you wish to say hello to our hosts."

I followed, shrugging. Xaron scowled, but came behind.

Talan led the way down the corridor, which skirted the edge of the amphitheater. Eventually, we would reach the large backstage building. Though we stepped lightly, the wooden walkways of the Claw defied silence. That I carried a heavy rope made walking quietly no easier. I winced with every creaking footstep, expecting guards to come pouring out on either side of us at any moment. But as none came, I dared to hope we were in the clear.

The corridor finally ended, and a door emerged from the gloom. Halting before it, Talan considered it for a moment.

"Between the two of you, surely we can open a lock," I teased quietly.

"Allow me," Xaron said snidely, stepping forward.

But before Xaron could get close, Talan placed two fingers inside the lock. A moment later, a small puff of air blew out of the hole, then a click sounded. Nudging it with his shoulder, the door swung open. Talan looked at Xaron with a raised eyebrow.

I shook my head and began to pass through, but Talan held out an arm and entered first. It shamed me, but I was glad he led the way.

Inside the room was even darker than outside. I peered around us, wondering who might be lying in wait in the shadowed corners. With a creak, Xaron shut the door behind us, leaving us in pitch black. Then a light flared to life next to me, white and pure. Talan held up a hand, and between his fingers, an orb like a star shone and unveiled the room around us. I blinked at the sudden sorcerous light, eyes adjusting, then studied the room. The room was sparsely decorated. A single table with two rickety chairs were tucked into a corner next to a cabinet. A covered pyr lamp was mounted near the door. Stepping around the room, I saw small signs of habitual use scattered about the place. Two cups with the dregs of liquid at the bottom. A cloak draped over the back of a chair. The floor free of dust.

"People pass through often," Talan observed quietly. Nodding toward the passageway beyond, he began to move on.

Following him, I found the archway led to a narrow corridor, with room for no more than one person to comfortably fit at a time. At the end of it, Talan's light illuminated a door. No light shone from underneath, indicating it was unoccupied, unless we'd stumbled upon sleeping quarters.

Talan glanced back with a raised eyebrow, and I nodded. Putting his hand to the keyhole, it only took another moment before this door, too, unlocked at his touch. He pushed it open, and Xaron and I followed him in.

This room was better furnished than the first. Setting down the coil of rope to ease my aching shoulder, I looked around. Opposite us, a door promised to continue our journey. Two windows faced out over Oedija, glittering city lights shining in. Before them, a small platform elevated a wicker wood chair. And hanging off one of the gnarled ends rising off the back of the chair was the leering mask of a dragon.

An uncomfortable feeling stirred in my gut. I glanced at Talan. "Do you know what that is?"

He shrugged. "The mask of the Visage of the Wyvern, perhaps. They say he always wears a white peplos and a mask with the aspect of a dragon. Explains his name, doesn't it?"

Though my anxiety had increased, I continued to look around. In the center of the room, a large map was spread across a table. Approaching it, I saw it was a careful rendering of the Four Realms. Several marks defaced it in dark ink. A crossed-out circle marked Oedija. Avvad had one circle over its capital, Erimis, though this circle remained open. The Qao Fu jaitin had no circles, but one lay out in the wasteland to the far northeast, encircling what seemed to be a poor sketching of a tree. The Bali plateaus had many open circles, nearly as many as there were ishakas. Littered across the map were figurines, crudely carved, but plain in their depictions. Soldiers. Horsemen. War machines. Even, I guessed, the Tefra and their enslaved pyr, Silks.

"Xaron, Talan," I called softly. "Come look at this."

They approached and stood around the table, studying it for several long moments. Xaron pointed at the circles. "It has all of the Four Realms marked. I'd guess these are plans for starting new cults, except for the circle deep in the Wumofu."

Talan shook his head. "The figurines tell the tale. Cultists do not concern themselves with armies and nations."

I lifted my gaze to look around once more. The unease

that had haunted me since entering the Claw crystallized. The map. The wicker wood chair. The fortified position looking out over Oedija.

"This is a war room," I said quietly.

Talan suddenly raised his hand and went stiff, listening. Xaron stilled as well, brow drawn together. Finally, I heard it myself: footsteps echoing along the hall, making the floor vibrate.

My chest felt so tight I could barely breathe. "The next door," I whispered. "You have to unlock it."

Talan was already moving toward it, using his unlocking trick again. As soon as the click came, he pushed on the door, but it resisted him.

"Barred from the other side," he muttered.

"I could blow it off," Xaron suggested, his voice high with anxiety.

Talan shook his head. "They'll know we're here anyway, and it could trap us further. We make our stand here."

I didn't know what to make of the words. *Make our stand.* For a moment, I stood in indecision next to the barred door. What was I supposed to do to take a stand?

Talan noticed and took my arm. "Find cover. I'll make sure they notice me first. You just make sure to stay out of the way."

His chivalry finally roused my spirit. "I'll fight as much as I can," I promised him. Not waiting for an answer, I scanned the room for a hiding spot. Only two were readily apparent: crouched behind the map table and behind the wicker wood chair.

Xaron shifted in indecision next to me, eyes darting between the open and closed doors.

"Duck behind the chair," I advised him, giving him a push in that direction.

He looked glad to be told what to do and moved quickly behind it.

I went to my own position behind the map table and drew my knife. Crouching there, it suddenly felt much less covered than it had first seemed. I could only hope it would be enough. Talan moved to the corner just beyond the door and pressed against the wall, then extinguished his light.

Left in darkness, I stared at the only entrance to the room and waited. Waited, grinding my palm into my blade's grip. Waited, listening to the footsteps grow ever closer. Waited, knowing how helpless I was in a fight, knowing there were far too many Seeker guards in the compound. Fear, cold and craven, rose in me. I would have fled if I'd had a choice.

We'd left the door open, so I saw their light first, creeping down the hall. Then figures emerged from the darkness. The man who came first didn't look like a guard. Balding and thin, he wore spectacles over the violet tatu around his eyes. But it was the light projecting from his fingertips that amazed me most of all. Fear squeezed me harder, and breath came shallower. He was a warden.

The man stepped into the room, his brow drawn as he gazed around him. Two more figures loomed in the hallway beyond, light projecting from their own hands. Two more wardens.

Before the lead warden could glance his way, Talan struck.

15

IN RUINS

Daemon run far
Daemon jump high
Daemon breathe fire
Daemon drop sky

Daemon come find you
If you run
So don't call daemon 'round
Keep him hung

- Children's rhyme, origin unknown

Talan lashed out, a knife flashing in his hands as he stabbed into the man's gut. The Seeker warden shrieked and stumbled back, his light extinguishing as his hands fell to his stomach. From the light in the hallway beyond, I could see blood, black wetness in the gloom, staining his clothes.

The two Seekers in the hallway shouted and rushed forward, hands outstretched. From the lights in their hands, I saw one to be a Qao Fu female of middling years and the other a stout Oedijan youth. Spotting Talan, they both leveled their hands at him, and fire and force leaped toward him.

Talan dove, but was sent tumbling across the room by their assault. The two Seekers stalked after him, hemming him in with a barrage of magic. Talan dodged or blocked most of the blows, but a kinetic wave found its way through his defenses, slamming him back against a wall.

I couldn't crouch in fear forever. Forcing myself up, I crept around behind the two seeker wardens. The hilt of my knife felt so slick with sweat that I thought it would slip from my fingers. Gripping it tighter, I rose and charged.

The young man glanced back, his eyes widening. Fear struck me anew, yet I continued forward and raised the knife with a scream.

Something knocked hard into me from the side, sending me crashing into the wall. My head knocked against the wood, and stars sparked into my vision. As I staggered back to my feet, my body felt drunken and clumsy. I turned toward the direction of the attack, focusing my unsteady gaze. The balding man leaned against the wall, one bloody hand raised toward me. As I stared, another kinetic wave came barreling down on me.

I threw myself to the ground. As the wave passed, it beat me against the floor, knocking the wind out of me. But I'd avoided the worst of it. Gasping for air, I pushed myself up and dove behind the map table, hoping it would give some protection while I recovered.

A glance Talan's way showed that Xaron had joined the fray. Blinding light flashed from his fingertips as he contended with the middle-aged woman from behind the wicker wood chair. Talan engaged the young man. As I watched, he sent the Seeker flying backward with a powerful kinetic attack, a snarl on his lips.

"Watch the one in the corner!" I called to Talan, then

threw myself toward the young man. He had hit the wall badly and was slow in rising. Not letting myself doubt or think, I stabbed at him.

My poorly aimed blow caught the Seeker in the shoulder and, biting in, glanced off bone. The young man howled with pain and anger, then punched his fist into my gut.

It hit with the force of a kicking horse. I crumpled, all breath and fight in me gone as pain spread throughout my body. I crawled away, knife lost, barely able to see for the darkness creeping up in my vision.

The young man stood over me, hand outstretched, when his head suddenly kicked back. As he slumped over, I saw dark liquid leaking from his eye. Or where his eye had been — all that was left now was a jagged, bloody hole.

"Take cover!" Talan roared as he leaped over the map table, scattering figures as he passed.

I fell to the ground at once, too weak from the Seeker's blow to go anywhere else. From beneath the table, I glimpsed Talan landing on the other side, then the Qao Fu woman's feet lifting as he hit her with a kinetic attack, slamming her into the opposite wall. Xaron's feet danced across the floor as he, too, channeled at the woman.

Something tickled my nose and throat, making my eyes water, and the back of my neck felt uncomfortably warm. I turned and noticed smoke billowing up from flames licking across the wood floor and walls. Pushing aside weakness, I rose, coughing as smoke filled my lungs with each shallow breath.

"Fire!" I gasped, though I wasn't sure anyone heard me.

"Back away from it!" Talan commanded.

I staggered toward the door. A glance at the first Seeker in the corner showed he was dead. The Qao Fu woman had similarly gone still, her head craned back at an unnatural angle and her body sprawled upon the floor. And I knew the youngest of the Seeker wardens was not likely to rise.

Now, we just had the flames to worry about.

"What do we do?" I asked, fear making my voice high and sharp.

Talan shook his head. "Run. There's nothing else we can do."

"But Linos might be in here!"

"Wait! Let me try to shred it!" Xaron swayed where he stood, but he held his hands toward the fire. The flames already rose nearly as tall as me, and smoke and heat poured out from them.

"Hurry!" Talan said sharply.

Xaron's eyes screwed up in concentration, arms trembling as he held them out. A moment passed. Two. Still, the fire continued to grow and consume.

Talan backed up to the doorway, pulling me with him. "We have to go!" he shouted.

"I can do this," Xaron said through gritted teeth. He hadn't moved, though the flames advanced across the room toward him.

"Xaron!" I pleaded.

Suddenly, the fire spluttered, then began to dissipate. As suddenly as they'd spread, the flames died out. Soon, all that was left behind were glowing embers and smoke hanging thick in the darkness.

"I did it." Xaron coughed, staring dazed into the smoke.

"You did," Talan admitted grudgingly. A light blazed to life in his hand again. "Now let's go."

Xaron shook his head, then staggered toward us, stumbling and nearly falling. I moved forward and steadied him, though I felt none too steady myself.

"Are you alright?" I asked him as we followed Talan through the doorway.

His eyes were vacant as he glanced at me. "Airene, I... I killed that woman."

My throat closed shut. All I could do was squeeze his arm and press forward.

We made it out of the corridor, then through the next room. The night air outside brought cool relief and fresh air to my fevered skin. But as shouts from the Seeker guards filled the air, I knew we couldn't stop to catch our breaths.

"Move quietly, but swiftly," Talan commanded over his shoulder as he slowed his pace to a fast walk. "Could be they don't know where to find us yet."

We obeyed, moving along the outside of the amphitheater. The wood creaked with each step, driving anxiety through my gut. The shouts faded in and out below. I didn't dare glance over the railing lest they see me.

The pounding of feet sounded ahead. Around Talan's form, I saw figures racing toward us. The foremost leveled his spear and charged, eyes wide with fear, mouth pulled back in a snarl. Talan didn't back down, but raised his hands. Kinesis barreled forward from his fingertips. The Seeker crashed into the others behind, collapsing them in a tumbled heap. Talan swiftly followed the first attack, hands jabbing forward again and again. Concentrated kinesis pounded like arrows into the guards, dealing death everywhere they landed.

Then Talan dropped to the floor. "Duck!" he bellowed.

I obeyed at once, hoping Xaron would do the same. As my knees hit the wooden planks, something hissed overhead with terrible speed. As wood splintered behind us, I grasped what it had been. The guards had brought crossbows.

Talan cursed and rose, channeling with a fury. The Seekers screamed and fell away. A second crossbowman tried to get in a wild shot and missed. Soon, the few guards still standing were fleeing back the way they came. Even then, Talan did not relent, but shot at their backs, felling a few more.

I gagged as the stench of burned flesh filled my nose, but

held myself upright. I tried not to look at the dead guards as I stepped over their bodies. I could not help but count them. *Seven*. Seven more Talan had killed. I tried focusing, tried remembering how many guards had been at the entrance. Eight, I was fairly certain.

"One escaped," I told Talan. "He'll call for reinforcements."

"Then we'd better get the hell out of here." He glanced back. "When we reach the edge, I'll carry you over."

I nodded, though I felt far from certain about that prospect. Even for Talan, such a feat seemed a stretch. Yet with time pressing short, the rope back in the war room, and no idea what reinforcements might be coming, I had no choice but to agree.

We left the bodies behind, then the lip of the wall appeared ahead. Skirting to the end to make sure no one lay in wait, Talan turned back to me. "Ready?"

Repressing my fear, I nodded and stepped toward him. Bending, he scooped an arm under my legs and back. Barely giving me time to wrap my arms around his neck, he lifted me off my feet, stepped over the lip of the wall, and leaped.

I clung to him as the air rushed past, the torches blurred, and the dark ground reached up to swallow us. The impact of landing was so powerful and sudden that I nearly bit off my tongue. But though Talan bowed under the impact, he didn't let me fall, but set me back on my feet again.

"Thanks," I said breathlessly to him.

All he could do was grunt in response and move out of the way as Xaron leaped down to land beside us, his landing much softer.

Talan staggered forward a couple of steps, then shook his head and drew himself upright. "No time to waste. We have to get out of here."

Following him, we stumbled away from the Claw and back into the dark forest.

WORTH

The tale of Kyno, the man who wished to be a warden, is often told by parents to children to explain why Tyurn's gift should not be desired.

In the story, Kyno, a man with a wife and many children, wishes one day he had a warden's magic to make his life easier. If he were a warden, he reasons, he could use magic to carry the wood to his hearth and light a fire, and his home would ever after be warm. Magic could ease his aching back, and put food on the table. Magic, he thinks, could put to rest all his cares and concerns.

That night, he wakes to find his little finger flashing with sparks. Panicked, he thrusts his hand into a bucket of water. But rather than putting out the spark, a charge like lightning zips through him.

Dazed, Kyno reels and falls to the mud, rolling around like a pig to dampen his magic. But though his little finger stops spark-ing, it now begins thrusting out such forceful air that he's tossed about in the mud to and fro, becoming bruised and battered as a fish in a dry bucket.

Finally, exhausted and beaten, Kyno decides it's a dream and returns to his bed just as he is, mud-splattered and bruised.

But it is not a dream. When Kyno wakes, he finds his house

burning down around him and his wife and children screaming for him to get out. But it is too late.

The story ends with Kyno looking at his little finger and saying, "If I had known all the trouble you'd cause, I never would have wished for you." Then he burns down with the house.

- Tales of Wardens: A brief study of Oedijan folk stories; by Acadian Helene, Master Historian; 1160 SLP

We were three shadows as we stole up the night-shrouded hill, all moving slowly from our wounds. I suspected that I had suffered the least. Though my muscles protested and my gut throbbed, nothing was broken, and I had not suffered any burns. I could not see much of my friends, but what little I did see horrified me. Xaron's face was dark with bruises, but he had at least recovered enough of his wits to climb his way up. Talan looked less battered, though his stony expression betrayed deeper wounds. Yet we had to press on, lest the Seeker guards who shouted from beyond the forest find us.

"Where are you taking us?" I asked Talan, keeping my voice soft.

"Another of my hiding spots." His head remained down as he picked a path through the dark woods. "As I said, you can never have too many."

Though the expression felt foreign in that moment, I smiled. At least he retained his sense of humor. But as I thought of what he had done back in the Claw, the smile quickly dissipated.

We labored our way up the rest of the hill. As we neared the end of the tree line and the tents appeared above us, Talan reached out to stop us. I flinched at his touch. His hand was still wet with blood.

He spoke as if he had not noticed my reaction. "Up ahead. Guards watch the forest. To reach my tent, we must pass by them." He looked at Xaron. "Are you ready to fight again? We must kill them quickly and quietly."

I seized Talan's arm, fighting back the discomfort at touching him. "No. No killing."

Talan looked at me, darkness hiding his expression. "Then what do you propose?"

I had no immediate answer. But if there was a way to avoid bloodshed, I had to find it. I cast my gaze along the line of tents, desperately hoping to see something. The guards, many more than we had seen before, were spaced a dozen feet apart, and each carried a torch. I could see no way to slip between them.

But then, maybe we didn't have to. "We need a diversion. Xaron can set one of the tents on fire with his trick from Eltris. Right, Xaron?"

He looked around at me, and even in the darkness, I saw hollowness in his eyes. "Yes," he said softly.

"Can you do it?"

He seemed to give himself a shake. "Yes," he said more firmly. "I can do it."

"Fine," Talan relented. "We'll try it your way."

Xaron looked between us, then nodded to himself and turned away. As he faded into the shadows. I started to follow him, but Talan stopped me with a touch. "We'll need to enter on the other side of the diversion," he reminded me. "It will be quicker for him to rejoin us when he's ready."

I nodded, though I suspected he was hedging his bets. No need to lose me if Xaron botched the job. I tried to have more confidence in my friend.

A minute passed, then two. I stared at the tents lining the hill above us. They had to be at least thirty paces away from the tree line, much farther than Xaron had been able to channel radiance in Eltris's tower. Doubt gnawed at me. I wondered if I had put too much pressure on him.

Just as I resolved to go check on him, calls of "Fire!"

sounded down the line. Guards from along the tents rushed to the calls.

"Amateurs," Talan sneered softly as Xaron rejoined us. I half expected Xaron to be wearing a wide grin, but he was sober as he stopped alongside us. Talan nodded once in approval to him, then pointed. "We make for that gap. Right… now!"

He darted forward, keeping low, and Xaron and I followed on his heels. Breath hissed between my teeth as we ran up the last stretch of the hill. I expected to hear shouts of alarm, but as we passed between the tent shops, the guards still seemed focused on the fire half a dozen tents down. We slipped onto the street unnoticed.

Talan led us across the road and into a field of squat tents, then began a disorienting path through them. The further we went from the street, the deeper the darkness became around us, as clouds had choked out the moonlight. To keep us together, I grabbed hold of Talan's coat in one hand and took Xaron's hand in the other. "Stay close," I whispered to them.

It took an excruciatingly long time to arrive at Talan's tent. In the thick darkness, I didn't know how he could tell it apart from the others. It barely looked large enough for two people, much less three. Still, as he bent down and opened the flap, I ducked my way in.

It was even darker inside the tent. Xaron and I crouched in the far corner, our backs pressed against the heavy cloth, until Talan entered. Folding closed the flaps, he pulled off the lid to a jar of pyrkin, and a green glow like the radiant winds lifted the edges of darkness in the tent. A blanket spread across much of the dirt floor but didn't quite reach the edges. Other than the blanket and the pyrkin pot, the tent hosted only a small basket of clothes and a small pitcher of water we had narrowly avoided overturning.

Talan crawled to the pitcher and lifted it to his nose,

sniffing, before he held it out to me. "It's not fresh, but it doesn't seem to have fouled yet."

I accepted it from him and drank from the spout. He was right that it was far from fresh, but after the long night, I was happy to drink water of any quality. After I finished, I handed it to Xaron, who also drank a hearty fill, then handed it back to Talan. The Guilder finished it off, then set it back in the corner.

For many long moments, we sat in silence. The quiet settled heavy and thick in my lungs until it felt like I couldn't breathe. Guilt pressed down on me so I thought I would drown.

"I'm sorry. I'm sorry for getting you both wrapped up in this."

Talan looked up. "Don't apologize. We knew what this might lead to."

"But we didn't even find Linos," I continued miserably. "He's still lost here, somewhere. And you two got hurt, and had to…" I trailed off, not wanting to face the truth of what had just happened.

"I killed them." His voice was flat and emotionless. "I killed them because they meant to kill us first."

I shook my head violently. "*I* killed them. If I hadn't rushed us into the compound and the Claw, none of this would have happened."

"Airene." Talan leaned across the tent to touch me in comfort, but I recoiled.

"And I can't stop seeing you kill them." I whispered the words, not daring to meet Talan's eyes. They were callous and unreasonable. Yet that didn't change the horror of what I'd seen, how I'd witnessed my friend transforming into a man I didn't know.

Talan withdrew his hand and studied me. "Airene. I killed them to protect you."

"I know. Don't you think I know that?"

"What I'm saying is that it's not your fault. It was me, not you. I need you to understand that."

"So what, I can see you as a killer?" I swallowed hard, the next words inevitable. "You slaughtered them. They didn't stand a chance. I heard their screams, their pain, their fear. I can't forget that."

Talan's gaze wandered to the canvas above us. For a moment, we watched the roof of the tent shift lazily from the breeze outside.

When he spoke, his voice was tight with bridled emotion. "Many people kill. Drunk patrons in tavern brawls. City watchmen on patrol. Tribunes ordering executions. I have killed many times for many reasons. You knew that. Why should witnessing it change anything?" His gaze lowered to meet mine. "Especially since you have killed for me."

I looked away, unable to deny it. Nearly three years before, I'd slain a warden who had been trying to kill Talan after he'd intervened on my behalf. I drew in a shuddering breath. Even if it didn't banish the ill feelings I had toward Talan, it did give me pause.

"You're right," I muttered. "And I'm sorry for that, too."

Talan shook his head, a small smile playing at his lips.

Not yet ready for levity, I turned to Xaron. "How are you doing? Those bruises look painful."

"I'm fine," he responded without looking up. His hair, dirty with mud and ash, hung about his face.

I sighed. I knew what plagued him. The same thing had haunted me for the last three years. But I didn't push him. Xaron rarely held his feelings back for long. He'd talk when he was ready.

Turning my gaze back to Talan, I forced myself to meet his eyes. "What did we learn from our excursion?"

He shrugged. "The Manifest have grand designs for Oedija and the Four Realms. If they can accomplish them."

"War." I breathed the word, unable to truly believe it. War

had been a thing of the past for the Four Realms. Now only butchers like the Kahin-Shah indulged in it, and only then in faraway lands. I couldn't imagine purposefully orchestrating it and breaking the Concordance.

I focused my thoughts. "The figurines. I'd assumed they represented where forces currently were in the world. But thinking back, they weren't positioned as I would expect them to be. Avvad's armies were not near the Rift, but along our border. And I could have sworn there were Tefra and Silks positioned within Oedija city itself."

Talan's eyes gleamed strangely in the green light. "They could be projections, or intentions for what they seek to accomplish. Or perhaps things are not as they seem."

A shiver ran through me at the thought. I remembered again the mask hanging from the back of the wicker wood chair. "Who is the Visage of the Wyvern?" I murmured. "And the Dishonored who stands by him? What do they want?"

"Blood and power, it would seem. We can only truly know if we discover their identities."

"Find out who they are." I nodded. "They are at the center of it all. If we can stop those two, perhaps the movement will fall apart."

Talan inclined his head. "Perhaps."

"But Linos… What part could he play in this? In politics and war? Why bring him onto the Claw's stage? Why hold him among the elite Seekers?"

"My orphans will not be able to tell us that. They see and hear much, but understand little. To know, we must see your brother ourselves." He glanced thoughtfully aside. "The Seekers at the compound entrance. They mentioned a gathering in two nights. Perhaps that would be such an opportunity."

After the chaos of the night, I had nearly forgotten. I nodded. "That sounds like the perfect opportunity. But, Talan… I would understand if you don't want to be involved."

Talan's lips twisted into a wry smile. "Ah, Airene. When will you learn better? I am with you, now and always."

I smiled, chest warming. "I'm glad to hear it."

My smile faded as I glanced at Xaron. I doubted he'd feel the same way. He'd curled up on the ground, facing the tent's side so I couldn't see his face, but I suspected he was awake, reliving the moment when he'd killed the Qao Fu warden. I looked aside.

"Could all this have been worth it?" I asked softly of no one.

Talan smiled bitterly. "We'll soon find out, won't we?"

BEYOND THE CLAW

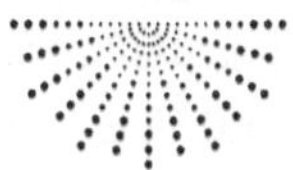

Oedija is a society with four distinct classes: the honors, the under-class, the citizens, and the patricians.

At its foundation are the honors, or the Kalthuae, as they are named in the histories. A distinctly Oedijan caste, they are a people unpaid for their labors, but well-treated and respected for their service. Yet for all their good treatment, the rigidness of the caste, which deems that honors cannot marry outside of it nor possess any wealth of their own, puts many ill at ease.

- Oedija: A History; by Acadian Helene, Master Historian; 1167 SLP

We settled down to rest, but sleep evaded me. I lay between Xaron and Talan and struggled to keep still while my thoughts raced. Again and again, my actions seemed to make matters worse. Yet I couldn't tell where I'd stepped amiss. What more could I have done, only knowing what I did then? I forced my thoughts down a different path. No point in regretting the past. No amount of guilt would change anything.

I thought back to the Claw's map. I wondered what the

circles meant and why Oedija's was crossed out. Perhaps the Manifest meant to assassinate the leaders of each nation. But though it fit for Oedija, and could apply to Avvad and the Bali, the circle for the Qao Fu was far beyond their jaitin. There had to be something I was missing.

A thought came upon me with such clarity that I nearly bolted upright. As if it had been placed in my head by the hand of a god, I had a plan. One that could resolve both the puzzle of the Despot's disappearance and save my missing brother. One that could tear down the Manifest and restore stability to Oedija. Perhaps, in time, it could even help us weather an Avvadin invasion, if it truly were impending. I even had the means to take the first step.

I lay there for a long time, burning to begin. But we could not yet rise. We hadn't left a clean trail behind us from our foray into the Claw. Besides the battle and bodies, I'd left the rope in the war room and my chiton in the forest. The Seekers would be on high alert. If we were to have any chance of escaping the compound, we would need to wait for its occupants to be fully awake and bustling about their business. With an effort, I held myself still, coaxing my budding plans to blossom.

Many excruciating turns later, golden morning came wholly upon us. Outside, the compound was bustling with noise and life. I allowed myself to sit up, desperate energy staving off exhaustion, and moved to settle a hand on Talan. A moment before I touched him, I glimpsed the blood dried on his sleeve, and I hesitated.

"I'm already awake," he said without turning. "You need not touch me."

I startled guiltily, then steeled my resolve and touched his shoulder. "I don't hold it against you, truly. I'm thankful. I just... need a bit of time."

Talan shifted to look at me from the corner of his eye. "I

understand. It took some while to look at myself after the first time."

His words twisted sharply inside me. I drew in a breath, trying to calm myself. "We'd best be going."

Talan nodded, then sat up without looking at me.

I withdrew my hand to wake Xaron. When I turned back to him, however, his eyes were open, staring at the ceiling of the tent. I studied him with growing concern. He had said little since leaving the Claw.

"Xaron?" I said hesitantly. "How are you feeling?"

He glanced briefly at me, then resumed staring at nothing. "I'm not going to fail again," he said calmly.

His words jarred me. That wasn't what I thought had been bothering him.

"I've been training with Eltris for the last two months," he continued. "Two months of intentionally learning how to use my talents to contend with other wardens. But last night, when it came time to use that knowledge, I lost my head. Someone who couldn't have been more than a four-shift and could only channel kinesis nearly had me."

Every thought that occurred to me promised only to make him feel worse. Yet I had to say something. "Xaron. No one expected you and Talan to get attacked by wardens. Deep depths of the 'Thae, who could have expected that? It's not your fault."

Xaron jerked his head at Talan, who was bent over the small basket of clothes. "He was ready. He killed the rest of them, and easily. And he's a seven-shift. I'm *shur*, a ten-shift. I should be capable of more." He rose and muttered, "I will be."

I didn't like the thread of his thoughts, but all I could do was look helplessly at Talan.

He nodded at Xaron, a small smile on his lips. "You can. You are capable, Xaron, just inexperienced. Stay alive long enough, and you'll find where you stand."

I glowered at Talan.

He shrugged. "We are what need makes us. And now, we are escapees. We had best leave as soon as we are able. I have a change of dress for myself, but I will have to find clothes for you two. Give me half a turn, and I shall bring back some serviceable items."

I nodded grudgingly, and turned away as he dressed, despite his mocking invitation for me to watch. The truth was, I shied more from seeing his wounds than seeing him exposed. In the light of the morning, I had to witness what my rash decisions had inflicted upon my friends.

Talan soon dressed and left, warning us not to exit until he returned. Xaron and I sat in uncomfortable silence. I stewed over his earlier words until I found a safe question. "You never really explained how you met Eltris."

"Trying to get me to talk, are you?" He looked up. The pain in his eyes struck arrows through me.

Before I could answer, he nodded. "I suppose you deserve some explanation. It started about two months back, just after that job that involved the house-break."

I remembered it all too well. "With that merchant who sold those elixirs made of bat feces?"

He gave a hollow laugh. "Right. And you were so against the house-break you wouldn't even come."

"I stand by that."

"Anyway. After entering into his home, I didn't make it far before an old woman stopped me. I was so startled when she appeared that I channeled. To defend myself, I suppose."

"From what I've seen of Eltris, I don't think that would have ended well for you."

A ghost of a smile touched his lips. "I didn't attack, fortunately. Once Eltris convinced me she wasn't turning me in to the Shepherds — at least not at that moment — and she'd told me who she was, I decided it was worth hearing her out. She quickly made it clear what I could gain, first by chiding me for being inefficient at channeling kinesis, then promising she could improve my ability to channel tenfold."

I frowned. "Surely that sounded suspicious. For one, how did she find you? And why offer to teach you?"

Xaron shrugged. "She's a powerful warden, Airene. It's said that Kyros Brighteyed can see traces of channeling. I think she can see even more. I believe she can see the strength of a person's attunement, and maybe even the potential of those with loci closed to the Pyrthae."

Such an ability teased my imagination. I couldn't help but wonder what Eltris had seen in me. But it was foolish to dream of such things now.

"As for teaching me," Xaron continued, "I was intrigued, and agreed to meet her at a neutral location—"

"Intrigued? Xaron, that's a pretty flimsy reason to meet someone who could have called down the Shepherds on you. She could have been leading you into a trap."

"Yes, well..." He ran a hand through his tangled hair. "You can't understand, Airene. I have this gift, a strong one. I could be one of the best wardens this age has seen with training. Yet to have to keep it secret, to hardly use it, to stagnate... You can't know how that feels." He stared at his hands. "To not be able to use it when I need it most."

"I can. Of course I can. But you have to remember the risk. You could be locked up in the Acadium, or outright killed."

Xaron glanced sidelong at me, then looked away. "What you just said tells me you don't know. If you were forbidden from using your right hand again, how would you react?"

It wasn't the same, I wanted to argue, but the words died on my lips. His attunement wasn't just a tool. It was a part of him. I couldn't imagine Xaron not being a warden. But the feeling still burned in my gut that the risks he took weren't worth it.

I conceded as much as I could. "I understand where you're

coming from. But that doesn't explain why you had to start meeting in the Acadium."

"She couldn't teach me properly outside of it. Small displays of channeling can go unnoticed outside the Acadium, but for extensive, ongoing training, it would be much riskier. After meeting a couple of times at the old river-port, I decided it was worth the risk. I trusted her." He bowed his head and stared at his hands. "For all the good that training has done me."

"Why now? You've channeled for all this time, yet she only now approaches you. It has a foul smell to me, Xaron."

He glanced up at me. "Oh, it does, does it? And what about your new medallion — that's not a mite convenient?"

I blinked, and a hand went to touch the medallion hanging under my clothes. "That's not the same. Vusu knew our reputation. But with Myron's disappearance, he only just now needed our help. It's a mutually beneficial agreement. It's nothing like your and Eltris's arrangement. What does she benefit from that?"

"Perhaps she needs me," Xaron said icily. "And only just now decided it was worth the risk."

"Needs you? And why would she need to teach you martial channeling? I'm liking this less and less. She's an Acadian master, Xaron. She should have turned you in as soon as you entered the grounds."

He gave me a scornful look. "She doesn't believe wardens should be locked up. She doesn't believe we should allow others to determine our lives, or sway how we use our abilities. Eltris believes that gifts such as ours should not go to waste among smoldering tomes, but be explored to their fullest capacity. So we can stand ready when we're needed."

His words struck a chill through my heart. "She believes like a Seeker then," I said quietly. "That the power of the Pyrthae should reign unbridled."

Xaron turned his head away in disgust. "I knew you wouldn't understand. Why do you think I never told you?"

"Oh no, I'm very sympathetic," I continued hotly. "I, too, wish for the great Tyrant Wardens of the past to rise and rule the polis again. It worked so well last time, didn't it?"

"You know that's not what she means."

"Well, it ought to be, because that's where we'll end up with if we stop regulating wardens."

He was silent for a moment. "And what about me?" he asked quietly. "Should I be locked up with everyone else?"

I gritted my teeth. "Of course not. You have more sense than to lord your power over others."

"But I don't use my gift for good exactly, do I? I break into people's houses. Last night, I used it to fight, to… kill." His voice shook, but he drew a breath and pressed on. "I'm not a shining example of the good warden. Yet you don't think I should be locked up. Shouldn't we give everyone in the Acadium the same chance? Shouldn't we let them be people and not criminals before they have the chance to decide?"

It felt as if another spoke through him. His master had ingrained her philosophies in him well. I shook my head. "No one gets a fair shot at life, not even patricians and Wreaths. We're all what need makes us, like Talan said. So you haven't had the chance to develop your channeling. At least you haven't been forced to serve an Acadian master carting books back and forth across the campus, studying a discipline you care little for. No one gets everything they want. Maybe the way things turn out is the best they can be."

I didn't believe the words even as I said them. They'd been repeated to me a thousand times in a thousand ways, but there was always something flawed in that argument. Was stability such a noble aspiration when the fate of so many was determined by where or to whom they were born? By mere chance?

Xaron stared at me like I'd become a stranger. "I thought

you of all people would understand. Particularly while we take refuge in a cultist compound. Look around us, Airene. Oedija is changing. The world is changing. And if I don't adapt ahead of it… Then I can't protect the ones I care for."

Words failed me. I lowered my gaze and studied the edges of the worn rug. What a fool I'd been. All this time, he hadn't just been doing it for himself. And I'd been blind to it.

"I understand," I said softly. "Just… be careful. You're not the only one who wishes to protect your friends."

He looked like a thirsty man given water. He surprised me by pulling me into an awkward embrace in the small space. A moment later, he broke it off with a groan. "I forgot it hurt for a moment," he said, gingerly touching his side.

I winced. "We'll get you looked after just as soon as we get out of here."

He nodded. "Then we'll watch out for each other."

The only smile I could manage was small and sad. I knew how little I could protect the ones I loved. "Yes. We'll watch out for each other."

A QUARTER-TURN LATER, Talan returned with clothes and a fresh pitcher of water. After rinsing off the soot — and blood — as much as we could, Xaron and I dressed, then left the tent. I peered around nervously, expecting Seeker guards to appear at every corner and apprehend us. The Manifest compound seemed to buzz without any unusual alarm, but I felt that a trap must be waiting.

Even once we'd joined the crowds on the main street, I felt only marginally better. People jostled us as they hurried past, most showing more urgency than we dared to. As we passed the blackened row where Xaron had set the tents on fire, the crowd thickened. Some people, perhaps the owners of the tents, gesticulated angrily at the Seeker guards standing silently before them. I bent my head and hurried Xaron and Talan past them. One guard had escaped, and I didn't want to chance that our descriptions had been passed on to all of them.

Once we were safely past the destruction, my attention was drawn to a man in shabby robes as he stood on a stand, shouting to a half-moon of intent listeners. "We must not flinch before our fates, my fellow Seekers! We must not back away! No, we must run and embrace our destiny and become who we were always meant to be! We must accept the power of the One, and wield it in his name!"

Now that I had seen wardens truly were among the Manifest's flock, his proselytization was unsettling. Though I still doubted they could make wardens, for most, seeing a warden openly would be enough to inspire belief.

It had been enough for Linos, apparently.

We quickly approached the fence marking the end of the compound. I leaned toward Talan. "What do you have in mind? We can't just walk through."

"Look again, my Finch. During the day, the compound is open. All may come and go as they would."

"Even us?"

He shrugged. "We shall see how well information disseminates among their guards."

I held my breath as we passed through the opening. I didn't look at the Seeker guards, but kept my eyes forward, willing them not to see me. Around us, a small caravan of people also passed, disguising our approach.

"May the One grace you."

Dread filled me as I glanced over. A young guard, his face covered in the Manifest tatu, smiled slightly at me. I stared in return. For a moment, I thought it was Linos who smiled at me, but the fancy quickly passed.

I blinked and paused mid-step, realizing he expected a reply. "May you seek — may you find what you seek, and the

One not pass over you." I thought that was more or less what Talan had said the night before.

The man only smiled at my blunder and waved me through. I hurriedly followed after my companions.

Outside the compound, we quickened our pace until the fence was out of sight, then ducked into an alley. Xaron wiped a hand across his brow but said nothing, his eyes still hard and pinched.

After we'd caught our breaths, Talan spoke. "I don't know what else we can do right now but wait for the gathering tomorrow night. I'll try to find a better way inside the Claw, but it's not a task for which my orphans are well suited, and the Seekers will be on higher alert now."

"Of course. Don't take unnecessary risks. But anything you can do, you know I'll appreciate."

He nodded.

I drew in a breath. "In the meantime, I have a plan to begin."

Xaron looked up with a spark of interest, but it was Talan who spoke, an eyebrow arched. "What plan?"

"A drastic one. But a measure our leaders should have taken long ago." At his doubtful look, I flashed him a smile. "It will take too long to explain, so you'll just have to trust me."

Talan snorted and stretched like a cat, then stepped toward the entrance of the alley. "I'll leave you with your secrets, then. Just remember not to take any risks that I would."

With one last lazy smile, he disappeared around the corner.

Xaron leaned closer. "What do you mean to do?" he asked quietly. "Or are you going to exclude me from your plans as well?"

I took his arm and led him out of the alley. "No, I won't leave you out. But I can't tell you where ears might overhear. So how about I just show you?"

He pulled me to a halt, and I complied, though not gracefully. "Airene," he said seriously. "Stop for a moment. Have you really thought this through? We just fought for our lives. We're injured. We're wearing borrowed, ill-fitting clothes and haven't had more than a few moments of sleep. And Nomusa isn't even with us — who knows where she is." He stared imploringly at me. "I know I'm prone to rashness, but don't you think this goes well beyond that?"

I was in no mood for a lecture. "And this coming from the man who trusted his life to an Acadian on a whim. Xaron, my brother is still trapped back there. The Manifest is—" I cut off abruptly and looked around. "This isn't the place to discuss this."

"Then let us go somewhere we can. Back to Canopy, or wherever else you think is best. But we need food and rest. We need to stop and think."

For a moment, I wavered. My decisions had gotten him injured last night. I owed him recuperation. Yet I found myself shaking my head, slowly but firmly. "There's no time. Not for my brother, not for us, and certainly not for Oedija."

Though it wrenched my heart, I pulled my arm from my friend's grip and turned away, then began walking down the street back toward the city. I walked alone.

Despite my firm words, I felt my energy flagging now that the immediate danger was over. Guilt and shame replaced fear now, spurring me past exhaustion and into desperation. I had few allies and fewer friends, and here I drove away one of my closest. Yet I didn't see how I could do any differently.

Footsteps pattered on the street behind me. As Xaron walked up beside me, my faltering hopes rose once again. I smiled over at him with genuine warmth, but all he could return was a shrug.

"I'll follow you, Airene, into the dark depths of the 'Thae. You know I will. Just don't get us lost down there."

"I won't." I wondered how much he would believe that when he saw where we were going.

Though my empty belly grumbled and my feet dragged, we pressed on through the morning, entering back into the inner city and walking through the demes. Xaron asked no more questions, but walked by my side, looking around warily as if he expected to be attacked at any moment. It wasn't an unreasonable suspicion. With my next step, Feiyan might finally make good on her promise to expose him to the Shepherds. It tore at me to do it, but it was a risk he had accepted, and a measure I had to take.

As our destination came into sight, Xaron's eyes widened. "You can't be serious." He looked down at himself, dazed. "I never dreamed I'd be walking up to the Laurel Palace looking like this."

I gripped him by the shoulder and kept him moving forward. "That's more like the Xaron I know. Don't worry. With the news I have for the Archon, he'll barely notice."

UNSPOOLING

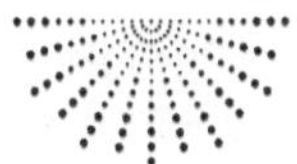

As the next closest kin to Myron's line, Jaxas Wreath remains an important figure in the royal line. Related through the sister of Gandyrion Wreath, Myron's father, the early deaths of many of the royal line have left him third in line to inherit the Evergreen Wreath. Little can be said about him, as he has been quiet in his actions. Yet what he has set his mind to, he has done well and with sound morality. Until Asileia's appointment as a governor, Jaxas was often seen by his cousin's side, assisting in her projects and tempering her worst impulses. Many times, he intervened for a whipping girl before Asileia's impudence took her punishment too far...

- A Modern Account of the Wreaths; by Acadian Helene, Master Historian; 1170 SLP

The Laurel Palace sat atop its many-tiered hill like a gilded dragon on its hoard of riches. There were enough columns and domes and towers to befit an Avvadin prince, with roofs and palisades of bronze and walls of white marble and limestone. The pillars before the double wooden doors loomed like a beast's maw, and a thousand eyes glittered with the windows reflecting the light of the morning sun.

I glanced down at myself. Xaron was right about one thing: we were far from adequately dressed. My hair felt a mess, and new cuts and bruises showed from beneath my ill-fitting and stained chiton. Xaron was in even worse shape, his tunic little more than a burlap sack. I suspected Talan had brought him such shabby clothes intentionally. Were I a guard at the palace gates, I would turn us away in a heartbeat. I could only hope Vusu's medallion would work as promised.

"Ready?" I muttered to Xaron as we approached the two men standing before the gates.

"This isn't what I thought I'd be doing this morning," Xaron murmured in reply. But he stayed by my side as we moved forward.

The laurel guards caught sight of us approaching from the bustle and watched with growing amusement. "Halt there," one of them said, the shorter of the two. "More plebs thinking to see the Despoina, eh?"

"I am Airene of Port." I paused, hardly believing what I was about to say. "I'm here to see Archon Jaxas Wreath."

I didn't need to see their eyes under their visors to sense their astonishment.

"Best not be foolish," the second guard said, his voice soft but firm. "You know we can't allow that."

I reached into the collar of my tunic and drew out the Verifier medallion. I was surprised to find my hand was shaking. Great forgotten gods, could I be so nervous to use it? At least my voice didn't quiver as I spoke. "My companion and I are of the new Order of Verifiers, sent by Tribune Vusumuzi to speak with the Archon about certain matters to which he is privy."

I held out the medallion. The heavy, metal circle slowly

spun at the end of the chain, Finch symbol glinting in the sunshine.

The shorter guard drew it up in a gauntleted hand. "And I don't suppose we get to know of these certain matters, do we?" he asked sarcastically.

I met his shadowed gaze steadily, though the shaking in my hand caused the medallion to dance. "I don't suppose you do."

The taller one suddenly startled. "I think she's telling the truth. Missive came a couple days ago regarding it. The First Laurel told us to keep an eye out."

The guards exchanged a lingering look. Unease crept along my spine. Had Lykos made inquiries after our run-in with his guard in the Valemish temple? But even if he had, I didn't see how he'd discovered who I was. I set my jaw and held my ground.

"Ah, yes," the shorter guard said as he glanced at me. His expression was inscrutable as he released my medallion. "Come with us, then, both of you."

He nodded to his comrade and motioned back at guards on the other side of the gates, who began to crank the heavy metal doors open.

I glanced at Xaron, and he shrugged. It was as warm of a reception as we could have hoped for, and better than being thrown in the dungeons by far. Still, I couldn't help but feel we walked into a wolf's den as we followed the guards through the open gates.

It was a long walk up the hill. As we ascended the endless stairs, we passed tier after tier of manicured gardens, each level more ornate than any yard I had seen before. Trickling fountains, intricately carved statues, and striking plants drew the eye. But, tired and preoccupied, my interest failed me, and I dropped my gaze to the ground, striving to keep one foot in front of the other.

Finally, the high doors to the palace drew nearer, and none too soon. Between the steep hill, the long night, and half a day without food or drink, my head felt light and dizzy. I set my jaw and braced my legs while our escorts signaled for the doors to be opened, then followed behind as they admitted us.

The doors were opulent, but the massive atrium introduced a new meaning to the word. Gilded surfaces glittered in the light of a thousand pyr lamps. White marble and veined silver stone were waxed to brilliance. The effect was softened by plush Avvadin carpets, red as a Stratechon's cape, and laced with the Wreath's colors of green and gold. From this great hall extended many winding staircases. At least six were in sight, and an archway promised more just beyond it.

There were many bright and promising hallways and staircases to choose from, but the laurel guards selected the darkest one. As we headed toward the corridor, my sense of foreboding increased. I stopped at the threshold, self-preservation calling too strongly to continue.

"Come on now," the shorter guard said. "We wouldn't want to keep the Archon waiting." In the brightly lit room, I could see his mocking grin under his helm.

"Are you sure that's the right way?" I felt sure it wasn't, but I needed to keep them talking until I figured out what to do next.

"Oh yes, very sure. He and I are old friends. Knew each other when we were in our cribs, side by side, we did."

I bowed briefly. "You know, I think we can find our own way. Thank you for your escort." Motioning to Xaron, I turned on my heel.

A hand snaked out and held me fast.

"No one is allowed to roam the palace without an escort," the taller guard said anxiously. He had seized Xaron, and I worried he might do something rash from the black look he cast at the guard.

"Especially not you," the shorter guard said, who held me. "You have another appointment to keep."

I tried to break free. "Take your hands off me. What gives you the right?"

He laughed and tightened his grip. "Here in the palace, we have absolute right. It's best you remember that for your own health, girl."

"No need for that," the taller guard muttered. "Just doing our duty."

"If you'd like to continue to do your duty, you'll unhand me," Xaron said darkly.

They tried pulling us back into the dark corridor, but not hard enough to overcome our resistance. I knew their patience wouldn't hold out for long.

"Why arrest us?" I demanded. "What have we done wrong?"

The taller guard was about to speak, but his comrade cut him off with a glare. "Can't say. We're under strict orders. Now let's go — it'll be better for you if you come quietly."

I gritted my teeth and resisted, expecting a punishing blow at any moment. Yet before they could become violent, voices cascaded down a stairway to echo in the lofty entrance hall. I redoubled my efforts, pulling at my captured arm with my other. Anyone talking that loudly here promised to be exactly the sort of people the guards wouldn't want to make a scene in front of.

I knew what I had to do. Suffocating my pride, I drew in a breath, then shouted at the top of my lungs.

My scream cut off as sparks exploded in my vision. The back of my head smarted where the guard had hit me. I suddenly felt queasy.

"No more of that," the guard snarled in my ear. Before I could say another word, he clapped a gloved hand over my mouth and pulled me roughly back into the corridor. I struggled and bit at his hand, but all I received for my efforts was the taste of grimy leather. Darkness began to fall around me.

"What is the meaning of this?"

The guard abruptly released me, and I stumbled upright, dazed. As figures approached down the stairwell, I gathered my wits, caught my breath, and quickly brushed back my hair to look marginally less like a mad woman. Two people stood at the front of a procession of honors, gazing at me with expressions as opposite as their appearance. Lykos, the First Laurel, didn't wear a helm, revealing a balding pate and peppered beard. His steely gray eyes, catching me in an unblinking gaze, made my skin crawl.

The other I had not seen so close before. Archon Jaxas Wreath was as thin as a corpse, his eyes shadowed, cheeks sunken, and veins showing through his sallow skin. In contrast to Lykos, his gaze was calm and considering.

"I asked you a question," the Archon said, his voice soft, his gaze shifting between the two guards. "For what reason are these two held?"

The shorter guard shook me, though not as roughly as before. "Let's see it, then."

I drew out my Verifier medallion and held it out, hand shaking anew.

The Archon stepped forward and curled a hand under the medallion. As he examined it, a faint smile blossomed on his lips. "A Finch," he observed. "Surely I must speak with the first of the Order to reemerge in a century. Release her and her companion."

"Archon," the First Laurel spoke in his hoarse voice, "I do not mean to contradict, but—"

"I'm well aware of your suspicions, Lykos. I have always made it a point to listen to your briefings. But your reservations give me all the more reason to speak with her."

Lykos stared at me for several moments longer. He was a

hard man to lock eyes with, but I managed it. Finally, he gave our captors a nod, and the guards unhanded Xaron and me.

"Come with me, if you please," the Archon said, then turned and walked down a much brighter hallway. The honors following in his wake streamed past us with many a curious glance.

I exchanged a look with Xaron, then we wordlessly followed, leaving Lykos and his guards behind.

THE ARCHON

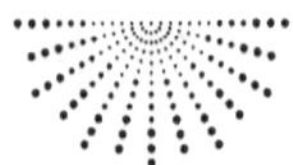

Since Asileia departed three years ago, Jaxas has flourished in his own right, though not always in ways that please those of Preservist inclinations. It is said that he garnered support for the Equalist measure to provide public granaries for times of famine, and he secured further rights for the women on the Lotus Ships, who were notoriously mistreated in their night work. He has, however, also fought to continue public funding for Eidolan temples, an effort older generations would most likely appreciate amidst the growing skepticism of the younger patricians.

Should he ever come into the Evergreen Wreath, Jaxas's rule might promise stability, but also significant changes. However, should Asileia produce an heir, he would be further supplanted from inheritance. Yet, loyal as he has shown himself to be to both Asileia and Oedija, I find it likely he will be content to serve at her side.

- A Modern Account of the Wreaths; by Acadian Helene, Master Historian; 1170 SLP

W e caught up with the Archon, walking around the contingent of honors to follow at his heels. For such a frail-looking man, he moved swiftly.

"He came not a moment too soon," Xaron muttered. "I was about to send those two beyond the 'Thae if they hit you again."

"Your violent rashness is sweet." I glanced at the Archon. "Let me do the talking. That is, if you can rein in your impulsivity."

He flashed me a sly smile. "We'll see how I feel."

We continued at Jaxas Wreath's heels for a few more paces before he glanced back and slowed to fall into step beside us. "You need not act so formal," he said with his phantom smile. "After all, you did shriek to catch my attention."

I flushed at the memory. If it wasn't the most horrifying thing I'd done, it certainly ranked high among them. "My apologies, Archon. I didn't have rotting in a dungeon on my list of tasks for today, and that seemed the quickest way out."

"It's a small thing to apologize for. At the very least, I won't imprison you for it."

The Archon did not treat me as someone below him, but as an equal. I swallowed and decided to do the same. "I did not know if you would or not. The whispers I hear of you are thin and insubstantial. For such a prominent figure, you surround yourself in silence."

"A mysterious man — I like the sound of it." His eyes slowly scanned the rich decorations in the corridor surrounding us before settling back on me. "Perhaps it makes me quite the eligible bachelor as well."

"Oh, quite. Hardly another topic occurs among the women at the baths."

He laughed softly. "You have a glib tongue, Airene. I'm sure it serves you well as a Finch."

My pulse quickened as he used my name, even as I deduced who had told him. "Tribune Vusumuzi sent word."

"Indeed he did. But you had come to my attention before that." His gaze flitted between Xaron and me.

My tongue worked around my dry mouth. "Few people in deme Port gain much attention from the Laurel Palace."

"True. But few people assault laurel guards in Valemish temples within a span of the Despot's disappearance."

My heart thundered in my chest. Little point in denying it now. "Assault is a strong word," I murmured.

Jaxas laughed softly again. "I'm inclined to agree. He may not seem it, but Lykos can be dramatic when his hackles are raised. Which, as I'm sure you've guessed, is quite often."

I felt my knotted shoulders slowly relax. "Dramatic seems a curious word to assign the man."

"Yes, there's something about him, isn't there? Something metal behind the eyes."

We emerged from the hallway into a tiered garden, one layer falling away under another. White stone paths shone in the sunlight and curved under the slender limbs and bright green leaves of laurel and olive trees. Pyrkin shimmered over statues and in cascading fountains. The garden seemed a fractured, hazy rainbow. Its arches and columns extended into the distance.

The Archon started down one of the winding paths, and Xaron and I fell back into step with him, the honors never far behind.

"Fortunate that I came by," Jaxas observed. "It is unlikely I would have chanced upon you in the dungeons."

I caught a glimmer of mischief in his face and suspected he said more than his words. "Fortunate indeed."

"Vusu has spoken of your talents. If what he says is true, I have need of you and your associates, Airene." His gaze abruptly sharpened as he looked at Xaron and me. "What were you searching for?"

I was taken aback by the sudden question. "We came to speak with you," I said carefully.

He stopped walking. Behind us, the honors stuttered to a halt. As if just noticing them, the Archon waved a hand, and they shuffled back out of earshot. He returned his gaze to me, and his eyes, soft and sunken, seemed to burn with resolve.

"That night at the temple," he clarified. "What were you hoping to gain there?"

I forced myself to hold his gaze. "We'd heard rumors," I said slowly. "Of certain activities."

"Activities." He shook his head. "Airene, now is not the time to withhold. If I wanted you in chains, I would have let the guards take you."

The statement had enough truth in it to loosen my tongue, if only a bit. "I don't know what I hoped to gain. But a nighttime visit by the First Laurel to a Valemish temple so soon after the Despot's death was too promising an opportunity to let slip away."

"So you were tracking Lykos's movements? Following where he went?"

"Call it a happy accident. Like you saving us from the dungeons."

A smile ghosted upon his lips. "Except that was no happy accident. I have eyes in this palace, ones loyal only to me. Without their warning, I would have had little reason to go to the atrium, as there are a hundred more convenient routes to my usual spaces."

In that moment, Jaxas seemed to possess all the hardness of the First Laurel and none of the Despoina's fragility. I struggled to keep his gaze.

"I ask again, Airene," he continued. "Why did you follow Lykos to the Sandglass temple that night?"

I sensed the sharp blade of the guillotine hovering above my neck, and one wrong word could bring it crashing down.

Yet I had to say something. "I had been investigating Myron's disappearance for the past half-span, as I didn't trust the reports of his natural death. Myron was too hale a man to die so suddenly, even at his age. Then the rushed private funeral, and the Despoina's Ascension so soon after... It didn't settle well with me. Yet I'd had no leads in that time. None, until I heard of Lykos's planned excursion to the Sandglass temple that night."

It was a gambler's throw to admit it all. If I believed the rumors, Jaxas was the Despoina's pet, serving her in every capacity — even desires of the flesh, according to the more salacious tongues. But the Archon had not been the man I'd been expecting. Though weak in body, he possessed a strength of mind that brimmed from his shadowed eyes.

I studied his expression, hoping I had judged correctly, but I could not catch the emotions that flashed in it. Eagerness? Regret? My fate — and Xaron's — hung on the balance of his judgment.

A silence extended over us. Wind whistled through the arches and rustled the leaves. Water pattered in the fountains. Xaron fidgeted with his hands. I shifted my weight from one foot to the other, breath coming quick and shallow. All the while, I stared at Jaxas, waiting for an answer.

The Archon, whose gaze had dropped, looked up. "You are correct. Our official explanation doesn't suit the facts."

I blinked. Was that an admission?

Before I could speak, he continued. "We wanted to contain panic. To present a sense of normalcy during a time of transition. But I cannot ignore this any longer. I cannot turn aside from what has truly occurred. Which is why I brought you here. Yes, it was I, though Vusu orchestrated the meeting on my behalf. He expressed great confidence in your abilities. Now that I have met you myself, I find myself swayed to his belief." He turned to fully face me, the loose sleeves of his robes billowing slightly in the wind. "So I must now offer you a proposition, Airene Finch. Are you prepared to hear it?"

I turned to face him as well, the situation gaining a strange formality. "Yes, I am, Archon Jaxas," I said, feeling slightly faint.

"I call it a proposition, but it is not one I expect you to refuse. Do you still wish to hear it?"

I forced myself to maintain eye contact as his gaze vacillated between steel and sadness. "I believe I've already accepted it, Archon."

His shadow-smile returned for a brief moment. "Then for clarity's sake. As the first of the new Order of Verifiers, you, Airene of Port, are to investigate the murder of Myron Wreath, the late Despot of Oedija. You are to have whatever resources you require at your disposal for your search, and you are to look into anyone of suspicion, without being bound by rank or decency." He stared at me a moment longer. "Investigate anyone of suspicion. Do I make myself clear?"

"Yes, Archon," I murmured, though words were nearly stolen from me. It was so clear as to be confusing. *Anyone without bounds.* Including himself. Including the cousin who was almost a sister, who wore the Evergreen Wreath.

The Archon nodded at Xaron. "Vusu spoke of you as well, Xaron, and of your third companion, Nomusa, who has preceded you here."

In an instant, the glow of success faded.

"Nomusa is here," I said, trying to make it sound like a statement rather than a question.

The Archon's eyebrow rose. "Yes. She was admitted for the same reasons you were, but as I was busy at the time, Low Consul Feiyan elected to entertain her on my behalf. They are still wandering the gardens last that I heard."

My heart hammered in my chest. How Nomusa had come here, and why she was meeting with Feiyan, were questions I could not begin to answer.

"We will encounter them soon, I expect," Jaxas continued. "But you are my concern for the moment, Xaron. I would confer the same responsibility and title upon you, if you will accept it."

Xaron startled, as if not expecting to be addressed. Or perhaps he was as distracted by the news of Nomusa as I was. "Ah, yes, Archon," he stumbled to say. "That is, I accept."

Jaxas nodded. "Good. Then it is settled."

But my thoughts were far from settled. Pushing Nomusa and Feiyan from mind, another burning question spilled from me. "Why now? It's been nearly a span since Myron's death. If you wished us to investigate this, why not summon us earlier? Why let us meander our own way here?"

Jaxas nodded slowly as if he'd been expecting the question. "There are things I know that you have yet to hear. The Manifest have secured the borders of Thys, and enforce it through their arms. Rumors have it that wardens are among their ranks, yet Vusu has ever counseled patience and delayed sending in the Shepherds. He wishes for stability, but I fear it was swift action that would have served us better. The Stratechons have raised taxoi to man the inner city walls, but too few and too late, and they lack the boldness we now need.

"As for our Despoina…" He paused and closed his eyes for a breath's count. "She has officially ejected the Avvadin diplomat and threatened war with the Imperium. And despite assurances from the Council and myself that we would never take such an action, the Kahin-Shah will take offense."

Fear crept up my spine. "Will two horns soon blow from the palace?"

He shook his head. "It will not come to that, I think. A

concession of tax remittance is underway within the Conclave, and some agreement will be reached. Nevertheless..."

I wanted badly to believe politicking would suffice. But I had seen the map inside the Wyvern's Claw. I'd been attacked by the Seeker wardens, and the wounds they'd inflicted still pained me. War, it was beginning to seem, was an inevitability.

Jaxas shook his head again, as if trying to banish the ill tidings, then motioned the honors back to us. "We should formalize our agreement."

One of the honors produced three goblets on a platter, which he promptly filled with a bottle of wine and handed to us. Archon Jaxas held up his cup, and Xaron and I followed. Without a word, we drank, as was the old Oedijan way when deals of commerce were struck. Apparently, the same held true for agreements of subterfuge and justice.

He lowered his cup a moment later and dabbed at his lips with a cloth. "Rooms have already been prepared for you to stay within the palace. It is traditional for Verifiers to take up residency at the Aviary on the Conclave grounds, but sadly, it has fallen into disuse since the Order was dismantled. Until such a time as it can be refurbished, or the Council reaches out to take hold of you themselves, you may stay here on Wreath property at our expense."

I exchanged an astonished look with Xaron. It was a boon I hadn't dreamed of receiving, and one that we sorely needed. "Thank you, Archon. Words cannot express our appreciation."

He smiled thinly. "It is for my convenience as well as yours. I wish to have my Finches at my disposal. Besides, keeping you within Wreath boundaries limits the number of eyes and ears who know that I use you."

Once again, cold clarity reasserted itself. Now that the Archon had us, he wouldn't easily let go. We were in a cage still, if more comfortable than the palace's dungeons. And here I'd begun to think Jaxas Wreath was a kind man.

The Archon turned away to look out over the sea, and with a nod at Xaron, we stepped up next to him. Though he was surrounded by people, I had the sense that Jaxas was far away and alone. And as I contemplated his position, I remembered my own. An unforeseen windfall had appeared to me, it was true enough. But as long as Linos was in the hands of the Manifest and the mystery of Thero's death went unsolved, I had no right to any measure of elation.

"Do you believe in the Pyrthae?" the Archon asked suddenly. "That it exists?"

I raised an eyebrow as I looked up. "Of course. We see it in the sky above."

He waved a hand dismissively. "There are other explanations for the radiant winds than a haven for lost spirits. At another time, I might recommend texts on it. But even without skepticism, I find myself hesitant to believe in it. Believing in things immaterial… It can cause a great deal of trouble."

In my experience, such statements were often said by those troubled by things immaterial. But I knew when to hold my tongue.

He looked to me, expression soft as the high tide shore. "Bring me more than ghosts to fret over."

I nodded, unsure whether it was a command or a plea.

He turned back to the gardens. "Ah. The last of our Finches has returned to the roost."

I tried to hide my surprise as I looked around. Standing on the tier above us were two familiar figures. Nomusa stared down at us with a somber expression, while Low Consul Feiyan wore a self-possessed smile.

"The other two of our new Verifiers, I see," Feiyan said with calculated derision. "When the Archon is finished with you, I'd like a word. I believe we have a few matters to settle."

I didn't look at Feiyan, but at my friend standing beside her. Nomusa stared back, her expression flat and unreadable. She and I had worked together for nine years and lived together for nearly as long.

Yet I couldn't help but wonder if all our shared lies had finally caught up to us.

TRUTH'S COST

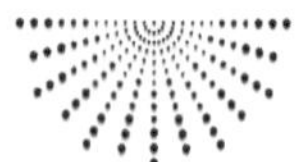

There is much discrepancy about the spirits of the Pyrthae and their origins, including whether or not anything resides within the realm at all, or indeed if it truly exists as a separate plane of existence parallel to our own Telae. Yet assuming spirits and their realm exists, there are a few things agreed upon.

The first is that there are lesser and greater spirits. In Oedija, we refer to the lesser spirits as pyr and the greater as gods, and believe a discrepancy in power exists between them. In some texts from the Age of Despots, there are mentions of a third being of spirit called Quintyr. How these beings differ is not clear, though influence and origin certainly appear to be important. Pyr, for example, can be of Pyrthaen or Telaen origin, such as our deceased ancestors, whereas Quintyr are said to be born only of the Pyrthae, and cannot reside outside of it. Gods, like pyr, are not restricted by origin, and there are tales in many lands of men and women performing heroic deeds and attaining divinity.

Those, however, can safely be dismissed as mere folk tales with little truth behind them.

- The Traditions of the Eleven: Eidolan worship in the demotism of Oedija; by Oracle Iason of deme Iris; 1164 SLP

A irene of Port," Feiyan said sweetly as she started down the stairs toward the Archon, Xaron, and myself. Nomusa followed in her wake.

"Feiyan," I said flatly, refusing to acknowledge her title or look at her. I didn't pull my gaze away from Nomusa. "What were you two discussing?" I addressed my loftmate.

Nomusa's mouth tightened. "What we were forced to."

"Yes, she was quite forthcoming." The Low Consul turned her smile on the Archon. "Perhaps we should speak later. I believe I can tell you many things you'll be interested to hear."

Jaxas gave her a stiff bow. "I would be happy to hear anything you might have to say."

I wondered briefly at their relationship. With both of them bonded tightly to the Despoina, they were bound to have regular interactions. And if this occasion was any sign, they weren't on the friendliest of terms. But that was a matter for another time. "Archon Jaxas, if would you excuse us, I'd like to talk over what we discussed with our associate."

He frowned, but after a moment's consideration, he nodded. "Of course. The Low Consul and I should converse before our Council meeting. We will speak more this evening. We each have more to say, I do not doubt."

I bowed deeply as I struggled for a response. I wasn't sure I should feel the depth of gratitude that I did for a man I barely trusted, much less express it. So I simply said, "Thank you, Archon."

As Jaxas nodded his dismissal, I took hold of Xaron and pulled him unceremoniously to the side. Nomusa frowned, but followed as we moved to another corner of the garden, sheltered from sight and sound by a laurel hedge and a glittering fountain.

As soon as we were alone, I rounded on Nomusa. "What did you tell her?"

Nomusa crossed her arms. "What I thought would keep us out of danger."

Xaron paled, but his expression remained determined as he asked in a low voice, "You didn't compromise us, did you?"

"How could it be I who compromised us?" Nomusa demanded in return. "Was it I who ignored her threats? One of us had to do something, or Feiyan would have done worse than sack Canopy."

I gritted my teeth, but held back my acid thoughts. "So you went to talk to her."

Her eyes blazed as she met my gaze. "Yes. I tracked Feiyan to the Laurel Palace, and her name gained me admittance. She was quite eager to speak with me."

"No doubt enjoying the opportunity to gloat," Xaron noted.

Annoyance crossed Nomusa's face, but she continued as if he hadn't interrupted. "She proposed that we make a mutually beneficial deal. In exchange for information, she would no longer antagonize us, nor turn in 'our feral,' as she called it."

My eyebrows shot up. "And that's it? You tell her a few whispers, and she lets us off the hook?"

"There was one additional condition. That we stop investigating the Despot's death, no matter the Archon's insistence on the matter."

I shook my head and rubbed at the bridge of my nose. My head was starting to ache. "Just what information was she so interested in anyway?"

The muscles in her jaw worked for a moment. "All that we've learned in our hunt," she admitted.

"*Our* hunt? You're talking about the hunt you impeded at every turn, and now throw away?"

"I'm trying to save us from your foolishness!" Nomusa hissed through clenched teeth.

"Easy, both of you," Xaron said, turning sideways to step between us. "Nomusa, what exactly did you reveal?"

Nomusa exhaled sharply. "I told her our suspicions and how we'd come to them insofar as they concerned the Despot. Of the Valemish, the Manifest. The Despoina herself."

I rolled my eyes. "Little wonder she wanted us to stop investigating."

"She always wanted that," Nomusa retorted. "Nothing I said changed that."

Xaron sighed and stepped back again. "At least we have a dialogue with our favorite hive queen and know she still doesn't intend to turn us in without provocation."

"Then I assume you won't do anything to provoke her? Like meet with the Archon this evening?" Nomusa's eyes bore into me.

I shook my head. "I'm still going."

"Let's go find our rooms before we talk about this further," Xaron interjected. "I'm sure one of Jaxas's honors can point us in the right direction."

I relented to Xaron taking command of the situation and was relieved when Nomusa did the same. As we followed after him, I studied my old friend. Anger still ran hot through me for her rash actions, but beneath it, there was a small strain of relief that she had acted in our best interests, misguided though the attempt may have been.

But when she glanced back at me, I turned away. If she expected an apology, she'd be waiting a long while.

THE HAND OF CLEPSAMMIA

Clepsammia is eighth of the Eidola, the daughter of Tyurn Sky-Sea by his infidelity with one of the deep-dwelling Sandwatchers. Nearly from birth, she was given Telae's Sandglass and put in charge of keeping the time of our world flowing at a steady grain. One of two deities born of another race, Clepsammia has ever been an outcast.

It is uncertain if it was her position or her origins that gives her such a unique insight into the streams of time. By turning her sandglass, she may visit any epoch of the world that has occurred or is still to come. Yet though she possesses unique knowledge, the Keeper of Time has in most of our stories contented herself with little more than the occasional enigmatic warning. Only in one tale did she do more, when she tried turning her father away from the mistake that would lead to his demise...

- The Traditions of the Eleven: Eidolan worship in the demotism of Oedija; by Oracle Iason of deme Iris; 1164 SLP

Two honors from Archon Jaxas's regiment led us to rooms on the opposite side of the palace. The hallways leading up to them were orderly, but not opulent like the main atrium we'd first entered. After informing us of the locations of various necessities, the two honors left us to our own devices. Though hunger gnawed at my stomach and weariness dragged at my limbs, it was the filth and the lingering memory of blood on my skin that sent me to the baths. Xaron, ravenous as usual, urged Nomusa to go with him to the feast hall, which left me on my own. That suited me fine; I needed time to think.

It was only once I was alone and walking down the hallway to the baths that I questioned my decision. Just a turn or so before, Lykos had tried to detain me and throw me in the dungeons. Even now that the Archon had claimed me as his own, a nagging paranoia persisted, especially when I passed between the guards scattered throughout the palace. Their eyes followed me with what seemed more than idle curiosity, and their words felt laced with secret venom. But for the moment at least, none laid a hand on me.

By the time I reached the baths, I was nearly shaking, though it could have as easily been from hunger and exhaustion as fear. I stripped off my ill-fitting clothes, keeping only the Verifier medallion with me, and relented to being oiled and scraped by an honor. Once she was finished, I slipped into the water. Though a roof sheltered the bathhouse from the elements, it was open on three sides, providing marvelous views of the sea and coastline, though it also admitted a chilling wind. No one else was at the baths at this turn of the day, so I had the view all to myself. Idly wiping the clinging oil from my skin, I stared out over the sea at the hazy horizon.

Somber thoughts accompanied me. Of Thero, and the lingering mystery of his death, and the dark master behind it. Of Linos, and my failure to retrieve him, and my fear that he'd meet the same fate. As I bobbed in the water, rubbing my hands over stinging cuts and bruises, I wondered if I'd given up too easily, if I shouldn't have pushed to infiltrate the Claw no matter the cost. The Verifier medallion, which I'd kept clasped over my neck, unable to trust parting with it, felt cold and heavy against my skin.

I closed my eyes and listened to the breeze rustling off the cliff and the lap of water on the edges of the pool. Slowly, my guilt's sharp edges dulled, and clarity returned. I couldn't have done anything more, not at that moment. I would have just gotten Xaron, Talan, and myself killed. What I'd done already had been foolish enough. To let the guilt hinder me now would only do my brother a greater disservice. I sighed slowly and let myself relax.

"Airene of Port. Or should I say, Verifier Airene."

I startled and spun around, arms crossed over my breasts. Nikias stood with hands clasped behind his back, dressed in all the finery of his station as steward to the Archon, and a severe expression to match.

"Hello, Nikias," I said drily. "Could you not wait until I'd dressed?"

His cheek twitched. "I come in regards to your dress. My master has had garments delivered to your rooms. I took the liberty to have some sent here as well as to dispose of your old clothes." He didn't bother hiding a sniff to show what he thought of their state.

That was a kindness I hadn't expected. "Thank you. Is there anything else?"

"As he conveyed before, my master will meet with you this evening to discuss your tasks. Your meeting will be at the Laurel Groves. Are you familiar with their location?"

"Vaguely." I knew where the royal gardens were, but as it was a place for patricians, Servants, and Wreaths, I'd never had occasion to visit.

"A carriage will await you at the sixth turn of the evening

outside the palace doors. Be there promptly; my master is not to be kept waiting." Nikias bowed stiffly, then turned on his heel and left.

I let my arms fall. The calm of the bath had been disturbed, so I rose from the water and hurried to the changing room.

A peplos had been laid out for me, far finer and more elegant than anything I'd worn before. I ran a hand over the soft silk and marveled at the expense. It made me uncomfortable to think about donning it, especially since I rarely wore peploses, which exposed one shoulder and therefore eliminated the possibility of wearing a tunic beneath.

Even more discomforting was the jewelry laid out with it, an assortment of silver bracelets, rings, and earrings, altogether worth twice as much as what Feiyan had stolen from Canopy. I put on the peplos, but was loathe to touch the jewelry. Did the Archon honestly want his Verifiers dressed in such finery? Perhaps I was meant to serve a different function than I imagined, a puppet in a plot I had yet to discover. It was uncomfortable to consider Jaxas in this new light, but I knew too little of him to rule it out. Another possibility was that this was a test, though what its purpose might be, I could not tell. Whatever his reasons, I decided not to wear them, but took them in hand. Perhaps it would be an insult to the Archon, but I couldn't abide wearing jewelry that announced my arrival in every new room with its rattling.

I returned to my chamber and entered without inquiring after Xaron and Nomusa. Weariness, which had prickled at my consciousness during my whole stay in the palace, now seized hold of me. Closing and locking the door, I collapsed onto my bed with barely a cursory look around. The fine furnishings could wait to be appreciated until I awoke. With a vague hope that I wouldn't sleep too late for our appointment with Jaxas, I drifted off.

~

A KNOCK WOKE ME. Disoriented, I bolted upright and stared about the strange room in confusion.

The knock sounded again. "Airene," Nomusa's voice came through the door. "We have half a turn to be outside the palace doors."

"I'm up." I looked around blearily, trying to orient myself to my surroundings. Slowly, I remembered where I was, and the twists and turns in my fortunes that had brought me here.

"You might hurry," Nomusa said, annoyance clear in her voice.

"One moment!" I rose, groaning. Where before I'd been exhausted, now I was sore and stiff as well. Not to mention ravenous. It promised to be a long day yet. At least I was already dressed. I found a mirror resting on the bedside table and examined myself. I was clean, but my hair was a messy cloud around my head, as I hadn't bothered to arrange it after my bath. Fortunately, a comb had been provided, and I used it in an attempt to tame the tangled bush.

As I tailored myself back into a presentable condition, I tried working my mind around my plans again, but the hunger was too great. Too little time to do everything necessary, as usual. I threw down the comb in frustration and, strapping on my sandals and donning the Verifier medallion, I bolted out the door.

Xaron and Nomusa were waiting outside. As I stepped into the hall, Xaron yawned widely. "Morning," he said miserably. He was even more of a sight than myself, his face swollen and scabbed. Even stranger was that he'd been provided robes for the occasion in place of his usual coat and trousers, which made him squirm in discomfort.

"It's evening. And don't moan," Nomusa chastised him with a fleeing smile. As usual, she looked radiant, with her hair smartly done and a rich silver peplos clinging to her figure. She hadn't spurned the jewelry as I had, but wore it all, bracelets jingling on her wrists and rings clinking on her fingers.

"Come on, Airene," she said, turning away. "We'll be late."

"I'm famished. Is the dining hall near?"

"No. You'll just have to cope."

"I guess I can relinquish part of my stash," Xaron said grudgingly.

After I'd restored myself from the mound of food Xaron had stolen from the kitchens, him grumbling about losing his late-night meal the whole time, we hurried through the palace to the front doors. Xaron and I chatted of small things, not daring to touch on more pertinent topics. I much preferred Xaron in his current high spirits to the brooding man he'd been the night before.

As promised, Nikias had ordered a carriage to wait for us, with an honor holding the reins to a pair of mules. "If we might hurry, master and mistresses," the man said with a low bow. "We are past the time Steward Nikias instructed me to depart."

Nomusa glowered at me and climbed into the carriage, Xaron and I coming after. As soon as we were seated, the honor shook the reins, and the mules started clopping down the marble path.

We were quiet at first, and I stared out of the barred windows of the carriage. I'd never ridden in such high style, yet I hadn't hesitated to climb in and accept the privilege like a born patrician. It made me uneasy how quickly I was adapting to this new lifestyle.

"Why are we meeting Jaxas in the Laurel Groves?" Nomusa broke the silence, reluctance plain in her voice. She spoke softly enough that the clamor of the horse and carriage would mask her words from our driver.

I met her gaze. If she was willing to talk, I'd meet her half-way. "I don't know. He didn't say."

Xaron shrugged. "Something to do with the Despot job, no doubt."

"With Despot Myron's death?"

I nodded. "It's what he's hired us for. To get to the bottom of things."

Nomusa was quiet for a moment. "That will go against Feiyan's demands," she said quietly. "Xaron, are you prepared to accept that?"

Uncertainty flashed across his face, but I saw the man I'd glimpsed the night before return as he sharply nodded. "Yes," he said in a rough whisper. "I won't live in fear."

I clenched my jaw and turned my gaze out the window. I hated what necessity made us risk, but I couldn't think of any way around it.

"What did you find in Thys?" Nomusa pressed.

I spoke before Xaron had a chance to. "What did you tell Feiyan?"

She scowled, but it was Xaron who answered. "Let it go, Airene. She did what she thought was best. We can settle all that later. Right now, we have to work together. Or are you forgetting what's on the line?"

"No, I'm not," I answered coolly.

"Good. Then let me do the talking."

Xaron recounted the events of the night before with enough embellishment that it took all my self-control not to cut in. When it came to the violence, though, he was conspic-uously brief. After he finished, Nomusa nodded, her expres-sion thoughtful.

"That does seem serious," she admitted. "But the Manifest doesn't have the means to take over the city, much less start a war with Avvad."

"Perhaps not. But they must have significant resources to

erect and support an encampment of that size in the midst of an oncoming famine." I paused, considering. "They've been shielded from all echelons of the government. Which means someone must be protecting them. One of the Stratechons, a First in the city guard, or someone in the Tribunal, possibly."

Xaron's eyes widened. "Jaxas said Vusu had counseled him not to send in Shepherds to the Manifest. But we saw wardens there. You don't think...?"

"No, I don't," I replied sharply. "We'd never have gotten as far as we have without Vusu. What possible reason could he have for aiding us if he's a Seeker?" I shook my head. "More likely it is someone from the Preservist faction among the Council. Jaxas said they'd also advocated for little to be done."

Nomusa leaned forward. "Unless the Preservists are more connected to Avvad than any of us suspected. All of them have ancestry from the Imperium."

"We can't assume that," I murmured, but there wasn't much heart to my words. It made too much sense to me to deny it. "But unless the Manifest and Avvad are somehow connected, I don't see why they'd want to foster them."

"Chaos," Xaron guessed. "Undermine the city's stability so that it makes it easier to conquer."

"Then what about the Despoina's strange behavior? And Feiyan's plotting and protectiveness? It seems too far a stretch to wind them in."

Xaron shrugged. "Asileia's crazy. What else is there to figure out?"

I suspected it was the truth as the Manifest loomed ever larger in my mind. But it wasn't an assumption we could safely make, not with our limited information. And it didn't solve one central question: if Asileia wasn't the master at the center of the Manifest, who was?

The carriage finally rumbled to a halt. I looked out to see

we'd arrived at our destination. The Laurel Groves were known as a horticultural wonder of the Four Realms, and I saw they lived up to their name. Fountains, marble walkways, and manicured aisles wove together in dazzling arrangements. Flowers of orange, periwinkle, and violet emerged amid emerald green leaves and trees hanging with gold-limned moss. Laurel trees in the peak of their summer bloom filled the air with a wonderfully sweet scent and dotted the groves with white flowers like stars. As in the palace gardens, pyrkin was used to highlight effects, but on an entirely different scale. Where in the gardens everything was kept tightly in check, here a balance had established itself between the tidiness of architecture and the chaos of creation.

The approach of the Archon with his usual group of honors drew my attention. "I am glad to see you made it," he said as he arrived, sounding slightly out of breath. "We'll go on foot from here. If you'll come with me…" Jaxas Wreath's words trailed off, but he turned sharply on his heel and started back the way he'd come, sending his honors scattering before him.

My accomplices and I disembarked and hurried after him. Unlike earlier that day, I immediately walked by his side. "What are we here for, if I may ask, Archon?"

"Ah, so you haven't guessed?" His eyes gleamed with mischief. "And here I thought your wealth of information was endless."

I shrugged. "We're not seers."

Jaxas only chuckled softly.

"Archon, if I might speak of a subject that is of vital importance…" I trailed off. The request sounded too formal and stiff. I'd never get around to my point if I didn't state it bluntly.

I started again. "There's a danger to the city, and nothing is being done about it that I can tell. I hope the information we have will change that."

Jaxas glanced at me, then at Xaron and Nomusa behind us. "I believe I know of what you speak," he said in a low voice. "We will talk of it later. But now, I must show you why I've brought you here."

I repressed an urge to share a skeptical look with Xaron and Nomusa. What could he have to show us in the Laurel Groves? "As you wish," I relented.

We turned the next corner to find a strange sight. Asileia Wreath lay under an olive tree, staring up through its leaves. She had never seemed a woman to be caught unawares, but as we approached, she didn't seem to notice our presence. Her oracles were a different story. Three in number, they crowded around her like vultures over carrion and gazed up at our party with jealous possessiveness. I ignored the syco-phants and watched our Despoina. She could have been dead for all she moved or blinked. I wondered if the glass-thin sanity of our Ruling Wreath had finally cracked.

I rounded on the Archon. "Why didn't you tell us we were meeting the Despoina?"

Jaxas Wreath shrugged. "Surely you have many questions for her. Now is your time to ask."

I turned my gaze away from him and looked back to my friends. Nomusa stood with as haughty a posture as I'd ever seen her don. Xaron slouched and cast his eyes about nervously, looking as unsettled as I felt. I wanted to confer with them and ask what questions we should pose to her. But the Archon was already beckoning us forward.

"Come — it's not fit to keep the Ascended Wreath wait-ing." He and his retinue of honors pushed closer, leaving us no choice but to follow.

As we approached the Despoina, the situation became yet more bizarre. I expected her to shake off whatever stupor gripped her and resume her royal manner, but she didn't move. When we were a dozen paces away, the oracles finally moved to stand before her. They were cowled in dark brown robes, their faces hidden from view. All I could distinguish them by were their disparate sizes, with several cubits between the smallest and largest.

"You are not worthy," the middle one said.

"She is listening and is not to be disturbed," the largest one continued.

"Leave and never return," the smallest finished.

Jaxas ignored them all. "Leia," he said softly. "Leia, I've brought you guests, ones who won't hiss poison in your ear."

"You are not worthy," the first oracle repeated stubbornly.

I stood there, uncertain of what to say. Jaxas slowly peeled his eyes from Asileia to settle on the oracles. "Move from our way," he said quietly.

A pause. "You are not worthy," the first oracle said once more.

"I know," the Archon replied. The humility in his tone surprised me. "But we must speak to her all the same. Move and let me see her."

The oracles barely shifted, yet I sensed their unease. The middle one stepped aside first, the other two following after. They muttered something as we passed between them, but I couldn't hear the words.

Approaching the Despoina, Jaxas knelt next to her under the boughs of the olive tree. "Leia," he said softly. "We have guests. Some people I'd like you to talk to. Will you stand?"

The leader of our nation didn't bat an eye. Her lips barely parted, and a wordless moan escaped.

Jaxas closed his eyes for a moment. When he opened them, his gaze had grown hard as granite. "Leia. You must rise now."

Her eyelids fluttered, then closed. "Why do you bother me?" she said faintly. "I am trying to rest."

"With your eyes open?" The Archon's anger spilled forth

in cutting words. "You don't need any more rest. You need to rise."

"Indeed?" Leia's eyes snapped fully open, and her face adopted the hard lines I'd initially expected. "Because my war to save our city from invading pyr is inconsequential? Because I don't stay up, day and night, guarding you and every other small mind in this polis from their grasping claws? And you wish me to pause my watch to do, what? Speak more with the Avvadin ambassador?" She squeezed her eyes shut again. "We have spoken enough. I will hear no more of his talk of commerce and *mutual benefit*. He is a weak man, a paragon of a nation in decline."

Jaxas opened and closed his mouth, his shadowed eyes smoldering. But I could see his anger was getting us nowhere. I'd long ago learned to trust my gut, even if it sometimes led me to strange places. Before he could speak, I boldly stepped forward and slipped down to the ground.

Asileia Wreath stared at me with slitted eyes. "And you are?"

I crossed my legs under my borrowed peplos, ignoring how dirty I was making the delicate fabric. "Trying to get comfortable."

Her hard expression didn't flicker. "You are not worthy to sit here."

So it wasn't just the oracles who thought so. "I'm sorry to disturb you, my Despoina. I have heard of your… hardships."

She stared at me a long moment, then her eyes slid back into her head. "You don't know the half of them."

"Then tell me. What is this war to save Oedija?"

She sat bolt upright so quickly I nearly scrambled away in surprise. "I am the Hand of Clepsammia," she declared so loudly it was almost a yell. "I will cast you down from your unholy throne, daemon! Begone, before I grow angry! Begone, before—!"

She stopped as suddenly as she started, going as rigid as a

plank and eyes staring wide and straight ahead. I was hesitant to speak, but I had to make the most of this conversation. Jaxas might cut our talk short at any moment.

"Despoina Asileia, I need you to tell me—"

"I don't need to tell anyone anything. *I* am the Hand of Clepsammia."

I swallowed my pride. "Of course you are. As the Hand of Clepsammia, do the gods speak to you? Do they ask you to do anything for them?"

"I do what I wish. And what I wish is their will." Her eyelids fluttered. "But it is I who is in control."

"Was it your will or theirs to kill your father?"

The oracles hissed and stepped forward, only stopped by a sharp reprimand from Jaxas. Xaron chuckled inappropriately. Yet no one spoke against my accusation.

I kept my eyes on the Despoina. Slowly, she met my gaze and smiled. "Wasn't it marvelous? The first test of my power. There he went, gone without a trace."

I stared at her, searching her eyes, not daring to believe her words. I found nothing there but the certainty of madness.

I rose, thoughts tumbling about my mind like marbles in a cup. Glancing back, I saw the Archon staring at me with a strange twist to his expression. Nomusa wore begrudging respect, while Xaron's brow was knitted in consternation.

I turned back to Asileia, who still lay on the ground, and bowed. "Thank you for your time, my Despoina."

She had already resumed staring up through the trees and paid me no mind.

Jaxas Wreath took a deep breath. "If you'll give us a moment," he said in carefully measured tones, then turned to his cousin.

The honors, Xaron, Nomusa, and I shuffled back along the path until we were out of earshot, but still within line of sight. The oracles lingered behind until the Archon cast a withering look in their direction, then they walked over to stand next to us stiffly. The whole company watched the silent pantomime between Jaxas and Asileia, her ignoring him, him gently pleading.

"You misunderstand her," an oily voice said from next to me.

I looked over to see the largest of the brown-cowled oracles staring down at me. Under his hood, I found beady, glittering eyes staring from beneath peppered eyebrows and a prominent forehead.

"Pardon?" I asked politely.

"She is the savior of our city. You would do best not to question what she does in service of it."

"You are not worthy," the middle-sized oracle intoned.

I shrugged. "I'll take that into consideration."

The oracle nodded as if my reply was enough, then he and his fellows moved further away.

Xaron and Nomusa pressed in closer. "Did she admit what I think she did?" Xaron asked dubiously.

"Yes, we all heard it," Nomusa said impatiently. She nodded toward the oracles, who had turned their backs on us. "What I can't figure out is why they're still following her around."

"Lingering opportunists," I said with a shrug. "We've got bigger concerns than them."

But Nomusa still wore a thoughtful expression as she looked away.

Xaron glanced between us. "Are we not going to talk about what the Despoina confessed to?"

I smiled and put a hand on his arm. "Later will be soon enough."

After several more minutes, the Archon finished his piece to the Despoina and rejoined us. From his slumped shoulders and her continued position on the ground, the conversation had not gone well.

"We move on," the Archon said as he swept past us. His posture showed defeat, but his voice was still full of command. "You have another appointment to keep."

"Another appointment?" I glanced at Nomusa and saw my question echoed in her eyes. "With whom?"

"A ghost," the Archon said with the shadow of a smile. "One I'm sure you're eager to meet."

2 2

REMNANTS

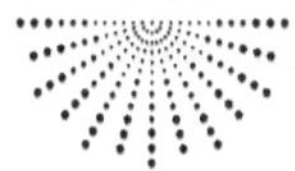

If spirits do exist in the Pyrthae, they do not have much interaction with us of the material plane. At certain festivals, such as Oedija's Carnival of Veils, trickster pyr are said to appear and cause mischief, though little evidence supports that such pranks are truly of Pyrthaen origin. Some Eidolan sects believe that rituals can call forth pyr to provide aid or do harm to others, though again, I remain unconvinced that any perceived intervention isn't simply in the minds of the ritualists.

- The Traditions of the Eleven: Eidolan worship in the demotism of Oedija; by Oracle Iason of deme Iris; 1164 SLP

Jaxas kept us in suspense for the ride back up to the Laurel Palace. In our separate carriage, Nomusa, Xaron, and I quietly debated what the Despoina's subtle admission of guilt meant, but our next appointment begged speculation. I had my suspicions, and when I shared them, Nomusa and Xaron nodded along in agreement, apprehension and eagerness battling in their expressions.

When we reached the palace, we ascended the stairs to a grand hallway with a lofted ceiling and plush, red carpet over the stone. At the end of it lay a pair of large, wooden doors. Whereas everything else was gilded and glimmering, these doors were scratched and plain. A matronly honor waited by them, whom I understood to be a head of the palace staff. She informed us that the doors were a remnant from the Wardens' War, when the newly freed people of Oedija raided the palace and gutted it of all its value. All else in the palace had been restored, but this reminder of those dark times had been ordered to remain.

The Archon stopped before the doors. "These are the Ascended Wreath's official living quarters. Myron, however, preferred to have his chambers elsewhere." He shook his head. "He claimed it was too ostentatious for his liking, but I believe he always feared assassins in the dark. A poor irony, isn't it?"

Nomusa and I shared a look, while Xaron chuckled irreverently. Jaxas didn't comment, but led us down the hall to a smaller door. This one had figures carved into it. I recognized Tyurn Sky-Sea in the center of it, his star-crested mantle sweeping over the rest of the mural.

"Did Myron believe in the Eleven?" I asked, curious.

Jaxas nodded. "He believed we'd lost something when we abandoned the old ways and beliefs. The way his daughter behaved only served to reinforce this belief."

I tucked the fact away for later and stared at the doors, imagining what was beyond them.

The Archon sensed my eagerness, and he smiled faintly. "Chiri, please open the old Despot's chambers."

"Yes, Archon," the matronly honor said. Trepidation filled her voice, yet she complied, producing a ring of keys and turning an iron one in the lock. She gave a push, and the door swung slowly open.

My heart pounding, I stepped forward at Jaxas's inviting gesture. Nomusa and Xaron walked next to me, staring past the frame and into the room beyond. But as the door opened fully, my stomach lurched, hard and sudden. Bile burned the back of my throat. I swallowed hard to keep it down.

"Airene?" Xaron touched my bare shoulder. "Are you okay?"

His touch was unbearably hot. I gave a wordless cry and shrugged off his grip, taking a step back and breathing hard. As I stepped away, the pain ebbed, as did the fire from Xaron's touch.

He stared at me in astonishment, not daring to come closer. It was Nomusa who slowly approached next. "Aire?" she asked cautiously. "Are you well?"

My cheeks flushed as Jaxas, Chiri, and the other gathered honors stared at me. I swallowed hard once more before I trusted myself to speak. "I'm fine." I turned to our host, trying to pretend that nothing had happened. "Have the rooms been disturbed?"

Jaxas studied me carefully for a moment, then gestured to Chiri. "I'll let the matron of the palace speak."

Chiri looked less certain of my wellness. Still, she replied, "Not a man or woman has been permitted to enter since the first night."

"But someone entered that night?" I followed up quickly. My stomach still turned, unsettled.

The honor eyed me, sizing me up, or perhaps wondering if I was about to create a mess that she'd have to clean up. At a nod from the Archon, she continued. "The Archmaster Kyros, the Tribune Vusumuzi, and the First Laurel Lykos were the only ones to go within. I saw myself that they did not put anything amiss."

"You didn't enter yourself?" I asked Jaxas. "Nor the Despoina?"

He shook his head, eyes shadowed by the pyr lamp mounted behind his head.

"May we enter?" Nomusa spoke. "We won't learn much by standing in the doorway."

The honor looked scandalized by the suggestion, but Jaxas nodded. "Of course."

Xaron and Nomusa glanced at me, and I felt a new flush settling over me. Setting my jaw, I stepped determinedly forward, even as I tensed for the coming blow. I was not disappointed. My stomach thrashed again, and hot bitterness hit the back of my throat. But instead of recoiling, I barreled through the doorway. At once, the feeling faded, leaving my organs mangled and throbbing.

The Archon entered with us. "Are you well?" he murmured to me as Xaron and Nomusa spread out to look around.

I nodded. Though the danger of retching seemed to have passed, I didn't want to risk opening my mouth.

Seeking a distraction, I peered around the room. It was modest for a Wreath, only a few dozen paces across. Dominating the room was a four-poster canopy bed that looked fit to sleep a giant, its sheets and blankets undisturbed and tidy. The Despot had not yet been to bed the night of the three horns, it seemed. I tucked the thought away for later.

Other doors led off from the main chamber. I wondered if he'd gone to any of them when a breeze drew icy fingertips along my exposed shoulder. Glancing over, I saw the doors to the balcony were slightly ajar.

"Have those doors been open since his disappearance?" I asked Chiri, who had remained by the door.

"As I said," the honor stated, sounding more than a bit annoyed, "nothing has been disturbed since His Majesty's disappearance."

"Thanks," I said, not bothering to hide my sarcasm, then approached the balcony.

The balcony faced west over the sea, affording an excellent view of the brilliant sunset. Pink lined the horizon, and orange caught on the clouds above, then faded to a lighter blue etched with the green rivers of the radiant winds. This room was high up on a cliff and positioned over the sea, so the wind was cold and biting, and I had little in the way of shelter from it. As gooseflesh spread over my skin, I set discomfort aside and scanned the foreboding cliff below us and the sheer walls of the Laurel Palace to either side. Having seen Xaron and Talan at work before, I knew wardens were capable of incredible acrobatics. Yet ascending this wall seemed beyond even the most skilled warden. Even they had to have occasional handholds. Though the stories told of other abilities like walking the Pyrthae, I dismissed them as legend. If such things were possible, the restriction in the Four Realms on channeling likely meant such abilities were beyond any living warden's reach.

I discovered another barrier to entry when my gaze fell to the turrets on the island below. While a palace mounted on a cliff above the sea would ordinarily be vulnerable to naval attacks, the Laurel Palace was sheltered by a narrow island just off the shore. The guard towers built there would no doubt have eyes on the Despot's rooms at all times. Even if someone did manage to ascend the walls, they'd be spotted by half a dozen different men.

Unless, of course, those guards were no longer loyal to one they were supposed to protect.

Stepping back inside, I approached Jaxas. "Have you questioned the guards stationed that night? On the towers and outside the door?"

He frowned. "Yes. They reported seeing the Despot step out on the balcony for a moment, then step back within. Nothing else."

They were lying. The night of Asileia's Ascension, Nikias had told me that an honor had overheard the guards talk about arguing and a sound like snapping fire from within the room. More had transpired than the laurel guards had admitted to their Archon, or perhaps than Jaxas had admitted to us.

I closed my eyes, thinking it over. I heard the other three in the room gather closer, but they didn't speak, and I didn't look at them. Only when the pieces began to fall into place did I open my eyes again. My friends and the Archon stood waiting.

"I think we should close the doors," I said quietly, "and talk among ourselves."

The Archon studied me with an inscrutable look, then gestured to Chiri by the door. "Please, Chiri, if you could give us a moment alone."

The honor looked aghast. "In here, my Archon? There are restless pyr still astir."

"We'll be perfectly fine, I'm sure."

With one last disapproving look, Chiri pressed shut the doors.

Jaxas turned back to me. "What do you make of this?" he asked quietly.

"Much is uncertain. But we do know some things. Things that can't wait to be discussed any longer."

I stared at the Archon, and he met my gaze unflinchingly, as impassive as before. I continued. "What remains unknown is how the Despot was killed, if he even was killed."

Xaron's brow creased, but he remained silent. Nomusa looked less surprised. She, like I, must have worked it out as we looked around his quarters.

I gestured around us. "There doesn't appear to be signs of a struggle, which might mean any number of things. He might have been pushed from the balcony. Or maybe he was killed and his body smuggled out. For the moment, we'll set the matter aside. We can't draw conclusions until we know more."

Jaxas's facade cracked for a moment, a flicker of curiosity crossing his thin features. "Go on."

"About who might have done it, we know more, including some of the connections and motives behind the players." I shifted from one foot to the other, unable to completely contain my nervousness. The accusations I was about to level might have grave consequences if Jaxas wasn't the man I thought he was.

He seemed to sense my hesitancy. "I know this is a delicate matter, Airene. You have my word, you won't be punished on account of suspicions alone."

I noticed that didn't preclude consequences. Yet I found myself speaking nonetheless. "We have reason to suspect Archmaster Kyros Brighteyed in Myron's disappearance, as well as First Laurel Lykos. Not only were they both some of the first to enter the Despot's quarters, but they have also displayed suspicious behavior in the time since."

I told Jaxas of how I now saw Lykos's investigation into the Valemish temple as a sham, a show for a false trail. The loyalty I'd sensed in the First Laurel had to be loyalty to someone else, someone he thought he owed greater fealty to than the Wreaths. I also explained how while the laurel guards had reported one thing, the honors had heard them speak of another, and how the guards mounted on the island across must have seen something of what occurred on the balcony. The Archon didn't make any motion of agreement or disagreement but simply listened in silence.

Then I explained the Archmaster's involvement, including the disturbing rumors of Kyros gathering and training Acadians to use their attunement to fight. I also explained our interpretation of Hilarion's supposed assassination attempt at the Ascension, and how Kyros was the closest other warden, and how he might have set the man up.

At this point, Jaxas spoke just one word. "Why?"

I drew in a breath. I felt lightheaded with the implications of these revelations, but I'd said this much. There was only one way to proceed.

"Kyros must be associated with the Manifest, perhaps

even the leader of it. It's said the Visage of the Wyvern claims to be a warden and has built his image to seem that way."

"Kyros as the Visage himself," Jaxas mused. He seemed thoughtful. "And do you have suspicions as to why he might do this?"

"Power," Xaron spoke up. "You don't have to listen to him for long to see a man like him chafes at chains."

The Archon glanced at Xaron, then looked back to me. "Then you believe Archmaster Kyros to be an enemy of the state. That he seeks to destabilize Oedija through the organization of a dissident movement, the assassination of our leader, and the re-militarization of wardens within the Acadium."

I hesitated, glancing at both Xaron and Nomusa. When I saw my own belief mirrored back to me, I nodded.

"And what of the Despoina?" he asked.

I saw in his minute expressions how closely he'd kept this question. How much he feared its answer.

I shook my head. "She wishes for power and significance and seeks to expand her position. But I do not believe her capable of her father's disappearance." I hesitated. "That is, I do not believe she has the ability to execute it as quietly and smoothly as it has been accomplished."

Jaxas nodded gravely as if he understood my unspoken sentiment. Nevertheless, relief shone in his eyes. "I will take these thoughts into consideration. Is there anything else? For Chiri's sake, I would not wish to overstay our welcome."

Xaron, Nomusa, and I shared a look. I almost asked for a moment to speak among ourselves, but before I could, Xaron forged ahead. "We do have one more thing to say, Archon. You have an enemy whom you've ignored for far too long."

Nomusa's eyes widened, mirroring my own reaction. But the Archon only wore a small, sad smile.

"Yes, I suspect I have," he murmured.

Xaron took it as a sign to continue. "The Manifest plan to

overthrow the demotism. I saw the war map for myself, Archon. As you said, Kyros and his lackeys want to destabilize you and the Despoina, then take over when Avvad invades from the south."

A pregnant silence filled the room. "Then you are saying," Jaxas said calmly, "that not only have we ignored a threat within our nation, but a threat from without. And that we must deal with both immediately. Is that correct?"

Xaron still wore his determination as armor, but his eyes flickered to me. I said reluctantly, "We believe them to both be significant threats. The sooner they are dealt with, the better for all."

Jaxas nodded once more. "This, too, will be taken into consideration." As if we hadn't just announced the impending demise of Oedija, he gestured politely toward the doors. "You may take your leave now."

Xaron and Nomusa started to comply, and the Archon turned away, but I stayed where I was.

"And when can we expect your decision?" I asked. "A significant Manifest gathering is occurring tomorrow night. It might be best if a course of action was decided by then."

Jaxas glanced over his shoulder. "As far as I'm aware, when the Order was still intact, Verifiers of Truth did not determine the demotism's policy."

The rebuke was no more than I deserved. Even as a nominally appointed Verifier, why should I, not even a citizen in my own right, question the Archon? I flushed but didn't look away. I almost confessed the real motivation behind my urgency. But if I admitted my brother was held hostage, he might question my motives and conclusions. I held my tongue and curtly bowed.

The Archon barely seemed to notice as we exited, but stared out over the balcony into the coming twilight.

RUDE AWAKENING

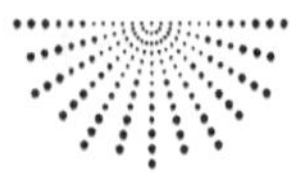

It is uncanny, what happens to a warden's mind when they are forged into a Shepherd. Not even the honors are so servile as they. It is as if another occupies their mind, moves their limbs, governs their thoughts...

- Tribune Yalissa before the Demos Council; 1071 SLP

He won't do anything," Xaron muttered as we descended the staircase from the Despot's quarters and headed back to our rooms.

"We did all we could," Nomusa said firmly. "And we will continue to do all we can."

"This isn't over," I said, almost to myself.

By the time we reached the chambers, my stomach was rumbling again, and I convinced Xaron to go with me to the feast hall. Nomusa decided to retire early, claiming to have little appetite after the meeting. Xaron and I ate our fill of what remained from that night's dinner and chatted of menial things, even as my mind wandered back to the many problems weighing me down.

They pressed in closer when we returned to our rooms.

As I lay down, I thought of Talan, who no doubt worked tirelessly to learn all he could of the Manifest and Linos's whereabouts. I hoped he would be able to get in contact if he learned anything. I also remembered with a start that Corin hadn't had word from the rest of us in days. I was failing as a friend as well as a sister. I turned on my side and clutched the blankets close, trying to banish the guilt and fears that hounded me.

They chased me into dreams, where fragments of the day and night before floated about me. The faces of the Seeker guards with their bright, violet tatu. The flashes of channeled radiance and waves of kinesis bursting around me. I suddenly found myself running, fleeing the broken memories.

"Flee," a boy's whisper sounded in my ear.

I jerked my head around, but I saw and felt nothing but mist.

The whisper came in my other ear. "Flee, Airene. He has his claws in you."

I whipped my head around, terror making the world around me pulse. Then I saw it. The creature emerged from the fog in hazy detail. The face of a lizard loomed dozens of cubits tall and looked as if it was made of smoke. Its mouth gaped as it swam through the dream toward me.

"He feeds," the boy's voice said, fear etched into his voice. "He comes."

"Who?" I yelled as I ran. My feet carried me nowhere. Abruptly, the ground was stolen from under me, and I ran on light and air. I glanced over my shoulder and saw the lizard's forked tongue dart out, tasting the air. Tasting for me.

"Flee, Airene," the whisper finch murmured. "Taozu comes."

The lizard's maw made the world black behind me. I ran, but not fast enough. I felt the mouth closing, the long, sharp teeth blocking escape—

I jerked awake, sweating and breathing hard. For a moment, I lay there with my heart racing. The dream had already started to fade, the logic of it unraveling as the day pressed in through the windows. I shook my head and rubbed at the aching in my temples. As if I didn't have enough to worry about when awake, my mind had to invent terrors in my sleep as well.

Pushing away the fragmenting memories of the dream, I rose and went to the huge closet in the room. I was relieved to find that Nikias had supplied chitons for my wardrobe. Selecting a dark green robe, I dressed and resolved to ask the steward about obtaining a tunic and trousers as well. I blinked as I realized again how swiftly I was adjusting to someone else providing for me. I shook my head and planned instead to buy them myself as soon as I could find a moment — and the coin — to do so.

Shouting from just outside my door jolted me from my thoughts. My heart began hammering once again. Had Lykos and his guards come for us? Jaxas had said he would protect us, but I didn't know whether he actually could or not. I pressed my ear to the door and listened to the shouting. Xaron's voice was distinct from the rest. Without strapping on sandals or fixing my tousled hair, I unlocked the door, wrenched it open, and spilled into the hallway.

If my heart had hammered before, now it thundered. Three cowled men in aqua robes stood before Xaron's open door, manacles trailing from their raised hands. My friend must have been just within, for I heard him shout, "I swear by all the gods, I'll attack if you come in here!"

I stared, unmoving. I'd had nightmares of this happening in Canopy. But with everything that had been occurring, I never thought they'd catch up to Xaron here. I saw how stupid I'd been now. We hadn't stopped investigating the Despoina, not from the way Feiyan saw it. And now she'd carried through on her threat.

"Hold!" I snapped, marching up to the three. The Shepherds looked around at me with shadowed eyes. If I'd hoped to cow them, I was disappointed, for I saw no fear in their eyes. They were hollow, emotionless pits that seemed to stare through me.

The Shepherd in the middle answered me. "Another Finch," he said with a thin smile.

"Stay back, Airene!" Xaron shouted from around the doorway.

The Shepherd continued as if he hadn't been interrupted. "But you do not sing as pretty of a song as this one. Stand back, foolish girl."

Suddenly, it felt as if I hit a wall. My body smarted from the impact, but I tried not to let it show. I knew one of them must have formed a wall from kinesis — the one closest to me, if his subtle gesture was any indication. They could easily do more if they had half a mind to.

My body trembled with fear, but I couldn't abandon him. "Xaron is a Verifier under the protection of Archon Jaxas Wreath. I don't know what you think he did, but you'd better take it up with the Archon if you're going to try arresting him."

The Shepherd laughed without mirth. "I don't need the Archon's permission to dispose of ferals."

I forced an astonished look. "Xaron? A warden? You must be japing." I jabbed my finger at the doorway. "I've lived with him for six years. I think I'd know if he was a feral."

"And you would tell us, I suppose?" There was a glint to the warden's eyes. "We have ways of knowing, I assure you, Finch."

I had as much effect as I'd expected. Yet despite the Shepherd's confidence, something held him back, for none of the enforcers moved into the room. From all I'd heard of their abilities and what I'd seen of Xaron's fighting, I didn't doubt that they could handily take him down. But they didn't know that. Perhaps they were proceeding cautiously, waiting for an opportunity to present itself, or hoping to convince Xaron to yield peacefully. Or perhaps they were waiting for permission from someone.

Whatever the truth, I knew I had to keep trying. "You take commands from Tribune Vusumuzi, do you not? It just so happens that we know each other well. How about we call him over and see what he thinks about Xaron being a warden?"

There — a glimmer of uncertainty in their postures. The two silent Shepherds exchanged glances, while the middle one continued to stare at me. "Tribune Vusumuzi need not weigh in on clear matters like these," he said.

Before I could respond, he spasmed. One of his eyelids twitched, then a corner of his mouth. The twitching spread. All along the Shepherd's body, his muscles jerked until he could barely stand upright. I watched in horrified fascination as he collapsed to the ground. His companions looked down at him, but made no move to provide aid.

I looked between the two still standing, wondering who to address next, and what had caused the reaction in the first. "Do either of you want to countermand Tribune Vusumuzi?" I asked them impetuously.

They didn't look at me, but stared into Xaron's room. Neither of them fell to the ground incapacitated, though the one closest to me negated his wall of kinesis. Emboldened, I took another step forward. The closest Shepherd's head snapped toward me.

"We await his judgment," he said in a hoarse whisper.

Just then, I heard footsteps hurrying down the hall.

"Hold!" Vusu's voice echoed from the corridor. Trailing after him was the clerk from the Tribunal, clutching a binder of vellum to her chest.

"Hold!" the Tribune repeated. His forehead shone with sweat, but he wasn't out of breath. Vusu stared calmly around him, eyes pausing on me for a moment before settling on one of the Shepherds. "Explain what is occurring."

The Shepherd closest to the Tribune pointed into the room. "We were told a feral had taken up residence in this room by the honor of a Low Consul. We came here to see if it was true. We know this man, Xaron, to be attuned to the Pyrthae. We were executing the detainment protocol when you arrived."

Vusu glanced at the collapsed Shepherd. "He tried to disobey again," he said, his words more a statement than a question.

"Yes," the same Shepherd answered.

The Tribune sighed and walked around the Shepherds to stand next to me, glancing into Xaron's room as he passed. "I apologize, Airene. But I must believe them. Your friend Xaron is a warden." He shook his head. "I know this must be distressing to you."

Frustration and despair washed through me. "You can't take Xaron away. Whatever else he is, he's a Verifier under Archon Jaxas's protection."

"I'm afraid that is beside the point here," the Tribune said almost gently. "Wardens are not allowed outside the Acadium's influence, nor even their compound, besides the masters. This is the way it has to be. For the good of all."

"You don't understand," I said, desperation tinging my words. "I need Xaron for the task you set before me. Things are going on here, things I can't even begin to tell you about, that could affect all of us." My mind whirled, searching for the answer. "At least discuss it with Jaxas. Perhaps you can work out a compromise."

Vusu glanced toward Xaron's doorway for a long moment. "Perhaps," he said slowly. "he could stay here for a day or so."

Hope surged inside me; I didn't dare speak.

"It does not seem your friend would go willingly, as

matters stand," Vusu continued, "so it is small as far as concessions go. But I can promise you this much: no Shepherd or any person under Tribunal authority will seek to arrest Xaron for a day and a night."

It was a relief, if a small one. But even as I took Vusu at his word, a colder part of me wondered why he would grant us this favor. Even as Verifiers, who were we that he would bend the law for us? I didn't dare question him on it though. I couldn't afford to have him revoke the reprieve.

I bowed to the Tribune and turned back to the room. "Xaron, did you hear that?"

"Yes." His reply was terse. Evidently, he hadn't relaxed at the Tribune's words.

"Thank you." I bowed to Vusu again.

Vusu gave me a small smile. "I must keep Shepherds here to watch over him, but as I've said, they will not enter for at least a day. And you will know beforehand if they intend to."

He gave a small bow, then turned away. Not knowing what else to say, I stared at his retreating back down the hall, the clerk following once again on his heels.

PREPARED

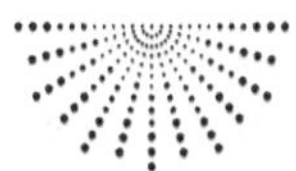

The underclass outnumber the honors. Composed of plebeians too poor to be considered citizens, they are miners, cooks, sailors, and more. The underclass are often the first to feel hardships of natural disasters like drought, for patricians keep their honors fed, while plebs must care for themselves.

- Oedija: A History; by Acadian Helene, Master Historian; 1167 SLP

Though Vusu had left, the Shepherds remained where they were, two standing and the third twitching on the ground. Turning my mind from one inscrutable mystery to another, I considered them. I'd never been in such close contact with Shepherds. Now, I saw the strangeness that people spoke of. They acted with inhuman rigidity, and seemed physically incapable of disobeying a command from their Tribune. And that was to say nothing of the way they spoke and stared with those empty eyes. It reminded me of Talan's theory, that Shepherds were yoked in much the same way that the Avvadin Imperium controlled their elite warriors, the Damask Esir — by using a pyr to forge a bond that compelled them to obedience.

That knowledge and what I'd just witnessed of their rigid loyalty were enough to renew my courage. I took a deep breath and started forward. The closest Shepherd immediately gave me a sharp look. "You should not enter," he said in his hoarse voice.

"But I will." I stepped around him, tense, but they let me pass through the doorway unimpeded.

As I entered the room, the sight of my friend almost brought laughter and tears at the same time. Xaron was clad in nothing but underwraps. His lithe muscles were still tensed with his hands slightly raised, no doubt ready at any moment to channel. His gaze was hard, but I could see the strain of maintaining his vigilance from the shiver that ran through his body.

I walked up slowly to him and placed my hands on his wrists, pushing his hands down. "You have to relax."

He resisted for a moment, his eyes never leaving the Shepherds in the doorway. "I can't," he said through clenched teeth. "I need to be ready." The shiver ran through him again. "Shepherds, Aire. They're actually here."

"I know," I said, guilt rising higher inside me. "But you need to stop channeling, Xaron. They can't disobey Vusu, and he gave his word that they won't enter until tomorrow."

Xaron held on for a moment longer, then sighed and let his arms fall. He didn't relax, however, until he slouched out of sight of the doorway. "Close the door. I don't want them staring at me with those dead eyes."

I obliged, turning back after the door was closed and locked.

"And, er… if you could grab my clothes…"

With a small smile, I handed him a white tunic with a vibrant yellow coat and tan trousers. It seemed Nikias had paid attention to Xaron's style as well as his measurements.

Looking away until he dressed, Xaron drew my attention back with a touch on the wrist. "What do I do, Aire?" he asked miserably. He glanced back at the window opposite of the door. "Try to escape while I might still have a chance?"

"They'll chase you down. Vusu's command won't protect you then." I shook my head. "We should at least wait until Vusu speaks with Jaxas. Perhaps something will come of it."

Xaron's expression was drawn, the doubt on his face a mirror to my own, yet I tried not to let it show. Perhaps all we could do now was think of other things and forget the things we couldn't change.

"Where is Nomusa?" I asked him.

He shrugged. "You think I know? I woke to those three banging on my door. Talk about a rude awakening."

"At least they knocked." I gave him a weak smile. "I suppose I'll have to go find her. And hunt down Jaxas as well. The sooner we get this sorted out, the better." I thought of a few other things we needed to sort out as well. With the Manifest gathering tonight, we couldn't afford any delays in our planning.

Xaron seemed to read my mind. "Go. I'll appreciate you talking to them, but don't worry on my account. You have plenty of other worries besides me."

"Of course I'm going to worry about you," I said, aghast. "Besides, you're only in this position because of me."

"I accepted that this might happen, remember? This isn't your fault. Stop trying to put all the responsibility on your shoulders, Airene. You can't control everything."

I smiled wanly. "But you know I still have to try." I pulled him into a sudden hug. He must have stolen a bath some-where in the past couple days, for his hair smelled faintly of olives. "Everything will be okay," I whispered, as much to myself as him.

"I know."

I broke the embrace and stepped away. His warm touch

lingered on my arms as he let go. I smiled and tried to fight back the sadness at leaving him there, the wolves howling at his door.

"I'll be back as soon as I can," I promised him.

"I'll be here. Unless I'm not." He gave me a rueful smile.

"You'd better be."

I turned and left, marching between the Shepherds without a sideways glance. Then, stopping by my room only to gather my sandals and a tie for my hair, I went off in search of an honor. Finding one outside of the dining hall, I convinced her to lead me to the Archon and followed her down the familiar path to the palace gardens. We headed to a copula that projected off the palace to hang over thin air. The Archon stood staring out over the sea, strong winds tousling his short, curly hair. At least my own messy tresses wouldn't look amiss.

Thanking the honor, I approached him. "Archon Jaxas."

"Airene. I've been waiting for you."

He gestured for me to come forward, and I approached cautiously to stand by his side. Perhaps it was the wind catching his voice, but he sounded strangely distant.

Jaxas continued to stare out over the sea in silence for a long moment. "Why did they come here?" he finally said.

It took me a second to understand whom he was referencing. "Our ancestors?"

He nodded absently. "Why leave instead of fight whatever threatened them? And the gods who were said to lead them — how could they so easily abandon their home?" He shook his head. "It makes me wonder. Are there some threats out there so great, so terrible, that nothing can stand before them?"

Perhaps it was the wind that drew my skin into gooseflesh. Or perhaps it was the memory of being chased by the giant beast from my dream, and the whisper finch telling me to flee. But superstition would gain us nothing now. "With all due respect, Archon, the threats that face us are not so grave as to call for that. We know more or less what they are. Now we must stand and fight."

"So you say." He finally looked at me, and I saw that his eyes were nearly as empty as the Shepherds'. "Yet how are we to fight with no army and no authority?"

Fear gripped me. I forced myself to ask the question, though I suspected I didn't want to hear the answer. "What did the Council say?"

His eyes fell to his hands, knuckles white from gripping the limestone banister. "As they said before. That the Manifest movement is unsustainable, and that it must soon buckle in on itself as its food and coin start to run dry. That raising the taxoi and attacking our own people would fan the flames, not dampen them, and might lead to a city-wide rebellion." His eyes slid over to meet mine. "And that you and your associates are to continue your investigations into the former Despot's death and present to the Council what you have discovered on the morrow."

My eyes narrowed as I studied the Archon. "What do they expect by then? That I'll give them a convenient suspect that they can present before the people and call the issue closed?"

"Not even that much. The Low Consuls much prefer keeping the truth of Myron Wreath's disappearance behind closed doors. All they want are reassurances that no further harm will come to the Despoina."

I shook my head in disgust. "And if I tell them the Manifest is behind it?"

"Then I am sure they will call you a liar and throw you out onto the streets, never to seek your services again. At best."

I considered the options before us. It hurt me to say the words, but I knew I had to. "Jaxas, I won't lie about this. There's far too much at stake for me to deceive the Council, no matter how much they delude themselves." I paused. "Your pardon, Archon. I did not mean to speak so harshly."

"You did," Jaxas observed drily, "as I mean to agree with you. And as you mean to help in any way you can, so do I seek to help Oedija."

I didn't mention the limits of his power. As the Archon, he was the representative for the Despoina in the Conclave. But the Laurel Palace had far less power than the Council. He could not call armies, could not command the city guard, and had no control over the Tribunal or Shepherds. All he had was influence, the limited resources of the Wreaths, and the laurel guards. Not nearly enough to dismantle the Manifest, much less deal with the Imperium.

I wanted to thank him, but all I could do was look away. I felt nearly as sick to my stomach as when I'd entered the Despot's quarters. "What do we do?"

His voice was surer than mine. "Only what we can."

The same thing I'd told Xaron, I noticed. It brought me back to another urgent matter. "Jaxas, have you spoken with Vusu? Something has happened."

He blinked at the abrupt change in topic. "Yes. We just met."

I turned to face the Archon fully. "And?"

He drew in a slow breath. "Verifier Airene, I cannot countermand the mission of the Shepherds, nor will I. I am sure your friend Xaron is not a criminal, nor a danger to our nation. But that doesn't change that he's a warden." He hesitated, then amended, "A feral warden. To make an exception for him would be to throw away a hundred years of institutions that protect against Tyrant Wardens rising again."

My heart pounded hard. "How long does he have before they take him?" I asked quietly.

"The day and night Vusu promised. Beyond that..." Jaxas shook his head. "I'm sorry. There's nothing more I can do."

A dozen arguments sprang to mind. I grasped at the least

offensive of them. "Then don't let them kill him. Let him become an Acadian."

Jaxas shook his head again. "He's far too old to be introduced there, and if I read him correctly, far too willful. He would never submit to a cage, however gilded."

He had only met Xaron a couple of times, but he'd noted his disposition accurately. I gritted my teeth, the other arguments falling to pieces before me. No matter how sympathetic he might be, Jaxas wasn't going to budge. Xaron and I would have to make other arrangements.

"I know he's your friend, Airene," he said softly. "But there is nothing you can do for him now."

I didn't want to speak of it anymore. "Then let us do what we can. What do you intend to do about the Manifest gathering tonight?"

Jaxas considered me again for a long moment. "What I believe you intended to do no matter what I instructed. I will send you and Verifier Nomusa to be my eyes and ears there and report back what occurs."

Reconnaissance. Perilous forces were moving within and against our city, and all our leaders intended to do was watch and listen. I tried to push down my anger. Not only would it ill serve me, but I knew it was misdirected. Jaxas acted as much as he believed himself able. I could hardly expect others to be as rash as myself. The knowledge did little to lessen my frustration.

I gave a perfunctory bow. "Then we will make ready to leave this night. Where may I find your steward? I have requests to make of him."

Jaxas's eyes narrowed, but if he was suspicious of my capitulation, he didn't voice it. "At this time of day, he will likely be in the larders, scribbling in his ledger. But I should give you one last detail for your mission tonight. Another will go with you, someone who I think will be useful for navigating the Seeker compound. He will meet you in the atrium at the seventh turn of the evening."

I wondered who it was, but only nodded. Jaxas didn't seem willing to tell me, and I wasn't going to beg. "If I have your leave?" I requested stiffly.

The Archon sighed. "You may go."

I turned and walked away.

"And Verifier Airene?"

Reluctantly, I turned back. "Yes?"

His eyes bored into me. "Remember: only do what you can, and no more. I would not lose an asset so newly gained."

I clenched my jaw so hard my teeth hurt. All I could manage was a sharp nod before I left the gardens.

I FOUND Nikias in the larders and requested a tunic and trousers from him, despite my earlier resolution to buy them myself. At this point, I wasn't even sure if I'd be allowed to leave the palace without permission, and with all I had to do, I didn't want to waste time trying. Nikias ungraciously complied and said the clothes would be found and brought to my room before I departed that evening, evidently having foreknowledge of our trip that night. I thanked him and left.

Despite worry gnawing away my own appetite, I knew Xaron would be starving. It was the least I could do to bring him food. Visiting the kitchens, I soon bore a platter of egg tarts, flatbread, spiced meats, and fruit to his room. The Shepherds were still standing before the door when I arrived, including the one who had earlier collapsed. I faintly made out Nomusa's voice from within. My heart in my throat, I maneuvered my way around the immovable Shepherds to open the door.

My friends spun around at my entrance, tensing until

they recognized me. That didn't lighten their expressions, however.

"Where have you been?" Nomusa demanded. Her robes today were a deep turquoise with a low dip in her neckline. As before, silver jewelry glinted across her body.

"Doing what I can," I retorted, carrying the platter over to the bedside table and setting it down. "Which is apparently little more than an honor."

Xaron sat on the bed and reached over, his movements sharp and nervous. "At the moment, that's the best I can hope for," he said morosely.

I took a tart and studied my friend as I chewed. His mood had only worsened in my absence. What I had to tell him wasn't going to make him feel any better.

I sucked in a breath and dove into my conversation with Jaxas and our excursion that night. As predicted, Xaron's mood turned as black as the Lighted Sea in a storm.

"So you'll leave me here," he said flatly. "Alone."

"We don't have a choice," I replied in a low voice. I remembered how keen Eltris's hearing was and worried that the Shepherds' might be as sharp through some trick of channeling. "We have to get you help, Xaron. Finding Talan is our only chance."

Xaron snorted and bit savagely into a skewer of meat. "As if that will help," he muttered.

Ignoring him, I looked at Nomusa. "Do you at least agree?"

She considered for a moment. "Yes. We have to do what is expected of us, and we have to get you help. Airene and I won't be of any use here even if they do come."

"They won't until we return. Jaxas and Vusu both assured me." Still, I couldn't help but fear it was all a ruse. But even if it was, I saw little else that we could do. Xaron couldn't stay on guard all night.

He turned his head aside. "Then go. I'll be fine."

"But if they do come," I continued. "You still have your lodestone, don't you?"

"Of course."

"Give us a signal. Alright?"

Xaron nodded, though he didn't meet my eyes. I turned to the door, yet I couldn't help glancing back at Xaron, who watched us with hooded eyes from the bed. I couldn't find the right words to say, so I gave him an uncertain smile before leaving him in the room that had become his cell.

THE GATHERING

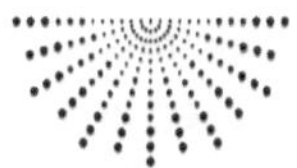

Next are the citizens of Oedija, those who own a plot of land of at least twenty-five cubits on each side, and have resided within Oedijan borders for two consecutive years, or have family members who have resided here for eleven consecutive seasons. These are often successful artisans, merchants, as well as many of our public servants. They often have little significant family wealth, but live comfortably, elect their Servants, and vote on measures of law brought before the public.

- Oedija: A History; by Acadian Helene, Master Historian; 1167 SLP

The seventh turn of the evening took its time in arriving. Even with the necessary preparations that Nomusa and I undertook, it felt as if the beads in the sand-glasses mounted in the palace halls fell ever slower, each turn lasting longer than the one before.

Finally, the seventh turn was announced with the long tolling of the bells. Both Nomusa and I were dressed in tunics and trousers, and she looked as common as I'd ever seen her. Knives were secreted against the small of our backs and lashed under our sleeves, though I knew they'd be small use against Seeker wardens. True to his word, Jaxas met us in the soaring chamber of the atrium soon after the toll. His usual line of honors trailed him, but it was the figure next to him that drew my attention. A thin, gangly boy with dark hair that hung in front of his eyes, he wore a frown like it was a shadow he couldn't shake.

"Verifiers Airene and Nomusa," the Archon said as they approached, "here is the accomplice I mentioned will be accompanying you. Meet the latest man to bear the name Hilarion."

I couldn't help but stare at the boy. He sulkily met my gaze, then turned his eyes aside.

"Archon," I said carefully, "what made you think his attendance is a good idea? He's still half a boy."

Jaxas acknowledged it with a dip of his head. "Of this, I am well aware. Yet you don't become the Despoina's Hilarion without having certain commendable qualities."

Studying the boy again, I thought it unlikely that those extended beyond his attunement to the Pyrthae. "Which is why he is by her side now, I suppose."

"Ah…" The Archon's eyes shifted. "She has been a bit… wary since her Ascension. But truly, I was not sure you had devised a reason for your attendance of the gathering. Hilarion provides the perfect excuse."

"A reason? Half of Brinecoast and Thys will be in attendance. It's true that guards checked my companions and me at the compound gate, but that was at night, and not during a gathering."

"Perhaps not. But consider: if the Manifest worship the idea of every man and woman channeling, and you bring them a warden, who do you think you'll get to talk to? Where might you gain access?"

I met Jaxas's gaze. We both knew what offering up

Hilarion might mean for the boy. Nomusa's hardening eyes told me she guessed as well.

The Archon turned. "The guards will be watching for your return."

With that, he left, his entourage following after, leaving the morose boy alone with Nomusa and me. I addressed him. "Did he even ask if you wanted to come?"

I didn't expect him to answer, but Hilarion looked up sharply through his bangs. "That's the joke no one seems to get," he said darkly. "No one ever asks."

I exchanged a glance with Nomusa. Our long walk promised to be longer still.

As PREDICTED, the journey to deme Thys was not wholly enjoyable. The events of the past span and my role in them weighed on me, and my Verifier medallion felt heavier with each step. It did not make it any easier that I was sore and tired as well. Yet I had to carry on — for Linos's sake, and Xaron's. Deep depths of the 'Thae, I had to go on for the polis itself now, as strange a thought as that was.

I led my small party to deme Bazaar. When he realized we weren't headed straight for the gate outside the city, Hilarion stopped. "Where are we going?"

"I'm thirsty," I lied. "We're visiting a favorite tavern of ours."

The boy scowled. "Fine," he muttered, following again. "As usual, no one values my time."

I turned away from him to hide my eye roll, and Nomusa smiled briefly. Neither expression went unnoticed, for when I glanced back at him, Hilarion's frown had deepened.

The tavern was far from my favorite, but I still felt easier as the Ignorant Intellectual came into sight. If anyone could help with the problems facing us, it was Talan.

"Wait out here," I instructed the boy. "You're too young for spirits."

He crossed his arms and leaned against the wall, heedless of the grime that dripped down it. As Nomusa and I entered, I wondered if he wouldn't just run away. What bound any Hilarion to stay loyal? This boy didn't have the dead look of the Shepherds. Strange that a jester should have more freedom than his enforcers.

The Intellectual was fuller and noisier than I'd seen it before, though the clientele was the same shady stock as usual. I slipped between two men to get to the bar, which was crowded with men calling for drinks. "Watch it," one of them snapped at us. A sharp look from Nomusa made him scowl and turn away. I tried flagging down the barkeep unsuccessfully for a few minutes until I finally reached over and tugged at his sleeve. The normally mild-mannered man looked around with irritation, though when he recognized me, some measure of it faded.

"Ah, you," he said, his eyes flitting to either side.

"Yes. I'll have my usual, please."

He stared at me for a long moment, ignoring all the other men shouting for his attention. I wondered if he hadn't heard me and was about to repeat myself when he responded. "I'm afraid we're out. Come back some other time."

I watched him as he turned to help others, uncomprehending. "A chalice!" I shouted stubbornly after him. "You know what it's filled with!"

He turned back with fire in his eyes. "I told you, we're out!" He resolutely ignored me as he began filling his patrons' drinks.

I knew a hopeless cause when I saw one. Pushing away from the bar, Nomusa and I forced our way back out of the tavern. Her eyes were full of questions, but Hilarion turned toward us as we exited. So I shook my head, mouthing to her, *Later.*

As we headed for the gate, I worked through what Talan's absence meant. Either he was unavailable as he'd never been before, or the barkeep no longer worked for him. Neither scenario boded well. I knew Talan could take care of himself, but he wasn't the most cautious of men. And when dealing with the Manifest, I worried he'd bitten off more than he could chew, especially after he'd killed their wardens and guards.

On the other hand, his meddling might have finally gotten him kicked out of the Underguild. Or his network could be eroding, just as mine seemed to be amid all these sudden changes. Even with a Guildmaster as his advocate, he was not insulated from punishment. Particularly if the Underguild was aligned with the Manifest.

I shook my head. Uncertainty haunted me at every turn. I didn't know how I would tell him of Xaron's plight. With no other choice, I carried on, hoping something would come to me, and soon.

We reached the Sandglass gate where a swell of people waited to exit the inner city. Pulled from my thoughts, I stared around in mute amazement. I had known the Manifest movement was large, but I hadn't realized it extended to this many people outside of the compound.

"*Faresh*," Nomusa swore under her breath.

I glanced at her. "At least we won't need an excuse."

Hilarion scowled. "Then I'll return to the palace."

"No," I replied sharply. "The Archon sent you with us. Stay close by."

He shot me a black look, but he stayed with us as we wove through the crowd toward the gate.

It took well over a half a turn before the city guard waved us through. He and his comrades looked harried and irritable and didn't bother examining anyone passing by. Such laxness made me feel uneasy, even if it aided us for the moment.

Once through, I clung to Nomusa and Hilarion as

Nomusa forged a path through the crowd. It was only when we broke free of the reek of the masses that I could properly breathe again. "I thought there were public baths for a reason," I muttered.

"You're one to talk," Nomusa said snidely.

I considered her for a moment. A chilliness lingered between us. The trust we had forged over nearly a decade would be long in mending. I repressed a sigh and touched her arm. "Come. Whatever performance the Visage and the Dishonored have planned will probably start soon."

Nomusa nodded, then led us back into the stream of people winding toward the Manifest compound.

As we walked, I found that my errant comment had resurfaced past thoughts. Who *were* the Visage and the Dishonored? I'd given little thought to the identity of the Visage other than my suspicions of Kyros Brighteyed, and none to the Dishonored. For Kyros, it would seem a tricky balance to strike. Surely someone would have noted his crossing into the compound. Or did he have another way of reaching the Claw? Perhaps a boat lay ready to take him across Lake Thys so that his comings and goings were kept secret. Or perhaps he had some mystical means of travel.

Then there was his second-in-command, the Dishonored. I wondered what that title was supposed to mean, and why I'd had so little report of him. Wisp, the keenest of my contacts, would likely be able to tell me something, but it had been a long time since I'd been able to track her down. Perhaps it was best that I saw for myself.

The crowds were thick and crushing around us. I tried not to breathe too deeply, the air ripe with the unwashed bodies of the underclass. We twisted, tumbled, and swirled among the people like kelp in a turbulent wave. I clung to Nomusa and Hilarion, holding fast despite the boy's flinch at my touch.

It felt like an eternity before the river of people flowed

through the compound, then down the hillside to the Claw, easing and spreading out. The reprieve didn't last long, as we were funneled back together at the entrance to the Wyvern's Claw.

I was somewhat distracted from my misery as the amphitheater rose around us. It had been an impressive building at night, but by the illumination of evening light, I balked at its immensity. Tier upon tier ascended above us, with row stacked on row of benches in each section. I strained to make out the people in the upper tiers. How many could those stands seat? Thirty thousand? Forty? Fifty? Easily a quarter of the population of Oedija could fit in the wooden bleachers without rubbing elbows, to mention nothing of the amphitheater floor where my companions and I stood. It defied comprehension.

But why were all these people here? No doubt for some, idle curiosity was reason enough, to see a spectacle outside their usual routine. But for the others — did they, like Linos, harbor childish dreams of claiming a warden's power? But no; I had but to look around me to see the truth. Thin children holding to their famished mothers. Men with bent backs and hollow cheeks. Famine gnawed at the polis, and those people living in the peripheries were the first to feel it. Loyalty had been bought with simple promises. *Food. Shelter. Certainty.* These were what the common people strived for, as they had not the means to strive for anything more. And these were the very things that the Conclave had failed to provide.

I found myself staring up at the sky as it drained to a bruised blue. Above us, the eleven spires of the Claw curved overhead, leaning over to almost touch each other in the center, like the long, sharp nails of a leviathan trying to scratch free a piece of the sky. The Manifest had taken a dragon for its sigil, but it seemed a swarm of locusts would have been more suitable. I did not blame those who had joined as Seekers; I could not claim to know the right or wrong of any of their situations.

But I knew that, unchecked, their hunger would consume the polis, and all of us with it.

I held onto Nomusa and Hilarion as we continued forward. Midway through, the crush of the crowd stopped moving forward and pushed in even tighter around us. I fought for room to breathe, earning scowls and halfhearted curses. I reluctantly settled into my discomfort. This didn't promise to be a pleasant event.

Hilarion yanked his wrist away and rubbed it while Nomusa pulled me close. She spoke loudly, but I could still barely hear her over the clamor of crying children and loud talking. "What happened at the Intellectual?" she asked.

I explained as best as I could. "I don't know what else to do," I concluded.

Nomusa's brow drew down in consideration, but she made no reply.

The people around us began looking toward the stage, lively chatter giving way to muttering and staring. I could barely see the stage between the heads of the people in front of me. The platform beyond was unremarkable, though the two huge braziers that were mounted on either side and threw orange, flickering light over the stage floor filled me with nervous apprehension. Only then did I remember how precarious our safety was. One tipped torch, and the whole place would go up in flames. It did little to settle my already tattered nerves.

A roar cascaded from the stage, deafening and intoxicating. I gave a small cheer of my own to not look out of place, then cringed as lights flashed from hands around me. What caused them, I couldn't see.

The racket redoubled, and I strained to look past the seething mass of bodies to the stage. The dais erupted in light, and the crowd became deathly quiet. An ethereal light unmatched by a three-moon night emanated from the platform. A silhouetted figure stepped to the front.

"Brothers!" a pleasant baritone boomed over our heads, Pyrthaen-magnified. My pulse quickened. A warden, unbound by law, stood before us all and openly used their power.

"Sisters!" the man continued to shout. "Sons and daughters! Fathers, mothers, friends, and neighbors! We gather here not as individuals, but as a family! All of us are Seekers of the One who graces the sky above us!"

Cheering clapped like two bricks over my temples. A woman near me screamed and leaped up and down, eyes rolling into the back of her head like she were possessed. I felt my presence of mind slipping away in the crowd's emotions like a leaf in a swollen river.

"There are those who would not have us here," the man continued. "Those who would not see the common people become powerful. Well, what do we have to say to that?"

Jeers passed over like a storm, leaving me sweating with their dissatisfaction.

"No, they cannot keep us down. For we have the One's power inside of us, from the oldest gaffer to the youngest child. And it is emerging, isn't it? Soon, we will show them all who we truly are!"

When the cheers died down, the honey-voiced man continued. "Daemon-lovers, they call us. Worshippers of false gods. Cultists. But we know who we are. We are Seekers. We are the Manifest, wardens on the verge of expression. Soon, we will have our power. And with it, we will take back what is ours by right."

Silence stole over the amphitheater, tens of thousands of people hanging onto his every word. No Wreath had ever held such rapt attention. Between the heads of the people, I finally caught a glimpse of the speaker, a man swathed in robes of black. As the Visage was supposed to wear robes of white, this had to be the Dishonored. I did not see anyone holding a hand to his throat. Did that mean he was a warden himself?

"Now, we will hear from the man who led us here," the Dishonored continued. "The man who will lead us onward to our grand destiny. The man… but he is more than a man. He is half a god himself." The man fell to his knees and out of sight, yet his echoing whisper could still be heard. "The Visage of the Wyvern."

The crowd shifted, slender trees bending to a strong gust. They wondered if they, too, should kneel like the Dishonored. I clenched my teeth and hoped my pride wouldn't have to endure that.

But everyone stayed on their feet as a man in a white peplos slowly entered the stage. The brightness of his robes sharply contrasted with his skin, dark and rich like mossy earth. His face was covered with a red mask, no doubt the dragon mask I'd glimpsed in the war room.

The crowd leaned forward as he slowly stopped in the center of the stage. As he neared, the dark-robed prophet rose and stepped aside. We watched in silence as the masked man stood there, unmoving except for his head, swiveling to take us in.

Then came the fire.

THE VISAGE OF THE WYVERN

Last are the patricians, the wealthy nobility that has persisted largely since the Lighted Passage landed on Oedijan shores. Though their political influence has waned in recent years with the rise of demotism, patricians are still the backers of most commercial ventures within the realm and own the vast majority of its wealth. On them falls the responsibility of raising the taxoi in times of war as well as leading and arming their militias against the enemy. With their significant social and commercial influence, patricians have often occupied much more than half of the seats on the Conclave, and almost all of the Demos Council.

- Oedija: A History; by Acadian Helene, Master Historian; 1167 SLP

The flames rose from the man in a spire, thin as a needle, then spun out in a thousand graceful ribbons, like ripples from a stone in a still pool. Cries of fear and panic rose as it spread closer to the crowd. I stared at the blazing cyclone, beautiful as the three full moons over a red sunset, mesmerizing as the green radiant winds painted across a midnight sky.

Then came the inferno.

Comets split off from the tornado and landed with splashes of flames on the wooden supports. The heat that washed over us was as intense as Maesos's furnace. Panic set in. People around us jostled and pushed back toward the entrance. I didn't resist the flow, but fought to keep myself from being flattened, losing Nomusa and Hilarion as the crowd swept me up. But it wasn't enough. The entrance was too small and the people too many. The flames were speeding everywhere, too fast to escape. The meaninglessness of it all, the cacophony of terror, made me want to collapse in despairing laughter.

Then came the storm.

It crashed around us like a thousand cymbals, booming like ten thousand drums. It screamed like war itself. The sky split as if it were made of porcelain. Quick as blinking, bolts of lightning pounded the ground outside the amphitheater. I ducked down with the rest, cowering, waiting for the next one to fall on my head.

"Am I so callous as this?" called a voice different from the first, a voice used to the reins of command. Somehow, it seemed familiar. "Would I kill you as frivolously as your Conclave would? As your Despoina would? As your Strate-chons would?"

I risked a glance up just in time. All at once, the flames disappeared, falling away like torn strips of cloth, then dissipating into thin air. The intense heat died at once, and the cool night air crept back in. As the crowd stilled to look around in wonder, I stared with equal measures of awe and terror at the man on the stage. "Who are you?" I whispered.

"The Dragon!" shouted someone nearby. "The Dragon has come to save us!" Others took up the cry, passing it along until the amphitheater was echoing with the chant.

The Dragon. It was just another word for wyvern, yet my thoughts caught on it.

"No!" the masked man shouted, quieting the chant. "I am not the Dragon. I am he who comes before, who will usher in a new age. I am not the Dragon — *we* are the Dragon! We of the Manifest, deep in our cores, each have this power inside us! And what must you do?"

Confusion took over. The shouted answers made me laugh again. What could we do? Such power was impossible. No man should have magic like that at their fingertips. No Tyrant Warden had, nor any wardens before them. Not since the days of gods and pyr living among us had such strength existed. Nothing we did mattered; we were ants before this daemon-wrought man.

Yet even as I cowered at his power, I raged within at what he had brought to my city. A god's power he might wield, but he was still a man, with all a man's failings and flaws. Impossible as it seemed to match his might, I had to hope that this warden was fallible. *Somehow.* A smile twisted onto my face, a sliver of bitter humor growing inside me. Ridiculous to think anyone could overcome him after the display he'd just put on.

"You must rule yourselves!" the Visage finally answered his own question. "Follow me, and I will show you how. This night marks the first that we take back this city. This night, the men and women who call themselves Low Consuls and Servants of the people will tremble, for the true citizens of Oedija rise!"

The Visage raised his arms, and the Claw lit as bright as the sun. "This night," he shouted, "each one of you will begin to become gods!"

I grinned mockingly as the crowd's cheers reached a zenith. It felt like the smile worn by a skull.

Amid the fading light, the leader of the Manifest motioned for silence. "But I do not make promises without proof. You believe without seeing. Yet how much stronger will you believe when you see one of our own has succeeded in harnessing his power?"

"Show him!" some called from the crowd. "Let us see Vessel!"

"Yes," the Visage said, gratification plain in his voice. "Yes, you know him. Some of you have seen him before. But for the rest of you..." The man in white robes extended his arm to the side. "Vessel! Attend me!"

As a slim figure in gray robes walked onto the stage, my rigid grin slid away. I couldn't see much at this distance, little more than a blond shock of hair atop an adolescent's head. But I still felt as if I'd taken a blow to the gut.

The Visage clasped the boy's shoulder as he came near. The boy didn't react, staring out over the Claw.

"This is Vessel," the Manifest leader declared. "The first of you to receive the One's grace. Vessel, show us your gift."

The boy raised a hand. From it, a plume of fire erupted and shot halfway across the amphitheater. But I wasn't watching the display. I couldn't tear my eyes away from the boy, from the fear that held my heart in a deathly grip.

The boy continued to channel radiance until the Visage said in a carrying whisper, "That is enough, Vessel." The boy obeyed immediately, cutting off the stream of flames and letting his hand fall back to his side. He was as rigidly obedient as a Shepherd. Hollow. Empty. Just as a proper vessel should be.

"You see?" the Visage said to us. "If this boy can become a warden, then any of us can. All you must do is submit yourself to the One. Submit, Seekers, and the One will work wonders through you."

The sound rose, bit by bit, as each took up the chant. First a tide, then a wave, then a tsunami flowing inexorably forward. "Dragon!" they called. "Dragon! Dragon!"

The Visage stood calmly, accepting it all, as the Dishonored joined him at his side. But I did not look at either of them. I could not peel my eyes away from the boy who stood with them. I could not help but fear that despite all my efforts, I was too late.

Too late to save my brother. Too late to save Linos.

But I didn't know for sure. And though doubt was a poor replacement for hope, I clung to it as the world reeled and tumbled around me.

I DIDN'T LOOK AWAY from the stage until the Visage, the Dishonored, and Vessel had retreated into the eaves. Only then did I wade through the crowd to find a clear place outside the amphitheater's entrance. There I waited, stewing in my tumultuous thoughts, until I saw Nomusa dragging Hilarion in her wake. I waved and they made their way toward me.

For a few moments, we were silent as the hum of excited conversation emanated from the crowd flowing past us. Hilarion looked sulkily between us. "Can't I go back to the palace now?"

"No," I answered without looking at him. A glance at Nomusa showed my own fears reflected in her eyes. I hoped it wouldn't hold her back from what I'd resolved to do.

I motioned my two accomplices near. "Once the crowds thin out, we'll approach one of the Seeker guards."

"Why?" Hilarion asked, suspicious.

The Archon and I had shared an understanding. No doubt Jaxas Wreath had hid his intentions from the boy. "There's no time to explain," I said, bridling my impatience. "The Archon instructed you to do as I say."

"He didn't tell me to obey you," Hilarion argued. "He said to follow you here. I did that. Now it's time to go back to the palace."

He started to walk away, but Nomusa's hand snaked out

and seized his wrist. "I wouldn't do that," she warned in a low voice.

The boy's eyes flashed. "Maybe you forget what I am."

Nomusa didn't loosen her grip. "And maybe you forget what happens to a rebellious Hilarion. Or didn't you attend the last Ascension?"

The boy's expression spasmed, and my gut twisted. But I knew we couldn't relent.

"Fine," he muttered. He wrested his arm from Nomusa's grasp and rubbed at his wrist. "But no more grabbing."

I nodded. "Come on. It looks like our opportunity has arrived."

Weaving through the thinning crowd, I led them over to the nearest guard, a woman with a broad face and a dark braid draped over a shoulder like a snake. Summoning all the underclass charm I could, I said cheerily, "Eleven blessings to you! If you could spare a moment—?"

"Move along," the Seeker snapped, barely looking around.

"Now, no need to—"

Her glare silenced me. "If I chatted with every pleb passing through here, this gate would still be jammed," she said. "Now move along."

I struggled to keep my expression pleasant. "I have a cousin here, Hilly, and he wants to join you. He's a war— that is, you know…"

That caught her attention. "Hand," she said to the boy.

Hilarion stepped forward and gave her his hand. After a moment of intense concentration, the guard threw it aside and scowled. "You would try and trick me? The One has clearly passed over him. Leave, before I have a mind to do worse."

"What?" I grabbed both of Hilarion's hands and understood at once. Hilarion only had his shifts on one hand, and he'd given the ordinary one to the guard. "He thinks he's a clever boy," I said apologetically and held out his other hand. "It's this one that shows his talent."

The guard eyed me suspiciously, but accepted it again. After a moment, she nodded sharply. "You should hope he isn't so cheeky with the Visage. It won't end well for him. Come, Hilly. I will show you the way. Move!" Seizing Hilarion by the wrist, she started to drag him through the crowd. I could tell the boy was tired of being towed around, but he was smart enough to go along with it. Or trusting enough. The pair moved quickly, the crowd parting for them, while Nomusa and I struggled to follow.

As they climbed the stairs to the next tier, the guard noticed us and turned back with a snarl. "Not you two fools! Just him. You did your duty bringing your cousin here. Now he's in the care of the Visage."

I thought fast. "It'd be best if we came with him. Hilly was so nervous coming here — you saw how he acted out. I'd hate to see how he'd behave if we weren't there."

"Save your air, woman. I've heard it all before. Come, boy." The guard turned back up the stairs.

"Wait!" I took the stairs two at a time after them, ignoring the guard's glare. "Let me explain! He has a condition. Falls to the ground in spells, see. I know how to hold him down so he doesn't hurt himself."

"I can hold a bucking invalid as well as any," the guard said drily. "What were you planning to do once you'd brought him here? Stay with him?" The Seeker laughed. "You're not half as special as to warrant that."

The guard turned and tugged Hilarion after her again, eliciting a muttered protest from the boy. They strode down the wooden corridor along the long curve of the amphitheater, the same way I'd travelled with Talan and Xaron two nights before.

I glanced back at Nomusa and saw she hadn't followed. "Come on!" I hissed at her. "They'll get away!"

Nomusa looked aside. "I'm not coming."

"What? What are you talking about?"

"This is going to get you killed. Me as well, if I were going with it. I won't do it, and you shouldn't either."

I didn't have time for her excuses. The guard and Hilarion were already disappearing out of sight. "Fine," I snapped. "I'll go by myself."

I turned away and ran after the pair, trying to push away fear and frustration. Though I couldn't blame Nomusa for not jumping off the brink with me, the surprise still felt as sharp as betrayal.

When I caught up with the guard and Hilarion, an edge had crept into my voice. "Fine! I'll admit it!" I called to them. "I want to see him, the Visage. I want to know him, know his might—"

"Get in his bed?" The guard gave a harsh laugh. "Not the first." She rounded on me again, all humor faded. "Listen, lady. If you don't walk back the way you came, we're going to have to settle this another way."

"And how's that?" I dared to ask.

She scowled and glanced back at the Claw's entrance, no doubt looking for reinforcements. But a glimpse behind showed no one had noticed us below, nor was anyone close enough to hear her shout over the remaining crowd.

The Seeker realized it too. "Fine," she snapped. "If you don't turn back before we reach the door at the other end, you may not leave here alive."

She continued to drag Hilarion on, and I set off after them. My throat was so dry that it was hard to swallow, but we were too close for me to give in now. I had to continue. I had to see Linos.

We reached the door, and the Seeker turned. "This is your last warning."

I crossed my arms, trying to appear more certain than I felt. "Open it. I'm not going anywhere."

"On your head." The guard knocked sharply, then leaned into the door to whisper an entry phrase. I held my breath as we waited, pushing away my doubts. Too late to turn back now.

The door opened, and a woman answered it. She was young, and might have looked comely had she cared for her appearance.

The guard spoke softly to her for a moment before pulling Hilarion forward and gesturing back to me. The woman at the door turned to study me. "Who are you?" she asked.

"Jaxale of Hull," I lied.

The woman looked about to speak, then stiffened with her mouth open. She held rigid for so long even the Seeker guard grew uncomfortable. "Honor Seda?" the guard prompted her, eyes wary.

I stared at the woman in confusion. The guard named her an honor, yet her name and features seemed Avvadin, and she lacked the shaved head and tin spiral earrings. The dissonance did nothing to ease my nerves.

The woman finally stirred. "He wishes to see you," she muttered. She stepped aside from the door, holding it open. "If you'll come with me. The boy as well."

Gooseflesh spread over my skin. The greater part of me wished to turn and flee. But as the woman led Hilarion within, the boy cast me an uneasy glance, and I knew I could do nothing but follow.

"Watch your step," the supposed honor warned us from the darkness. "If the boy wishes to channel any light, he may."

Hilarion immediately complied, a bright glow emanating from his fingertips. The sparse surroundings were revealed under the faint illumination, little changed since my recent visit. My breath came quick and shallow as we entered the hallway, approaching the door at the end. From beneath the door, light escaped from the room beyond. My heart pounded harder.

The woman Seda set a hand to the handle. "My master will see you now."

She opened the door, spilling light into the dim corridor and blinding me. I blinked and followed mutely forward. My heart threatened to escape my chest. My folly struck me in full force. But I couldn't turn back now.

The room bore scars from our battle with the Seeker wardens, wood splintered and blackened along the walls and floors, but the main elements were still intact. The map table stood with its red circles, the stage bore its wicker wood chair. But now, the chair was occupied by a man with dark skin in a white peplos. A red mask with the aspect of a dragon hung on the back of the chair. The man sat before the windows, back erect, eyes sharp and studying me. My breath hissed out as my eyes settled on him. The Visage of the Wyvern was unmasked.

And I knew him.

Recognition dulled my wits, and I could do nothing but stop in the doorway and stare at him. The Visage smiled sadly back, and I saw him as I'd known him before.

Tribune Vusumuzi.

"Please bring her closer, Seda," Vusu said with a motion. "Airene and I have much to discuss."

BEHIND THE MASK

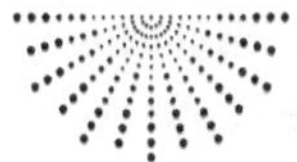

You cannot pen us in. You cannot bind us to your will. We have the power of gods at our fingertips. Try to cow us with your hounds — we will strike them down. And you along with them.

- Augur Naldeia, Daemon, at her trial shortly before her execution; 1065 SLP

I stared at Vusu. He sat straight-backed on his throne. Clad in his sleeveless white peplos, his white gloves were gone, his arms and hands left bare, his tatu visible. They were the familiar vibrant blue of Nomusa's, but they extended far beyond hers, all the way up to his shoulders. They also moved before my eyes, slithering like a mass of worms along his skin. The whole of his arms composed his shifts. Even having witnessed his displays before, it was only now that I fully grasped the extent of his power. And the extent to which I'd deceived myself.

I looked away from Vusu to the stranger to his right. A man swathed in dark robes — the Dishonored, I assumed. His name suddenly made sense as I took in the shaved head and spiral earrings of an honor glimmering beneath his hood. The Dishonored nodded slowly to me, and in his blue-green speckled eyes, I sensed familiarity, as if this was not the first time we had met, though he was a stranger to me.

I thought the room otherwise empty, until Vusu, his dark eyes still on me, made a beckoning gesture. "Vessel," he said. "There is someone here I'd like you to see."

An adolescent boy stepped out from behind the throne. Gray robes clung to his thin frame, but even with the unfamiliar dress, he had the same mop of blond hair, the same nose he shared with myself and our mother.

Linos.

Many changes had been wrought upon my brother. I had to cling to the doorframe as I observed them. His blue eyes, ordinarily alive and intelligent, were dull amid the spiderweb of lavender tatu. The inked lines were jagged and erratic, not straight-edged like the designs Seekers painted onto themselves. Jagged as Thero's had been, fourteen long years before.

"What have they done to you?" I whispered.

"This must be a shock," Vusu said mildly, drawing my attention back. "I apologize for the falsities I perpetuated. But sometimes lies are necessary for the truth to be unveiled."

I didn't look at him, but continued staring at my brother. "Linos," I said, voice trembling. "Linos, look at me."

"He won't respond to that name anymore. He is Vessel now." Vusu glanced at my brother. "Vessel, tell your sister what you are."

"I am Vessel, empty in preparation for the One." His voice was monotone, eyes staring at the wall behind me.

The anger simmering beneath my fear caught fire. "Linos!" I snapped. "*Look at me!*"

Vusu held up a hand, and I flinched. I remembered the inferno that had come from those fingertips. "Calm yourself, Airene," he said softly.

His words only inflamed me further. "Why?" I demanded, glancing back at Linos, my heart rending a little more. "Why do this? He's a boy, just a boy."

Vusu shook his head. "You crave understanding in all things. To you, an unanswered question is as good as a festering wound. Soon enough, you will learn the necessity of it. But that will come in time. I have other work for you."

My emotions simmered so near the surface, I almost laughed. What else could I do when the world had become an absurdity? "You have work for me? You're too kind."

His eyes narrowed slightly, betraying his annoyance. It gave me more satisfaction than it should have. "You jest, but you will obey. Not willingly, I know all too well. Your loyalty to the realm is strong, if misguided." His gaze slid over to my brother. "But I believe your loyalty to your family is stronger, is it not?"

Rage almost stole words from me. I managed to choke out, "What do you want?"

His eyes studied me for a moment. "Consent. Fear. Admiration. The three pillars to a strong rule. The foundation for a necessary resistance. I need these, Airene, for the sake of all. And I will acquire them. With your aid."

"I don't understand."

"Then let me be clearer. You have been investigating Myron Wreath's disappearance. You need not wonder about that anymore. I am responsible."

The bald admission astonished me. For once, no further questions came to mind.

The false Tribune smiled thinly. "Perhaps you think you understand now. But full understanding will come later. What you must focus on now is the task I lay before you. While I am responsible for the Despot missing, you must interpret the evidence as if Asileia Wreath is responsible. I know there is ample evidence to frame her. Including her own admissions."

I listened, straining to understand what the man behind the Visage wanted, what he hoped to gain. But my anger burned away any reason still within me.

"Finally," Vusu continued, "you will leverage your burgeoning relationship with Archon Jaxas Wreath to summon a trial of the Despoina within the next span. There, you will present your case against Asileia Wreath and convince the High Tribune to convict her of Myron's death."

My fragmented thoughts struggled to put themselves together. "And if I refuse?"

Vusu shook his head, a sad smile on his face. "Of course you would ask. I knew you might need convincing to understand the depth of my convictions. Yet I wish you hadn't forced me to it." He looked slowly over at Linos. "Vessel. Demonstrate your obedience. Kill the boy."

My brother, still a moment before, whipped into motion. His hand shot out toward Hilarion, whom I'd nearly forgotten was present with us, and a plume of fire erupted from his fingertips. I stumbled back from the blast of heat and fell to the floor as the room filled with screams. Hilarion fell to the floor, writhing, as flames eagerly consumed his blackened body. I stared in horror, stomach churning.

"Do not toy with your prey, Vessel," Vusu said through the noise. "End it."

I looked back at my brother, his vacant eyes watching the tortured boy. "Linos," I said weakly.

Linos didn't make any sign he'd heard me. The air rippled around his fingertips, grew sharp, then whipped toward Hilarion with a crack. I closed my eyes and looked away, but I heard the snap of bone all the same. The screams ceased at once. But the hissing of hot fat, the stench of burned flesh, the crackle of the dying flames—

Next I knew, I was retching onto the floorboards. But it was the guilt washing over me that left me weak and shaking.

"Have I provided enough instruction?" Vusu asked quietly when I finished.

I wiped at my mouth with the back of my hand and, trembling, stood once more. "You're a monster," I whispered. Out of the corner of my eye, I saw Hilarion twisted on the floor, his neck like the bent stem of a trampled flower.

He gave a sudden laugh, a laugh full of sharp, broken glass. "You do not know monsters, Airene. My sins are many, but they pale to the evil of others." He shook his head. "But some must be sacrificed for any to survive."

I couldn't look at the boy's body. The Archon had been the one to bring him to me, but I had used him willingly. I had told him all would be fine. And now he was dead. "You do all this so you can rule. But a land of ashes is all that will remain."

Vusu smiled thinly. "Perhaps that is all I desire. But I would not presume to know what I want, Airene. False assumptions, as you should have learned, can draw people down dangerous paths."

I clenched my fists and stared at Vusu. The man had manipulated me at every turn. He had helped only to aid his own cause. He had taken Linos from me and turned his mind inside out. He had likely done the same to Thero all those long years ago, then killed him when he failed. Rage ran through me like wildfire. It was the only thing holding me upright, feeding me the strength that all my sorrow and misery and guilt threatened to leech away. I wanted to burn his carefully constructed plans to the ground.

"They won't flock to you," I said with forced calm. "Even if you discredit Despoina Asileia, Jaxas Wreath is next in line. He'll wear the Evergreen Wreath in her stead."

"Perhaps that would be true, but for one thing." His smile was paper thin. "They will not need to raise a new Despot. They will have their old one returned to them."

I remembered what I'd seen in the Despot's quarters. The

empty room. The open balcony doors. The guards who reported seeing nothing, only hearing a loud noise like thunder. For a man who could raise an inferno and call down lightning, kidnapping the ruler of Oedija must have been simple.

"You didn't kill him," I said slowly. "You took him to be your puppet ruler."

Vusu nodded. "Partly correct, at least. But that is enough for now. You have your task set before you. I expect I'll have your compliance." He smiled thinly. "I will be there in attendance myself to ensure you have done as I have instructed."

My stomach suddenly roiled again. Clutching a hand to my gut and grimacing, I glanced at Linos. "Accuse the Despoina and take her to trial. And if I do that, you will set Linos free?"

Vusu almost looked as if he pitied me. "I fear you misunderstand me on purpose. No, I will not set Vessel free. He is mine now." He leaned forward on his wicker throne. "If you succeed, Vessel won't burn your family and friends before you. Your mother, father, sister. Corin. Xaron. Nomusa." He smiled thinly. "I have already taken two of your brothers. Do not force me to take the rest of those you love."

As his words sank in, I found something growing inside me, a festering desire like nothing I'd felt before. I didn't just want to stop Vusu to save Linos and the others, or keep Oedija safe from him. I wanted to see him hurt. I wanted to see him lost to despair. I wanted to know what he treasured most in life and crush it before him. I yearned for it. I burned. It was a hunger burrowing its way into my heart and hollowing it.

For now, I contained it. I held it in. There was nowhere for it to go. Not yet.

But I could not hold back a despairing question. "Why do this to us? To Thero? To Linos? To me?"

"Why you and your kin? It is a mystery I am still piecing

together myself. Something grows in you, a seed..." He stared beyond me for a moment, as if remembering a distant memory. "We are all seeking to fill the holes riddling us. The lingering hungers that never fade." He shook his head. "The thirst I must slake will take a world, I imagine. But I must start somewhere."

Vusu looked away, sagging back against his wicker throne. His voice was suddenly weary. "I expect to see progress in the coming days. If she is not on trial within the span, I would not depend upon your loved ones' safety."

He flicked his finger again, and the Avvadin honor who had guided me in took me by the arm and led me back through the door. I looked back one last time at the people in that room. The Dishonored. Vusu. Linos.

"I'll save you," I whispered to my brother.

Even to my ears, the words rang false.

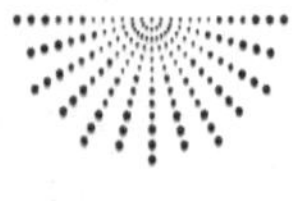

EAZAL

azal descended the last of the stairs, licked his cracked lips, then passed through the doorway. The windowless chamber was dim, lit only by smokeless torches, with the low ceiling lost in shadows. It evoked the familiar, oppressive feeling the Subjugated were supposed to feel. The bag in his sweaty hands threatened to slip and spill the heavy coins across the dark stone floor. He tightened his grip, stood up straighter, and walked to the attending scribe's desk.

The scribe looked up from his scrolls. As he was cross-eyed, Eazal could only assume he was looking at him. "Here for a loan?" he asked in a bored, expectant voice.

Eazal tried to speak, coughed, tried again. "The opposite, actually. I'm here to pay mine off."

The scribe stared at him, his wandering eyes trailing to the sides. "Pay it off?"

"Yes." Eazal lifted the sack of coins and rested it on the desk with a clinking of metal. "Here is my debt, plus the agreed-upon interest."

"Pay it off," the scribe muttered. "You know, you just might be the first."

"What is, ah, the process for doing so?"

"I'm not sure. If you'll wait one moment..." The scribe's gaze strayed to the bag, but with his eyes, it could have been an accident. Eazal suspected otherwise. With the silver in that bag, the scribe would be able to leave his thankless position for good. It had to be tempting, even for one of the Subjugated. Yet the man left it on the desk as he turned and swept through a curtain at the back of the room.

Eazal shifted nervously as he waited for the scribe to return. To keep his mind busy, he thought through his commerce. When to deliver his last shipment of carpets to Riverport. When the next shipment was coming in. Where the guards would come from, who had recommended them, how much he could trust them...

But no matter how he tried to focus, his thoughts, as always, strayed back to his family.

When he'd returned to Oedija after his two-year exile, he had hoped at least to come back to a wife, a daughter, and a home untouched by lost time. Of the three, only the home remained, and that barely, for it had been stripped bare, and the whores squatting there had turned it into a brothel.

They didn't leave you, he reminded himself, not for the first time. *You left them. Your negligence. Your guilt.*

He had tried to make things right. He'd gone to his connections, begged and pleaded for a second chance. All had turned him down — all except for one, who relented when he finally reminded her of their past affections for one another. Despite her own dire straits, she financed him one ill-fated trip. Eazal had sent the caravan to Avvad, seeking to purchase fine carpets that would have secured his position once more as a merchant of middling capacity, and perhaps even have attracted the eye of the master merchants in the Ten-Tiered Bazaar.

But he had, once again, failed. Unexpected storms had caused delays, and highwaymen, who had increased with the droughts now common throughout the Four Realms, had carried off what little hadn't been ruined. Eazal was left bereft and friendless once more, estranged even from his last friend, and without a prayer of a second chance.

He had thought of returning to the profession that had landed him in trouble in the first place, but quickly dismissed it. His days of brewing tinctures were over. After the things he'd been party to, he couldn't return to being an apothecary without wondering if he was disabling — or killing — those who drank his potions. To make no mention that it might tip off those better left unaware of his return to Oedija.

Though it was the last place he'd wished to return to, he'd turned to the temple for aid. To his surprise, he had heard whispers of a service unheard of in the Violent Father's halls before: moneylending. A shameful practice perhaps, but Eazal had long since been disillusioned to the faith, and found few qualms if they handed money out to dishonored men like himself. So he'd walked up to the desk, to a scribe like the one who had disappeared through the curtain, and taken out a loan. A sizable loan. A loan large enough to finance a second caravan, this one making the trip successfully, and catapulting him back into respectability.

But that hadn't brought his wife and daughter back.

In time, they will forgive, he told himself. *Lost Mother willing, they will forgive.* But even as he submitted the prayer, he knew it fell on deaf ears.

After the last of the money he'd left them two years ago had run out, both his wife and daughter had been forced to take desperate measures. His wife had moved in with a widower, a former partner of Eazal's. They had lived together as if they were married for nearly the entire time he'd been absent. Even so, Eazal held onto a sliver of hope that she was not forever lost to him. His wife could not marry another man, and she would ever be in uncertainty; the widower might tire of her and cast her aside for a younger, prettier woman if he so desired. If she returned to him, Eazal told himself he would forgive her. After all, hadn't he had his own dalliances in the past? She would see reason. Eventually.

His daughter was in a more precarious position. She had spoken her vows to a sailor, one who took Valem's mandate of dominance far too literally. Eazal's throat tightened to think of it. Before his exile, he might have killed the man for harming his daughter, consequences be damned. But somewhere along that long, lonely walk through the wilds of the lands, caution — or cowardice — had seeded itself in him. He had precious little he could call his own, but at least he had something once more. He would wait and hope that his daughter would forgive him and return home.

His thoughts were interrupted when a woman entered the chamber. He stared at her for a moment, her size catching his eye, as she rose well above him and had the stolid look of a laborer. Even more, her skin was the pale color of sea froth on a stony shore. An outlander, here in one of Valem's temples. When she returned his gaze and approached, he flushed and looked away, cursing his inquisitive eyes.

"I am looking for the clerk," the woman said to him, her voice not as deep nor loud as Eazal had expected, though it did have an outlander accent.

He gave her a polite nod. "And I am waiting for him to return. He's just gone back to see if the Kul is available."

The outlander was silent for a moment. "The priest?" she asked finally.

Eazal nodded, realizing too late that "Kul" wouldn't be a familiar term to those outside of the Subjugated. She wasn't here for faith, but the same reason he was: debts owed, or soon repaid, in his case. He wondered what had driven her to such madness.

He and the woman waited in awkward silence until the scribe finally emerged from the curtains. A second person followed him out. A thrill of fear went through Eazal as he stared at the Kul. The skin around the large priest's eyes was still bubbled and red, though it had been years since the calderas of the Father had been burned into his flesh. Once a priest was made, he could never leave Valem's service; just as the scars lent the priest authority over his fellow man, it lashed him to the Father's chains for life. Chains — Eazal could not be rid of them soon enough.

"Sakin Faldul — how pleasant to see you return," the priest said. His size was intimidating, though not as large as the outlander woman. His voice was warm and rich with the sly manner of a shopkeeper. "I had just been wondering after you."

His skin crawled at hearing the false name he'd given the temple. It had been a necessary lie, even if it still made him uneasy. "Me, my Kul?"

"Of course you, my good man! And why not you? When you have such marvelous... talents."

Eazal shifted his foot before he could think about it. "Valem leaves such crumbs as he can spare, my Kul. I possess no more talent than any other."

"Such modesty!" The Kul's eyes gleamed, then slid over to the outlander. "Ah, and another welcome face. I will speak to you after, if you will wait a moment."

The woman's voice creased into a deeper frown. "You promised safe passage for my sister. But I've not had word that she sails."

"Because she does not sail," the Kul said, his tone as patient as an adult speaking to a child. "When you made your request, you did not mention her reasons for fleeing, nor the complications. That was... ungracious of you."

The tall woman grew very still. "You will still bring her?" she asked uncertainly.

The priest smiled broadly. "If you agree to our revised terms, I'm sure we can come to an understanding. But first, I must speak with this man. All depends on his answer. Come, Sakin Faldul. We will discuss your situation in private."

Eazal had listened with a growing unease, and wondered what depended on him as he followed the Kul behind the curtains. He glanced back one last time at the woman and saw his discomfort reflected in her eyes before the curtains obscured her from view.

"This way." The priest led him down a narrow hallway until they reached a small door, then opened it and gestured him inside. As with all the rooms in the temple, it was dark and cramped, with an altar of stone and a small rug before it. Eazal hoped that his knees, wearing out with age, wouldn't be made to endure supplication before the altar.

The priest closed the door behind them. "You have kept the prayers, have you not, Sakin Faldul?"

Eazal carefully considered his next words. The priests of Valem had always shown an eerie sense of the truth, and he didn't want to lie any more than he had to. "I keep them as well as I can."

The priest's eyes gleamed. "Worshipping with the sun's movement might be difficult when you are constantly traveling, wouldn't it be? Have to arrive to your destinations on time! No matter — the effort at subjugation is what is important. An effort that I expect will continue."

"Of course, my Kul." Eazal cleared his throat and gathered his courage. "If I may ask, did your scribe mention my purpose in coming?"

"Yes, he did." The priest nodded at the bag Eazal still clutched in his hand. "Is this your remittance, then?"

Eazal offered the purse. Strangely, despite the wealth it held, he felt eager to be rid of it. "One hundred silver scions, in addition to an interest of ten silver. And, if you please, an additional donation of ten silver to the temple to convey my gratitude."

"Too kind of you." The priest took the bag and hefted it

experimentally. "It certainly has the feel of some hundred coins. I am happy to hear you have succeeded in your ventures."

"Thank you, my Kul." Every bone in his body begged to turn and walk away, but Eazal forced himself to stillness. Here in the temple, the Kul had to dismiss him before he could leave.

"However," the Kul said, "this payment is not what we are truly seeking. We are alone now, Sakin Faldul. It is time you are honest about the blessing Valem has given you."

He went rigid. He didn't dare contradict him, nor did he dare admit it. So he remained silent, staring at the priest as if in confusion.

The Kul smiled wider. "Show me your Branding, man. It is on your foot, is it not?"

His blood ran cold. There was little point in denying it. He wondered dully how the priest had found out.

"You wish me to show you now?" he asked, feigning dumbness in his reluctance. "To take off my boot and—?"

"Yes, all of it," the Kul said patiently. "I have it on good report, but I must see the truth for myself."

Slowly, Eazal leaned against the stone and pulled off his boot and sock, then held up his wrinkled foot awkwardly. The priest leaned down and peered closely at Eazal's toes. Finally, he nodded and straightened.

"It runs weakly in you, but I know Valem's signs when I see them. You have channeled before?"

"Yes. When the Brand first appeared."

"And it came to you when, exactly?"

He hesitated. He didn't want to speak of that night, and the other nights that had precipitated it. The despair that had swathed him in the darkness as he rocked back and forth in the bushes on the side of the road, with no comfort beyond a thin, ragged blanket and the occasional begged meal. He didn't want to speak of the curses he'd hurled at Valem for the misfortunes that had been heaped upon him. Nor did he wish to speak of that darkest moment, when he had stood at the edge of a cliff, his feet peeking out over a hundred-cubit drop.

When the blue-breasted bird had come to him.

How it had reached him out in the middle of nowhere, he could not comprehend, nor how it had spoken to him in a human voice. He had heard of whisper finches before, but he'd never visited houses wealthy enough to keep one. Nor did he understand the message that it had spoken to him in a boy's voice: *You are not alone, Eazal. I am here with you. I have not given up on you. I will not abandon you to yourself.* But despite the words, the bird had left soon after, leaving him more bitter than before. Someone — his wife, his daughter, a gloating competitor — must have sent the mocking message to deepen his misery. Yet how could they know where to find him? He himself had not known where he was.

His Branding had appeared that very same night. For the first time, Eazal had channeled. Just a bit, a small burst of sparks that sent his heart galloping and his boot smoking. But the flash of light had been enough for him to know. Valem had not left him to his fate. The Molten God still had uses for him.

Only he no longer knew if he believed it was Valem's hand at work. Eazal hadn't kept his prayers. He hadn't renewed his faith in the darkness of his travels, but lost it. If this was what happened to him when he kept faith, he had reasoned to himself, then what worse could happen if he broke it? Yet despite his renunciation, Valem's blessing remained. He wondered if Valem had ever had anything to do with it.

"Well?" the Kul prompted.

He'd been quiet for a long time. Sometimes that happened since his long sojourn; he lost track of the moment, like he often had during the countless turns of lonely walking.

"When I was on the road," Eazal answered, then added belatedly, "my Kul."

"You do not flaunt it. That is good. You could hardly be accused of misusing His gift." The priest smiled thinly. "But I have a better application for it. A matter for which you, Sakin Faldul, are particularly well suited."

Fear trickled down his back. He moistened his lips. "What is this task, my Kul?"

"There is a woman with whom you're intimately familiar." The priest paused. "The one who exiled you from the city."

Eazal tensed. He had given a false name. He had said nothing of the circumstances that had led to him leaving Oedija, nothing of the three people, including the young woman that the priest referred to, who had brought his life crumbling down.

"I do not know of whom you speak," he finally replied.

The priest eyed him, his expression searching. "Do not test me. Eazal."

Eazal clenched his teeth. He shouldn't have returned. He'd known he shouldn't have. Yet even for the safety of his family, he couldn't keep away from Oedija.

"Of course you remember," the priest continued. "I am sure you thought of little but your revenge during your years away."

Eazal didn't reply this time, not trusting himself to lie further, and not knowing how much the man knew.

The Kul frowned. "I thought you would appreciate this opportunity, Eazal." He shook his head. "Whether you do or not, I must lay this task at your feet. For it is you who must accomplish it."

Foreboding pressed down on him, but Eazal forced himself to nod and say, "Yes, my Kul."

The frown eased slightly. "Since she wronged you those many years ago, she has pried into others' affairs, including those of our faith. Yet she was useful in other capacities, airing the foul laundry of others and accusing them of crimes they likely did not commit, and so we left her alone. But now, she is at the end of her usefulness. It would be best if she did not pry into our affairs again." The priest eyed him. "Do I make myself clear, Sakin Eazal?"

His mouth was dry. His stomach tossed and turned. "Why me?" he finally asked.

"Why you? Because of your history. It must seem motivated by purposes beyond political ones, and must not be explicitly associated with the faith. After your long absence from any Valemish temple, you qualify in this capacity. And it must not be done by a hired man; that, too, would excite too many questions. No, Sakin Eazal. You are the perfect candidate to carry out this unfortunate deed."

But Eazal was already shaking his head. He could only play this part so long. Even for his family. "With all due respect and obedience, my Kul. My debt was one of monetary value. This debt I've paid in full." His courage almost failed him under the priest's cold stare, but he forced himself to continue. "This request... I do not want to fulfill it, nor do I feel I am obligated. I cannot help you."

There was silence for a long moment. Eazal bowed his head, wondering if his words had been too hard, if he could have refused in another way.

"You are one of the Subjugated, Sakin Eazal," the priest said in a low voice. "It does not matter what you want or what you think you are due. In your time of need, when all others abandoned you, the faith saved you. Do you forget that so quickly? You owe us your life. The time has come to surrender it."

"No." Anger smoldered inside him as Eazal raised his head to meet the Kul's gaze. "No. I won't murder an innocent woman."

"Innocent?" The priest snorted. "She is far from that. Or do you forget what she did?"

"I haven't forgotten."

"Then you remember how she murdered that woman in the alley, do you? Stabbed her through the neck, as I recall. Had you not run, who's to say she would not have done the same to you?"

His resolve was thinning. "She was protecting herself," he muttered. "She had no choice."

The priest smiled thinly. "No. Perhaps not. But neither do you. Or do you forget the penalty in this city for being what you are?"

The anger washed away in a moment, replaced by fear. Eazal finally saw the trap. Being Branded might mean being blessed by Valem. But he didn't doubt the Kul would turn him in to the Shepherds if it served his purposes.

Still, he shook his head. He was not a brave man. But even a coward could stiffen his spine. "I won't kill anyone."

The Kul's expression became ugly. "You disappoint me greatly. Then you leave me no choice." He leaned in close. "It is not just you who will suffer, Eazal. Or did you think we didn't know your wife and daughter?"

The words broke him. His head fell, eyes stinging with tears. He'd been weak and returned when he knew he should not have, hoping to be with his family. But now, he'd endangered them once more.

He couldn't fail them again.

He sighed. "How am I to do it?"

THE WHISPER FINCH

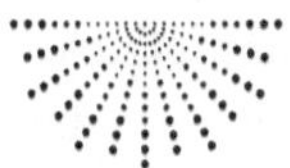

VERIFIER: So have my convictions been formed.
HIGH TRIBUNE: Your convictions. That the
leashing of Shepherds puts too much power in
the hands of the Tribunal. In my hands.
VERIFIER: Yours, High Tribune, and the Tribunes
acting as their handlers.
HIGH TRIBUNE: Thank you for your report, Veri-
fier. As always, you have been thorough in your
investigations. However, I must inform you that
your fears in this case are misguided. No one
wishes for the return of the Tyrant Wardens, my
Tribunes least of all, which the improper use of
the Shepherds could only facilitate.
VERIFIER: I am sure that is true now. But the truth
I hoped to convey is that an institution must be
solid from its foundation. This is a flaw that will
one day be exploited.
HIGH TRIBUNE: That is enough. I trust you will
find your own way out.

> *- Verifier Jaxale before High Tribune Krynollon;*
>   *1067 SLP*

I held on for Xaron.

The cracks were quickly spreading. As the honor Seda led me out of Vusu's war room and back into the amphitheater corridor, the pieces of myself threatened to fall apart. But I held together, clutching at my one remaining goal, the one atrocity I might be able to prevent.

What I could do to help Xaron, I had not the slightest clue. But I knew he was still alive. The lodestone in my pocket hadn't twitched that I'd felt. There was still hope. And as long as I had hope, I had to keep going.

Halfway down the amphitheater, Nomusa materialized from an alcove. "Airene," she said, relief and guilt warring in her eyes. "You made it out. You can't know how—"

She stopped, suddenly noticing the woman next to me. "Where's Linos? And Hilarion?"

Before I could answer, Seda bowed. "I leave you here," she murmured. "Do heed my master's words."

She turned and walked back the way we'd come.

Nomusa looked baffled as I resolutely stalked past her. "Airene, speak to me," she said, following. "What happened in there?"

Anger leaked through the fog of despair that had settled over me. "You would know if you had been there."

"You really expected that I would go in there with no idea of what dangers lay beyond?" she exclaimed, incredulous. "That I would risk my life on — what, a hunch? Where is Hilarion, Airene? Why did he not come out with you? And your brother—"

I rounded on her. "Vusu has him, Nomusa. He made Linos a warden, and he made him kill Hilarion. And now he's as empty as the Shepherds. There's no righting that." I swayed. The cracks inside me opened a little wider, and the hunger to make Vusu feel the pain I felt grew greater. But I was growing thin and tired. I had too little hope left. After what I'd seen him do, the power he'd wielded, the impossibility of harming him made the dream of vengeance impossible to sustain.

Nomusa put her hands on my shoulders. "Airene, look at me. You're not making any sense. What do you mean, he made Linos a warden? And that he killed..." She shook her head as if denying the words. "And what does Vusu have to do with this?"

I closed my eyes and drew in a shuddering breath. "Not here. We have to get out of the compound and back to Xaron. Vusu commands the Shepherds. He will break his word, if he hasn't already."

Nomusa's eyes widened. She seized me and dragged me toward the stairs. "No time to waste then."

The Seeker guards were surprised to see us descend from the Claw, but with the same laxness they'd shown the rest of the evening, told us not to linger at the next gathering and waved us through. We walked quickly up the hill and through the rest of the compound, not daring to go faster lest we attract the wrong sort of attention.

Once we were through the compound's gate, we ran. Even though defeat had exhausted me to the bone, somewhere in me I found the strength to press on. Nomusa easily kept pace beside me. We passed through deme Thys and had nearly reached the gate to the inner city when a shadowy figure emerged from an alley and made straight for us.

Nomusa cried out and leaped toward it, adopting one of her Ixolo stances, while I, panting and wild-eyed with confusion, reached for one of my hidden knives. But the shadow held up its hands, and a familiar voice said, "Wait! I've had enough violence tonight without fighting you two."

"Talan," I said with a relieved gasp. I released my knife and stumbled toward him. Before I knew what I was doing, I fell into him and wrapped my arms around his middle. The Guilder caught me and held me, surprising me by running a hand through my hair. His body was lithe and strong pressed against me, comforting in its surety.

"I've been watching for you," he murmured in my ear. "And I'm glad to see you safe. But your brother is not yet."

The momentary comfort dissipated. I pulled away. "No, he's not. I saw him. I stood in the same room as him."

Talan's eyebrows rose. "You did?"

"She has yet to explain it to me as well," Nomusa said drily.

I shook my head. "There's no time. Xaron is in trouble. Shepherds had him cornered in the Laurel Palace when we left. They may try seizing him at any moment now."

"You left him surrounded by Shepherds?"

I clenched my teeth. Both of them needed to know everything I did, yet there was no time, nor did I seem to have the wit capable of proper explanation. "Tribune Vusumuzi is the Visage," I said hurriedly. "He said before that they — the Shepherds, I mean — would wait until tomorrow morning to enter Xaron's room and arrest him. But now…"

The Guilder nodded, accepting the revelation with astonishing composure. "Then I'll go ahead and do what I can." He pressed my hand one last time, then turned away.

Though time pushed down hard on us, I stopped him. "How will I reach you again? The barkeep at the Intellectual wasn't compliant."

He paused, turning halfway back. "There is much I need to tell you as well. Guildmaster Hax is dead, as is Peralda." He shook his head. "The Underguild is tearing itself apart, and my network has suffered for it. I must expect that all of my hiding spots are compromised and that any of my contacts might turn on me."

I stared dumbly at Talan for a moment, the words

washing over me. "Two Guildmasters, dead tonight?" I shook my head. "Another time. How will I contact you?"

"I will seek you out at the palace as soon as I'm able. Now, fly back there, my Finch." He flashed me his half-smile, then turned and ran back into the dark alley from which he'd emerged. He wasn't headed toward the gate; I wondered if he meant to scale the fifty feet of the city wall, or if he had other ways around.

Nomusa seized my arm and pulled me toward the gate. "He's right — we need to hurry. Come on."

I nodded and set off at a jog.

The city guards, as disinterested as they had been before the gathering, waved us through without a second glance. We broke into a faster trot when we turned out of sight. The palace wasn't far, but the distance seemed to stretch on. I pressed on, clinging to the hope that we weren't too late. I seized onto a desperate idea. If we could convince Jaxas that Vusu was the Visage, he might be able to overrule the commands that the Shepherds had been given. I dismissed it as quickly as it occurred to me. I could do nothing that endangered my friends and family further than I already had. And undermining Vusu's authority and exposing his true alignments would be going against his will. Vusu was right; he had known where to strike his dagger.

Finally, we made it to the palace gates. Panting, stitches stabbing my sides, I held up my Verifier medallion as we approached the laurel guards standing watch. I hoped they weren't the same men who had tried kidnapping Xaron and me earlier.

"We're Verifiers for the Archon," I said between breaths. "We need to get through."

The guards exchanged looks. "We were told to watch out for you—" one of them began.

"Save it," I cut him off. "A pair of you fools tried taking us yesterday. It didn't work then and it won't now. So how about you just let us in and save everyone the trouble?"

Surprisingly, the guards relented, and soon, Nomusa and I were passing through the gates and ascending the many stairs to the glittering palace above. "You're becoming as ill-tempered as me," Nomusa observed, as breathless as I'd ever heard her.

I couldn't answer. Air hissed between my teeth, and I felt faint. I took the stairs as fast as my leaden legs would allow. The guards at the doors admitted us, but called after, "You're too late! The action's already over!"

My heart wrenched at their words, and we pressed on faster still.

We sprinted through the atrium, then down the hall toward our rooms. As we approached the doors, I saw that the Shepherds no longer stood watch in the hall. My hopes plummeted further as I saw Xaron's door hanging open. But it was only as I entered his room that my hopes were crushed.

The bed still smoked, little more now than charred wood and ashes. The other furniture was pressed against the walls in crumpled heaps. Not even the broken window, a potential sign of escape, could relieve the stupor that claimed me. Even if Xaron had temporarily fled, I knew it wouldn't last long.

I sank to my knees, hardly noticing the hardness of the marble floor. My mind went numb, feeling as if I fell away from myself.

"Airene!" I heard Nomusa cry, but it came from far away. I could not find it in me to respond.

I did not lapse into unconsciousness as I wished; that would have been too great a relief. Instead, I stared at the latest of my long list of failures. My fate was sealed. I was chained to the path Vusu had set before me and could do nothing but stumble along it.

"He didn't give me the signal." I felt in my pocket and

drew the lodestone out, staring at the smooth, gray stone. Maybe he *had* given the signal. Maybe I'd been running, or jostled in the crowd, and hadn't noticed the lodestone twitch.

As I moved the lodestone in my hand, I noticed movement in the corner of my eye. Startling, I gained my feet and stared at the ashy corner of the room. A suspicion made me feel sick to my stomach, and I twitched the lodestone again.

The movement came again from the ashes.

Approaching, I bent over and swept the debris aside. There, laying among the ruins, was Xaron's matching lodestone. I took it in my hand and rose, staring from one to another in my hands. Much good they'd done him in the end. Closing my hands on them, I turned and left the ruined room.

"Airene," Nomusa said again, following. "We have to find him. You saw the window. Maybe—"

"It's over." My voice was leaden. "You know what the Shepherds are capable of, and what Xaron is. He doesn't stand a chance."

I didn't wait for an answer, but continued to my room. Without another word, I shut myself within.

I DREAMED AGAIN of the whisper finch and the gargantuan lizard. *Flee*, the bird urged me. *He has his claws in you.* This time, I didn't run, but turned to face the huge creature looming out of the mist. I did not flinch as it reared and rushed forward, then closed its gaping mouth around me.

I was drenched in sweat when I awoke. The nightmare made all too much sense now. Even my dreaming mind had seen that the Visage of the Wyvern had been the threat looming over Oedija, and that I'd been dancing to his tune. I squeezed my eyes shut in the darkness of the palace room. Suddenly, the foreignness of the place closed in. I longed for something familiar, for my bed in Canopy, or even the room I had shared with my oldest sister, Sophene, as a child. Yet even if they had been available to me, I could not make myself stir and rise. I was drained, empty. Not even the hunger for revenge found sustenance.

"You are not alone, Airene."

Instincts of preservation found strength where nothing else could. I bolted upright, my hand clutching something. A knife, one of the two I'd hidden on myself earlier.

"Who's there?" I called out in a quavering voice. In the darkness, alleviated only by a sliver of light from a capped pot of pyrkin, I could not see the intruder.

"I am with you."

I spotted the speaker at the same time as I recognized the boy's voice. The whisper finch had perched on my window sill, shadowed but for the glowing patch of blue on its breast. Yet I sensed that its eyes were unerringly focused on me.

"You." I lowered the knife but didn't sheathe it. I felt dazed. "You spoke in my dreams."

"I have not given up on you," the whisper finch continued resolutely. "I will not abandon you to yourself."

I laughed hollowly and turned my head aside. But as I looked away, I glimpsed out of the corner of my eye something else standing with the bird. I looked back, blinking, but nothing was there. Yet I couldn't shake the feeling that I'd seen the faint outline of a boy cast in blue standing next to the bird.

"Who sent you? And how did you get in here?"

"It is too late to flee," the boy's voice said. "So we must turn and fight. Will you fight with me, Airene?"

A helpless rage sparked to life within me. "Why don't you answer my questions?" I demanded. "Who are you? How do you know my name and where to find me?"

I rose, leaving the knife on the bed. I would need both my hands to catch the bird. But the whisper finch sensed my intentions. As I approached, it took flight and settled on the top of the dressing cabinet on the opposite side of the room.

"Be ready, Airene," the bird said, continuing as if it had not been interrupted. "He has his claws in you. His change will come soon."

"Answer me!" Ridiculous as it was to demand this of a bird, I could not bear yet another mystery flitting beneath my nose.

"Be ready," the whisper finch warned me one last time. Then the blue patch disappeared from the top of the cabinet.

I advanced, straining to see where it had gone, but could not find it. Stalking over to the pot of pyrkin, I ripped off the cover and cast the light around me. Nothing. The bird had disappeared. If it had ever been there.

I sank onto my bed and leaned back on my hands when pain cut across one of them. Yelping, I looked down. The knife, unsheathed, had sliced into my palm. I stared down at the blood oozing from my hand, the yellow light of the pyrkin giving it a strange orange cast. It throbbed with the beat of my heart, trickling down my hand to drip onto my trousers.

The pain focused me. Ignoring my wound, I searched through the whisper finch's mysterious words. Perhaps it was right. I could not flee. Maybe it was time to turn and fight. Strange that I should find strength in the words of a bird sent by a stranger when all else had failed.

I picked up the knife and sheathed it, then settled back onto the bed, heedless of the blood I might spill on it. *Fight.* Chained to a path I might be, but I didn't have to go complacently. I would make Vusu struggle for every inch he took me down the road he'd planned for me. Even with my loved ones' lives at stake, I couldn't put aside this... duty, I supposed. Loyalty to Oedija, he'd called it. Maybe it was. With the foundations of our society cracking underneath us, to stand by and let it bury us all, my friends and family included, was something I could not allow myself to do.

I closed my eyes, but I did not sleep. Slowly, thoughts began to stir, unfold, bloom. The sandglass must have turned many times as I thought through and tempered my ideas into something that resembled a plan. Threads I had not considered suddenly wove into a net sturdy enough to cast. There were loose ends. There were weak lines. But it was a start. A way to begin to fight back.

When the glow of dawn crept in through the window, I rose and bound back my hair. I washed my face in the washbasin set out for me, then the blood that had crusted over my hand. I settled a chiton over the tunic and trousers I still wore from the night before. I painted the expected veneer over my hardened resolution.

I touched the Verifier medallion, still hanging from my neck, as it had since I'd received it from Vusu. He had given it to me so I would do his bidding. But I didn't think only of my gullibility. I remembered, too, the whisper finch in the night and the boy's words that had come from it. And I remembered the mission set long ago before the first Verifiers of Truth. They had been killed and ignored and finally cast aside. But they had not swayed from what they knew to be right.

I turned from the room and set out to spin my net.

TYING LOOSE ENDS

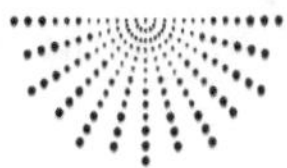

The isikhayha trees are singular, both in look and function. My time with them was brief, but poignant...

The sight of the trees was immediately enchanting. I was dazzled by the light emanating from rivulets of pyrkin down the isikhayha's sides in green and gold and tangerine. The trees were large and most oddly formed, for their trunks did not rise up in a single unit, but expanded into a web of smaller trunks that bound themselves into a great orb without any gaps between. I could not see if anything was bound inside the spheres. The trunks were lined with thorns both great and small. A man thrown against the tree would be impaled to his death, and indeed, I was informed that this was the punishment for some crimes, though no signs of gore lingered.

Above the sphere of trunks and thorns extends a canopy of branches, cascading up and out like a thick head of hair. The leaves are golden all year round and know no season, and are small and shaped like spearheads. The tops of their branches would likely reach through the oculus of the Conclave, were one to grow within it.

*- An Oedijan's Account of the Bali Ishakas; by Manenes of Gate,
an itinerant scholar; 1140 SLP*

I opened the shop's door and stepped inside without invitation. The glass pieces displayed on pedestals glowed in many hues, casting the dim room in eerie, shifting light. Closing the door behind me, I turned into the hall to the workshop, where I heard the forge burning, and the grunts of a man at work.

Maesos didn't notice me enter. He sat working his jacks around a wad of orange-hot glass that I could already tell would become a vase. His bald pate dripped with sweat from the thick heat of the room, making his remaining curly hair hang limp and slack. The work apron over his yellowed tunic and trousers was riddled with ashy holes. Glancing over, Maesos didn't startle, but smiled up at me as he continued working his jacks around the molten glass.

"Maesos," I said, staying by the door and out of the oppressive heat. "It's good to see you."

He stole another look. "You look like you've spent all night in a forge. What are you up to, little Finch?"

I drew a breath. "I need your help."

His brows furrowed as he continued his work. "It wouldn't be concerning our Low Counsel, would it? I've been working out something for her should the occasion arise. A beautiful, ornamental orb that may or may not explode in a few days." He flashed me a boyish grin.

I returned him a begrudging smile. "Feiyan's not the problem. Not at the moment." I pushed down thoughts of Xaron and pressed on. "My younger brother, Linos, got caught up with the Manifest. And I need your help to save him."

Maesos's smile faded, and he worked silently for many moments longer. Withdrawing the blowpipe, he placed it on a pair of forked stands, then moved over to another furnace to withdraw a blowpipe that had been sitting with one end in it. "You feel responsible," he finally said as he moved back to his seat.

"Of course I do."

"You're not." He darted a look at me, one bushy eyebrow cocked. "Every man and woman leads their own life and makes their own decisions. You can't be with your brother at all times, Airene, nor should you. You have to make a living and find a bit of happiness for yourself."

I turned my head aside and stared into the corner, where a sliver of darkness had escaped the glow of pyrkin. *Happiness*. How far that was from my mind now.

"I didn't come here to talk about that."

"Fine." He rose and replaced the second blowpipe in the furnace. "What do you need my help for then? I'm an old man who makes ornaments and vases for a living. Hardly the kind of man you'd ask to rescue a boy from a cult."

"There's something happening to the city, Maesos. Something that I don't have time to explain. But there's going to be a coup, and wardens from the Manifest are behind it." Giving voice to the suspicions I'd held these past few days made it sound crazy even to me.

"Coup? Wardens trying to take hold of the polis?" He raised the fully formed vase for a closer look. "Eidola above, I've lived too long."

"I think you can help."

"Can I?" He bellowed a laugh as he rose and moved toward the far corner of the room, where he opened the door to a dark clay lehr for cooling. "And I thought I was the mad old gaffer!"

I gave him a slight smile. I'd thought he was the mad one as well. But with what I had in mind, I wasn't so sure any longer.

"In Zotikos's shipment, you were receiving a pyrkin strain rumored to dampen a warden's channeling, right?"

He placed the new vase in the lehr and shut the door. "Yes. So I was told. Pyrkin scraped from the trunk of an isikhayha, one of the Bali spirit trees."

"I didn't believe it could be true before. But now, I need it to be."

Sitting, he studied me. "What do you mean? Do you have something in mind?"

I sighed. "Only a plan for the desperate. If I asked you to make crossbow bolts with glass orbs affixed to the ends, could you do it?"

"I suppose so."

"Good. Then I have a visit to make. If I succeed, I expect I'll be back shortly."

Maesos shook his head with a resigned chuckle. "And here I thought I'd go to my grave a bored, happy man. Very well. I'll await your return."

Nodding grimly, I left his shop.

FEW VISITORS STRAYED INTO HULL. Located in the southeastern corner of the inner city, it was so named for the skeleton of a beached ship that leaned over a dry branch of the Walano River. That image epitomized the whole of the deme. Lichen and vines ate away at the stone and wood of its buildings. Most seemed not to have seen fresh paint in my lifetime, and a few looked on the verge of collapse. It had not been as long as I preferred since my last trip. Yet here I was, a span later, visiting for the same errand as before.

I knew the way to the smuggler Zotikos's manor, having earlier wormed his secret from his serving staff with a few well-placed coins. Less than a turn after leaving Maesos's shop, I had arrived before the manor and stood facing it. It was not unimpressive, rising several stories high, but the merchant seemed to have fallen on hard times. No guard stood at the gate, and trees and bushes along the path to his door lay untrimmed. I marched through the gate and up to the door, then knocked loudly.

Several long minutes later, the door opened to reveal a tired-looking woman. "Yes? How may I help you?"

"I need to see your master. Please tell Zotikos that Airene the Finch has come to see that he completes his task this time."

The woman blinked at me. "Oh, my dear, I'm sorry. I've grown so used to answering my own door that I've forgotten how strange it must be. But if you need to see my husband, I can bring him here."

A flush crept up my neck. Zotikos's scorned wife was the last person I wanted to insult. "My apologies. But if you would do that, I'd be grateful."

"Of course." She smiled and began to turn away, letting the door close behind her.

Inspiration struck me then. "And please, if you'd return with him, I'd appreciate speaking with both of you."

The merchant's wife looked back with a quizzical look, but she nodded before closing the door.

I waited impatiently, thinking. If Zotikos's wife answered the door herself, times were hard indeed for their household. Perhaps Zotikos wouldn't even have that giant of a body-guard he'd had before. That would make this much easier. But how had the smuggler been ruined so quickly? I doubted my interference could have had such a dire impact.

Minutes later, the door opened again, this time to reveal both Zotikos and his wife. Anger already smoldered in the smuggler's expression. "What are you doing here?" he snapped.

"Hello, Zotikos. What a lovely manor you have." I held back other insults for his wife's sake.

Her face grew pale even at that small slight, while her husband's purpled. "You come to my house and insult me," he said in a low, threatening voice. "I should have you thrown off my yard."

I gave him a knowing smile. "You won't do that though, will you, Zotikos? Even if you had a man to do so. After all, we have unfinished business to discuss. I held up my end of the bargain. It's time that you held up yours."

The merchant's angry gaze fell on his wife. "As I told you, it is merely business. You may leave us."

"But she asked me to…" Her nerve faltered as his glare intensified. "Very well. Excuse me, Airene the Finch." She bowed and swiftly departed.

I let the silence stretch between us as Zotikos glared at me. "I don't know who told you those filthy lies you threatened to tell my wife," he said in a low, harsh voice, "but rest assured they paid for it. I threw them all out — steward, cook, servants, and guards. All!"

"Even your tall, well-muscled admirer?"

"Even him," he snapped. "And now you come and tell my wife to stay while you insult me—"

"We had a bargain," I interrupted, my patience quickly fraying. "And you broke it. Yet, as despicable as I find you, I am still willing to uphold the deal. I will not speak of your injustices against your wife so long as you, here and now, deliver the shipment promised to the glassblower, Maesos."

Zotikos laughed bitterly. "So it was he who hired you. Well, too late for that. Now go away. You've done your worst."

He moved to slam the door in my face. Acting without thinking, I threw my shoulder against the door and opened it wide, then shoved the merchant back against the wall behind him to pin him there. The man's eyes bulged, and words failed him as he spluttered. He and I were of a height and build, but the contest was far from even. The merchant had grown too used to others doing his dirty work for him. Or perhaps, with blood pounding inside my skull, I was more dangerous than I realized.

"How about we strike a new bargain," I suggested with a sharp smile. "Go fetch the shipment yourself while I wait here, and I'll leave you alone."

"God-touched bitch," he spat. But I noticed that he didn't make any move to dislodge himself.

I pressed harder into his chest until he gasped. "Now!" I snarled.

"I can't!" he practically squealed. "I sold it!"

My stomach sank. "Liar."

"Sold it!" he repeated frantically, clutching weakly at my arm.

"Who? Who did you sell it to?"

"The Low Consul! Feiyan of Port!"

The fight went out of me. I released him and stepped back. *Feiyan.* Of course. My far-fetched plan hinged on the woman who had likely had Xaron killed.

"If you lied..." I left the threat hanging as I turned away and went quickly back to the street.

30

SPINNING

Yet seeing these isikhayha trees did not answer my question of what they protected their ishaka against. When I posed this question to the Shaka, she shook her head and did not answer in words I could understand, and though I sought a translation, none was provided. I must settle on speculation. With their plateaus largely peaceful and free from disturbance by both spirits and wardens, I must assume the isikhayhas protect against influences of the Pyrthae. Perhaps daemons are trapped within their spheres.

It is one mystery I am most happy to wonder at, and never discover.

- An Oedijan's Account of the Bali Ishakas; by Manenes of Gate, an itinerant scholar; 1140 SLP

I t was well into the afternoon by the time the Laurel Palace came into sight. I had known no better place to return. Feiyan was as likely to be here as at the Conclave or her own manor, and Talan might be waiting nearby with news. Besides, after the day's hindrances, exhaustion and doubts weighed me down. But I kept going. As unlikely as my chances of success were, I had to try to stop Vusu.

302

As I approached the gates, a figure came out from an alcove toward me. My stomach fluttered with hope as I turned, expecting to greet Talan. Instead, I blinked in surprise. "Corin?"

"Airene." Canopy's last loftmate trudged over to stand before me. She looked the worse for wear, which was saying something, as her job usually kept her coated in dust and mud, and she smelled as if she hadn't bathed since the three horns had blown.

Even with everything else pressing on my mind, I suddenly realized how deeply I'd wronged her. "Corin, I can't say how sorry I am about everything." My gaze slipped from her face; looking her in the eyes had become unbearable. "I know you'd been saving up to bring your sister to Oedija. Now all your savings are gone. Because of me."

"It was not you who broke into Canopy."

I forced myself to meet her eyes. "But it's my fault, Corin. I brought Feiyan's henchmen down on us. She warned me, and I ignored it. And now we're both without our home." Unexpectedly, I felt a hot pressure on my eyes. After everything else, it seemed strange that this small ache would be the one to bring tears. Corin averted her gaze, clearly uncomfortable.

As I wiped at my eyes, an idea occurred to me that cheered me, if only slightly. "I'm staying at the Laurel Palace and have the Archon's ear. I'm sure you could stay with us. And after things calm down, if you still want to bring your sister here, maybe I could get Jaxas to finance her ship."

Corin's eyes widened, and she lifted her head to stare at me. I returned the look, puzzled. Had I said something to offend her? Perhaps it was her strange sense of honor, which compelled her to earn the coin necessary for her sister's passage without aid from anyone else.

"No," Corin said at length, looking away again. "I will find a way."

I let it lie for the moment. If we survived what was coming, there would be time to discuss it later. "At least stay at the Laurel Palace. I know you can't have money for another place to stay."

A long pause followed. Slowly, the cartwoman nodded. "Thank you," she whispered, the words seeming to cost her.

I reached forward to take her arm, but she drew back. I didn't understand what was going on with her, but the time I had for her troubles had dried up. "Come. I'll see if Nikias can't find you a room."

Corin kept three paces behind me as we approached the palace gates. The guards eyed us, but admitted us without complaint. I was glad to see my position as a Verifier was worth that much at least.

Passing through the palace doors, I found we had a greeting party. Nikias stood in the middle of the main hall with a pair of honors, hands folded behind his back, his expression severe.

"Nikias," I greeted him as we approached.

"Verifier Airene, you are late in reporting to the Archon. Your companion Nomusa has already given her account, but my master informs me that it is vastly incomplete. He has summoned you to his solar at once."

I was in no mood to bandy words with the prickly man. "Fine. You can take me to him in a moment. But I'll need a few things from you in return."

Nikias's eyes narrowed. "And those would be?"

"First, my friend here needs a room in the palace."

The steward scowled. "This is not an inn, Verifier Airene. We are not required to provide lodging for your every passing acquaintance."

"Just give her a room, Nikias. If you want to argue about it later, fine. But I have to report to Jaxas now, and I'd like to know that Corin is treated well before I go."

The steward sniffed, his mustache bristling. "Fine. Name your other requirements and be on your way."

"Bring Nomusa up to the Archon if you can. I want her to hear everything as well."

"Very good. Is that all?" His sarcasm was not lost on me.

"Nearly. Should you receive a report of a disreputable-looking Avvadin man hanging around the front of the palace, please notify me."

"I would be happy to act as your messenger finch," he snapped. "Now, if you please, do your duty and go to the Archon."

I glanced over at Corin. "They'll take you in now. Just ask if you need anything."

The big woman didn't nod or respond, but remained with her head bowed. I imagined it was shameful for her to be in this position, taken care of by not only me, her friend, but also served by honors. But Corin's pride was the last thing I could be concerned with now.

As an honor stepped forward and led Corin away, I turned back to the steward. "Take me to him."

Nikias motioned sharply to an honor. At her indication, I followed her up the stairs.

After many twists and turns through chambers and hall-ways, the honor and I arrived before a simple wooden door. The honor knocked lightly, then opened it and ushered me inside. The room I entered was bright, light streaming through a wall of windows, catching on the dust hovering around stacks of books and scrolls. Plates of fruit, meats, and bread were set out on a table in the middle of the room.

The Archon sat in one of the dark corners amid the books, his pen scribbling on a piece of parchment. He continued writing for several more moments, then slowly set the pen in its stand and lifted his gaze.

"Verifier Airene," he greeted me. He looked tired, and the

shadows on his face made his appearance seem even more wasted than the day before.

"Archon." I gave him a brief bow.

Jaxas gestured to a seat adjacent to his writing desk. "Please, sit. Or we can step onto the balcony if you prefer. Even in the daytime, the view of Oedija is excellent."

"Sitting is welcome." My rumbling stomach begged for me to pick up some morsels, but I resolutely ignored my needs and sat.

Pushing the parchment before him aside, the Archon leaned forward, forming a steeple with his hands. "Nomusa gave an interesting report, but I'll need your account to fully understand it."

"Yes." My throat tightened as I thought over what I'd witnessed the previous night, and how I'd now have to relive it. "I'll help you make sense of it. But first, I have to ask. What happened with Xaron?"

"Ah, yes." Jaxas's eyes were hidden in the hollows of his skull. "The Shepherds invaded your friend's room sometime around the mid-turn of the night. A fight ensued. Some claimed to hear claps of thunder from the room. Others saw him fleeing the grounds with two Shepherds in pursuit."

I closed my eyes, emotion choking me. For a moment I couldn't speak. I drew in several shuddering breaths.

"I'm sorry, Airene," Jaxas said softly. "Even if he was a feral warden, I know he was your friend. Yet I do not know that anyone can escape a Shepherd."

I fought for control. "He understood the risks," I said, my voice shaky. "We all did."

He looked at me and slowly nodded.

A light tapping sounded at the door. I turned, grateful for the distraction. A moment later, Nomusa was escorted in. I halfway stood, suddenly uncertain. She paused at the sight of me, then rushed over and wrapped me in an embrace.

"You scared me last night," she whispered in my ear. "With

everything that happened, and how you just seemed to drift away… And then you were gone this morning!" She abruptly pulled away and shook her head with a small smile. "I'm just glad you're all right."

I nodded, tears suddenly stinging my eyes. "But Xaron…"

"I know," she said simply. "But we can't lose hope. Maybe he escaped."

I shook my head, but didn't respond. There was no point in dwelling on it. I couldn't help Xaron. But I might still aid Oedija.

Turning, I met Jaxas's gaze. "I should give report."

Jaxas exchanged a look with Nomusa, then gestured for us to sit. "Please."

I did not give them the complete tale, though it was nearly so. I told of our approach to the Wyvern's Claw, the size of the crowds, and the laxness of the guards. I spoke then of the show the Dishonored and the Visage of the Wyvern put on, and how very close everyone there came to burning alive. Jaxas nodded, and Nomusa indicated she had covered as much.

After a moment's hesitation, I told them of Linos, though I did not yet admit to the Archon that he was my brother. Instead, I spoke of him as a credible case of the Manifest turning an ordinary person into a warden.

Jaxas's brow creased. "And how do you know that the attunement was not just buried within him, waiting to be expressed?"

I glanced at Nomusa, and at her nod, I felt a sliver of gratefulness. She hadn't already told him. I drew in a breath. "I know because... He's my brother."

The Archon was still for a long moment. "I am sorry, Airene," he said softly. "Though words can ill convey it, I truly am."

I didn't acknowledge it. I couldn't yet. Instead, I barreled on with my report, the details becoming lost in the blur of revelations that followed. When I unveiled the Visage's identity, Jaxas nodded, seemingly unsurprised.

"Tribune Vusumuzi," he murmured. "I never would have suspected the old man. He always struck me as kind, if resolute."

"His attunement is more powerful than I've ever seen. The whole of his arms moved with his shifts."

"I wish I had gone with you," Nomusa said quietly. "I would have liked to have seen his arms."

"To see his shifts?"

"No — his tatu. Zipho told us he'd shown her them before and that they were of the Yorandu, but it always seemed strange to me. He never showed deference to me beyond the formal address — not that he needed to," she amended quickly. "But Zipho and the few other Yorandu in Oedija all do speak to me that way. It just didn't fit."

"Well, now we know why," I said heavily.

"Almost. I suspect he's not Yorandu. But that raises the question: which ishaka is he from?"

That question might have fascinated Nomusa, but it was the furthest query from my mind.

"When you encountered him," Jaxas interjected, "did Vusumuzi say anything of note?"

I hesitated. Now I stood on the precipice, with deadly consequences either way I chose. I studied the thin, sickly Wreath sitting across from me and wondered once again why he had done as he had. The choice before me hinged on Jaxas being true to the realm.

I glanced at Nomusa, but she had no answers. If I were to trust Jaxas, trust him with my friends' and family's lives, I had to know the one thing holding me back.

"Why did you let us investigate Asileia Wreath?"

Shadowy emotions flitted across his face, so quick I couldn't identify them. "You know why," he said quietly. "Because, no matter what I might wish to believe about her,

Leia will do anything to achieve her goals. No one — myself, her father — no one means as much to her as herself. I believed she was capable of killing her father if it served her goals, and I needed to know the truth of it." He sighed. "That she showed symptoms of insanity upon her return from the Peninsula only heightened my suspicions."

Jaxas looked away. I stared at him, realization settling in. He loved Asileia. Mad as she was, she was still his family. Yet rather than protect her, he had sought the truth behind her father's disappearance. No matter the cost.

How could I hold myself to anything less?

"Vusu instructed me to accuse Asileia of Myron's murder, then have her convicted in a trial. And if I don't comply, he'll kill my family and friends."

I glanced at Nomusa, and she stared back at me, her mouth slightly parted. She seemed more surprised than upset.

The Archon's expression was inscrutable. "It was risky for you to tell me this."

"Just as it was risky to bring on three strangers to an investigation that could break Oedija."

He bowed his head in acknowledgment. "I appreciate the trust you've placed in me, Airene. I swear to you, it is not misguided."

Nomusa's gaze had fallen to the floor. I hoped she had the same conviction as Jaxas did.

The Archon rose, folded his hands behind his back, and began to pace. "Vusu wishes to have Asileia pushed out of the way," he mused. "But that would leave me in line to be the next Despot."

"It would, if not for one other thing. Myron isn't dead. Vusu kidnapped him, to present him as soon as the Despoina is discredited. He means to send the whole system spiraling."

A small smile worked its way onto his lips. "I've been aiding your cause. If Leia is convicted by your testimony, it will cast suspicion on myself. After all, what better motivation would I have to take away the Evergreen Wreath from Leia than to wear it myself?"

That piece hadn't occurred to me yet, nor Nomusa, from her reaction.

"I must hear your report in its entirety," Jaxas continued. "What else did he say?"

I thought back. "It isn't so much what he said as what he did. He… he killed the boy Hilarion." I did not mention it was by my brother's hand that the deed was done.

The Wreath bowed his head and was quiet for several long moments. "I sent him with you," he said softly. "If you blame yourself for his fate, don't. His blood is on my hands."

"His blood is on Vusu's hands."

Jaxas inclined his head. "Anything else?"

I shook my head. "Nothing of significance." I didn't mention our brief encounter with Talan afterward. I had kept the Guilder secret thus far and had no intentions of revealing him now. He had always valued his anonymity, and I meant to honor that for as long as I could.

"I'd hoped to put off our decision until later." Jaxas continued to pace, the creases in his brow growing ever deeper.

"We have to deal with him here and now." I braced myself for the words. "And I think I have a way to do it. To make it seem like we are implementing his plan, but will in actuality foil him."

Both Nomusa and the Archon looked over in surprise.

"You do?" Nomusa asked skeptically.

"Don't hold us in suspense," Jaxas said with a faint smile.

I hesitated a moment. A plan to trap the most powerful warden in Oedija. I was even madder than I'd thought.

Taking a deep breath, I began to speak.

THE DEMOS COUNCIL

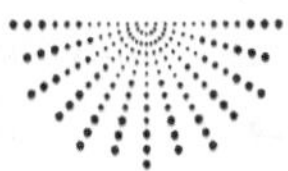

...And from the Conclave will be elected a Council of eleven Low Consuls, each elected by ten Servants, who will determine matters of expediency. To them are ceded powers of swift military action, response to disasters, the management of foreign entities, and criminal matters of the highest order. In matters of commerce and the wealth of the realm as well as laws of lesser haste, the Council is to cede responsibility to the greater Conclave...

- Charter II of the formation of the Demotism of Oedija; 1063 SLP

Afternoon was bleeding into evening by the time Nomusa and I departed from Jaxas's solar. We'd discussed, refined, and finally committed to my scheme. There were still many risks involved. There were still loose threads. Yet, together, we had begun weaving a web that might just be strong enough.

But there was much work to be done. Once we'd honed the details to as fine a point as we could, Nomusa and I took our leave of the Archon. We took with us his promise of setting up a meeting for later that evening, a meeting that I once would have fawned over attending: a meeting with the Demos Council and the other heads of Oedija's institutions. The ten Low Consuls would be there, as would the Stratechons, the High Tribune, and Archmaster Kyros. Significant as they all were, though, the conference was just another piece in the puzzle now.

As we descended the steps to return to our rooms, Nomusa touched my arm. "I know we've been avoiding this, but we have to find Xaron. Everything else has been set in motion. Now, we need to find out what happened to our friend."

I didn't answer for a moment. As desperately as I wished to know if Xaron had survived, fear that he had not was stronger. But fear was a poor excuse to do nothing for him if something could be done. "You're right. Where do we start?"

"Shepherds chasing after a feral warden would likely draw many eyes and ears. Perhaps we should ask in the usual places?"

I sighed. "We don't have the coin to pay them, remember? I barely have two magnes to rub together. The Archon's mercy is all that's keeping us fed and sheltered."

Nomusa drew out her purse, setting it jingling with a shake. "I have my own stores, as well as the bit I took to buy food for Canopy. We'll have enough for this."

My excuses exhausted, I nodded. "Then let's see what the city is whispering."

A FEW TURNS of plying our contacts yielded more intriguing results than I'd expected, if not in the direction we desired. As food costs continued to climb, disputes were breaking out among the agricultural guilds, which only made the situation worse when even less food was brought in than before. In even more worrisome news, ever since the night of the gathering — the Dragon's Dusk, some silver-tongued fool had named it — the Manifest was said to be stirring like a hornet's nest, the people within the compound seeming to have awakened with innumerable activities. They built bonfires; they built houses; they sowed the ground for fields and dug trenches. Vusu and his Seekers were fortifying their position. The Manifest was preparing for war.

Others whispered of the Despoina's absence from the public scene after her erratic behavior, but none could say what it meant. Some said she grieved her father's death. Softer, it was murmured that she hid from her guilt, though no one outright accused her of the deed. I smiled bitterly at that. It would make the web we spun all the more convincing to the common people. We heard, too, that to show their displeasure at Asileia's insult to the Avvadin emissary, many of the Valemish priests had mounted blazing braziers before their temple doors.

But of our immediate concern, we heard only enough to tantalize. A feral warden, it was said, had fled into the heart of Iris with Shepherds in close pursuit. If it was Xaron, the news wasn't good, for no one had seen the warden leave the deme, nor had they glimpsed the Shepherds again. Having few leads, Nomusa and I wandered Iris aimlessly for a turn, but happened upon no further clues. My hopes lay solely with Talan, though it worried me that we had not heard from him since the night before.

Returning to the palace as the sun hung just over the sea, I hoped to see him waiting outside the grounds for us, but no such luck was to be found. We walked back up to the palace and to our bedchambers. There, Jaxas Wreath himself stood before our doors, while Nikias hovered nearby wearing a severely offended expression. The usual gaggle of honors lingered behind.

"Verifiers," the Archon said mildly as we approached. "I expected you to be more easily summoned. We must hurry;

the meeting occurs within the turn and on Conclave grounds."

"Our apologies, Archon," I said with a slight bow. "We were looking into the fate of our accomplice."

"Ah." Jaxas's neutral expression clouded with conflicting emotions. "And do you have news of him?"

"Little of use," Nomusa said tartly.

"A shame." The Archon actually did sound regretful. "If you had found him, I had an idea to…" He shook his head. "But no need to rouse restless pyr. We must depart at once. It will not do to keep them waiting."

I nodded and forced the matter from my mind. "We're ready when you are, Archon."

Two carriages were waiting out front for us. Jaxas took the first one, while Nomusa and I slipped into the second. Before our driver took us after the Archon, his steward saw it fit to give us one last stern lecture. "It does not bode well to keep my master waiting, nor the other leaders of our nation. Be more timely in the future, Verifiers."

"We will, Nikias," I said wearily. "But it is you who delays us now."

With a scowl, the steward stepped back, and the driver set off.

Our carriage took us over the bridge that connected the Laurel Palace to the Conclave grounds, a graceful construction of white marble, with arches and columns supporting it over the chasm that fell to the sea seventy cubits below. But it paled in comparison to the structure to which our carriage pulled up.

The Conclave's massive dome bloomed before us like a flower bulb on a godly scale, rising hundreds of feet high with shining bronze plating and white marble that still gleamed as if newly set and waxed. A sanctuary to the Eidola built by the original settlers of Oedija, it was said to have been forged partly by magic. Seeing the impossibly seamless curve of the dome, the agelessness of its stone, and how the bronze had not ceded to a green patina even after many long centuries, I found myself believing it.

We exited the carriages to rejoin the Archon. Jaxas noticed our awed expressions, and his mouth quirked in a slight smile. "Yes, it is impressive. I remember craning my head back the same way as you when I first came here as a boy."

I drew my gaze from the edifice to the Archon. "The Council is within?"

He nodded. "The Low Consuls don't meet within the main chamber, but we'll need to cross through it." He motioned to a few attending honors who had traveled on the back of his carriage, and they pulled open the doors to the building at the heart of Oedija's demotism.

I found myself once again slack-jawed as we entered through the two grand doors. The dome's tremendous height looked even higher from within, its peculiar and unnatural architecture made clear by the lack of supporting beams or columns on its smooth, curved ceiling. Ringed balconies spiraled down the dome, supporting gilded effigies of old heroes and yet more gods. At the top was a shining oculus that admitted the dying golden light of the day through it. Each ring down was trimmed with a dull gold, and where the sunlight hit it from the oculus or the many windows below, it glittered faintly. It was as wide across as it was high and dizzyingly massive.

While the ceiling curved up, the floor sloped down like an amphitheater, rows of seats layered and offset so that the speaker's platform below was visible. On the platform was mounted a podium and a gargantuan mounted bell. This, I realized, was where the Archon presided over Conclave sessions.

Late in the day as it was, I had not expected to see many people, but the Servants of the Conclave, elected officials from every deme of Oedija, still filled the soaring chamber with a susurrus of murmurs. At our entrance, many glanced up, their expressions mildly curious. As we passed, whispers died down and eyes cast aside, yet I had no doubt as to where their attention lay. I was surprised to find that my stomach fluttered with nervousness. I had always worked within the shadows of the polis's most powerful. Now I blanched at being the object of their attention. If I was forced to work long within the Conclave, I doubted I would enjoy it.

Jaxas led us down the many tiers to the small, shadowed space behind the speaker's platform. There, a small, humble door presented itself, hidden from view from the rest of the chamber. As we stopped before it, Jaxas again smiled at our surprise. "Yes, the Council meets within. Humility is often the best guise for hubris." He continued quieter, "Are you ready to begin?"

Studying the Archon, I wondered if he was asking it more of himself than us. I nodded. "We're ready."

Jaxas motioned to an attending honor, and she opened the door. With one last lingering look, the Archon led us inside.

The chamber looked to have been adapted from a cave. Its windows were little more than natural openings with no glass covering them, so the scent of salt and seaweed filled the room. As we entered, the Low Consuls of the Demos Council looked up. There were ten of them, all seated around a slab of stone smoothed so that its surface reflected like glass. Conversation ceased as we entered. I didn't meet their eyes, but dropped my gaze to the strange table and the goblets of wine set before each member.

There were ten of them, the Low Consuls, though there were supposed to be eleven. One of the seats remained empty due to political deadlock. Thus, it fell to Jaxas as the Archon to break tied votes. The Servants were the official representatives of Oedija's citizens, and the Ruling Wreath was given the glory. But the Low Consuls commanded all of Oedija's politics from the shadows.

I recognized their faces, both from the notices posted in the forums of each deme as well as from the recent Ascension. On one side of the stone slab sat the five members of the Preservist faction, the faction most closely aligned to Avvadin ancestry and policies. As their name implied, they sought most of all to preserve the state of the polis, holding change to be more detrimental than how matters were presently.

On the other side of the table was a more eclectic group. Three comprised the Equalist faction who, when they managed to draw a majority in the Conclave, passed legislation like basic protections for prostitutes and establishing public granaries. But the famine showed the holes in their accomplishments. Though the granaries existed, the Equalists had only managed to secure a fraction of the grain needed to supply them to stave off disasters. So it was that starvation was proceeding unchecked as the current drought progressed.

I couldn't help but suspect one particular Equalist in having a role in this duplicitous outcome. Feiyan stared at me with a small smile, her narrow eyes crinkled in consideration. Her peplos was unassuming, her only concession to frivolity a silver necklace adorned with glittering emeralds, but I knew better than to believe her humble. It was just as Jaxas said; humility was ambition's mask. I imagined Xaron, dead in a ditch somewhere in the city, and had to clench my teeth hard to hold back words I could only regret.

The Low Consuls weren't the only ones present. Around the edges of the cave-like room stood other notables of Oedija. Before one window were the five uniformed and white-haired Stratechons, their red lacerna thrown over their shoulders. The half-cloaks distinguished their elite military status along with their laurel-crested breastplates.

Next to them stood High Tribune Photina, staring severely over the heads of the others. She, like the Stratechons, often preferred Preservist policies. I couldn't help but feel irrationally angry toward her. While it was true that the Shepherds were under her command, she had little choice in the mandate being carried out. Anyone who sought to change the way that wardens were managed in Oedija would quickly lose their authority. Yet she was the head of the institution that had likely killed my friend. I could not easily forget that.

The man who stood in contrast to that institution was under another window. Kyros Brighteyed glared over the gathering, his sagging jowls making his scowl even more pronounced. As my eyes slid over him, I considered once again what to make of the Archmaster. If what Xaron had said was true, that Kyros was training wardens to fight, we still had good reason to be suspicious of him. As he met my gaze, his scowl did not shift, and I saw that his eyes glowed eerily. I averted my gaze, wondering what the Archmaster saw as he peered at me.

Orhan of Bazaar, the leader of the Preservists, spoke first. "Jaxas, how good of you to join us." He smiled brilliantly, looking the picture of an Avvadin patrician in his diamond-patterned, velvet robes.

"A good turn after you said you would," growled Berker of deme Sandglass, Orhan's secondhand man, whose pock-marks were barely disguised beneath his curly beard.

Daelya of Saltpeter, leader of the Equalists, snorted and leaned back in her chair, her willowy body curving into it. "As if you keep any of your promises."

Berker flushed as he leaned forward. "And what do you mean by that?"

"Berker," Orhan said with a laugh, placing a hand on the bigger man's shoulder and pressing him back into his seat. "Peace, my good man. We're here on serious business, not to quarrel with each other." He eyed Daelya from across the table. "Isn't that correct, my dear?"

Daelya raised an eyebrow, but nodded silently.

Jaxas walked slowly to his own chair and sat. Nomusa and I remained where we were by the door, seeing no obvious place for us.

"Low Consuls," the Archon said, raising a hand toward us, "this is Verifier Airene and Verifier Nomusa."

All shifted their gazes toward us. My stomach fluttered, but I forced calm onto my expression.

"Ah, the little Finches who have been causing such a disturbance," Orhan said with a smile. "You are most welcome."

"Very welcome," Feiyan reiterated. She, too, smiled at us, but it was tinged with frost. "And dressed so prettily for us — we appreciate the effort you put into your presentation."

I ignored her, keeping my focus on our task. "If you have heard of us," I began, "then you may have also heard of our purpose in being here." At a nod from Jaxas, I continued. "For the past span, since the first of Odaon, Nomusa and I have been looking into the murder of the late Despot Myron Wreath."

The Low Consuls shifted, as did the rest of the attendees. I felt the gaze of Kyros Brighteyed most keenly, but it was Orhan who spoke. "Murder, you say?" the Preservist leader observed, his head tilting. "But I do believe Despot Myron was declared to have died of natural causes."

"And yet here we are."

Orhan's mouth quirked. "So we are. Perhaps subterfuge isn't necessary before someone with such incisive perception. Very well, Verifier Airene. We will drop the pretenses within this room."

"L-looking into it?" stuttered Iason, a nervous, old man of Preservist inclinations. "What m-measures have you taken?"

I hesitated, but there was no path but forward. "We have

investigated the possible motives and actors behind Myron's murder. Recently, we visited the Despot's chambers and spoke with the Despoina."

"You spoke with her?" Daelya leaned forward, her eyes alight with interest. "She hasn't been to a Council meeting since her Ascension."

"Though after what she did with the Imperium's ambassador, it's best that she stays away," Berker rumbled. "Does she mean to start a war we cannot win?"

I glanced at Jaxas and saw his head bowed and eyes obscured. I wondered if my remarks would hurt him, even knowing this plan. But before I could speak, Nomusa stepped up beside me. "Yes, we spoke to her. And what she told us was as good as an admission of guilt."

"Guilt?" Zehaar, a beautiful Avvadin woman of the Equalist faction, repeated with skepticism. "What precisely was said?"

"I asked her directly if she killed her father," I responded. "She said in return that it had been a test of her power, a test that had gone well, as the Despot had completely disappeared."

Murmurs started around the room. Jaxas dropped his head into his hands, so full of despair I doubted it was wholly an act. Zehaar looked about her, seeming to measure each reaction, the Archon's most of all. "I, for one, am not convinced," she declared. "Delusion seems her crime more than regicide. Why admit guilt if she truly were guilty?"

Orhan spoke up. "It's true that it is not a direct admission. If we were to proceed with a trial, I would be more comfortable if an explicit confession were brought forward."

"She admitted it." The Archon slowly raised his head from his hands, his face stiff as a waxen mask. "She told me in words as clear as you could want. 'I killed him,' she said the night of her Ascension. When she still appeared... sane."

The muttering around the room escalated to confused

chatter. I shifted, trying to contain my nervous energy. *A trial* — it had come to this point without even our suggestion. The lines of our net were twisting fast now. I hoped they would hold.

Orhan sighed heavily, barely audible among the noise of the disbelieving Council. "Then we have the beginning of our proof," he spoke loudly. "Even if it is with heavy hearts, we had best proceed while the fire is still hot."

My gut clenched again as the rest of his faction nodded along. Daelya, however, shook her head. "No. I will not comply with this."

Berker was nearly trembling with rage. "An admission of guilt! Three witnesses on two separate occasions! And one of those the Archon of the Conclave, and practically her brother! Is that not enough for you?"

"We have all seen her." Daelya leaned forward, her expression hard. "We know how far gone she is. Do you truly think she is capable of it, of murdering her own father, then hiding it until now? No. I believe she is mad, and that she should not be punished further for it."

"She was not mad before that night," the Archon said softly to the stone table. "She was not mad."

"Perhaps her crime drove her to this point," Orhan offered. "In any case, such a confession can hardly be ignored. We have found no better explanation for Myron's death."

As the rest of the Low Consuls took up the debate, I studied the leader of the Preservists. That Orhan seemed convinced of the Despoina's guilt with so little information, and none of his faction spoke up to dispute it, was unsettling. Another game was being played here, I was sure of it.

"My fellow Consuls!" Feiyan suddenly stood, chair scuttling back across the stone floor. "Are we not forgetting something? A threat that is much more likely to be behind our Despot's death?"

"Don't tell me you're concerned about Avvad again," Esen sneered.

Feiyan stared at her flatly for a moment, then looked to the other members of the Council. "Not Avvad. I speak of the threat that we have allowed to fortify just outside of our city's walls. The enemy that has stolen the hearts of the underclass, even of honors, and fomented unrest among them in their aim to undermine the very foundation of our demotism." Her gaze turned smoothly to me. "The ones who harbor and train wardens as we turn our eyes aside."

"The Manifest?" Berker said in disbelief.

Even as anger flared in me at her clear reference to Xaron, the analytical part of my mind turned. Of all of the Low Consuls, I had suspected Feiyan as the most likely to be working with the Manifest. Yet here she was, openly speaking against them, and laying the Despot's supposed murder at their feet. In one swift speech, she'd become the one person on the Council I could be most certain was not aligned with Vusu.

As the clamor among the Council flared up again, Jaxas and I briefly met each others' eyes. The net would soon be cast. But for my family's sake, and for Linos, I knew it could not be aimed at Vusu and his Seekers.

Before I could intervene, Orhan clapped his hands. "We stray from our purpose here. Whether or not the Manifest is an issue is irrelevant to Asileia's guilt. With your permission, Archon, I propose we move this issue of putting the Despoina on trial to a vote. Simple majority."

"Granted," Jaxas Wreath said, perhaps a tad too quickly, though no one else seemed to notice.

"All in favor?" Orhan asked as he raised his hand.

As expected, the other four Preservists followed suit. Orhan frowned slightly that he did not have the majority he sought, but continued. "Opposed?"

Feiyan immediately raised her hand, and Daelya and Zehaar followed a moment later.

"Abstain?"

Verchlesa and Tychon, the two independent Low Consuls, predictably voted as such.

"Then with the eleventh seat as yet unfilled, it falls to the Archon to decide." Orhan shifted to look at him. "Well, Jaxas, what will it be?"

Jaxas didn't look up for a long time, steepled fingers playing one over the other. I thought I knew what held him back. Even a fake condemnation of his cousin must be difficult. It did not make me feel any easier about what he would do. I stared at him, willing him to look at me and honor his word, but he continued to watch his slowly moving fingers.

"Jaxas?" Orhan prompted. "Remember what you said of her confession. Remember your duty to your polis."

The Archon's swallow was visible even from where I stood. "We shall have the trial," he said quietly. "I vote in favor."

Orhan nodded solemnly and stood, and the rest rose with him. "Then it is decided. Prepare the Tribunal, Photina. We expect her trial in two days. No need to delay this any further than is necessary."

They filed out of the room while Nomusa and I stood by. The true rulers of the city, who would so easily throw a Wreath to the dogs if the situation called for it. Unease spread in me as I turned the possibilities over in my mind for why Orhan and his Preservists had done it. But I could think of no better explanation than the obvious. The Wreaths had always been mere figureheads, and a symbol that no longer served its purpose had to be cut away.

Kyros Brighteyed lingered a moment longer than the rest. It took all my resolve not to cringe away as he leaned his generous bulk in close. A faint aroma of sweat and sulfur hung around him.

"Tread carefully, Finch," he sneered softly. "I've heard of you sniffing around my Acadium. I know what you're about. And I'll be watching you."

My thoughts spun, but I kept my expression neutral. "I serve at the pleasure of the Archon."

"I'm sure you do." He shouldered past me to exit the room.

"What did Kyros say?" Nomusa whispered as she came up next to me, Jaxas just behind her.

"He's suspicious," I murmured. "Of what, I don't know."

"Then we'll remain cautious." Jaxas's depression seemed to have lifted, and he held his thin frame upright again. "I do not believe we can trust him."

"No," I agreed. "Not in this." Nomusa also nodded in agreement.

After we left the room, the three of us started our way up the Conclave's great chamber. Many of the people who had occupied it before had left. Other than the departing Low Consuls, only a few honors lingered, sweeping and wiping down the surfaces of the benches and tables before them.

So I was startled when, halfway up, Feiyan and her honor Kako stepped out from the eaves.

Feiyan wore a lazy smile. "You seem to be missing one of your number, Finches."

Fury immediately resurged in me. Before I could respond, Nomusa hissed, "You *fareshi* whore of a *kaluae*—"

"Nomusa," I cut her off. My own temples pounded with anger, but I kept my words measured and controlled. "What do you want, Feiyan?"

"Oh, many things." Her gaze wandered about the chamber, while Kako's remained hard upon me. Her eyes settled on the Archon. "Most of all, I wished the Despoina to be left alone, a security she has commanded that I ascertain." She shook her head slowly. "Yet I find that difficult to achieve when her closest confidantes betray her."

Jaxas flinched, but retained his composure. "We all know

what she's capable of, Low Consul," he said quietly. "I cannot look away from the truth before me."

"You mean the truth you have constructed?" Feiyan's gaze slid over Nomusa, then settled on me. "If it has come down to manufactured truths, then perhaps I should no longer stay my hand. What do you think of the matter, Kako?"

"The same as you, mistress," the honor replied at her shoulder, not shifting his unnerving stare from me. "Our Despoina deserves to be protected at all costs."

"Precisely my thoughts," Feiyan said with another viper's smile. "You'll be hearing from me soon, I expect, Verifiers."

The Low Consul and her man began to turn away. Nomusa spoke to their backs. "You think to threaten us into silence when all of Oedija hangs in the balance? You'll ruin it all, Feiyan!"

Feiyan glanced over her shoulder. "Will I? Or is that your intention?"

As she stalked up the stairs, I stared after her, considering. Something about the conversation struck me as strange, yet I couldn't put my finger on it.

"*Fareshi* whore," Nomusa muttered. She was as stiff as an offended cat. "With what she did to Xaron…"

At her mention of him, it finally came to me. I seized Nomusa's arm and drew her close. "Does Feiyan think we're part of the Manifest?"

Jaxas's brow knit in consideration, while Nomusa's eyes widened. "Ah," she breathed. She glanced around. "We shouldn't discuss it here."

"No," I agreed. I looked at Jaxas. "Should we return to your solar?"

The Archon nodded. "Briefly. We have much that needs to be done."

He didn't need to tell me that. Though the web threatened to unravel at any moment, still we had to weave it.

3 2

PYRKIN

The sole interaction of spirits with the material plane that has credibility is the attunement of wardens. That some have the ability to channel magic is indisputable, and it can be seen at every public event due to the antics of the Wreaths' jester Hilarion. That some are born with this ability while others attain it later, too, has been proven time and again. That such an event might take place randomly certainly implies an interaction of some kind with Pyrthaen beings. But why, then, does it appear to be in the blood-lines of others?

I suspect that those who wield the Pyrthae's elements might be able to gain more insight into these mysteries. Yet, for the good of all, their magic is restrained, and even with knowledge lost or never recovered, I must agree that such a cost must be paid for peace so that the Tyrant Wardens never again return.

- The Traditions of the Eleven: Eidolan worship in the demotism of Oedija; by Oracle Iason of deme Iris; 1164 SLP

Having returned to the Laurel Palace, Jaxas, Nomusa, and I discussed Feiyan's suspicions. Why she thought we were part of the Manifest was obvious enough. We had been harboring a feral warden, Xaron. We had entered the Seeker compound not once, but twice, and I didn't doubt she was aware of both forays. If Feiyan happened to know the Visage's identity, she would be very suspicious of the fact that Vusu had been the one to recruit us as well as grant me the Verifier medallion.

The realization did little to make me like her more. But it did lead us to an uncomfortable conclusion: Feiyan was one of the few people we could trust not to be part of the Manifest. So I was forced to consider the unthinkable: to ask for her help. The chances of it yielding anything were close to none, but still we agreed that Nomusa and I would try before we parted ways. At the very least, I might recover Maesos's pyrkin. Perhaps it was a long shot that it would do anything to a warden's channeling. But it was our only chance of coming anywhere close to thwarting Vusu.

For his part, Jaxas agreed to continue the official preparations for the trial, including nudging the Council toward a conviction. I didn't think he'd need to do much in that respect, at least. In addition, he would try to determine if First Laurel Lykos had been duped by Vusu, just as we had, or if he was loyal to another. This information was particularly important to secure. The laurel guards wouldn't attend the trial unless specifically requested, as the Conclave had its own guards whom only the Low Consuls and Stratechons could command. Despite his determination, I sensed that Jaxas's conflicted feelings on the situation hadn't fully resolved. I understood them well. Our fake condemnation could result in very real consequences for those close to us. But there was little we could do but move forward. I could only hope Jaxas would stay strong.

Nomusa and I left his solar late that night and found our own beds. But as I lay there, still wearing my soiled tunic and trousers in case I had to rise quickly, sleep evaded me. My thoughts were too full of Linos and Xaron and how I'd failed them both. I saw images of the rest of my family killed the same way I'd doomed Hilarion: screaming and wreathed in flames cast by Linos's hand. Somehow, I clawed the pictures from my mind and settled into an uneasy slumber.

I rose early the next day and met Nomusa in the feast hall. While we ate, we discussed our plans once again and settled into our tasks. She would do what she could to find Talan and discover Xaron's fate. I would visit Feiyan and ensure everything was progressing well. That afternoon, we would meet again and try to sway what allies we knew we could rely upon.

Nomusa left before I did, for I first had to visit the palace aviary. I started composing a message to my family. Even if I'd had the time, I hesitated to visit them in person, fearing it would somehow make things worse. Since I didn't have the specific scent for their house here in the palace, I would have to send it to the public aviary in Riverport, the deme where they resided, which meant my words would have to be vague. In the end, I kept it brief, but asked them to leave their house for the next few days. I had little faith in my mother acting on my request, but still I made it, if only to ease my conscience. I doubted there was anywhere they could go where Vusu would not find them. But I had to do what I could.

I started to compose a letter to Vusu next, anxious to ensure he'd received news of the trial, but I stopped short of completion. If it was intercepted, Vusu might interpret it as an intentional betrayal. I burned the half-scrawled parchment in a nearby brazier and left the aviary. If he had as wide of a reach as he seemed to, he would hear of it soon enough. My small tasks done, I left the palace and headed toward Port.

A couple of turns later, I stood in front of the most substantial estate in Port. Feiyan's manor had a view over the bay and the port from which the deme gained its name. The docks were busy this time of day, commerce hardly slowing despite the brewing trouble. Trade had treated the Low Consul well. Though clearly larger than others, her home was not a patrician estate as of yet. A successful merchant, one might think. The limestone was well-treated, but lacked the decoration of old money. There was a fountain in its open-air garden, adorned with only a small statue. Rich, but not half as rich as the owner wanted to be.

I was admitted at the gates, but as I set up the stairs to the manor's doors, I was stopped by a waiting man. "Business?" he asked in a tone halfway between boredom and annoyance.

"I need to see your mistress."

"Feiyan? 'Fraid that can't happen. She's with a very important client, she is."

I gave him a studying stare. From the look of him, I guessed he didn't know how to tell anything but lies. "She'll make an exception for me. Why don't you go ask her?"

"Right. I'll just saunter up to the mistress and ask if she wants to see some dirty twat off the streets." He spat at my feet. "Guess I'm playing it too coy. Let me put it this way: If you don't have coin for me, you don't get past. Got it?"

I barely had enough in my purse for a meal, much less a bribe. "You seem a straightforward man. So let me be blunt with you." I drew out my Verifier medallion and held it up. "Employed by Feiyan or not, I can have you thrown in the dungeons. How's that for a bribe?"

The man's eye flickered from my face to the medallion. "You're not a Tribune. Ain't got the right symbol."

"No, it doesn't. But it does have the authority I claim." I slipped it back over my neck. "So either you can risk a cold cell, or you can let me through."

The man stared at me for several long moments, then turned away. "Stay here," he muttered, then walked into the house, closing the door behind him.

The ill-mannered guard kept me waiting long enough

that I started plotting other ways in. But eventually he came back and ushered me inside with a short wave. "Come on, then. My mistress wants to hear what you have to sing after all."

I silently followed the guard within.

He led me through an atrium barely more impressive than the one in my family's house, then through the inner garden, and finally out to a courtyard with a view over the sea. There, a woman reclined on pillows piled on a stone bench. Most striking of all was that she lay stark naked. I quickly looked away. Nakedness outside of the baths was considered shameful to those who saw it. My face flushed at the insult.

"Not bad on the eyes, eh?" the door guard said with a leer at the woman. "But I think you came for the sight over here."

The guard led me around a series of pillars to where a familiar woman stood staring over the water. I tried not to let my teeth clench as I approached Feiyan on my own, the guard staying back to make eyes at the nude woman.

I stopped just short of the edge, standing behind her left shoulder. "Feiyan."

"Ah, the little Finch," the Low Consul said without turning. "I hope you enjoyed the sights on the way in."

I held my tongue.

"I'm not always inclined that way. Toward women, that is," Feiyan observed absently. "Sometimes, I have a man in her place. I find it a good reminder of what we are underneath it all. All the clothes, titles, privileges." She turned and smiled lazily at me. "Just flesh and bone, aren't we? Nothing that can't bruise or break."

I decided it was best to ignore her strange words. "We need to talk."

"So I hear. But it's odd. I thought I'd said all I needed to when I set those Shepherds on your friend. Xaron, wasn't that his name?" She chuckled. "I suppose it doesn't matter now. Though I must say, it was a good guess on my part. After I spoke with your other friend Nomusa, I thought it must be him. The Bali seemed too proud to remain in hiding her whole life."

My teeth clenched, and my fists bunched at my sides. As much as I might want to, pushing her off the balcony wouldn't help Xaron, but only make his death in vain.

"Let's say that's in the past," I managed to say.

Feiyan's eyes widened, her surprise seeming genuine. "How… magnanimous of you."

It took all my self-control to continue. "The Despoina's trial is tomorrow."

"Yes, even the cobblestones know. I should have suspected a Finch is good for no more than repeating the messages they are given."

"But the trial is not just about the Despoina's guilt or innocence. Someone in particular will be in attendance. Someone we have to stop for Oedija to remain whole."

Feiyan laughed, her voice shrill. "Oh, Airene. Stones don't shift because your star rose and fell, and fantasies do not become reality. Really, you seem as mad as Leia these days. But then, to have aligned yourself as you have, you'd have to be." She shook her head. "I think I've heard enough. You weren't nearly as entertaining as I'd—"

"Listen!" I hissed, stepping so close that our faces were barely a foot apart. "The Manifest is moving to take power, and you know it."

All humor fled the Low Consul's face, and she stared hard back at me. "You would know, wouldn't you?" she said softly.

"I know what you suspect, but you're wrong. I'm no Seeker, nor are Jaxas or Nomusa. We've had no part of them."

Her eyes widened in mockery. "No? Considering all you've done to wrongfully accuse Despoina Asileia, I find that hard to believe."

"Then let me explain." I drew in a deep breath, readying

myself. "Their leader, the Visage of the Wyvern — he's the most powerful warden I've ever seen."

"I expect you would know, having seen much of him in the past span. Or have you not visited the compound twice since Myron was killed?"

"Myron was not killed. He was taken. And the Visage was behind it."

Feiyan studied me. "If you know so much, then perhaps you can explain just who the Visage is. Who is the man behind all of this? And what does he want?"

"I know as little as you why he does what he does. But as to who he is…" I braced myself for the words, knowing what they might cost me if I was wrong about Feiyan. "The Visage is Tribune Vusumuzi."

Feiyan's face went strangely still. "Ah. An interesting choice, I'll grant you that."

"He's the reason that Archon Jaxas pushed for a trial. Vusu wants the Despoina condemned for her father's murder to disrupt the polis. He himself will come to speak her final sentence. And when he appears, we aim to put an end to all of this."

Feiyan glanced over the water, which glittered in the morning sunlight. "If he is what you say he is," she said slowly, "then you have not a prayer of a chance of stopping him."

"I have a plan."

"Oh, good. Since your plans have worked so well in the past." She glanced back. "Forgive me if I do not beg for the details."

"You don't have to believe in it. You don't need to know anything about it. But I need your help if we're going to stop him. Fighters, weapons, gold — the Laurel Palace has some reserves, but it will arouse the wrong sort of suspicion if too much is used in one night."

She laughed again, but this time it was low with disbelief.

"You don't tell me your plans, and yet you expect me to aid a hopeless cause and condemn myself in the process. Is this your poor attempt at revenge?"

I grabbed for her, hardly knowing what I was doing. All I knew was that I couldn't let her turn me down. But even as I gripped her arm, I was hauled backward. The door guard clucked his tongue as he wrenched my arm behind my back until I cried out.

"Now, now, it won't do to touch the mistress," he chastised in my ear, greasy locks brushing against my face.

"Feiyan!" I drove desperately on, struggling to twist my arm free. "You know what's at stake! You can't ignore what is happening!"

The Low Consul turned away. "Take her from my sight."

I wanted to rage at her, hit her, throw her off the cliff and watch her splatter across the stones below. She had hurt me, destroyed my home, and as good as killed Xaron. But no matter what bad blood remained between us, this wasn't about her or me. This was about the fate of the realm. This was about saving Linos.

"At least give me what Zotikos sold you!"

Feiyan stiffened, then turned back. "Wait, Gaoxo. Hold her there. Why would you want that contraband?"

I frantically thought of how much to reveal. "There are rare strains of pyrkin from the Bali highlands within it. I have need of one of them."

"Why? Don't play coy with me, Finch. It's long past time for that."

Her guard Gaoxo twisted my arm harder against my back for emphasis. "Tell the truth to the mistress, now."

"It dampens a warden's channeling!" I blurted. "We need it to ambush Vusu!"

Silence fell but for the whistling wind off the sea. Feiyan seemed frozen as she studied me. Then a slow smile spread across her face. "Someone has been telling you pyr stories,

Airene. You will rest the fate of our realm on a few vials of pyrkin?"

I shrugged, the motion awkward with my arm held behind my back. "What choice do I have?"

The Low Consul shook her head. "Gaoxo, please escort the mad Finch from my manor. And give her some seed for her trouble."

"No!" I tried to wrench free, but the guard had too firm a grip. Ignoring my protests, he wheeled me around toward the entrance and took me away from his mistress.

Gaoxo was not gentle as he threw me down the entrance steps, and even less so when he peppered the stones around me with cullets and magnes. "The mistress's seed," he called down to me. "Eat up, little Finch. Oh, and here's a little water to wash it down." He spat in my face and grinned.

I wiped the wet globules from my cheek and stared back at him. "I'm not leaving till I get that shipment."

"No? Then you'll have an uncomfortable wait. Don't see a chamberpot around, do you?"

I stared defiantly back up at him. I had no real plan. No matter how I turned the matter, there was little I could do now that Feiyan had refused me. But I couldn't give in. This was the crux to the ambush. Without it, Vusu had as good as won. And Linos would remain in his clutches.

The door opened behind the guard, and he whirled in surprise. A man in serving robes emerged with a crate in his arms.

"What's this?" Gaoxo demanded. "The mistress told me to send her from the property."

"And she sent *me* with this gift," the manservant replied stiffly. He descended the stairs and stood before me. "Airene the Finch?"

I could only nod.

He held the crate forward, its contents clinking softly inside. "My mistress wishes you to have this. She sends words as well: 'Let the cockerels fight each other.' If you'll take it..."

I accepted the crate silently. *Let the cockerels fight each other.* So she meant to stand back and watch. From her, I could scarcely expect more. But with a healthy heaping of luck, it would be enough.

I hefted the heavy crate and began my long walk across the deme.

MAESOS ANSWERED ALMOST AS SOON as I knocked at his door — or kicked at it, as it so happened.

"You confronted Zotikos? I just heard the merchant had a run-in with a madwoman." He saw the crate in my arms and his eyes widened. "And you recovered it?"

"It's heavy," I offered, voice strained.

"Of course! Allow me..."

The old glassblower took the crate and ushered me to the back of his workshop. Securing the door behind me, I followed him, arms aching after the long walk from Feiyan's compound. I could still scarcely believe she'd relented, though how much the gesture would matter remained to be seen.

After he'd set down the crate, Maesos turned back toward me, holding his back and wincing. "I don't envy you carrying that from Hull."

"It wasn't in Hull."

I explained what had occurred in brief. At my facing Feiyan, he whistled softly. "Not an easy woman to face down, our Low Consul. But you did it."

"For all the good it will do us. Are you sure the tales tell true of this pyrkin? And if they do, why would its use not be more widespread?"

Maesos had bent over the crate and pried it open,

revealing rows of vials packed with soft cloth to keep them from breaking. As he drew one out, I saw it shone with the soft blue-green of the shallow waters on the northern coast of the city. "I do not know if its properties are real, but I do trust my supplier. As I mentioned before, this is pyrkin from the Bali spirit trees, the isikhayha. It is a capital punishment to scrape the pyrkin that grows on its trunks, so few would risk it, even for such properties. And as far as I know, only the Thulu trees host this strain."

I stared at the vial as Maesos unstoppered it and wafted the scent to his nose. It was pungent enough that I could smell it from where I stood, the scent of moss after a fresh rain filling the room. It seemed to calm the roiling anxiety that had swirled inside me for the last few days. "It has some effect at least," I admitted. "Just smelling it settles my nerves."

He nodded encouragingly. "But to know if it will truly work, we must test it on a proper subject. But where to get such a warden, I do not know."

I thought morosely of Xaron and Talan. If only I knew where they were, this would all be much easier.

"Maybe I can ask an Acadian I know," I suggested without hope. I doubted Eltris would be willing, but I had no other option.

Maesos seemed to sense my hesitation. "Take a vial and do what you can," he said kindly. "In the meantime, I'll finish out these bolts. Just need to put in the pyrkin and affix the heads now."

I nodded. "I'll be back soon."

He raised an eyebrow. "So you said yesterday."

I shrugged and smiled, then turned to leave. But as soon as I'd turned away, Maesos suddenly gasped. I spun back around, expecting him to be hurt somehow, but he just stared at me with wide eyes.

"Airene! I almost forgot to tell you!"

"What? What is it?"

"Your Guilder friend came by here. Said he had a message for you, that you were to meet him as soon as you could down at the 'Children's Cave.' He said you'd know the one."

My heart pounded. "Did he say whether the news was good or bad?"

Maesos shrugged helplessly. "No. I would have asked, but he was gone almost as soon as he came. Seemed in a big hurry."

Talan at least was alive; my knees went weak with relief. But what of Xaron? Even though it was blazing hot in Maesos's furnace room, I clutched my arms at the sudden gooseflesh that rose off my skin. "Thank you, Maesos. I have to go, but I'll see you tomorrow at the Conclave gates when dawn breaks?"

The glassblower bobbed his head. "You will, my Finch." He grinned like a child. "I'll get this down pat, don't you worry. If I don't have three dozen of the bolts, I don't deserve to be called the finest glass smith in Oedija!"

"Let's not get ahead of ourselves," I said with a small smile of my own.

He waved his hand. "Go, go. You know where to find me."

I left his shop at a run.

WARDENS

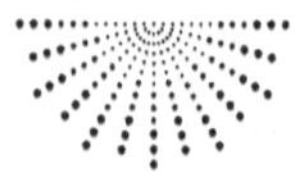

...And so, despite the admirable courage and dedication shown by our self-named Finches, the Council has deemed it necessary to disband the Order of the Verifiers of Truth. This is for the good of all; for the commerce, so its monied families and factions are not cast needlessly into the dungeons; for the demotism, so its Servants are not frivolously run out of office; and for the Finches them- selves, who have suffered, I am told, a startling number of deaths among their members...

- Archon Cameos, announcement of the dissolution of the Order of the Verifiers of Truth, 1067 SLP

My heart was in my throat as I departed for the far end of Port, questions of Xaron's survival and Talan's news spinning in my mind. Why he had chosen the Children's Cave as a hideaway became obvious enough as I thought about it. Though it was not much of a cave, barely thirty cubits deep, it was dug into the side of a cliff off of Oedija's main ports, and was infrequently visited by only the most daring of children. I had heard of it when I was first establishing myself as a Finch, and had even had a child take me to it once, but I was surprised that Talan knew of it as well.

Several turns later, I reached the cliffs where I thought I remembered it lay. Afternoon had arrived in full. Nomusa would already be back at the palace, impatiently waiting for me. If I had been thinking straight, I would have sent a finch from Maesos's shop to tell her to proceed without me. But at the moment, that was the least of my concerns. I had to know what had happened to Xaron.

Traversing along the top of the cliff, I searched for the cave's marker. It had been a red rag tied around a mounted stick when I'd visited nine years before, but I doubted it would be the same now. Gray boulders were piled around me, and uneven stones beneath my feet made the trek difficult, cutting at my exposed toes as I walked with haste. But I didn't see the red rag. Leaning against a boulder, I caught my breath and plotted how to find the new sign. I could try and hunt down a child in the area who might know, but it would take time, and time was something I had precious little of. Still, I couldn't leave without hearing what Talan had to say.

I started moving again, but instead of looking for the red rag, I searched for anything that seemed out of sorts. A new generation of kids visited the cave now, and they would have their own way of marking it. It wasn't long before I saw it: a small cairn piled on top of the largest boulder. I smiled to myself and made my way past the stone to peer down the cliffside.

Knowing where to descend was only half the battle. Now, I had to navigate the precarious hand- and footholds, time-worn and broken by the many children who had clambered over them. At least I could identify the path; scratches in the cliffside made it clear where I should place my hands and feet, so long as I could grab on. If I remembered correctly, the cave wasn't far down. Steadying myself with several deep breaths, I bent over the edge and slowly, carefully, let myself down.

It was a torturous quarter-turn as I crawled down the cliff. Sweat beaded my forehead and ran into my eyes, but I didn't dare let go of the stone to wipe it clear. My hands and forearms burned with the exertion, and the rest of my body protested as well. But finally, the mouth of the cave came into sight, and I pulled myself inside.

Within the shadowy mouth, a figure leaped to its feet. There was a pause, then, "Airene? Airene, is that you?"

I rushed forward at his voice. "Xaron!"

We met in a tight embrace. For a moment, all I could do was hold my friend and bury my face in his shoulder. Only his gasp of pain made me release him.

"Sorry. Are you alright?"

"Oh, it's not so bad." Xaron flashed a rueful grin. "After all, I made it out alive."

I shook my head in amazement. "How? Three Shepherds came after you."

His smile slipped away. "We killed them."

"You and Talan?"

He nodded. "Really, he killed two, and I got one before that. But that's still a lot more than most people can claim. Certainly more than my old feral friends. They didn't even manage to take down one."

"What matters is that you're alive." I took his hand and squeezed it, eyes burning. "No thanks to me."

"Airene, don't. I told you, I accepted the risks." He tried to pull me into another hug, but I pushed him away.

"It's not just that. Xaron, you barely escaped with your life. You've almost died twice in the past few days." I couldn't meet his eyes. "And I'm about to ask you to risk it again."

His face stiffened. I didn't need to see his eyes to know the conflict waging behind them. He nodded once, swallowed, nodded again. All I could do was watch him from the corner of my eye, hoping he would agree and hating myself for that hope.

He gave a third nod, and this time he spoke. "Yes." He cleared his throat and said louder, "Yes — of course I'll do it."

I didn't meet his eyes. "Thank you," I murmured.

"It's just who I am," he continued as if I hadn't spoken, his gaze traveling beyond me. "Or who I need to be."

I finally lifted my head. Not so long ago, he'd been my wine-guzzling, starry-eyed friend who happened to be able to channel. Now, he was becoming a warden like the stories of old. It was who I needed Xaron to be. Even if it wasn't what either of us wanted.

Pebbles and dust suddenly spattered the entrance of the cave. I startled and spun around. A moment later, a silhouette swung into the cave and sauntered toward Xaron and me. I didn't draw my knife. I'd know Talan Wraithsbane's swagger anywhere.

Despite my somber mood, I pulled him into an embrace as well. "Thank you," I whispered in his ear.

The Guilder chuckled softly as he folded his arms around me. "I wouldn't let the little man die," he replied, pitching his voice loud enough for Xaron to hear.

I pulled away at the reminder and glimpsed Xaron's scowl before he turned his head aside. A pang of guilt passed through me, and I let go and stepped back.

Talan's gaze passed between us, but his half-smile never faltered as he leaned against the cave wall. "You've saved me a few words I see. Now you know my news."

It was only then that I took in their shabby state. They didn't look as bad as the night we'd tried infiltrating the Claw, but between the cuts and burns and bruises, they weren't far off. "Tell me what happened."

Xaron ran a hand through his messy hair. "Not much to say. The Shepherds came for me in the night. I was dozing at the time, so they had the element of surprise, but fortunately,

I used what Eltris taught me this time. I turned aside their first few attacks and managed to flee out the window before they came to terms with what happened." He shrugged. "From there, it was cat-and-mouse. I headed toward Iris, keeping to the rooftops. If my life hadn't been in mortal danger, it might have been exhilarating — I've never channeled like that before. From there, I broke into a few manors and tried to shake them off my trail, but it didn't work. Those bastards were like hounds with the scent. No matter what I did, they just seemed to know where I was."

"Maybe they can sense channeling like Kyros," I guessed.

Talan shrugged, as did Xaron. Even though they were both wardens, they knew little more than I about the full range of possibilities of their magic.

"In any case," Xaron continued, "they were starting to catch up and got a few hits in. One kinetic wave clipped my leg and made me miss my landing on a rooftop." He straightened the leg with a grimace. "Still hurts, but at least it didn't break. That might have been it if Talan hadn't shown up."

The Guilder gave a mocking bow. "It's true," he said extravagantly. "I swooped in and saved the damsel."

I pushed him lightly in protest and looked at Xaron, expecting to see another scowl. Instead, a reluctant smile had taken hold. I couldn't have been more amazed had alchemists transformed lead into gold before my very eyes.

"Alright," I demanded. "What exactly happened out there?"

Xaron laughed softly. "Look. I'd still rather spend time with a full chamberpot than him. But when a man saves your life two times in three days, you can't hate him *that* much."

"It seems I still have much to teach you," Talan said with a smirk.

Xaron shook his head with a rueful smile of his own. "But anyway, we've told you what happened with us. It's time you tell us what you've been up to. Talan said Vusu could no longer be trusted, but beyond that, we're both in the dark."

I sighed and told them all I knew. The retelling was not as painful this time, but the sharp reminders of my shortcomings were far from pleasant.

At the end of my tale, Talan nodded slowly. "I'm not surprised."

Xaron rolled his eyes. "Of course you're not."

The Guilder continued as if he hadn't been interrupted. "I'm sorry, Airene. I should have caught sight of this."

I laid a hand on his arm. "No one could have anticipated this. Vusu must have a means of traveling unseen. Perhaps he uses a radiant illusion like you've used before, Xaron. He's certainly capable of far more than that." I shook my head. "The power he has… I fear for both of you."

"Fear for us?" Xaron blanched as he realized now what my earlier request had meant. "Gods. You mean to set us against *him?*"

Talan's brow knit, too, as he looked to me. I raised my hands. "Not as things are. But I have a weapon that might even the odds."

"And what would this weapon be?" Talan asked.

I gave him a coy smile. "Pyrkin."

"Pyrkin?" Xaron arched an eyebrow. "What, to make him easier to see?"

"Your faith in me is heart-warming," I noted drily. "Since our run-in with Iela nearly three years ago, Maesos has been seeking to acquire a certain strain of pyrkin, just in case we ever faced a warden again. Recently, he found the strain and paid to have it smuggled out of the Bali highlands. He claims it can suppress a warden's ability to channel."

"And you believe that old gaffer?"

I drew out the vial of pyrkin from my purse. Where my fingers touched the glass, the strange substance glowed a brighter green. "Not exactly. But, on the slim chance that it does work, I need to test it on both of you."

Talan sighed and held out a hand. "I'm sure I've touched worse."

"I'll bet you have," Xaron muttered, but he followed suit.

Breath coming quick with anticipation, I unstoppered it and again smelled its pleasant, mossy scent. Tilting it, I dotted a small amount on each of their fingertips where the skin moved with their shifts. "Now try to channel."

For a moment, nothing happened. Then, as one, they cried out and clutched at their hands. Talan hissed and wiped his hand madly on the side of the cave, skin tearing and leaving a bloody smear behind. Xaron tore off his shirt and used the ragged garment to scrub furiously at his fingertip, then threw the shirt to the cave floor.

I stared in amazement at the two panting men. "It worked," I breathed.

"It burns!" Xaron moaned, peering at his finger. "It *still* burns!"

Talan, meanwhile, had calmed and now stared at his bleeding finger. "I think that will do," he said mildly.

Something inside me unwound. This had been the crux of the plan. And it was real. I steadied myself on the cave wall. "This might work. We could actually win."

"What might work?" Xaron demanded. He held up his reddened finger to me. "What exactly did I do this for?"

I took a breath, then told them the plan that Nomusa, Jaxas, and I had devised. The web that would, if we had woven it carefully enough, ensnare Oedija's enemy and render him helpless.

The plan that would kill Vusu.

Talan had gone very still by the time I was done, while Xaron was quivering with nerves. "Are you sure about this?" my fellow Finch asked uncertainly.

I nodded. "We have no other choice."

"He won't fight alone," Talan observed quietly. "We've seen what he has at his disposal. The Seeker wardens. The Shepherds." He shook his head. "And I do not know what allies we might recruit."

Xaron suddenly straightened. "Eltris! Have you gone to Eltris yet?"

It was my turn to stare skeptically. "Before I'd heard from Talan, I was going to have her check this pyrkin. But no, I haven't gone to her."

He shook his head. "I've told you, Airene, she's a warden to match Kyros. If we could get her on our side, it would go a long way."

"I suppose I could check." I looked between the two of them. "You should both probably stay here, though."

"But when it comes time," Talan said in a low voice, "we'll be by your side."

"And to let you know when that time arrives, you might need this." Fishing in my pocket, I drew out Xaron's lodestone.

A grin spread across his face. "You recovered it!"

"I did. But you'd better keep a better hold of it this time."

His grin turned sheepish as he accepted it from me.

Stepping back, another thought creased my brow, and I turned to Talan. "There's no chance of aid from the Underguild, is there?"

Talan shook his head. "It seems that Kalindi is taking power and establishing himself as the sole Guildmaster," he said, anger sharp in his words. "Even if he is not in league with Vusu, I doubt he would be amenable to opposing him."

I sighed. "Then I'll have to seek out other allies." I glanced at Xaron. "Like your bird master."

"See? You have that much in common," he pointed out with a grin.

I wished I could linger, to joke and pretend like everything wasn't coming to a likely end. But the concerns of the trial hounded me onward. "Wish me luck. I'll see you both at the trial."

They nodded, then watched as I scrambled my way out of the cave and back up the cliffside.

~

A TURN AND A HALF LATER, I arrived at Eltris's tower. My Verifier medallion granted me access to the Acadium campus, and after a brief while wandering, I'd remembered the way to the Master Augur's den. I knocked rapidly on the tower door and waited for a response. With Eltris's sharp hearing, I expected she'd detect me wherever she was in the tower. But five minutes had passed before I stepped back and started to wonder if the recluse was at home.

"You here to see that crazy old bat?"

I turned to see a woman in Acadian robes addressing me. She had dark skin, not the earthy browns of the Bali, but the deep bronze of the Avvadin provinces in the southern reaches of the Four Realms. There was a presence about her, like she owned the ground she walked on, that set me on edge. Acadians were supposed to be sheep, but this woman was far more like the fox stalking them. Xaron had said that Kyros was training some within the Acadium to work battle magic. I wondered if this might be one of his pupils.

"I was just stopping by," I hedged.

The Acadian studied me. "Well, if you were trying to speak to Eltris, you're out of luck. She went missing two nights ago and hasn't been seen since." She nodded up at a window on the tower. "Someone even went in to check if she had just locked herself up inside, but they didn't find anything. She's just gone."

Chills ran up my spine. Xaron had made it clear that Eltris was set against the Manifest. If she'd gone missing, I suspected I knew what had become of her.

"That's... unfortunate. Thank you for telling me."

"Sure." The Acadian turned away, then spoke over her

shoulder. "If you're going to ask after her, I'd be careful. Strange things are happening. I wouldn't trust anyone you don't have to."

As if I needed the reminder, much less from a stranger. I nodded. The Acadian returned the gesture, then sauntered off on her way.

I lingered a moment longer and looked up at the tower window. A mad thought went through my head to check on the augur myself. I didn't know that passing Acadian woman, nor if she could be trusted. The next moment, though, I dismissed the notion. While Xaron had a great deal of confidence in his mentor, I was not so sure Eltris was worth risking my neck.

I had just turned away when a voice demanded from behind me, "What are *you* doing here?"

I twisted around, a hand reaching for my knife before I recognized who it was. "Master Eltris."

"Let go of that, girl," Eltris snapped. "If you think that would be of any use in the Acadium, you're even more of a fool than I thought."

I quickly released the knife, cheeks growing hot. Somehow, the frumpy, short woman made me feel like a naughty pupil at my schoolhouse lessons. "Where did you come from?"

The Master Augur snorted. "You wouldn't understand if I told you. What are you doing here? Why hasn't Xaron come to me of late?"

I opened my mouth to speak, but hesitated, not knowing where to begin or how much to tell. "He's been busy," I said vaguely. "You've been suspicious of the Manifest, isn't that correct, master?"

"I'm asking the questions, girl. How about you finish answering them."

I reined in my patience and stepped closer to the augur, desperately hoping Xaron's trust wasn't misplaced. "The worst has come to pass," I said in a whisper. "The Visage of the Wyvern is a Tribune named Vusumuzi, and he has the city in a chokehold. He took Myron Wreath captive and is coercing me and others to hold a trial against the Despoina to disrupt Oedija's confidence in the Laurel Palace. But instead of him trapping us, we'll trap him when he shows up to the trial—"

"I've heard enough," Eltris cut me off. "And my answer's no to the question you're about to ask."

I stared at her, stunned. "What do you mean, you've heard enough?"

The Master Augur shook her head. "You're looking in the right direction, girl, but seeing all the wrong things. It's right there in front of you, all of it, yet you're completely blind to it."

Even with my fraying patience, I tried to make sense of her words. "You're saying I don't see the risks? I know what danger Vusu poses." I pitched my voice lower. "He's the most powerful warden I've ever seen."

I jumped back as Eltris suddenly barked with laughter. "But that's *all* you see!" she exclaimed. "What of the questions behind it, girl? *Why* has Vusu become so powerful? If he has always been this strong, why has he done nothing for so many years?"

I had guesses, but I sensed that wasn't what Eltris was looking for. So I remained quiet and tried not to glare.

Eltris studied me for a long moment, then shook her head in disgust. "You think the world is within these city walls. Girl, look beyond them to find the questions you need to ask."

"And those are?"

She stepped so close that I could smell her breath, sour and unwashed. It took all my willpower not to lean away. "Why, in the whole of Telae, are there only the Four Realms that are of any significance? Even you must have learned the world is a sphere, and that the Four Realms occupy only a small space on it. Why, then, do so few people populate it?"

I didn't understand how this was relevant, and Eltris seemed to see it in my eyes. "Fine!" she continued. "A more pointed query then. Why did our Oedijan ancestors embark on their Lighted Passage? What made them leave their homeland and sail across the vast sea to make landfall here? A whole nation uprooted in a single moment. Yet no one wonders why."

I opened my mouth to reply, but Eltris bulled over me. "And to the northeast! What of the Endless Expanse beyond the Wumofu Desert? Once an empire reigned there, a thousand years ago. Yet now their cities lie in ruin, their lands sand and dust, their lakes and rivers dried up. And their descendants live in caves on the edge of that desolation, as absorbed by their ignorance as you."

Ignorant. Of all the insults she could have hurled at me, this was the one that cut the deepest. "You speak of empires risen and fallen in ages past. But I'm concerned with keeping our own realm from splintering apart."

"As am I!" Eltris snapped. "So then, girl — where else are you to learn how to keep a realm from ripping asunder if not from the lessons of history?"

I had no response to that. Yet my frustration, brimming and threatening to take possession of me, didn't allow me to admit it.

"The lands beyond the sea to the west; the deserts to the east; to say nothing of the Rift and the Riven Lands beyond it to the south," Eltris continued more softly. "Girl, you can't see a storm coming by watching for rain at your feet. You look up and see the dark clouds covering the sky. Look up, and tell me: What is coming?"

It was suddenly too much. "Riddles," I said bitterly. "I beg for aid and all you offer are riddles."

Eltris looked as disgusted with me as I was with her.

"Finches," she hissed. "And you're supposed to be a sharp lot." She turned away. "I've wasted too much time here. Leave me be."

"I don't suppose I'll see you at the trial," I shot back at her, a bitter edge to my words.

The Master Augur didn't bother to answer, her fingers tapping across her crossed arms.

I exhaled in frustration, not caring how it looked, and turned on my heel. She wasn't the only one who had wasted her time.

34

LOYALTY

To secure the illusion, some privileges were granted to the Wreaths. First, they were returned possession of the Laurel Palace, their ancestral home, as well as the lands granted to it. Second, they were given a guard of their own to defend it, never to number more than three score. And third, they were to act as Oedija's nominal ambassador with foreign entities, though all matters of importance were to be approved by the Conclave or the Council.

- A Modern Account of the Wreaths; by Acadian Helene, Master Historian; 1170 SLP

Upon returning to the palace, I found an honor waiting to inform me that Nomusa and Jaxas were expecting me up in the Archon's solar. As I entered, they broke off their discussion and rose to their feet.

"Where have you been?" Nomusa demanded.

"Attempting to find us allies." I walked over to the center table, again laden with food, and helped myself. I'd barely taken the time to eat or drink that day. "And mostly failing," I spoke around a mouthful of a fragrant, aged cheese and a crispy wafer.

My companion crossed her arms. "You could have told us."

I raised an eyebrow. "Sorry. I was busy finding out Xaron is alive."

Nomusa's expression lifted instantly. "He is?" she exclaimed. "He survived?" She rushed over and wrapped me in my third embrace of the day, almost knocking the plate of food from my hands as she did. "He beat three Shepherds, Airene! Three!"

I gave a small laugh. I didn't mention Talan. Tomorrow would be soon enough to expose him. "Yes. I can't believe it either."

"He's hiding out, then?"

I nodded. "Somewhere safe. Don't worry, he's fine now. And he promised he'd come to the trial. But..." I extricated myself from her arms, and my eyes flickered to the Archon, who still sat in his chair. "Even with his help, we don't have nearly enough manpower to take down Vusu tomorrow."

Nomusa's smile faded and the lines across her forehead returned. "No. We don't. After I realized you wouldn't be showing up for a while, I set out on my own to search for allies. I looked into whether we could get a faction of the Underguild on our side, but they're all falling in line with that Kalindi. I even looked into hiring mercenaries," she said with a small laugh, "but I couldn't find anyone I could stomach, much less pay."

"I had similar success with Feiyan and Eltris."

Nomusa's eyebrows shot up. "Those are two people I hadn't expected you to ask."

I shrugged. "Who else is there? Surprisingly, Feiyan actually came through. I obtained the pyrkin we need." A small smile spread on my lips. "And it works. Xaron confirmed it."

"It works." Nomusa's eyes were wide as she considered the possibility.

Jaxas nodded slowly. "Then all this plotting may yet bear fruit."

I nodded, studying him. He'd shown little in the way of reactions thus far, even at the news of Xaron defeating three Shepherds.

Before I could speak, he inquired, "And what of this Eltris? She is the Master Augur, is she not?"

"Yes. And Xaron's tutor as well. But for all that, she would not pay me heed, but spoke in riddles around me. I would not count on her aid."

The Archon looked thoughtful for a moment. "My own inquiries have failed. I had the opportunity to spend some time with First Laurel Lykos, but I could not determine whether or not he is loyal to us or to Vusu. There is still time to give him our trust if we think it necessary, but I still hesitate to do so."

"Better it remains a secret then. The same with Kyros. They'll both be at the trial, so we'll find out their loyalties soon enough."

"But unless Lykos instructs it, the laurel guard will not be present," Jaxas pointed out.

I nodded wearily. So few allies, so many powerful enemies, and several other parties who might sway either way. I did not see how the trial could turn out well. Yet there was no other way forward. When I obtained the pyrkin bolts from Maesos, we would have no soldiers to shoot them. And even if we tried firing them ourselves, a foolhardy idea, we would arouse suspicion if crossbows went missing from the armory.

Silence reigned while I finished eating, then lingered afterward as we stared into the flickering flames of the hearth.

"What if," Jaxas said slowly, "we do not move against Vusu at the trial?"

My chest tightened. I had feared that someone would

waver in their conviction. Until the moment came, I still did not know if I myself could stand firm. But I spoke despite my doubts. "We have to ensnare him at the trial. It's our only opportunity. And it's the turning point for the polis. After her trial, Asileia Wreath will be discredited, and Vusu will reveal that her father has miraculously risen from the grave." I rubbed at my temples. "If we let that happen uncontested, she may lose all her influence, and you and us with it."

Nomusa shifted, and I looked at her, expecting her to disagree. So I was surprised when she said, "I agree with Airene. This is the time to strike, if only because Vusu would not expect us to."

Jaxas shook his head. "You do not know that."

"No, we don't," I conceded. "But I think I know something of Vusu now. He's proud. He believes his plans infallible, and that he himself is untouchable. Of course he knows we plot against him. But he must think none of it will matter so long as he gets what he wants. That our resistance is as futile as a fly's to a spider."

"And maybe it will be," he murmured.

Despite his doubts, when we separated some minutes later, our plans remained in place. We bade each other a solemn good night, the weight of the morning already bearing down on us.

Upon reaching our rooms, we found someone waiting for us. "Corin," I said as we walked up to her. In the midst of everything else, I'd nearly forgotten she'd taken up residence in the palace. She wore now what I suspected were the palace's rudest garments, which was to say they were far finer than her usual cartwoman's clothes.

"I didn't know you'd come here," Nomusa observed mildly, making no other gesture of greeting. They had never been close, despite living together for several years.

The cartwoman nodded before looking back to me. "There is nothing for me to do here," she said softly as if afraid of being overheard. "Is there something you need me to do?"

Distracted as I was with everything else on my mind, the last thing I wanted was to come up with ways for Corin to feel useful. Still, I knew better than to turn away an ally when we had so few — and an idea had occurred to me. "You know, there is. Maesos — you remember the glassblower? — he's forging a certain kind of crossbow bolt and means to meet us at the Conclave gates tomorrow morning. Could you help him cart his wares in?" I knew Maesos could manage it himself, but considering this was the heart of our trap, it wouldn't hurt to have two people on the task.

Corin hesitated only a moment before nodding. "I can do that."

I touched her briefly. "Thank you, Corin."

With that, we each slipped into our rooms. I stopped only to remove my sandals and hidden knives before I collapsed onto the bed. My thoughts and fears whirled in my mind, too many to concentrate on any particular one. I stopped trying. What would be, would be. Resignation swiftly carried me off to a deep, dreamless slumber.

I woke to scraping. Metal against metal. I sat up on an elbow, my groggy mind working to make sense of the sound. Something rattled in the door. A key turning in the lock. As comprehension set in, my heart began to hammer.

I whipped out of bed. In the darkness, I couldn't see where I'd discarded my knives, so I settled for the pyrkin pot, visible by the sliver of light escaping from beneath its lid. Taking it in both hands, I moved behind the door and raised it overhead, ready to smash it down on the first intruder to enter. The chill of the night mixed with my fear so that I began to shiver as I stood there, waiting.

The bolt settled. The door pushed open to reveal a figure. By the flicker of torchlight from outside the room, I saw a copper helm with a twist of leaves carved into it. A laurel guard. I held my breath, waiting for him to see me, but his eyes went first to the bed. He crept toward it without looking around.

The second man who entered, however, looked directly at me and startled. "Tyurn's balls—!"

I swung my pot as hard as I could into the slot of his helm. The clay shattered as it connected, spilling brilliant light down the front of the soldier's muscled breastplate and into his eyes. As he cried out and stumbled back, the first guard looked around and spotted me in the sudden brightness. I recognized him: the man Talan had hit with his own sword in the Valemish temple.

He stalked back toward me. "You shouldn't have done that," he sneered, his short sword ringing as it left its scabbard.

I backed away, feeling at the cupboard behind me for other things to throw. But it was too late. A third guard dashed into the room and seized me, detaining both of my arms. "Enough of this," he growled in my ear as he bore me to the ground.

I tried to shout, but a gauntleted hand clapped over my mouth, filling it with the taste of sour leather. I tried biting through it, but only achieved an aching jaw for my efforts.

"You'll get your due soon," the squash-nosed guard chuckled as they hauled me bodily from the room. "'Thae above, you'll get it soon."

The guard I'd hit with the pot glowered down at me, his face dripping with yellow pyrkin, his skin fiery and red from the contact. His glare also promised vengeance.

They dragged me roughly down the hall. As we passed Nomusa and Corin's rooms, I heard nothing from behind their doors. I could give them no sign.

No one was coming to my aid.

Rage gave way to terror. And I'd thought I could save the polis. Bitterness mixed with the rest of my caustic feelings. I gave up my struggles, saving my strength for a moment when it might count.

I'd expected them to carry me down to the dungeons. They took me up instead. Desperate curiosity seized me, but I couldn't have asked where we headed if I'd wanted to. We arrived at the defaced doors of the Ruling Wreath, then continued down the hall to the chambers where the Despot had actually resided. My confusion only grew.

As soon as we were inside the doors, they threw me to the ground, the rich carpet only partially cushioning my fall. I drew in a ragged breath and clutched my hands over my middle. The same nauseating illness as my last visit washed over me.

As the sickness began to pass, I lifted my head to find a man waiting. He was silhouetted by the soft light of the moons with his back to me, but it was still simple to guess who he was.

"Lykos." I tried not to show how rattled I was, but my chattering teeth betrayed me.

The First Laurel turned, his steely eyes catching a glint of light before they were once again cast in shadow. "A story will be called on the streets tomorrow. Verifier Airene, over- come with guilt over her deceit of the Despoina, cast herself over the balusters of the Despot's old rooms to the sea below."

"I don't understand," I said through clenched teeth.

"Then let me make this clearer." Lykos approached to stand over me. "As the First Laurel, it is my duty to protect the wearer of the Evergreen Wreath from harm. You, along with the treacherous Archon Jaxas Wreath, mean to condemn the Despoina of a crime she did not commit."

I still didn't know where his loyalties lay. Perhaps he was

telling the truth. Perhaps he was a dutiful guard. Or maybe he was in league with Vusu, and this was a test of my resolve before the trial tomorrow. As far fetched as that seemed, I had no idea of what lengths the traitor Tribune might go to.

So I kept my response neutral. "Neither you nor I know who killed Myron Wreath. That is why we must hold a trial."

"You may not know," the First Laurel said coldly. "But I do."

"Then tell me. Unless you would condemn yourself."

Lykos's eyes didn't shift. "You mean to lay your sins on me as well."

Opposition didn't seem likely to get me anywhere. I shifted tactics. "First Laurel Lykos, listen to me. Archon Jaxas brought me into his service three days ago. I don't know the circumstances around Myron Wreath's disappearance, nor who had a part in it. But I must act now. Things are happening—" I fumbled for the right words. "—a coup is underway, and plans are being set into motion. So I'm forced to do what I can with the tools that I have."

The First Laurel stared down at me. "Then you mean to condemn the Despoina because she makes for the most convenient scapegoat."

He was like a wolf with the scent, implacable in its hunt. "Lykos, please. I can't tell you what is going on without risking others' lives. But I can say that if you don't allow me to proceed with this trial, many people will die, and Oedija as we know it will collapse."

One of the guards snorted behind me. "Just listen to the wench, sir. Now she wants to save the city!"

"Quiet," Lykos said without raising his voice. His guards' chuckling abruptly ceased.

His gaze never left me. "You convinced the Council that the Despoina is responsible for her father's death. You devised an expedited trial for her guilt. Yet you expect me to believe that you're trying to save Oedija from an unknown threat."

"I know how it sounds. I know I look guilty. But if you just give me a chance to — to—" I could not think of a way to convince him without betraying my secrets. And I couldn't do that when I was still unsure of him. Not when I knew what Vusu would do if he discovered I'd betrayed him.

"She's guilty," the squash-nosed guard spoke up again. "Sir, you have to see—"

"I told you to be quiet."

A long silence filled the room, broken only by the creaking of the laurel guards' armor. I dropped my head and wrapped my arms tighter around me as I thought desperately of a plan. But my thoughts turned in circles around each other.

"On the one hand," the First Laurel said at length, "you could be scrambling to save your life." He paused. "What were you doing at the Valemish temple?"

I looked up at him, startled by the disjointed question. "I was informed of suspicious activities coming through the temple and thought there might be more to it. Perhaps even something connected to Myron Wreath vanishing. That you were there was a coincidence."

His cold eyes gave no sign as to whether or not he bought my story. "But you do not believe them responsible. Who, then?"

I dropped my gaze again. "The Despoina," I whispered.

Lykos barked a harsh laugh. "It seems my interrogation has come to a close."

I didn't know if it was desperation or the strange sickness that burned in the back of my throat that compelled, but I threw my head back and stared up at him in defiance. "Lykos, I can't tell you who I am truly concerned about. But ask yourself: Who benefits from a city in chaos? Who would wish for the downfall of the Wreaths?"

The guards shifted, looking at each other, but Lykos remained still. For a moment, as he stared down at me, I thought I had gotten through to him. He would realize the truth of what I had been trying to tell him. This misunderstanding would be set behind us, and he would join us in fighting Vusu at the trial in the morning.

His next words put an end to hope. "Take her to the balcony."

I didn't struggle as the guards grabbed my arms, dragged me over to the balcony doors, and wrenched them open. The biting sea wind cut through my clothes, yet it was nothing compared to the cold fear that had frozen my limbs. I had failed. And now I would die for it.

"Why kill me?" What little self-possession I still had was swept away with the wind. "What does it gain?"

He stepped out beside me and my captors. "You are to be a key witness in the trial. Get rid of you, and I reduce the chances of its success. I defend my Despoina from false accusations."

"Please." Unbidden tears stung my eyes. "I'm just trying to do the right thing. I'm trying to save my friends and family. Please. Please don't do this." The words came tumbling from my mouth, one after another, barely considered. Only one secret did I hold back.

For a moment, I thought I saw doubt in his eyes. The next, the guards pulled me away, pushing me against the railing, rough stone scrapping against my exposed midriff. The pain awoke my survival instinct again. I suddenly kicked to life.

"I have to be there!" I cried through numb lips. I tried not to stare over the edge at the black waters below as they forced me to bend over it. "I have to stop him!"

Lykos brought his face close to mine. "Him. Who do you seek to stop?"

I clamped my mouth shut, afraid the truth would spill

from me as those first traitorous words had. Blood flooded my mouth as I bit my the inside of my cheek.

Lykos shook me hard. "Tell me!"

Tears were frozen on my nose. I clenched my teeth and remained silent.

The First Laurel stared at me for a long moment, then straightened and nodded. His guards began heaving me up, bracing their legs to get the leverage to force me over the railing.

Reckless rage overtook me. A scream ripping from my throat, I pulled at their hands and braced against the stone to kick back. They grunted and stumbled, but kept their holds.

"Please!" I screamed. "I swear by the Eleven, by the 'Thae, by whatever gods you want, I'm doing what's right!"

A fist slammed into my stomach and knocked the breath from me. Pain mixed with the sickness, and I curled up on the ground as the guards let go.

"Tell me," Lykos said as he stood over me.

Scraped skin burned with pain. Deeper pains lanced with fire. "I've said all I can," I whispered.

The guards grabbed my arms, and the fist came again. As agony spread through my gut, I spat up on the stone. One guard let out a disgusted grunt, but neither hesitated in hauling me back toward the railing. I couldn't catch my breath. Cold had penetrated me to the bone. Pressure built in my head like it would burst. The world pitched, and suddenly I was halfway over the baluster. I felt the weakness of fear come over me, and I went limp.

"Tell me, Finch!" Lykos shouted from behind me. "Tell me!"

I let my head hang as the craven part of me scuttled forward, whispering: *Tell him. What harm can it do? Tell him.* But I shut my eyes, bit my tongue, and held my confession back.

"Release her."

I waited for the long, weightless fall. Instead, they pulled me back and dropped me on the stone floor of the balcony.

Shock numbed my mind. All I could do was pant for several long breaths before I looked up at the First Laurel.

"I had to know." His hard eyes glinted with the purple light of the cloud moon. "Had to know if you would keep your word to the last. Archon Jaxas is no fool, but..." He looked away. "Cover her and escort her back to her room."

The squashed-nosed guard stared in astonishment at his superior, while the other fetched a blanket from Myron's old bed and draped it over my shoulders. I drew it around myself, but continued to stare at Lykos from a huddle on the ground.

"You knew?" I whispered. "You knew the whole time?"

He nodded curtly. "The Archon told me this afternoon. I swore him to silence until I determined for myself whether or not I believed him and would aid in your sham trial."

Sudden clarity came over me. I had held back the truth, unable to trust Lykos after too long of a suspicion. But all he had done was to protect the Despoina; his loyalty was with the Wreaths and always had been. As Asileia was not guilty, neither was he. And by holding back the plan, I had convinced him that I was worth trusting.

I stood slowly, staying upright through sheer force of will. "The ambush. The crossbow bolts." I forced myself to meet Lykos's gaze, though after what I had just suffered at his hands, I wanted to cringe away. "I need men to fire them."

He returned my stare. Fragile as I felt, it was almost enough to make me break. Finally, he nodded. "You will have them."

The guards stepped up to either side of me, but I ignored them, pretending like they hadn't nearly thrown me off the balcony. It was worth forgiving and forgetting all of it if the laurel guards would fight on our side tomorrow. It was what

I had to repeat to myself to keep walking steadily toward the door.

"Verifier Airene," Lykos said from behind me. "I… apologize. But I had to know you could be trusted."

I stopped and took a deep breath, forcing down my fear and anger. "We both want what's best for Oedija. The only apology I need is crossbows and swords tomorrow."

Then, chin up, shoulders back, ignoring the pain and weakness cascading through my body, I walked to my room, not looking back once at the laurel guards who followed.

ON TRIAL

*HIGH TRIBUNE: After careful review of the testi-
monies from all parties, it is with a heavy heart
that the Confessionary Tribunal finds Zalfene
Wreath, Despoina to Oedija, guilty of crimes
against the Charters, the demotism, and the
institutions which hold us true, by acts of aggres-
sion against foreign states, conspiracy, and
murder.*

*- The Trial of Zalfene Wreath, from the records of
the Confessionary Tribunal; 1087 SLP*

The glow of dawn stole through the window and
pressed on my eyelids, waking me from an uneasy
stupor. The trial would begin a few turns after dawn, and I
was to meet Maesos and Corin at the Conclave gates before.
Yet for the moment, I couldn't force myself to move. Aches
and wounds pained me all across my body. Scrapes and cuts
covered my skin, while bruises ran deeper. The worst of the
pain was in my abdomen, and not just from laurel guards'
fists. Twice now the illness had come upon me when

entering the Despot's quarters; I couldn't consider it a coincidence. But as to what caused it, I hadn't the faintest idea.

But strange ailments weren't my primary concern. The trial had come, and with it, a reckoning. For my family and friends, for Linos — 'Thae above, for the realm. I had managed to gather allies through, quite literally, blood, sweat, and tears. But it was still all too likely that none of it would come to fruition.

Yet one thing I knew for certain: staying abed would not delay the inevitable.

I rose slowly, trying to ignore the fresh pain that washed over me, and pulled out a clean chiton. Despite my tunic and trousers being stained with blood and dirt, I pulled the flower-embroidered robe over them. I smiled grimly to myself. The irony of my clothes was apt on the day our polis's own festering wounds would be revealed.

When I exited my room, I did so slowly. A moment later, I realized I watched for guards, the craven part of me expecting them to be lying in wait. Cursing myself to courage, I adopted a normal pace and visited the kitchens. There, I nibbled on a loaf of flatbread. It was all I could manage — my stomach was still halfway ill, and even the palace's rich coffee didn't have its usual appeal.

Upon my return, I found Nomusa waiting outside my room.

"There you are," she said impatiently. "I've been waiting… What happened?" Her eyes darted over my face and body.

I forced myself not to cover my arms, where cuts and bruises were plainly visible. "Negotiations. About which I need to have a word or two with Jaxas. But at least we have the laurel guards on our side."

"You have to stop telling stories halfway through. From the beginning, Aire."

"I'll tell you on the way. We're already late for Corin and Maesos."

I caught her up on the details. By the time I finished, she wore so fierce a scowl I was sure even the First Laurel would flinch to see it.

"Once this is over," she promised darkly. She raised her fist, shaking off a long flowing sleeve as she did, showing she wore steel punching rings across her knuckles.

"Won't be much good against a sword," I noted drily.

"We'll see about that." She hid them again and shook her head. "I can't believe I didn't hear any of it. I can't believe I wasn't there."

"It turned out for the best, though, didn't it?"

She nodded grudgingly. "I suppose."

I smiled weakly. "You'll be okay working with Lykos?"

She shrugged. "We'll see. At least Vusu is still more of a *fareshi* bastard than him."

"That he is," I said quietly, recalling to mind Linos's scarred face.

We went to the stables where, to my surprise, a carriage was quickly brought out for us. Jaxas's own had already left. Climbing in, we bumped down the road to the Conclave bridge. I stared out over the railing to the moody sea. Thick clouds, dark enough to be thunderheads, loomed along the horizon. The monsoons were still a month away, but those clouds promised tumultuous weather.

I startled as someone ran up alongside the carriage into view. As I recognized her, I cried for the driver to stop and threw open the door.

"Corin!" I would have drawn her into a hug had she not been sweating like hard-ridden horse. "Aren't you supposed to be with Maesos?"

She shook her head, beads of sweat flicking from her hair. "Conclave guards won't let him through. Suspicious of his wares." She motioned behind us. "I came in through the palace gates. They remembered me with you from before."

A pit formed in my stomach, and I grimaced. "I need

those bolts, Corin. Could you bring the cart through the palace gates?"

Corin shrugged. "Conclave guards are at the end of the bridge. But I brought what I could."

Only then did I notice the strange way she'd been holding a hand to her tunic. Reaching under with her free hand, she produced four crossbow bolts with glass orbs at the tips. I accepted them, staring at the green pyrkin shimmering inside the glass.

"Thank you, Corin," I said softly. "Could you bring in more the same way?"

The cartwoman nodded.

I smiled and reached out to grasp her shoulder, but Corin edged away. I withdrew, frowning, wondering why she was even more leery of touch than usual lately. Putting it from my mind, I climbed back into the carriage and faced her again. "We'll see you when you return."

She nodded again and took off at a jog back the way she'd come. Nomusa shook her head, but said nothing as our carriage took off rumbling again. I clutched the crossbow bolts in my hands, then thought to tuck them beneath my robes. I'd have to find out a way to pass them to Lykos as soon as I could.

Soon after, we pulled up in front of the Conclave. The courtyard was already full of people milling about. As I dismounted, awkwardly holding the quarrels underneath my chiton, I looked out over the shaved heads of honors and the glittering helms of guards, hoping to see Lykos. Then I heard it: a distant rumble, like the ocean was rushing to the shore, only coming from the direction of the city. Turning, I looked across the topiaries, fountains, and statues littered across the marble courtyard and saw beyond the black iron gate the movement of a crowd. I doubted they had gathered in support of our Despoina. But were they Seekers, or was this coming from the spite of the starving, neglected population at large?

Nomusa and I approached the Conclave doors to be admitted by the guards. As I looked to see if the crests on their helms were the sun-and-dome of the Conclave or the leaves of the Laurel Palace, I noticed the aqua cowls next to them. Two Shepherds waited, a man with a narrow face and teeth that protruded over his lip, and a woman with features soft and round. Both had the same dead eyes as the Shepherds I'd seen before.

"Verifier Airene," the male Shepherd said as we stopped before them. "Tribune Vusumuzi sends his regards."

Fear crept over me. I had known the Shepherds would likely remain within Vusu's control, but it was still unnerving to witness it — and even more as the female Shepherd's eyes fell to my hand, still clutching the crossbow bolts beneath my robes.

Not knowing how to respond, I ignored them and spoke to the guards. "I am Verifier Airene and this is Verifier Nomusa. We are to be admitted by Archon Jaxas's orders."

I saw now that the guards were a mix of Conclave and laurel guards. At least it seemed that Lykos had succeeded in bringing his guards into attendance. Part of me couldn't help but wonder if they would stay true.

"Into the dark depths of the 'Thae you go, eh, Verifier?" one of the laurel guards japed.

I wished I could somehow pass them the quarrels. Instead, I just nodded as he and his companions heaved open the doors to the Conclave, then entered after Nomusa.

We were not the first inside. Many Servants of the Conclave were seated on the stone benches, and honors stood inside the eaves, waiting with refreshments. I might have seized a glass of wine had I not already had my hands full. Nomusa, unburdened, accepted one and quickly drank down half its contents.

Sighing, I scanned the room. The Council was present except for Feiyan. I doubted she'd show up, knowing as she did what was coming. The Stratechons, too, were in attendance, as was Archmaster Kyros. His eyes met mine from across the room, but I quickly looked away. It drove needles of worry through me not to know which side he'd join. Jaxas, too, was in attendance, speaking to a knot of Servants. But one person was not yet there.

I leaned close to Nomusa and whispered in her ear. "He hasn't arrived yet."

She nodded, scanning the room herself. "But he will come."

I didn't know if I hoped Vusu would or not.

But first, there were preparations to be finished. Holding the bolts to my belly, I spotted the closest laurel guard. It would have been more reassuring to hand them to Lykos directly, but we'd look suspicious enough as it was.

Making our way through the crowd, I moved to stand before him — or rather, *her*, as I discovered as I neared. She had a strong jaw for a woman and bore her half-plate as easily as her male fellows. Her gaze was impassive as she looked me up and down, then nodded toward a relatively isolated alcove. Even among all those people, I couldn't help a spike of anxiety at being so near the laurel guard. But I forced down my fear and followed her into the shadows.

Another pair already in the cove glanced our way, then returned to their conversations. The laurel guard paused when we were in the far corner and met my gaze again, eyes shadowed. "Verifier Airene. I trust you have something for us?"

"Yes." With a glance to either side, I awkwardly worked the bolts out from the neckline of my chiton, Nomusa standing at my shoulder to block us as much as she could from view. The pyrkin orbs at the end of the quarrels flashed green as they emerged, then settled to a soft, mossy glow again. I held them out to the guard, and she accepted them wordlessly and slid them into a quiver resting at her hip, the pyrkin orbs hidden.

Not knowing what else to say, I nodded to her, then turned away with Nomusa.

"They'd better stay true," Nomusa muttered as we emerged from the alcove.

"They will." I spoke as much to my own doubts as hers.

Scanning the room again, we set our sights to our next quarry, who was walking down the stairs to the front of the room. Low Consul Orhan of Bazaar and his faction sat in the foremost rows of the chamber, chattering amicably among themselves. As we stopped before them, the portly man looked up, the very picture of pleasantness. "Ah, the Verifiers who made all this possible. What a happy occasion this must be for you. A true apotheosis of your career."

I kept my expression impassive. There was little point in acknowledging the absurdity that we both knew it to be. "Yes, of course, Low Consul."

"Of course, we're all grateful as well," Orhan continued, gesturing to his compatriots. "We never could have accomplished what you so swiftly have."

"You almost sound as if you wished for it," Nomusa stated, her tone just shy of impetuous.

"Perhaps we do, perhaps we do." He winked at me.

It was as good as an admittance of guilt. Yet, soon, it might not matter. Even if the Preservists had worked to bring the imperial rule of Avvad to Oedija, Vusu could overturn all their plans in a moment.

Orhan's grin grew wider at my expression. "But that's enough chatter for now. The trial will begin soon. After will be soon enough to discuss other matters."

I bowed silently, Nomusa following, then we turned away from the faction. How little he knew how uncertain that "after" was.

~

"Despoina Asileia Wreath, please approach the dais."

The High Tribune's warbling voice echoed throughout the massive domed chamber. Nomusa and I watched from among the colonnades lining the right side of room, standing with the honors, clerks, and guards. I scanned those present once again. All one hundred and eleven Servants and Low Consuls were attending as far as I could tell — except for Feiyan. Vusu, too, was still missing. Worry was beginning to gnaw at me. Had he discovered our deception? Yet there was nothing I could do but wait.

As she complied with High Tribune Photina's order, the Despoina was more composed than the last time I'd seen her. Her dress was a muted blue, and she wore little in the way of jewelry. No twigs adorned her hair besides the Evergreen Wreath. Her eyes stared about with distant scorn, vague enough that I suspected she was as deluded as ever.

Leia stopped short of the podium and turned to face those gathered. Her gaze lifted above them to the statues of the Eidola on the wall — looking to those she deemed her peers, I didn't doubt.

"Despoina Asileia," the High Tribune began, "the charges placed before you are grave. You are accused of the murder of your father, the former Despot Myron Wreath, by your own hand or by your orchestration. How do you plead?"

The Despoina's lips curled in a sneer. "You cannot touch me."

The High Tribune leaned forward. "I ask again, Asileia Wreath. How do you plead?"

Leia raised her chin. "Guilty."

The room erupted into astonished whispers.

"Guilty," the Despoina repeated, her voice cutting through the murmurs, "of taking my rightful place as the Hand of

Clepsammia, the arbiter of retribution's divine will. You cannot unseat me from my destiny."

"Indeed," the High Tribune acknowledged drily amid a second round of murmurs. "Then we'll proceed with the witnesses. You are dismissed."

Even from where I was, I saw anger flash in Asileia's eyes. Yet she obeyed and left the dais, if stiffly.

"If only it was the last we'd hear from her," Nomusa muttered.

Perhaps it would be, when Vusu came. *If* he came. I kept the black thought to myself.

I quickly grew familiar with the tediousness of trials. Witnesses summoned forth, one after another, beginning with Lykos and his reports from the watch the night of the three horns. Intriguing as it should have been to hear his perspective, I learned little, and was reminded when looking at him of sharp memories of the night prior. I shoved them down, ignored my aching body, and tried to pay attention as the First Laurel took nearly a turn of the sandglass to read through the testimonies.

Then the High Tribune called out for Tribune Vusumuzi to provide witness. After a ponderous pause, she noted with irritation that he had failed to attend. For a moment, there was a stir in the Conclave at the absence of this key witness. Anxiety that he had discovered our trap stirred in me anew. Fear, cold and sharp, cut through me at the thought of what might even now be happening to my family, to Xaron, to Talan. But I had to hold on to hope. I didn't have another choice at this point.

The Council soon decided to proceed with the trial in spite of Vusu's absence, with an assurance that if he appeared, time would be made for his witness. Then Kyros Brighteyed rose and gave his testimony. I listened carefully to the Archmaster. He reported seeing "Pyrthaen residue" in the Despot's chambers, which he claimed was an aftereffect either of a pyr's presence or a warden's channeling. I rubbed my temples. I knew all too well who had channeled in Myron's bedchamber. I learned nothing new from his testimony. And though I'd hoped to discover which way Kyros's loyalties leaned, it seemed as indeterminate as before by the time he left the dais.

As the former steward of the Laurel Palace spoke next, I glanced at the laurel guards stationed around the chamber. Interspersed between sets of Conclave guards, they numbered nearly two dozen. Most had crossbows leaning at their feet or strapped to their backs. If Corin could sneak in more pyrkin bolts, we stood a good chance of hitting Vusu. Yet a glance back showed no sign of the cartwoman or Maesos, much less Vusu himself.

"Verifier Airene of Port!"

I startled and met the gaze of High Tribune Photina, who, having just belted my name, stared at me with growing impatience. It was my turn. Taking a deep breath, I slowly made my way down the stairs to the podium.

I felt disconnected from my body as I began to speak, forgetting my words almost as soon as I said them. But I must have made a convincing case, for I evoked a reaction that echoed all the way up to the highest circles of the chamber. At my recollection of the Despoina's earlier admission of guilt, the outraged muttering rose all the way to the oculus. I left the dais with no accusations of my own — there was no need when Asileia had condemned herself. I couldn't help but notice Jaxas staring down at his sandals and felt a pang of pity for the Archon.

The end of the trial was growing nearer; we could all feel it. Anticipation and fear pulsed in me as the High Tribune called Jaxas to the dais. I couldn't hear the Archon's words through the buzz of my thoughts, couldn't concentrate on the reactions of the gathered Servants from my gaze constantly flitting to the doors. My heart raced. Sweat trickled down my hairline. My mouth went dry.

Yet for all my agonizing, I still wasn't prepared for his arrival.

My gaze had settled back on Jaxas and his hollow eyes when the air behind him rippled, then tore open. I stared, disbelieving. A crack, incandescent and jagged, grew wider with each passing moment, ripping apart the fabric of the world. Around me, Servants and honors gasped, and guards fumbled for their weapons with panicked shouts. The crack opened into a tear; brilliant light spilled forth from it. A wave of heat washed over us, turning the cool chamber into a hot midsummer day. My gut suddenly kicked and throbbed, and I bent double with agony. But I couldn't look away.

A figure appeared within the tear, silhouetted against the blinding light. At first, it looked upside down, then slowly righted itself as it came closer. *A daemon* — it had to be a daemon come among us. My numb mind could invent no other explanation. The dark figure grew larger within the gash until it blocked the whole of the light behind it.

Then it stepped through.

I could tell it was Vusu as he emerged and moved away from the light. He wore the red mask of the Visage and the same white peplos as he had at the gathering. His arms were bared, his blue tatu dim compared to the brilliant light behind him, but with a glow of their own as they slithered across his skin.

Then another figure emerged from the rift. As the thin boy with blond hair in gray robes walked up to stand at Vusu's shoulder, my heart wrenched, more painful than my heaving stomach and throbbing head. Linos stared forward, not looking to either side, seeming as empty as he had in the Claw. *Still Vessel.* The bitter realization curled through me.

As Vusu and Linos cleared the rift, it began to retreat and close, like a patch of frost before a flame's heat. Vusu stepped toward Jaxas, who had staggered to the side of the dais as he stared, open-mouthed, at the intruders. The former Tribune raised his hands up as if in surrender, his gaze traveling across the chamber. Following it, I saw him looking at the guards' leveled crossbows. From the tips of four of them emanated the green glow of the pyrkin bolts. My heart was in my throat. Vusu was Bali. Would he recognize what it meant that they pointed pyrkin-headed quarrels at him?

My hand fell to the pocket where the lodestone lay. Twitching it hard three times, I signaled Xaron. Hopefully he and Talan were not far. I didn't know how long we'd have.

"What is this? Who are you?" the High Tribune demanded, her voice cracking and betraying her. As if to hide her fear, she turned toward the doors. "Shepherds! Apprehend this feral!"

"I do not blame you for not recognizing me, Photina." Vusu's voice filled the chamber, magically magnified so that it dwarfed hers. "I am much more now than you've seen me before. I represent not only myself, but a people. A cause. A new reign of power." He gestured to the back, where the Shepherds stood, unmoving. "The Shepherds know this. They will not harken to your call."

"You don't represent the people," Jaxas said, his voice tiny compared to Vusu's, yet still carrying through the chamber. "The Servants are the voices of the people. They were chosen by them. They were selected by fair and representative elections."

"Elected by who?" Vusu strode across the stage, his tatu seeming to shine brighter with each passing moment. "The citizens of Oedija. A fraction of the true population, set above the rest by the fortunes of their ancestors. What of the common people? What of the honors, paid not in coin, but in scorn?"

"It is their honor to serve!" one Servant cried from the crowd. "Just as it is our duty to serve by ruling!"

"Have you given them any other choice? Slavery does not seem so honorable when you wear the chains."

Vusu paced back the other way. I watched him, teeth clenched hard. I longed for Lykos to give a command to fire and be done with this. I burned with hate as I stared at him, and all the more when my eyes fell on my brother behind him. Linos hadn't shifted and seemed little more than a statue.

More Servants stood, some objecting and shaking their fists, but most stayed seated and silent. They had seen the power of this warden who could tear apart the very fabric of the world. They could feel the thickening tension in the air and feared to be caught in the midst of it.

Vusu raised his hands. "I did not come to discuss political philosophy with you," he said, his voice carrying over the rising shouts. "I came for a purpose."

He turned to the Despoina, seated at the edge of the dais. From where I stood, I couldn't see her expression, but she didn't shift as he approached and laid a hand on her shoulder. Jaxas convulsed visibly, but he didn't try to intervene.

"Photina," Vusu said to the High Tribune below him, "after my years of service to you and our cause, I ask only one favor of you."

Photina suddenly seemed to recognize who he was. "Vusumuzi? You, a feral?" She shook her long mane in disbelief. "But how could you—?"

"Do this one thing for me," Vusu interrupted. "Condemn Asileia Wreath for the crimes of which she is accused."

The Despoina finally flinched under his hand, but he kept a tight grip. I wondered if he channeled radiance to burn her, for her face twisted in pain.

"I cannot," the High Tribune said uncertainly, then continued more confidently, "I *will* not. You cannot make demands of—"

She never finished her thought. Vusu raised his hand and,

like an overripe melon dropped to the floor, the High Tribune's head burst open. People scattered all about her, splattered with red and gray gore. Some curled under the benches in numb shock or sobbing helplessness. Others retched on the floor. But most remained where they were, terrified of drawing Vusu's ire. Around me, those nearest the doors began pressing toward the exit. I fought against the tide to remain where I stood, unable to look away from the bloody mess that was the High Tribune's cadaver. Only now did I fully comprehend the depth of my folly.

Vusu inspected his white garment and wiped at a red spot absently. His voice projected above the pandemonium. "I am sure I can speak for the High Tribune when I declare the Despoina of Oedija, Asileia Wreath, guilty of murdering her father—"

Through the noise, a string snapped. A bolt cut through the air, then produced a sharp crack as it pierced its target.

Right through the center of Vusu's mask.

3 6

CRACKED VISAGE

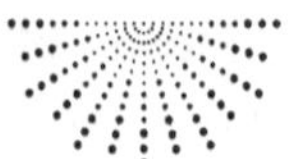

Short has been the puppet reign of the Wreaths, and for the greater part of it, they have played their role well. The first to accept the arrangement, the doddering Amanon Wreath, wanted any semblance of power he could manage, and was content with the mirage supported by a trough of wine a night. His daughter, Zalfene Wreath, was not so hazy-eyed. Her construction of the Half Wall, which was intended to encircle and protect even the outer demes, is now infamous for nearly provoking war with the Avvadin Imperium.

Other Wreaths followed, each swinging toward one end of the spectrum or the other, each struggling to accept that imagined power was not real power...

- A Modern Account of the Wreaths; by Acadian Helene, Master Historian; 1170 SLP

I stared at the pierced mask, breath freezing in my lungs. The bolt had entered just above the open maw. Pyrkin spilled out of the dragon's mouth like emerald fire, streaming down the fangs, down the jowls — and finally settled on the hand that held it, outstretched and away from his face.

378

"Well," Vusu said as he straightened. The resonance had faded from his voice. He held the mask before him and turned it back and forth as pyrkin crawled down his bare arm in green rivulets. "I can see my authority is not yet respected."

Somehow, he had pulled off his mask and used it to stop the bolt. I stared in numb wonder at his speed, but held my breath for another reason. Glancing at Lykos, I found him staring at me. I gave him the barest shake of my head, though I didn't know if he'd pay me heed. We had to wait and see if it took effect before we attacked, lest we find ourselves sorely outmatched. Whether or not he comprehended my line of thought, the First Laurel didn't order the attack.

"Airene of Port."

Those who had not already fled around me stepped away. I stood motionless at the top of the Conclave tiers, feeling the gaze of everyone remaining on me. But Vusu's shadowed eyes, staring up from the dais below, were the hardest to bear.

Even knowing that Vusu's power was draining away, I found it hard to respond. "Vusu," I said, unable to keep a tremble from my voice.

"Airene," he repeated with his head tilted. "Didn't I tell you the consequences of disobedience?"

My face burned. I didn't know the cost of seeming in league with Vusu should I survive this. But this wasn't only about surviving. "I didn't disobey," I said, speaking louder and regaining a measure of composure.

"No? Then your man, the glass smith — Maesos, I believe his name was. He wasn't coming here with more of these—" Vusu held up the mask, now teeming with pyrkin. "—meant for me?"

A pit formed in my stomach as I stared at the pyrkin now reaching his shoulder. It didn't faze him. Yet neither had it bothered Talan and Xaron, not until they had tried to channel. There was still hope.

"Did you mean to illuminate me up as a festival lantern? You should not have bothered, Airene. For the sake of everyone present." He held up his palm, casual, yet his slightest gesture held more menace than the leveled spears of a hundred soldiers. All around me, Servants, honors, and guards instinctively took cover. It took every ounce of my resolve to keep my feet rooted in place.

I licked my lips, closed my eyes, and took a deep breath. None of them slowed my racing heart. When I opened my eyes, Vusu still stared at me with a slight frown, like an uncle who had hoped for more from his promising niece.

I found myself rising to his challenge. "You say you're for the people, yet you set yourself above all others. You say everyone might learn to channel if they trust in your leadership, yet I've seen the cost of your power." My gaze lingered on Linos, but he had finally moved, tilting back his head to stare at the bright oculus above, where light poured in as the sun neared its zenith. Sunlight gleamed in his golden hair.

My eyes burned, and I fought to speak as my throat closed. "You say you wish to save this city, yet all you bring is destruction."

Vusu's expression didn't shift. "So it must seem. But you do not know all."

"Then why?" My anger made the words come out almost at a shout. "Why do any of this?"

Pyrkin crawled up his chin, yet Vusu didn't move to wipe it off. "We all have holes we must fill. We all have hungers for which we will give up all else." He shook his head and stiffened his upraised arm. "The cycle must be broken. No matter the sacrifice."

His fingertips, then his whole hand, began to glow with building radiance. My breath caught. I stared dumbly at him. I had failed. And now I would die for it.

The pyrkin crawling over him flared green. Vusu gave a pained yelp, staring at the pyrkin along his arm with wide eyes.

"What is this?" His gaze traveled up, latching onto me. "It cannot be... pyrkin from the Thulu isikhayha?"

For a moment, I was too stunned to do anything but return his stare. The realization that our moment had come brought me back. I looked to Lykos. The First Laurel made the barest movement of his hand.

Then came the chaos.

Twenty crossbow locks snapped forward. Twenty sharp points aimed for the usurper's heart. They would strike true; they had to. He had no magic to stop them.

Yet before the missiles could reach him, a wall of flames leaped up before Vusu. Linos stood with his hand outstretched and his empty eyes locked onto where Vusu had disappeared from sight. He channeled to protect the man he believed to be his master.

Fear for Linos roused me from my despair. "Don't hurt him!" I cried out. But my words were lost as the Conclave filled with the clamor of battle. As Conclave and laurel guards both surged toward Vusu and Linos with spears, swords, and shields, the crowd of Servants, honors, and notables of Oedija clawed to escape. I tried to follow the guards down, but was pushed back into the eaves and crushed against the wall. Nomusa had been lost in the din. Through the roiling mass of bodies, I caught a glimpse of spears leveling as they charged onto the platform.

"No!" I cried out, shoving with all my strength to form a path. I pushed against patrician and citizen alike, not looking back to see whom I knocked down, whose teeth my shoulder scraped against. My eyes were fixed on my brother. As Linos channeled to protect Vusu, three spearheads thrusted toward him. I rushed down the curved stairs, though I was too far away to do anything but watch.

As the guards struck forward, Vusu's voice rose briefly above the noise, and my brother snapped into action. As if he'd known they were there all along, he spun and slithered between two of the thrusting spears as he grabbed the third, sending it flying from the guard's hand with a rippling kinetic push. The other two spears were already stabbing forth again, but Linos leaped above them, the gray tail of his robe trailing behind. As he came back down, the guards set their spears to gut him. They never found the chance. Waves rippled from his feet, and the guards fell back screaming, their skin reddening with blisters.

Someone shoved into me, nearly knocking me to the floor. When I gained my feet, I saw that Linos had quieted the guards' screams and turned to engage others. Those were my allies he'd killed, but I couldn't help relief flooding through me at seeing him alive.

I closed my eyes. Linos would fight until he was dead, or Vusu was — I knew it to be true. He was more Vessel than my brother now. But somehow, I had to stop him, or the guards would surely kill him. I had to stop his channeling. Maybe then, he could be subdued without being hurt.

But to do that, I needed one of Maesos's pyrkin bolts.

As I turned to my new hunt, four aqua-cowled, manacled figures leaped through the middle of the chamber. Cursing, I scrambled back for cover again, cowering behind a column and watching the scene unfold. My cowardice saved my life. The Shepherds brought death with them, throwing waves of fire and force around them, breaking apart centuries-old stone and killing men and women by the handful. I felt the heat of the blasts wash over me. Guards fell from the nooks where they'd concealed themselves. The rafters around the oculus, stocked with a dozen laurel guards, crumbled circle by circle as concentrated waves of kinesis erupted from the Shepherds' hands. Men came tumbling down to hit the ground with sickening squelches. One fell close enough to me that I felt his blood spray against my skin as he split open. I wiped the droplets from my face, numb with shock.

Other guards were up on the balconies above and behind me; they fared little better. One Shepherd had leaped up and left waves of flames in his wake, rousting out any cross-bowman cranking their weapons behind the benches and sending them flailing and screaming over the railings. Another Shepherd pulled at the air, and swords, spears, and even armored guards came flying past him. It was as deadly a use of magnesis as I'd seen, far beyond Talan and Xaron's simple tricks.

Despite the odds, the guards continued to fight. I heard First Laurel Lykos shout from across the chamber, and the cheer of men rallying for a charge. One Shepherd took a bolt in the arm, then a second in the neck, sending him tumbling to the ground. Yet at least half of the guards must have been killed already. I couldn't tell which way the battle swayed.

"Enough!"

Another voice broke through the fray, mighty and amplified with Pyrthaen power. Wincing at the brutal wave of sound, I turned and saw Archmaster Kyros standing amid the chaos, untouched. His eyes shone bright as he glared about him. At his shoulders stood two Acadians, one a terrified young man, the other the woman who had spoken to me outside of Eltris's tower. I watched anxiously. Their entrance into the fray would turn the tide. But which way?

"End this!" Kyros commanded of his Acadians. Raising his hands, he turned himself to face the balconies, then sent out a wave of kinesis unmatched by anything else I'd seen. The balconies were blocked from my view, so I couldn't see if it was at soldiers or Shepherds that he aimed. The chamber shook as the wave connected, and dust and debris spilled anew from the balcony. Then a body tumbled to the ground, aqua-cowled and still. Hope hammered in my chest again. He'd killed a Shepherd. Kyros was on our side.

As the two young Acadians leaped up to engage another Shepherd, I turned back to the dais. There, Linos killed a guard with a sharp scythe of kinesis to the man's throat. My heart wrenched, fear and guilt driving through me. With only one Shepherd left fighting and Vusu still covered in pyrkin, the Acadians would soon turn to engage Linos. I was running out of time to save him.

Purpose steeling my will, I crouched low and darted out into the melee, questing for the place I'd last seen a guard with one of the special bolts loaded. Orange fire spat overhead, and smoke choked me at every breath. Twice I laid myself flat to avoid debris flying overhead. I was coughing from the dust by the time I reached where I thought the guard had been. The man was dead, his head split open by a broken piece of marble. Trying not to look at his ruined corpse, I checked the quiver at his hip, but found nothing but normal bolts. I took the quiver anyway, but found the man's crossbow had a cracked wing. Useless. I threw it back to the ground in frustration.

"Help." A man crushed by a collapsed column moaned from nearby. I clenched my teeth and dodged around him. He was beyond my help, but I could still save my brother. Misplaced guilt could wait.

The next two guards didn't hold a pyrkin bolt either, but I found a crossbow still whole. As I looked around, my fingers fumbled over the unfamiliar device. I didn't even know how to load a quarrel. Did I pull back on the string, putting my foot in the brace? Or was it something to do with the levers on the top and bottom? I cursed myself for not asking earlier. My eyes strayed to the faintly moving bodies around me. Soldiers, honors, Servants — their wounds leveled them to a single caste now, a bloody mire on the Conclave floor.

I slumped back against the last row of benches, crossbow falling into my lap. Everywhere, my body hurt. Any hope of saving Linos was fast fading. Even if the guards hadn't fired all their pyrkin quarrels, they wouldn't have survived long in this fight without shattering. The Acadians would finish off the last Shepherd soon. There was nothing I could do.

Why not flee?

I tried pushing away the cowardly thought, but it renewed itself at each fresh scream and bone-rattling blast rocking the stone. It was all I could do to remain where I was. I had little to offer in this fight. But I still had to try.

Then it came to me. Vusu was the one who held my brother captive. Perhaps I didn't need to restrain Linos's powers.

All I needed to do was kill Vusu.

I risked looking toward the dais. Though Vusu's powers were restrained, he was far from impotent. As I watched, a pair of guards advanced, taking advantage of Linos's distraction to attack what appeared to be a powerless old man. As one, they stabbed forth their spears in a move that should have trapped him. But with speed I'd thought impossible without channeling, Vusu narrowly dodged one spearhead and wrapped the other in the length of his white peplos. Though the guard ripped it away, Vusu danced forth with the vigor of a much younger man. Coming close, he kicked the guard's leg out from under him. As the man crumpled, the other stabbed at Vusu's back, yet somehow he spun and knocked it wide. With barely a glance around, Vusu's foot found the first guard's helm and kicked, forcing the man to stumble back or break his neck.

Tearing my eyes away, I stripped off my chiton and shielded myself from the debris as best I could as I set to figuring out the crossbow. With mindless desperation, I put one foot into the stirrup that hung off it and tried pulling at the string. It cut into my fingers, and I let it thrum back into position, panting, my fingers now slick with blood. I tried the other lever and noticed a satisfying tug of resistance. I'd found the right lever at least. Bracing myself, I pulled with all my strength and clicked it into place.

Loading a quarrel, I hefted the weapon slowly, careful of the two levers. Its power paled in comparison to the magic surging around me, but I was fully aware of how easily I could end a life with it.

Just as I set it, the grand double doors to the Conclave burst open once more. I crouched again, hope sinking. Four more Shepherds entered, crossing the chamber in great bounds and casting death around them.

"Come on, then!" Kyros Brighteyed boomed. A wave of kinetic energy cascaded overhead to crash into the wall, sending dust and debris flying.

Cowering among the benches, I faintly noticed two more shadows flit over the oculus. My ears were ringing, and the clamor surrounding me was muffled like I had a blanket pressed against my head. Yet I still heard Vusu's strained call, "Kill them, quickly!"

Cradling the crossbow, I ghosted to the end of the aisle and peered out, and my heart soared.

Xaron and Talan had arrived at last.

The next moment, hope turned back to fear as a Shepherd leaped toward them. My friends immediately reacted, attacking in synchrony. As Xaron channeled a flare of radiance and drew the Shepherd's attention, Talan cut through the air with a bright violet arc of light. It left no mark, but the Shepherd shrieked, then tumbled to the ground, unmoving but for a dim, silver wisp rising from her body.

"Hah!" Kyros projected from behind me. "The augur's pupil fights well! But more of them approach, wardens. End the Tribune quickly!"

Talan and Xaron exchanged a glance. Talan nodded toward the dais, while he turned to another Shepherd. Xaron complied at once, leaping across the chamber in two huge bounds. But before he could reach Vusu, a Shepherd leaped from nowhere to engage him.

I feared for my friends, but I couldn't help them. I could only do one thing to help turn the battle. I looked beyond Xaron furiously exchanging blows with the opposing warden to the dais beyond. With the Shepherds fighting for their own lives, Vusu had only Linos still protecting him from the guards, and my brother looked to be nearing the limits of his fledgling power. He swayed as two spearmen thrust at him, yet knocked aside their spears just in time to avoid being gutted.

Vusu fared little better. A spear had stabbed through his thigh and left a trail of bright blood down his leg. Pyrkin still smeared his chest and arms in green, but they had grown faint and thin. His peplos had been abandoned, leaving him shrunken in his underwraps.

Hefting my crossbow, I crept down the edges of the benches, knowing I would have to be close to be able to hit him. But as I neared the dais, a challenger stepped out to meet Vusu, and my stomach sank once more.

Nomusa had abandoned her long, flowing chiton to reveal dark, tight-fitting clothes beneath. Punching rings gleamed on her fingers, and she clutched a knife in one hand. She walked forward with a hunting cat's grace. I exhaled in frustration and lowered my crossbow. I couldn't risk a shot with Nomusa so near. I could only hope her Ixolo training would be enough.

Nomusa lunged, her feet sliding forward as she lashed out with her knife. But though Vusu was injured and no doubt wearied, he'd had many more years of practice than her. As he bent out of the way of her blow, he caught Nomusa's arm and twisted her to the ground. Their movements came fast and flurried as they tumbled and turned and lashed about the platform. They were like two hard winds twining, a storm forming between them, as they fought up the length of the dais.

Nomusa suddenly caught Vusu in a hold and flung him to the benches. But as she leaped down after him, Vusu gained his feet just in time to avoid her follow-up blow. Their deadly dance continued. Neither seemed to be slowing, but I feared it was only a matter of time.

Vusu leaped onto the dais again. As Nomusa tried to follow him, he served her a hard kick to the chest and sent her flailing back to the stone floor. Nomusa tried cradling her fall and succeeded only in twisting one arm painfully beneath her. She tried rising, but could barely move.

My time had come. I sighted the crossbow, leveling my shot — and yet another rose against Vusu.

First Laurel Lykos staggered up the dais stairs to the leader of the Manifest. The soldier's helm was gone, and red lines streamed down from his steel-gray hair. Yet as he raised his sword overhead, he did not tremble, nor did his hard eyes leave his foe.

Vusu kneeled on the platform, breathing hard and clutching his wounded leg. His exertions were finally catching up to him. Yet as the Visage of the Wyvern looked up and met Lykos's eyes, I knew he had not given in.

Before Lykos's blow could fall, Vusu spoke again with a resonance that trembled through me. "Taozu! I will give what you ask!"

Lykos swung his sword, but it was too late. Fire, red and yellow and orange, coiled around Vusu as he rose to his feet once again. As the blade entered the flames, it melted into globules of metal that splattered the floor around them. The inferno extended, reaching out for the First Laurel, and as tongues of fire stole up his arms, even his iron resolve broke. He threw himself to the ground, screaming and batting help-lessly at his arms as his men rushed to aid him.

Vusu rose from the fire and turned his gaze across the room. "Fools," he said in a whisper that carried. "Now see what you have wrought."

SACRIFICE

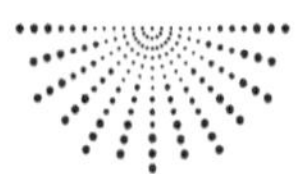

Praise be the wardens,
The hands of the Quintyr,
Who work the will of the gods,
Who forge great cities of stone and fire,
Who heal ills of mind and body,
Who keep at bay the daemons

Praise be the wardens,
They who save us all...

- Scroll fragment; origin unknown; estimated
*   256 SLP*

I raised my crossbow uncertainly. Now that he had regained his channeling, I doubted any shot of mine would help. Before I could decide to shoot, a third person stepped up in challenge.

"Let us test your mettle then, Vusu!" Archmaster Kyros bellowed, raising his hands toward the dais.

Vusu turned with his own hands raised, and their magic collided in a storm. Though they stood barely two dozen feet apart, with Vusu on the dais and Kyros on the floor below him, the wall of their contending power spanned the room and shot up to eat away the ceiling. Fire and lightning and force warred against each other, and it was clear which side was the stronger. Though Kyros threw all his will into the fight, Vusu eclipsed him. His sorcery bore down on the Archmaster, shrinking his wall. Kyros wore a snarl, but exhaustion was overtaking his fury. His loose skin stretched tight under the strain, and his limbs trembled under the weight of power.

A gap opened in the wall of magic, and a tongue of lightning flicked through and almost gently touched Kyros. He flew back, his channeling abruptly cutting off, and crashed into a bench. I only knew he was alive from his pained cursing.

Vusu ceased his own channeling for a moment, swaying. Even with the resurgence of his power, he was tiring. But it was only a moment before he gathered himself and raised a hand toward Kyros. I gripped my crossbow tightly, but still, I waited. I couldn't waste my shot. Once again, I could do nothing but watch.

"Vusu!"

The Visage of the Wyvern glanced up, and I followed his gaze. Talan and Xaron stood on the only unbroken balcony remaining in the Conclave.

Xaron, who had spoken, continued. "You have no more pets to protect you. You have no more allies. Submit, so no more have to die here."

Glancing around, I saw he was nearly correct. No Shepherds remained, though it had come at a cost. Few guards were alive, and I saw only the female of the two Acadians still standing. Only Linos, alone amid the corpses on the dais, remained by Vusu's side.

Vusu lowered his hand and shook his head. "You do not understand what is at stake here. You cannot, not with that augur having whispered in your ear." He looked around. "I do not relish what I've done. Yet to stop now would be to render their sacrifices void. I must carry this through, all the way." His eyes went skyward now. "For all of our sakes."

Sparks flew between Xaron's hands. *Lightning*. Xaron had finally summoned it after all his training and meant to use it against Vusu. My breath caught.

Xaron yelled and threw the lightning bolt forward. Vusu's hands shot up. As the lightning reached the usurper, it burst and scattered in rivulets around him. Vusu smiled. Sparks about his hands gave warning a split second before lightning, greater than what Xaron had summoned, burst toward my friends.

Xaron and Talan threw themselves to the sides, and the lightning burst where they'd been, shattering stone. In the shower of debris, I couldn't see what had become of them.

"No!" I drew up my crossbow again, even though it was too late. Reckless hate ran through me. I'd take my shot, the one I'd waited so long for. I'd pay him back for all he'd done to me.

But as I leveled it, Vusu convulsed and dropped to his knees.

"Not now!" Vusu croaked, his hands scrabbling over the dais. He seemed to speak to the ground. "You cannot defy me now!"

I didn't wait to interpret what his words meant. I took him into my sight, tightened my grip.

Then I fired.

As I pressed the bottom lever, the crossbow kicked back into my face. The spring gouged my cheek. I dropped the weapon and clutched at my wound, but ignored both as I looked up to see if I'd aimed true.

Vusu, still on his knees, sat up slowly. A hand traced over the quarrel lodged between his ribs. Blood trickled out from around the wound. His eyes rose and found me. A strange smile twisted his face.

"All this," he rasped, "and it is you who have doomed us."

Cold fear crept over me, but I thrust it aside. "Talan! Xaron!" I called. "Finish him now!"

I saw figures move out of the corner of my eye. Yet they did not surge forward.

Vusu shook his head slowly. "Vessel!" he wheezed.

My brother immediately approached, stepping over the corpses. Blood ran down him in a dozen wounds, yet his dead eyes did not show any pain.

Terror seized me. Dropping my crossbow, I ran forward. "Linos, stop!" I shouted. "Don't go to him!"

Linos glanced over at me and hesitated for a half a moment until Vusu commanded him again. "Vessel!"

"Don't go, Linos!" I ran to the stairs of the dais like I'd never run before, heedless of the rubble and bodies I had to step on and around. I slipped on blood and went down hard on one knee, but I barely felt it as I rose and continued my mad dash forward.

Part of me registered that Talan and Xaron had emerged from the ruins and leaped across the chamber to fling radiance and kinesis down on the prone Visage. Yet even with a crossbow bolt in his side, Vusu found the strength to disperse and shred the magic before it reached him. I ran forward, heedless of their attacks. My sights were set on Linos.

But my brother had reached Vusu and stretched a hand toward him. As Vusu touched his arm, my brother stiffened. A moment later, he spasmed and fell to the ground.

"No!" I screamed, crossing the last dozen paces. Vusu looked around at me, his face wan. All strength had faded, leaving him old and shriveled, even as Xaron's and Talan's magic continued to rain down to no effect. In his hand had appeared a knife.

"Taozu," he spoke in a whisper that carried, "I give to you your sacrifice."

He cut the blade across Linos's arm.

I screamed as I ran forward. My brother's empty gaze fell to the blood leaking from his arm.

The air above them rippled.

I didn't stop, even as I recognized what was happening. As he had entered the Conclave, so Vusu meant to leave. Reality tore open once again, but in a different guise than before. Reptilian jaws, the size of a carriage and shining with ethereal light, lined with teeth as long as a man, bit through the world. As the maw formed, the air bent around it.

Despite myself, I slowed before the head of the giant creature. I felt as if I were back in my nightmares, facing the beast that had pursued me back into wakefulness.

The daemon beast, or at least the head of it, bent toward Vusu and Linos as if it meant to swallow them. I stumbled forward again. I didn't know what I'd do. I didn't think of the consequences. I just couldn't let Linos slip away from me once more.

The Pyrthaen creation's jaws closed over them. I crossed the last few feet between us and dove. My hand shot through one of the beast's lips, its light-made skin giving no resistance, then closed on an ankle — *Vusu's*, I saw a moment later. I didn't let go. Debris tore at me as I hit the floor. Breath was crushed from my lungs. As I looked up, wheezing for air, I saw the Visage's eyes widen with surprise.

The jaws closed. The world ripped away.

Then — nothing.

Everything had ceased. All sound. All movement. All color, breath, heartbeat. Yet I existed. I was nothing *but* awareness, pure and true. I thought and felt without senses interceding. I was in a land beyond living.

Not knowing how, I opened myself to the dizzying reality

around me. Senses flooded back in, sharp and bright. I saw, yet what I saw didn't make sense. The world had doubled. Above me, a broken earth pressed in close. The world I'd left behind, I recognized it. Cracked slabs of stone seemed to form from nowhere just above me and fall up to crash into what had once been the floor of the Conclave, but now formed my ceiling. I saw my friends moving as slowly as swimmers through molasses through that upside-down world, running toward the spot where Vusu, Linos, and I had vanished.

The mirror world, the one in which I stood, shifted and swirled in defiance of the natural laws and order. I stood before the dais in the second Conclave, yet it was not the same. Though my senses were painfully keen, what I perceived seemed a misty veneer, like this world was a flickering candle that could, at any moment, blow out. Colors refused to remain their proper hue. Light bent and twisted, swirling in curves and spirals. An incessant wind whipped around me, deafening what hearing came back to me. My feet stayed planted to the stone floor, but I felt I might lift away from it if I didn't keep myself rooted.

I looked down at my body. All the pains I had borne in the real world had disappeared, as had the heaviness of the sky bearing down on me. I felt light and free. I looked at my hands, and like the world around me, my skin shone and was as thin and transparent as newly formed ice. Wonder at the creature I'd become filled me.

But then I remembered why I was here. *Linos.*

I looked up, and standing first before me was Vusu. Like me, he was a hazy shadow of himself. No quarrel bled in his side, nor did he bear any other wounds from the battle. Yet he alone seemed solid in this world, moored like a stone in a river. His eyes were bright in his earthy skin as he stared at me.

Beside him stood my brother, shining with a gray light. It

should have been him I looked to, but it was the beast that loomed behind them that finally drew my gaze.

I had heard stories all my life of the thing that towered over them. A legend gone from the world, restrained by the Eidola long ago, his appetite never to be sated again. A daemon I had always believed to be little more than fairy tale and myth, one to scare children into obedience, or to explain the world's cruelty. Now I knew the stories were true. Now I knew that everything that was occurring in Oedija was insignificant in comparison.

I craned my head back, but even as I gazed upon the monster, I could not fully comprehend it. I could not understand how it was possible, or why this was happening now. Yet I also could not deny it.

Famine had returned.

3 8

FAMINE

So with Aida of the Green as Sacrifice, the gods bound Famine, restraining his power and keeping at bay his endless hunger. And to ensure he stayed there until the end of Telae and Pyrthae, they threw him deep into the roots stoneward, where the days crawl into eternities, and his power would not touch any world again.

- The Seeds of Famine, a translation from the Lighted-tongue; by Oracle Kalene of deme Hull; 881 SLP

I stared up into Famine's black, slitted eyes as they glared down from a hundred cubits high. His great maw hung open, unhinged like a snake about to swallow its prey, and its throat was a black, depthless cavern that fell away behind the crumbling Conclave wall. Scales, each as large as a laurel guard's shield, shifted in the fickle light of the Pyrthae, morphing into scarlet, blue, and aubergine in turns. His snout, tapered like a mountain slope, was curled into a snarl above bared, white incisors as thick as columns and as sharp as spears. A violet, forked tongue flicked over his teeth, tasting as if in anticipation of seizing its prey.

I was frozen in place before Famine. I had followed Vusu

and Linos on a whim, and now I stood helpless before the daemon god who sought to swallow the world. Yet for the moment, he made no move toward me, but watched me with eyes black as a moonless night.

"Airene!" Vusu's voice brought me back to myself as it cut through the incessant wind of the Pyrthae. "You should not have followed! You will draw another of his seeds!"

I didn't understand, but at his voice, anger flared up in me again. As Famine continued to watch, motionless but for his whipping tongue and a slight sway, my fear was overrun by fury.

"You were a fool to think you'd get away!" I yelled back.

His hollow eyes were dark pits in the bright world. "You don't understand. What I do, I do for the good of all. For the continuance of all."

It was too much. A scream ripped from my throat, and I found myself charging at him. It was as if a daemon had taken possession of my body and drove it forward. My rage was a blaze out of my control, threatening to consume me. Above us, Famine shook his head back and forth. Terror, rising in me and setting my legs to trembling, almost won over as the great eyes peered down at me with narrowed interest. But if the god was going to kill me, I'd make sure he'd kill his servant as well.

Vusu didn't move as I ran at him. "He will take away far more than your life," his whisper cut through to me, speaking as if to my thoughts.

The words fell on deaf ears. Caught in my red anger, I flung myself at him. The sky's weight lifted from me so that I moved forward in a blur. Above, a shadow like a cliff fell over me. Famine descended, the daemon god's mouth gaping open, swallowing the sky and the Conclave walls alike as he came. I gritted my teeth and braced myself for the last rending even as I crashed into my enemy.

Something pierced my spine, then entered through to my

belly. My legs went numb; pain shot through the rest of my body. My rage burned hotter. Vusu, whom I'd sent sprawling, pushed at me, but I wrapped my arms around him. He didn't resist, but his shadowed eyes suddenly widened.

Something slammed into my side and carried me off of him, suspending me for far longer than nature's laws should have allowed. I felt short arms wrap about me and glimpsed gray hair whipping out from beneath a hood.

"I'll kill you!" I howled into the Pyrthae's gale, struggling against whoever had enwrapped me. But the world had begun pulling away, my body becoming heavier. My gaze fell on the gray figure behind the dark one. Thrashing against the figure who held me still, I willed myself toward my brother.

"Linos!" I yelled. "Linos, grab hold of me!"

My brother didn't move. His features were indistinct, barely recognizable. Still, I clawed my way forward. Above, Famine rose for another strike.

"Stop resisting!" the figure who held me snapped. "We must leave! Now!"

"No! Not without Linos!" He was almost within my grasp. I lunged for him, and my translucent fingers seized his wrist. I took hold of my brother. I didn't let go.

Famine roared. The deafening wave of it vibrated the world, shaking me so that I threatened to come apart. But I held myself together, and clung to Linos, even as the figure who had me from behind tried dragging me away. Famine surged down again, his maw trying to swallow us once more, but we had begun rising. The floor left as we fell into the sky. I closed my eyes as vertigo rocked my sight back and forth.

I slammed into stone.

Groaning, I pushed at the arms that held me with my free hand. My head pounded, and pain flooded my body. My gut heaved. The anger that had filled me in the Pyrthae drained away, leaving me weak and shaking. I rolled over and let loose the little contents of my stomach on the ground next to me. When I was finished, I lay my cheek on the stone. It was hard, but slightly warm. *From the battle*, I realized.

"Aire! Come back to us!"

Their voices called to me as they crowded around. They touched and held me, helping me sit back up as my paltry strength returned. But I looked first at the wrist still clutched in my hand. Linos sprawled out on the floor next to me. A weary smile stole over my lips. I'd done it. I'd brought him back.

Then I looked up at the people around me. Nomusa, one of her eyes swelled shut and her brow creased with concern, gently caressed my head like I were a child. Xaron had an arm around me, squeezing me in too tight of a hug. Talan kneeled before me, gripping my free hand gently in his warm grasp and wearing a half-cocked smile. It was all I could do to stare blankly around at them. My friends, here to hold me and check on me. Even as Linos lay senseless next to me, even after I'd stared a daemon god in the eyes, I found comfort in it.

Above loomed two more friendly faces. Corin, clothes even dirtier than before, loosely held a bundle of crossbow bolts with glowing glass balls at their tips. Next to her stood Maesos, the glassblower's face crinkled into a smile.

It was only then that I turned to see who had drawn me back to the real world, though I suspected I already knew. Eltris stared back with a sour expression and crossed arms. Her short, gray hair as messy as an untrimmed bush, and her robes were ragged with holes. I shook my head in disbelief. The Master Augur had come to our aid after all, and in the most spectacular of ways.

At my look, she broke off her glare to scan the scene around us. "You made a mess of this," the augur observed, though I didn't know to whom. She pointed at one spot among the destruction. "Xaron, was that black mark your bolt of lightning?"

Xaron winced. "Yes, master. I missed my target."

The augur harrumphed and began pacing the wreckage. I looked uneasily around as well. The stones had ceased to rain down from the ceiling, but from the precarious look of the fractured dome, it wasn't likely to hold for long. Bodies littered the ground all about us. I held to Linos, not trusting to let him go. Though his chest rose and fell, I didn't know what would happen when he woke. I couldn't bear to lose my brother again.

"That place…" I said at length. "Was it the Pyrthae?"

Eltris snorted. "The least part of it, but yes."

I shook my head as thoughts tumbled around in it. Stories told of wardens traveling to the home of spirits and gods, but I had never dreamed it might actually be possible. Especially not for me.

Then I remembered what I'd seen. "Famine. He's real. He's returned."

Eltris held my gaze amid the shocked expressions of my friends. "He's not returned completely yet," she said shortly. "But he will soon. Vusu has been weakened. He will not hold him for much longer." Her eyes slid down to Linos.

I shook my head. "I don't understand."

"I understand even less," Xaron muttered.

"Of course you don't," the Master Augur snapped. "Nor will you until I have the time to tell you." She looked around at the ruined Conclave. "Vusu has held Famine in his power for many years now. Ever since he laid siege to the united ishakas under the guise of Yama, in fact."

I scrambled to keep up. "Yama? From the Bali legend?"

"That was over a century ago," Nomusa said in disbelief. "You can't expect us to believe that."

"Believe what you will," Eltris replied shortly. "But open your ears to this: Though Vusu has gained great power from the Quintyr, he has ceded as much to him. And no warden has ever held him back forever."

Even amid the flurry of things I didn't understand, my mind quested back to the last strange thing Eltris had said to me in front of her tower. "You said there was a reason behind all the great disasters across the world. Was Famine the cause of them? The fall of empires? The destruction of the lands?"

The augur's face twisted into a mocking smile. "You solve my riddle after you've seen its answer. How insightful of you."

Annoyance flared in me anew. "You could have just told me instead of talking around it."

"You wouldn't have listened, girl. And don't expect me to believe otherwise."

Her words cooled my anger as quickly as it had risen. I sagged forth, not wanting to admit she was right, so I said nothing. I ran a hand along Linos's arm. His skin felt feverishly warm.

"I hate to rush such spectacular revelations," Talan cut in, "but we may wish to preserve our lives first. Shall we find the door?"

"Finally, a person with some sense." Eltris turned away, then turned back. "But put that Bali pyrkin on the boy first. No sense in risking it."

I startled at the suggestion and looked at him, chewing my lip. Linos still had a vague, empty look in his eyes. I suddenly realized I hadn't even addressed him since bringing him back. Unwittingly, I was treating him just as he appeared: a human statue.

I took both of his hands. "Linos," I said softly, trying to catch his eye. "Linos, look at me."

He didn't respond, but stared up at the broken dome, unseeing.

"Don't wait for the sky to fall," Eltris said drily.

"Which doesn't seem too far fetched now," Xaron muttered.

I took a deep breath. "All right. We'll do it."

Corin drew out a quarrel and broke the glass tip on a flat piece of stone. Then Nomusa stepped in, brushing aside the glass and scooping up the pyrkin with her good hand to spread it over Linos's hands and arms. "I think that should do," she said softly, wiping her hand clean.

Eltris nodded sharply, then stalked over the wreckage toward the entrance.

Talan and Nomusa lifted me and Linos to our feet. My brother could walk, it seemed, but there was no will behind it. The task fell to Talan to lead him to the entrance. Nomusa stayed by me, but I wasn't sure who supported whom. The wounds she had sustained from Vusu clearly ailed her, and her arm was braced against her in a makeshift sling. Xaron, who was more injured than I'd first noticed, limped next to us, while Corin and Maesos followed behind.

It was slow going for our crew, and after much effort and scraped hands and knees, we reached the door. Despite our haste, I paused to look back. The Conclave lay in waste. Half-burnt corpses littered the floors. Columns had been severed in half, and the great dome above was rent open. All of this had come about because of one man.

But now I knew Vusu wasn't just a man. He was a legend returned, backed by the power of a bound god. I couldn't doubt the sacrifices we'd made to stop him this time. Nor hesitate at the sacrifices still to come.

I felt a warm hand rest gently on my arm. "Airene?" Talan said softly.

I nodded and took a step forward, and we exited into the bright, noisy world.

ALL THAT SHATTERS

What world do we live in?
It seems a mean and feeble place
Yet the Four Realms are the last bastion of civi-
*   lization*
In a world spiraling toward chaos...

\- High Poetry of Lowly Things; by Hilarion the
    Second; 1085 SLP

As soon as we emerged, we were assaulted by questions. Guards, Servants, and patricians demanded answers of us. Just as I resolved to shove past them, Jaxas Wreath and his usual retinue of honors pushed their way through to us. Putting a proprietary hand on my shoulder, he led me and my companions away from the bustle, his honors clearing the way.

When we'd reached a more isolated part of the courtyard between two leaning laurel trees, he drew me away from the others. "Are you well?" he inquired gently.

"As well as could be expected." I glanced at Linos. The truth was, I felt better with each passing moment. Why that should be after all I'd put my body through, I couldn't say. Though who knew what to expect after visiting the Pyrthae. My head still spun at all I had just experienced.

"I worried when only Archmaster Kyros and his Acadian emerged. But I could compel no one to enter within, not even after all had fallen silent." He glanced back as well, drawing his arm away, his gaze lingering on the shattered Conclave dome. "I do not think our plan was wise," he said softly, and though his mouth quirked at the understatement, his eyes were sad.

"No. Perhaps not."

He stared at the ruined building for a long moment. "But we shouldn't speak here. Mobs are said to be ravaging the city. We should retreat to the safety of the palace before we discuss our next steps."

I nodded, dazed that I should be included in such deliberations. Though after the battle and the Pyrthae, it felt a very ordinary kind of awe. "Shouldn't the Low Consuls be present?"

"They are gathering at the palace as well, but I would hear your account first. I will see to them afterward." He looked at me again. "But we should get you into a carriage. You have much to think over, I'm sure."

"More than enough." Never had such an understatement been uttered.

Jaxas sent two honors back toward the crowd. "I won't pester you during the ride over," he said to me. "Your report can wait until you see me in my solar."

I gave him my thanks. As the carriages arrived through the noisy crowd, he climbed into his carriage, while my companions and I piled into the second. When it became clear that we numbered too many, Corin opted to take Maesos back to his shop, then meet us back at the Laurel Palace. I worried for her, but none of us could stay safe for long, and the glassblower couldn't be expected to stay away from his shop.

Eltris, too, was determined to part ways. "I have many things to attend to, girl," she snapped at me as Xaron and I tried to convince her to come.

"Greater things than telling our Archon of the threat we face?" I asked, incredulous.

She snorted. "You still have little idea of what that is. This is only the beginning, and someone must keep the watch." She glanced warily at Linos. "Keep an eye on that gray boy. And keep pyrkin spread on his shifts."

Without a word of explanation, the Master Augur stalked off toward the ruins of the Conclave. The rest of us exchanged glances, but we knew trying to stop her would be pointless.

So it was that Nomusa, Xaron, Talan, Linos, and I headed to the Laurel Palace in the carriage. Along the way, they urged me to tell them what had happened after I'd leaped into the rift with Vusu and Linos. Glancing at my brother, I gave them a brief account, but refused to dive into the specifics, saying they should wait until we met with Jaxas. The little I hinted at was enough to make their jaws drop.

Truly, though, even I didn't know what to make of what I'd experienced. Famine, the dragon god of old, had loomed above me. I had not believed the gods were real, not after they had been absent from the world for so long. Pyr had been hard enough to buy into. Now I found myself forced to consider the possibility that everything I thought to be legend and folk tale might just be real.

After I finished, my friends caught me up on their own stories. Xaron and Talan had intended to reach the battle sooner, but had been delayed by a handful of Shepherds standing guard. Once again, it defied my understanding how they could have taken on so many of the Tribunal's enforcers. "How are you doing it?" I pressed.

Xaron nodded at Talan. "It's him. I don't know how he does it, but he channels something that makes them collapse and… frees them, I suppose. Though mostly they die from it."

I looked to Talan with a questioning look. "Frees them?"

Talan quirked a smile. "Perhaps I'll explain more thoroughly another time. For now, let us say that I have a means of severing the connection that allows Vusu to control them. The process is often fatal, as the Acadian's apprentice observed."

Xaron and Talan had come a long way in their relationship, but the gibe still made Xaron scowl. I smiled. At least some things hadn't changed.

We arrived at the palace and made the long, weary walk up the stairs to the doors. Nikias greeted us there, the steward looking more anxious and sympathetic than I had ever seen him, though with far more fortitude than most after such an unimaginable situation.

"Come, come," he said as he bustled us up to Jaxas's solar. He eyed Linos strangely, but only said, "The Archon is waiting, as is food and drink. And the baths will be ready for you when you're done with your discussion."

We thanked him and ascended the stairs to find things arranged just as the steward had said. I had not expected to be able to eat, but at the sight and smell of the good food, I found myself wanting to heap as much on my plate as Xaron did.

But first, I went to my brother, bringing him a plate of flatbread and roasted lamb. "Linos, I brought you something."

Linos looked down at the food. Without taking the plate, he grabbed the lamb and shoved it into his mouth, heedless of the pyrkin that still dripped from his fingers. Hopefully it wasn't dangerous to ingest. I sighed. At least he still had that much will to live.

I left him with the plate and a cup of water in the corner of the solar as I returned to heap my own plate full and sit with the others around the hearth. As soon as I sat, Jaxas leaned forward and asked in a quiet voice, "That is your brother?"

I nodded. "We recovered him from Vusu."

The Archon glanced uneasily at the corner where Linos sat. "I don't think he should be here."

I stared at him, astonished. "Why not? He'll do nothing once he's done eating, I assure you. He'll be no trouble."

"Yes. But Airene, he is a warden. And he just fought for Vusu."

Cold fear crept down my spine. Suddenly, I felt it had been a terrible mistake to bring him here to the palace, where he was so utterly within Jaxas's power. "It was not his choosing. He was made this way."

"No warden chooses it," he said gently. His eyes flickered to Xaron and Talan. I wondered if he feared their reactions, since he now knew they were both wardens as well. Yet he'd invited them to his solar, and without any guards. Surely he didn't mean them ill.

"He fought for the Betrayer," the Archon continued. "Even if it was not his will, it does not change the danger he poses. What if Vusu were to seize hold of him again and try to kill all of us here?"

"His hands are covered with the pyrkin that brought Vusu to heel," I pointed out, fear sharpening my words. "He can't channel, I promise you."

Jaxas shook his head. "I wish I could say otherwise, Airene. But he must be kept away from where he can be a danger. I know these times call for extraordinary measures, so I will not exact what our laws would demand. But I would have him at least kept in the Acadium, where he might gain the help he sorely needs."

His thoughts echoed my own. Little as I wanted to, I knew I could not deny Jaxas this. "Fine," I agreed miserably. "But not yet. Let me stay with him a little while longer."

Jaxas hesitated, then nodded. "Very well. He can stay while you tell us what you saw."

I drew in a shaky breath and glanced at my brother. I felt guilty for the suspicion I bore for him myself. If Vusu could command him to kill, could he also use him to listen in on us? Yet I couldn't bear to send Linos away yet. I had to treasure what little time I had with him.

Without further hesitation, I launched into my story. I wondered if the Archon would believe me. If I hadn't experienced it myself, I knew I would have trouble swallowing the tale. As I reached the point where I leaped into the rift, I watched Jaxas for a reaction, but he kept his expression carefully composed. Even telling of Famine looming above me in the Pyrthae was only enough to produce slight twitches. The others were less restrained, and Xaron openly gaped.

When I finished, silence reigned over the solar for a long breath. Jaxas rose to stand by the window. Outside, the day was bright and cheery, a strange contrast to all we'd experienced.

Without turning around, Jaxas spoke. "I knew there was more that I didn't understand. But I did not suspect it would be... this." He shook his head, his expression hidden from me. "In light of all that has happened, what I have to say seems inconsequential. But I think we may find it necessary to formalize it sooner rather than later."

His words piqued my interest. "What do you mean?"

Jaxas turned to show a wry smile. "This evening, I will propose to the Conclave — whoever remains of it — that the Order of Verifiers be reinstituted. Not just as attendants to the Wreaths, but as a legitimate branch of the government. You will be named First Verifier and lead it, with Nomusa as your Second, should that arrangement suit you. If the measure passes, and I think it will, no one will be beyond your access, no matter how isolated or powerful. And you will find the truth that our polis so desperately needs."

I looked down at the tiled floor. Once, such an honor would have been everything I could want. Yet now, the offer felt hollow. I had barely recovered my brother, and then not even whole. We had stopped Vusu, but only for the moment, and at great cost. And now we faced a threat beyond any of our imaginings.

"I failed," I said softly. "I didn't know who was behind all of this until it was far too late. How can you expect me to find the truth now?"

"None of us knew the truth. But you drew closer to it than any other."

Not any other — Eltris knew far more than any of us had. Yet Jaxas didn't know that, and so he turned to me. But not only because of that, I realized. He trusted me. It was enough to make the difference.

"If you insist. But I have two conditions before I accept."

The Archon nodded gravely, though his eyes flickered to Linos. "Name them, and I will do whatever is within my power to ensure they are fulfilled."

I took a deep breath. "First, if I'm to be named First Verifier, Nomusa should be given the same title. She deserves it, and works better when she's the one directing others."

I glanced at her and was glad to see she shone with gratitude.

Jaxas looked between us, a faint smile on his lips. "I can tell she is well suited to authority. One might almost think she were born to it."

I startled and shared a look with Nomusa, wondering how much the Archon knew of her background.

"My second condition," I hurried on, "is that Xaron also be named a Verifier, and Talan be given access to the same resources, though he will not be a Verifier in name."

The Archon nodded. "I expected you would want to take care of your friends. But you must understand, wardens must abide by different rules."

Xaron tensed, while Talan's gaze grew hard. Yet as Jaxas turned to Xaron, he did not seem to notice. "While I am not able to make you a Verifier, Xaron, I hope you will accept a different position. Now that it is openly known that you are a warden, you must have a title that will protect you, yet still grant you a generous amount of freedom. I believe I have that solution."

Xaron stared at the Archon, his fluttering fingers betraying his anxiety. "And that is?"

"The Despoina is in need of a new Hilarion." His brow drew down, no doubt remembering what had become of the previous two. "I thought you might be the man for the task."

The look of astonishment and dread on Xaron's face would have been enough to make me laugh at another time.

Nomusa had no such qualms. "Oh, he'll be perfect for it," she said through her chuckles.

Talan's smirk showed he agreed.

Xaron tried to ease his frown, to little avail. "I thank you, Archon," he said stiffly. "I guess I have no choice but to accept."

Jaxas smiled faintly. "Do not fear. The Despoina hasn't been in much of a jesting mood of late. I doubt you'll be made to do flips and festival tricks."

"I had better not," he muttered.

Jaxas turned then to Talan. "As for you, Guilder Talan. Or perhaps it is former Guilder now."

It would have made me laugh to see the astonishment on Talan's face had it not made me fearful myself. How the Archon knew so much about each of us, I had not the slightest clue. It hardly seemed he needed an Order of Verifiers to learn all the secrets he wished.

"I am afraid the greatest gift I can offer you is freedom at this point," Jaxas continued. "As I have no other legitimate positions that wardens may occupy, you must either join the Acadians or face the Shepherds' justice. However, considering your service to the polis, I will not subject you to those today. You may resume your life outside the law as it was before, at least until such a time as I cannot ignore it."

Talan bowed his head. "It is more than I expected, and quite sufficient for me." He smiled wryly. "I prefer freedom to wearing a jester's bells."

Xaron scowled. "Just wait a span," he muttered. "We'll see how you feel then."

I didn't feel quite as sanguine about it. It rankled me to leave Talan without resources. Yet he had survived this long on his own. I had to hope he would remain capable of it, even devoid of his link to the Underguild.

Jaxas looked back to me and Nomusa. "Well then. If you two will accept, the position of First Verifier is extended to you, provided the Council agrees to reinstate the Order."

I looked at my friend once again, and she nodded. "It looks like we'll do it," I said.

"Then I will inform you of the results when I have them, though I do not expect much resistance." He looked between Nomusa and I. "There is one last thing on that matter. As of old, you and those you name as your Verifiers will be granted a place of residence on the Conclave grounds. You may have noticed us passing it as we came across the bridge, an odd-looking building situated near the cliffside."

I shook my head, but Nomusa said, "I saw it. It looks like a place pyr would go to die again."

"Yes, its maintenance has fallen off in recent times," the Archon admitted. "But as soon as the measure is passed to establish the Order, I will have renovations begin at once. I expect it won't be long before it is suitable for you to reside in."

The mention of living quarters made me realize I had forgotten someone again. "Corin. I need her to be named a Finch, too."

That raised the Archon's eyebrow. "The cartwoman? I do

not think we can justify a cartwoman in that role to the Council."

The reminder jolted me for a moment. If matters proceeded as they were supposed to, then we wouldn't have to answer to Jaxas, but to the Council. Which included Feiyan. And Orhan and his Preservists. Fear was becoming far too familiar a companion of mine lately.

I bit my lip. We'd already left Corin out after Canopy was ransacked. I couldn't do it again. "On the contrary — a cartwoman is the perfect Finch. She'll be the least suspected, and a cartwoman hears all sorts of conversations when people think they aren't listening." I braced myself for my next words. "Besides, I believe as First Verifier, I would have the right to appoint any to be a Verifier that I — and Nomusa — see fit."

The Archon met my gaze. "Yes, I believe that is true. My apologies for not seeing the value in such an arrangement. And of course, I will not infringe on an institution whose power is derived from the Conclave. Now, if that's settled..." He came over and sat in his chair again. "I believe that is all of immediate concern. You all have gone through many trials. It's high time you took care of yourselves. Go; rest, eat, and drink. Oedija will stand for at least one more day without any of you keeping watch."

The four of us shared weary smiles around at that. We all looked as if we needed the rest.

"We'll try," I promised with a small smile.

The Archon nodded, then gave us his dismissal. As one, we rose to leave, though Xaron stopped long enough to grab one more skewer of lamb, while I coaxed Linos to leave the plate of juices he'd been lapping up behind. Jaxas watched as we left, his eyes unshifting as he studied my brother.

Uneasy, I hurried Linos away.

40

ATTUNED

Beware, you of Telae
Who would stray into the Pyrthae

- Scroll fragment; origin unknown; estimated 100
PLP (Prior Lighted Passage)

The door had barely closed behind us before Talan murmured, "He makes extravagant promises."

I met his dark eyes, holding Linos's hand as I led him down the stairs. Even after the long days of fighting, they hadn't lost their shrewdness. Nor their mocking laughter.

"He does what he can," I said. "It's all we can ask of him."

"On the contrary. I could ask for a great deal more."

"Then what do you suggest? That we strike out on our own?" I looked him over. "You're already ragged and filthy. Leave you on your own for a span, and we won't recognize you from any other vagrant in the alleys."

He snorted. "I'll manage. Even if it comes to that."

I glanced at Nomusa. From the look she returned me, she knew what I had in mind. When she shrugged, I looked back to Talan. "Become a Verifier."

"Now hold on," Nomusa said with mocking seriousness. "I'd have to agree to that."

"Which you would." He gave her with a lazy smile before rolling his gaze back to me. "But you heard the Archon. He would never allow it."

I found it hard to believe Jaxas would turn him in after everything that had happened. But no matter what I thought, Talan would never trust him. "Then we'll make you a Verifier in everything but name. You'll have money, access, anything you need."

He was shaking his head before I'd finished. "Neither the Conclave nor the Laurel Palace will be able to protect me from Kalindi. And make no mistake — the Guildmaster will be after me once he's secured his hold on power. He never was one to leave loose ends, and I will be sure to make myself far more than frayed string."

"Don't be a fool," I warned him. "You don't jab a tiger outside of its cage."

"Nor do you let it roam free."

I shook my head. There was no dissuading Talan once he had his mind set. "I suppose we need someone watching the Underguild. Just be careful."

"Airene." His eyes were serious as they held mine. "Only a man with nothing to lose throws it all away. And I have something yet to hope for."

I looked away, hiding my rising flush. In another time and place, when a city wasn't falling apart around us, when my scarred brother wasn't following behind me mindlessly, perhaps it would have been the spark that ignited whatever lay between us. But here and now, it couldn't be.

Pushing down my disappointment, I turned to the others. "You heard our orders from the Archon. Who's ready for a round of drinks?"

Xaron, who had been distant during the conversation, suddenly lit up with a grin. "I thought you'd never ask!"

~

IT COULD HARDLY BE CALLED a celebration, but the time that Xaron, Nomusa, Talan, and I spent drinking wine that afternoon in the feast hall was enough for me. Even with all the concerns weighing down on us, and my brother sitting silently next to me with an unshifting, blank expression, we managed to speak of lighter topics. Like if Xaron was required to be drunk all the time as Hilarion. Or how Nomusa was supposed to find a good man to warm her bed when the city was in chaos. And how Talan was as likely to be sleeping in a sty as a bed if he didn't accede to becoming a Verifier. None of us forgot what we'd been through and what was to come. But for the moment, we were able to laugh at our hardships. And laughter gave us the strength to carry on.

In the early evening, the Acadians came for Linos. As I watched them lead him away, I wondered guiltily if I should have escorted him there myself. The streets were dangerous; violent mobs roamed the demes, to make no mention of Seeker wardens and Shepherds under Vusu's sway. But I wouldn't be able to protect him any more than the Acadians, and one of the Acadians who came was the hard-eyed woman who had fought by our side in the Conclave. If she couldn't protect him, no one could.

After he was gone, the rest of us went our separate ways. I held Talan for a long while before I let him go back out into the city, though I first attempted to elicit an oath from him to stay safe. He pressed my hand and left without another word. He never was one to make false promises.

Xaron, restless even when injured, went to see the quarters afforded him as the latest Hilarion, while Nomusa sought a bath. Though she implored me to come with her, I begged off and retired to my room. Exhaustion deeper than any I'd experienced yet coursed through me, and I wanted nothing more than to rest.

Yet, when I was alone in my room, sleep fled before the memories that flooded my head. I stared up at the ceiling, remembering what it had been like in the Pyrthae. I imagined the room as it would be there, mirrored above and below, but shifting and incandescent. I wondered if I would ever enter that ethereal place again. I wondered what it meant that part of me wanted to.

But it was the memory of Famine, and of my brother and Vusu standing before the daemon god, that haunted me most. I shivered and clutched my arms around me. I did not expect to shake the cold, yet my fingers felt oddly warm. Soon, the cold had fled, and warmth spread throughout my body. The afternoon's wine was settling in, I supposed. I was glad for its comfort.

A knock at the door startled me from my trance. Heart hammering, I rose and cautiously opened the door.

A female honor stood on the other side. "Verifier Airene?"

"Yes?"

"Someone waits for you at the front gates. Corin, she says her name is." The honor bowed briefly. "I am sorry, but they will not admit her, though she claims to have been granted access before. Security has increased, considering..."

I sighed. The rest of us had been reveling while Corin had, as usual, been doing thankless labor. And dangerous work, considering the state of the city. I glanced down at myself, still in my dirty and torn trousers and tunic. No doubt my hair was a mess, and I didn't smell clean. But they were frivolous concerns, and Corin no doubt suffered a worse state.

"I'll go now, if you'll take me to her," I told her.

The honor accompanied me down to a side gate in the northeast corner of the Wreath grounds. There, Corin waited for me, fidgeting with her hands and scuffing her feet. She wasn't usually prone to nervousness, but I didn't have to wonder what had upset her. In addition to everything we'd heard of riots and Seekers, plumes of smoke rose over the buildings in the distance. I wondered morosely if the shell horns would warn of widespread fires soon.

As I walked through the gate, I greeted Corin. Instead of approaching, she motioned me apart from the guards and down the narrow street leading away from the palace grounds. I followed her, my apprehension growing.

"Corin, is something wrong?"

She didn't stop and turn toward me until we were out of earshot of the guards, and even then, she didn't meet my eyes. "Maesos. He's hurt."

My mouth went dry. "What happened?" I demanded. "Where is he?"

"Thieves. They stole his cart and hurt him." She gestured down the street. "I took him to an abandoned house nearby."

"An abandoned house? Why didn't you—?" I shook my head. "Never mind. Is he hurt badly? Can he move? We need to get him back here. I'm sure we could have one of the palace healers attend to him."

"He hurt his leg. I couldn't move him alone."

"Then we need to get a cart, or a carriage—"

"No time," she cut me off. "We can help him together. Only one leg is injured. But we should hurry. The thieves might return."

I tried making sense of the situation. Corin wasn't acting herself, nor did her words add up. Whatever had occurred had clearly rattled her. I feared greater still for Maesos.

"Fine. We'll go now, and you can explain more on the way."

We set off at a jog back into the city. The streets were eerily empty, the people shuttered up in their homes, waiting out the riots. Distant shouts and screams told of the mobs' movements. With any luck, they'd stay far away from us. As we traveled, I asked between panting breaths about the details of their attack. Maesos, the old fool, had apparently tried protecting his wares when a group of young men had waylaid them, and they'd hurt his leg in vengeance. Corin had stood by; unarmed against their knives, she'd known she couldn't resist. After they'd left, she'd dragged the glassblower into a nearby house, which she'd found with the door open, and left him there to go fetch me.

As we turned into a narrow street of Sandglass, though, an uneasy feeling gripped me. The rows of houses on either side looked more decrepit than most neighborhoods in the deme. Nothing stirred behind the boarded-up windows. I couldn't decide if they were signs of safety or danger.

I glanced at Corin. "Why were you over here? This isn't on the way to Port."

She glanced up and down the street, perhaps worrying about the gang of boys returning. As she spoke, her words tumbled together, her accent more pronounced than usual. "We came here when they wouldn't let us through the Conclave gates. Thought it would be out of the way." She stopped and gestured to a house. "This is where he is."

Catching my breath, I looked up with apprehension. Crowded in close to the other buildings, the abandoned house was a dull sandy color, flat-roofed, with narrow windows. It didn't look inviting.

"Let's go get him then."

I started toward it when Corin grabbed my arm. "Airene."

I jerked to a halt. Her grip was tight enough to hurt. "What is it? You're hurting me."

She held my arm a moment longer, then released it. "Don't go in," she whispered.

I rubbed my arm where she'd gripped me. "Don't go in? But you just said Maesos is hurt and needs our help."

"I lied."

I stared, uncomprehending, as her words sank in. I

looked up and down the street. I saw nothing, but I had the distinct feeling that something lurked just beyond the shadows.

"What do you mean, you lied? Corin, I need to know what you're talking about. Right now."

She raised her gaze, finally meeting my eyes. "They have her," she said in a strangled voice. "They said they could bring her over from the islands, but they took her captive. And now, if you don't enter the house, they'll…"

My mind whirled. "Who was taken captive? And who did it?" The first part clicked into place. "Does someone have your sister, Corin?"

She nodded slowly.

"Who has her? Who?" I felt as if walls were closing in around me. Was it Feiyan? The Underguild? Or one of Vusu's henchmen, come to finish me off?

"The Valemish."

I stared at her. "The Valemish. You're sure?"

"Yes. Their priest threatened my sister. The Kul."

I scrambled to understand. Why would the Valemish wish me harm? Could they have found out I'd entered one of their temples and held a grudge for it? Was it to do with my association with Talan? Both seemed too flimsy of reasons to orchestrate such a betrayal.

But their motivation wasn't my immediate concern. It slowly dawned on me how difficult it would be to get out of this bind. If they had Corin's sister, and she failed to do as they'd asked — having me enter the house alone — then her sister would be killed. And for all I knew, if we tried leaving without entering, hidden watchers might stop us anyway.

Frustration flooded me as I stared at my friend. The Valemish might be the ones threatening us, but it was Corin who had landed us in this situation. She should have come to her friends before trusting the Valemish. Yet, as angry and betrayed as I felt, I could not fault her for being blind when it came to her family.

I drew in a shaky breath. After what I'd witnessed in the Conclave, I didn't think I could feel real fear again. But at least then, I hadn't faced my enemies alone.

One last desperate thought gave me pause. *The lodestone.* Perhaps I could signal Xaron, and he would come to my aid. But then I remembered the lodestone had been in the chiton I'd shed in the Conclave. Now, it was lost among the ashes. And even if I could have signaled Xaron, he wouldn't have known where to go.

I sighed, then squared my shoulders. "I'm entering."

Corin's eyes widened. "But—"

"We can't risk your sister getting hurt. And I don't see another path out. This is the only way to keep her safe, and for us to survive." *Or at least have a chance of it*, came my bitter thought.

Corin started to speak, then looked aside. I did the same. There was nothing really left to say.

Facing the house, its squalor took on a sinister air. Before I could lose my courage, I strode forward and pressed against the door, already hanging partly open. I hoped for a moment it wouldn't give, but it swung open to my touch with a loud creak that made me wince. Whoever waited within knew I was coming now. I continued forward all the same.

The entrance was tight and narrow with little room to do anything but kick off the mud from my sandals. I could see little, as the only light came from behind me.

"Maesos?" I called in. They knew I was coming already, but perhaps by playing my part, I might gain some edge. "Maesos, where are you?"

I moved into the atrium. It was tall, at least two stories high, if still narrow. The darkness was lifted slightly by a narrow slit of light from a high, boarded window. As I stepped in and strained to peer into every dark corner, I saw movement out of the corner of my eye. Blood hammered in my ears as I spun around. A man stepped free from the shadows.

"Who are you?" I demanded, voice quavering. My hand strayed to the knife tucked against the small of my back. Every part of me screamed to flee, yet I stayed. For Corin and her sister, and for my own sake, I had to stand firm.

The man took a slow step forward, moving into the slit of light. As his face became visible, I flinched in recognition.

"Eazal," I said, disbelieving. "The apothecary."

"Airene of Port." The man spoke in a cracked, deep voice. He was Avvadin, evident from his bronze skin, green eyes, and the cloth wrapped about his head. He wore a simple tunic and trousers in place of more traditional robes, though he looked clean and respectable. His hands were clasped behind his back.

Anger quickly filled me as I considered him. Three years before, Eazal might have helped me solve the mystery of Thero's death. Instead, he had fled the city, taking whatever he knew of my brother's murderer with him. Though I'd now paid Vusu back in part, his wrongs were far from righted. And but for Eazal, we might have uncovered Vusu's plans years before they came to fruition.

But for him, Linos might still be whole.

"I'm surprised you returned, Eazal," I said coldly.

The apothecary tried on a smile, but it slipped away. He looked as if he might become ill. "I'm not here over old wrongs, Airene. Believe me when I tell you that."

I gripped my hidden knife tightly. "But perhaps I am. I can't forget what you've cost me."

Eazal stared at me, buried emotion glimmering in his eyes. *Guilt? Regret?* He glanced away before I could tell.

"Perhaps it is best this way," he said softly. "After all, I cannot turn aside from my purpose, either. The Kul commands that I do this. Demands it. My last sacrifice to Valem."

His words sent ice through my veins. I had shot Vusu with a crossbow. I had come face-to-face with a daemon god. Yet here, in this dark shack of a house, I'd died at the hands of a man I'd inadvertently forced into exile. I was so afraid I almost laughed.

"Debts are owed," he said softly, and his hands came around. In one of them, a sharp knife gleamed as he crossed another narrow strip of light between us. The other he raised to his mouth, and I caught the glow of pyrkin before he closed it and swallowed. He coughed, then straightened. The sweat on his face shone as he stepped through the last patch of light between us. "I'm sorry, Airene."

As I wondered what he'd swallowed, my gut suddenly wrenched. Fire spread from it, more visceral than anger or fear. Despite the man stalking toward me, I felt my attention drawn inward.

"They used you to sow chaos," he continued. He was twelve paces off, eleven. "But now that you've served your purpose, you're expendable. As am I."

The heat spread, burning through my veins. The tips of my fingers itched with the feverish warmth. I ran them along the rough leather hilt of the knife. I narrowed my eyes and blinked off the sudden beads of sweat, trying to concentrate. I didn't draw the blade. I had one chance to strike, and I meant to make the most of it.

He sighed, slowing six dark paces off, as if reluctant to take the final steps. "This is how it ends."

"No." My head felt light like I were intoxicated. The fire inside me had burned away the anger, leaving a strange, disconnected clairvoyance. "This doesn't have to be how it ends, Eazal. We can settle this another way."

He took one more step, then another. "No, we can't. Not anymore."

Raising the dagger, he dashed forward with impossible speed. My mind in a fog and my vision hazy, I drew out my own knife and slashed wildly before me. As I flailed, I felt everything I'd held inside suddenly pouring out. All my helpless rage, my crippling fear, the guilt for all the things I did and did not do. All my failures and my successes. I struck blindly, and as I did, I felt something inside me break free. Heat flooded through me anew. My body did not feel like my own. My gut untwisted, and pain fled before the stream of fire that poured through me.

My fingertips no longer itched, but burned as they pulled at the stream and spread it forth. Flashes of light burst from my hands, blinding me. Vibrations built to a tremendous force, shaking and rattling my body. Sparks shimmered over my skin. From my feet, flames and force spread out in waves, disintegrating my sandals and blasting the dirt floor.

Suspended in the light and warmth, I stared in wonder at the energy flowing from me. I knew what it meant. Yet I couldn't yet put words to it.

Eazal had fallen back, cowering against the wall, as he stared at me with wide eyes. "You, Branded?"

The fear in his voice finally broke through my dumb wonder. "I'm not!" I cried.

But my hands and feet proved me wrong. Power continued to pour forth, ever greater with each passing moment. The circle of destruction around me was spreading. The knife in my hand melted before my eyes.

Before the impossible display, Eazal fled. Flinging the knife to the ground behind him, he cast back one more look, then disappeared out of sight. I felt little relief at his departure. I stared at my body, horror piercing through the calm aura that had until that point enthralled me.

"How is this happening?" I whispered. I'd always wished this day would come when I was a child. But now that it was here, I was terrified that it would never stop. "How?" I cried out.

The flames at my fingertips flared.

As if a dam had broken, fire burst forth to paint the walls and sear the floor. My skin blistered; my feet scorched. The house around me went up in flames. I watched, helpless to stop any of it.

Then, as suddenly as it had begun, the stream of energy stopped. All around me, flames died down, leaving the walls black and smoking. Exhausted beyond anything I'd experienced before, I collapsed to the floor and into the darkness beyond it.

Next that I knew, I was in Corin's arms, jostled with every step. My senses were dim. I saw she carried me along the street in her arms. Her panting sobs were loud in my ears. But though I saw and heard, my awareness ended there. I had no more command over my body than if I were asleep. I barely felt my limbs except for the pain slowly creeping at the edges of my mind. Trapped, my focus retreated within, where the ebb and flow of the energy still pulsed, like a glimmering light I could not look away from. I strained for its warmth like a drunkard at a wineskin. It was intoxicating, power undiluted. And I longed for more.

I did not think anything could draw me away from it, yet a sound cut through my stupor. It was a sound I had heard only a few times before. It was the sound that had set me on the path that had led me to this point.

The shell horns of the Laurel Palace, loud and long and mournful, blew once more.

The first horn sounded, and some part of me wondered if the fire had started with me. Then the second horn blew. I waited, expecting a third to come, if only because it had before.

But none ever did.

Three horns is nothing to fear, Father had once said. But he had not spoken of two. No one alive had heard just two horns call. Yet all knew what it portended.

I closed my eyes. Dread drew me away from the kindling magic inside me. *War.* We were going to war. But with whom?

The horns' call propelled our nation toward a cliff, beyond which Vusu and his daemon god waited, Famine stretching his mouth open to swallow us all.

War had come to Oedija. But war was only the beginning.

GLOSSARY

Acadians - The scholarly residents of the Acadium; often, they are wardens. While not all Acadians are wardens, any warden caught are forced to become an Acadian, or face the penalty of death.

The Acadium - Nominally, the center of learning and education within Oedija. The Acadium serves a dual purpose, however: the reeducation and containment of wardens.

Archon - The representative of the Despot or Despoina within the People's Conclave and Demos Council. Their powers are primarily limited to moderation, except when a member is missing on the Demos Council or a tie vote must be broken.

Avvad, or the Avvadin Imperium - The ever-expanding empire that lies to the south of Oedija.

Bali - The people who reside among the plateaus to the east of Oedija.

The Confessionary Tribunal, or the Tribunal - The judicial branch of Oedija's government, they are responsible for enforcing the rule of law, including the containment and punishment of rogue wardens. They are not elected, but are recruited by their own.

Daemons - Spirits who are considered evil or mean-spirited; also a derogatory term for wardens.

Demes - Districts of the city of Oedija.

Demos Council - The ruling council within the People's Conclave. Traditionally, it numbers eleven Low Consuls, with the Archon acting as a moderator, though often, the eleventh seat is disputed. Their responsibilities largely lie in determining the agenda within the larger Conclave. In times of strife, however, they are granted powers of military action and broad budgetary powers.

Demotism - A system of democratic republicanism in which representative officials are elected by citizens, or landowners, into a legislative ruling body.

The Despot/Despoina - The Ruling Wreath; a symbolic ruler who acts as a figurehead for Oedija. Small powers as the official emissary of Oedija and the nominal leader of Oedija's militia (when marshaled).

Eidola - The gods of the Eidolan religion.

Eidolanism - The religion of the original settlers of Oedija, in Airene's time, it is a fading religion, with many of its beliefs considered antiquated.

Energetic elements - The forms of energy present in the Pyrthae. Three energetic elements are commonly known: radiance, or heat and light; kinesis, or force; and magnesis, or the fields of magnetism. Other energetic elements are believed to exist, but are unconfirmed.

Finches (as a title) - Hunters and peddlers of secrets. While in purpose, their mission is to expose wrongdoing and uncover hidden truths, in practice they often perform small jobs recovering and threatening others with incriminating information for those who will pay.

First Laurel - The leader of the laurel guard, the soldiers defending the Laurel Palace and other Wreath properties.

The Four Realms - Considered the last bastions of civilization in a backwards world, four nations are united in peace by a concordance. These nations are: Oedija, the Bali ishakas, the Qao Fu jaitin, and the Avvadin Imperium.

Guilders - People who work on behalf of the Underguild.

Hilarion - The jester to the Despot or Despoina. Hilarion is always chosen from among Oedija's male wardens. Traditionally, he wears a crown of wheat, sackcloth clothes, and sandals bound with rope. Hilarion's nominal purpose is to entertain at the whim of the Ruling Wreath, but his true purpose is understood to be to diminish fear that people hold for wardens by making him an object of laughter and ridicule.

Honors - The lowest caste of Oedijan society. They are not permitted to own property, including money, nor choose their own employment, and are often housed and work within the estates of patricians. Honors are the descendants of the Kalthuae, the native inhabitants of the lands Oedija now claims, before settlers sailed from the west to found the nation.

Ishakas - The tribal kingdoms of the Bali people.

Jaitin - The matriarchal groups of the Qao Fu people; grouped by the caves in which they reside.

Low Consuls - The members of the Demos Council. Low Consuls are elected from the Conclave, requiring the support of ten of their fellow Servants to gain a seat.

Oedija - The "Pearl of the Four Realms"; the primary location of the story. A republican society undergoing significant turmoil, with threats from within and without.

Order of Verifiers - A branch of Oedija government tasked with routing out corruption. It was disbanded a few years after its founding, and a century before Airene of Port fashions herself after them.

The People's Conclave, or the Conclave - The legislative body of Oedija. Within their parameters lies the making and governance of laws, the taxing and determination of the treasury, the governance of commerce, and the defense of the nation.

The Peninsula - A rural area of Oedija to the north of the city of Oedija.

Prefectures - Areas of governance across Oedija's countryside.

Pyr - Spirits who are considered either benevolent or innocuous.

Pyrkin - A moss-like substance that is considered somewhere between plant and animal, it is supposed to have a connection to the Pyrthae, on account of its bioluminescence.

The Pyrthae - The plane of spirits, which is said to run parallel to the material plane, Telae.

Qao Fu - The people who reside among the desert caves to the northeast of Oedija.

Servants - The elected leaders of Oedija, with semi-proportional representation from across Oedija's ten demes. They number one-hundred and twenty-one, minus those Servants who are elected to the Demos Council. They are responsible for legislative actions.

Shepherds - Members of the Confessionary Tribunal, they act under the guidance of a Tribune to contain or punish any rogue warden.

Stratechons - The five permanent military leaders of Oedija. Responsible for the city guard and the taxoi (when they are gathered).

Taxoi (s. taxos) - The militia of Oedija. As Oedija has no standing army, the taxoi are organized and financed by patrician households whenever the need arises.

Tefra - Priests of Avvad who use Silks, or bound spirits, to fight on their behalf.

Telae - The material plane; or, the world as it is known, including The Four Realms.

Tribunes - Members of the Confessionary Tribunal, they act as arbiters of Oedija's justice.

The Underguild - A semi-legitimized criminal organization. Overseen by five Guildmasters, the Underguild has a great hold over criminal activity in Oedija, and is largely responsible for its relatively low crime.

Verifiers of Truth, or Verifiers - Members of the Order of Verifiers, who were tasked with routing out corruption in Oedija's government, and were met with often violent resistance.

Wardens - People who are attuned to the Pyrthae and are able to manipulate forms of energy as magic. Across the Four Realms, they are forced into hiding, killed, lauded, and enslaved, depending on the nation. In Oedija, they are feared and kept to specific roles, such as Acadians or Shepherds, that suppresses their freedom and use of their abilities.

The Wreaths - The royal family of Oedija, formerly the true rulers of the nation when it was a monarchy.

Valemism / The Valemish - Worshippers of the volcanic god Valem, the religion of Valemism began in Avvad. It is considered a strict religion with a heavy emphasis on subjugation and obedience to authority, and the punishments for disobedience.

OEDIJAN SOCIETY

SOCIAL HIERARCHY

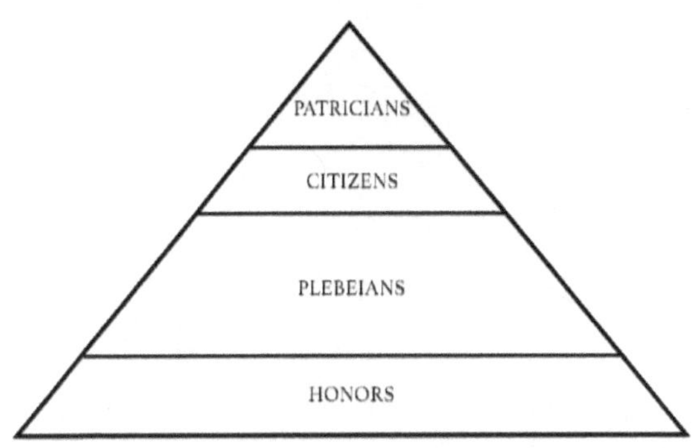

POLITICAL ORGANIZATION

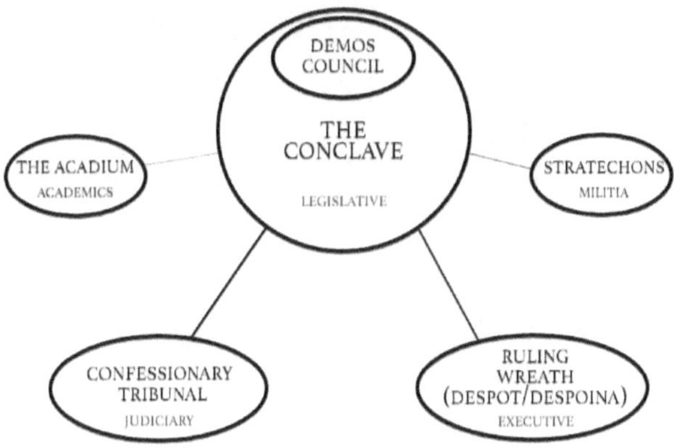

ACKNOWLEDGMENTS

Whispers of Ruin started, quite literally, as a dream. The first night after I'd moved to Seattle just over two years ago, I woke with the kernel of an idea in my head: an epic fantasy novel with a private investigator as its main character. Over the following months, Airene slowly started to reveal herself, becoming my first character who told me who she was rather than I create her. At least, that's how it seemed to me. And I was okay with that!

But from conception to published work, it took a lot more than Airene and I to write this book. As always, I couldn't have done it without Kaitlyn. As my idea bouncer, my alpha reader for both first drafts, and my relentless (in a good way) critiquer, thank you so much for sticking through all of the work that went into this book. I think we finally did it justice.

Thank you also to my developmental editor, Sylvia Cottrell, who told me the things I needed to hear in order to re-write the book the right way. Her insightful guidance was critical in *Whispers of Ruin* becoming the book it is. Go give her some business at exlibrisediting.com.

Thanks to René Aigner for the fantastic illustration!

Big thanks to my friend and proofreader Nick, with whose incisive comments and keen eye I've been able to write the best book possible.

As always, thank you to the rest of my family and friends, who support me every day in big and smalls ways. I need you all to keep going!

And finally, thank you, reader, for giving up some of your limited time to read *Whispers of Ruin.* I hope your journey with Airene was good one, and that you'll continue with us in the next book!

BOOKS BY J.D.L. ROSELL

Sign up for future releases at jdlrosell.com.

THE FAMINE CYCLE

1. Whispers of Ruin

2. Echoes of Chaos

3. Requiem of Silence

Secret Seller (*Prequel*)

The Phantom Heist (*Novella*)

RANGER OF THE TITAN WILDS

1. The Last Ranger

2. The First Ancestor

3. The Hidden Guardian

4. The Wilds Exile

LEGEND OF TAL

1. A King's Bargain

2. A Queen's Command

3. An Emperor's Gamble

4. A God's Plea

A Battle Between Blood (*Novella*)

THE RUNEWAR SAGA

1. The Throne of Ice & Ash

2. The Crown of Fire & Fury

3. The Stone of Iron & Omen

Godslayer Rising

1. Catalyst

2. Champion

3. Heretic

ABOUT THE AUTHOR

J.D.L. Rosell is the author of Ranger of the Titan Wilds, Legend of Tal, The Runewar Saga, The Famine Cycle, and Godslayer Rising. He has earned an MA in creative writing and has previously written as a ghostwriter.

Always drawn to the outdoors, he ventures out into nature whenever he can to indulge in his hobbies of archery, hiking, and photography. Most of the time, he can be found curled up with a good book at home with his wife and two cats, Zelda and Abenthy.

Follow along with his occasional author updates and serializations at www.jdlrosell.com or contact him at authorjdl rosell@gmail.com.

www.ingramcontent.com/pod-product-compliance
Lightning Source LLC
Chambersburg PA
CBHW030354200726
48286CB00014B/1396